Both men felt palpable relief when they reached cover

"Which way?" Ryan snapped as they came to a halt.

Jak paused, his impassive face refusing to betray the intensity of his concentration.

"There…there…" he said simply, indicating the direction.

Ryan knew what the albino teen was thinking: it was an obvious move. These people either credited them with no intelligence or had an innate confidence in the conditions, leaving them with little option.

"Let's do it," Ryan stated. "I'll go clockwise, you counterclockwise. See how many there are, and how they're spread, then meet at the mouth of the passage, fill in the others."

"What if they not want us meet up?" Jak queried.

Ryan grinned. It was cold, without mirth. "They'll want that—right now they're wondering where we are. They'll be so relieved we've turned up and they've got us all in one place that they won't wonder what we've been doing until it's too late…"

Other titles in the Deathlands saga:

JAMES AXLER

DEATH LANDS®

Ritual Chill

ALTERED STATES
BOOK ONE

A GOLD EAGLE BOOK FROM
WORLDWIDE®

TORONTO • NEW YORK • LONDON
AMSTERDAM • PARIS • SYDNEY • HAMBURG
STOCKHOLM • ATHENS • TOKYO • MILAN
MADRID • WARSAW • BUDAPEST • AUCKLAND

First edition September 2005

ISBN 0-373-62581-2

RITUAL CHILL

All spirits are enslaved which serve things evil.
—Percy Bysshe Shelley, 1792–1822

THE DEATHLANDS SAGA

This world is their legacy, a world born in the violent nuclear spasm of 2001 that was the bitter outcome of a struggle for global dominance.

There is no real escape from this shockscape where life always hangs in the balance, vulnerable to newly demonic nature, barbarism, lawlessness.

But they are the warrior survivalists, and they endure—in the way of the lion, the hawk and the tiger, true to nature's heart despite its ruination.

Ryan Cawdor: The privileged son of an East Coast baron. Acquainted with betrayal from a tender age, he is a master of the hard realities.

Krysty Wroth: Harmony ville's own Titian-haired beauty, a woman with the strength of tempered steel. Her premonitions and Gaia powers have been fostered by her Mother Sonja.

J. B. Dix, the Armorer: Weapons master and Ryan's close ally, he, too, honed his skills traversing the Deathlands with the legendary Trader.

Doctor Theophilus Tanner: Torn from his family and a gentler life in 1896, Doc has been thrown into a future he couldn't have imagined.

Dr. Mildred Wyeth: Her father was killed by the Ku Klux Klan, but her fate is not much lighter. Restored from predark cryogenic suspension, she brings twentieth-century healing skills to a nightmare.

Jak Lauren: A true child of the wastelands, reared on adversity, loss and danger, the albino teenager is a fierce fighter and loyal friend.

Dean Cawdor: Ryan's young son by Sharona accepts the only world he knows, and yet he is the seedling bearing the promise of tomorrow.

In a world where all was lost, they are humanity's last hope....

Chapter One

Blackness whirled around, some parts darker than others, some so deep they were no longer black but something else, something to which he couldn't put a name. Something that was sucking him in and tearing him apart at the same time: inclusion and expulsion in the same breath. Breath of what? This was just darkness: but a darkness that seemed to have sentience and life of its own.

Like a bellows that fanned flames, it seemed to puff and blow until finally it expelled him, sending him spinning upward, dizzyingly until...

He opened his eye, wincing at the light. It was, to all intents and purposes, muted, but to his vision seemed harsh and glaring. The icy blue orb watered as he blinked, slowly adjusting.

Fireblast, would there ever be a time when the mat-trans jump became easier? Would there ever be a time when he could look at the opaque armaglass and the disks inlaid on the floor of the chamber, without a feeling of revulsion or nausea? Without—yes, he had to admit it—fear? Fear that he wouldn't awaken from the vivid nightmares of the jump, fear that his disassembled being would be scattered into a dimension he couldn't comprehend, let alone name. A fear that the solution was becoming worse than the problem.

The problem being that to escape whatever firefight they had become embroiled in, to escape whatever wasteland they had been traversing, they used the mat-trans in the redoubt from which they had initially emerged. Of course there were exceptions: sometimes the redoubt had been destroyed in action, sometimes their journey had taken them far from their initial point of contact. Mostly, though, they would return to the chamber to effect an evacuation.

So where would they end up? They never really knew, only that there was a good chance it would be better than where they had recently departed. That's if the redoubt hadn't been damaged and they weren't transmitted into a mass of rock or a watery grave. Which was always a possibility. But it hadn't happened yet, and a continued existence was about riding your luck and playing the odds.

Sometimes, though, in the seconds that seemingly stretched into agonizing hours as they began to emerge from the unconsciousness of a jump, Ryan began to wonder about the effect it had on their bodies and their minds. To have your very being disassembled, scrambled and shot across vast distances before being reconstituted once more: what kind of damage did that do over time?

Ryan Cawdor pulled himself to his feet, shaky and unsteady, the world around him spinning rapidly one way, then slowly the opposite, as it gained equilibrium. He felt a rise of bile in his throat and spit a gob of phlegm onto the chamber floor, hoping it would halt the rising nausea. Breathing deeply, closing his eye, he felt his guts settle.

Around him the others were beginning to stir. Krysty

and Mildred were the sharpest, dragging themselves from their stupor, climbing unsteadily to their feet and checking their weapons and themselves, in that order. J. B. Dix took a little longer, choking slightly as he came around, his unfocused eyes seemingly small and beady without his spectacles, only coming to life when he placed them on his sharp nose.

Which left Doc and Jak, always the last to come around. And, as always, Jak greeted their new surroundings with a spray of vomit, bile spewing from his guts as he tried to adjust himself to being made whole once again. His body shook with the spasms as he braced himself, on all fours, against the floor of the chamber before heaving. Watching him, Ryan wondered how much more of this the albino could take before he was running on empty, with nothing left to do except to spew himself inside out.

But what options did they have? Without this mode of travel, they would have bought the farm long ago. There were too many enemies, too many troubles behind them to stop running, even if it did sometimes seem as though they never actually moved.

Doc muttered to himself, only the odd syllable breaking surface and making sense. Sense in that it was something recognizable, not that there was any kind of logic running through his discourse. Sweat plastered his hair to his forehead, smearing streaks across the pale skin, a pallor like a man who was already chilled.

Mildred moved across to him, slowly, still feeling her own way out of the jump.

"I don't know why he's still with us," she muttered almost to herself. "By rights, he should have crumbled to dust a long time ago."

Ryan gave her a skewed grin. "Doc's got no choice, like all of us. Stay with it or buy the farm. Who'd want to do that by their own choice?"

Eventually, Doc's eyeballs turned from in on themselves and slowly began to come to terms with the world around him.

"My dear Dr. Wyeth." His voice sounded husky as Mildred solidified in front of his eyes. "I had the most wonderful dream. That I was free—"

"You're free now," Mildred said softly. "At least, you're with us and you're okay. And you're still alive."

Doc grimaced. "Is that how you define freedom? Does it not occur to you that we seem to be at the mercy of some blind idiot deity who pushes us on, even when we would wish to stop? An entertainment for Olympians who would wish us to fight the same battles once and again, for all eternity? Never resting, never stopping, always being driven on to constant, repeated combat for nothing more than their own gratification."

"I don't think I would have put it quite like that," Mildred mused. "But I do wonder how much more of a battering a body can take before it just gives up. And for what?"

"Staying alive," Ryan answered. "That's all. Anything else is—shit, what did that old book say? Gravy."

Krysty gave him a curious glance. "What kind of an old book was that, and what the hell did it mean?"

Ryan shook his head, regretting it as some of the dizziness returned. "It was just some old book that I found once, but I figured that what it meant was that keeping out of shit was the main thing, and anything else good was extra and should be appreciated."

"Nice sentiment, strange expression." Krysty shrugged.

"Yeah. But any kind of words won't secure this shit, so let's get to it," Ryan replied, figuring that it was time to stop thinking and to see where they had landed.

IT WAS A SHOCK. All redoubts followed similar patterns, were designed from the same predark plans that meant the old predark sec forces could move from redoubt to redoubt and familiarize themselves with the layout immediately, know where everything was in the case of a sudden alert. Not that it had done any of them much good when the nukecaust had come, because no matter where you were, you had to surface sooner or later. And if you were sec, you were supposed to be fighting this war.

But within the fantasy world of the twentieth-century military, it all made sense: keep these things to a basic design and U.S. soldiers could live down there for as long as it took.

Which was, ultimately, good news for the companions, who could find their way around any redoubt in which they landed. Except that this time they wouldn't have to: they already knew it.

There were many similarities, but all the same every redoubt had its differences and unique points. Some of these were to do with the specific function allotted to the base in its predark life. Some were to do with the ravages of time in the period since. It meant that each redoubt that existed, no matter how long it had been silent, still had its own specific character.

This one hadn't been empty that long. No sooner had Ryan and the companions carried out basic maneuvers and secured the area than the familiarity of this particular redoubt impressed itself upon them.

"Can't be," J.B. said. "Hasn't happened all that often."

"If you consider that there are only a finite number of these infernal places and that the laws of probability dictate—"

"Doc, shut up." Mildred cut across him. "Are you saying that we've been here before? 'Cause I sure as hell don't get any bells ringing."

"You haven't been here before," Ryan answered with emphasis. "Neither has Jak. But the rest of us know this place only too well."

"Only too well indeed," Doc echoed with a touch of melancholy in his voice. He began to wander down the corridor outside the mat-trans control room. He appeared to know where he was going.

"Safe doing that?" Jak questioned.

"There isn't anyone here to harm us," Ryan told him.

"No one, but mebbe a few memories that aren't so great," Krysty murmured.

They followed behind Doc, Mildred and Jak exchanging puzzled glances. No one else spoke. They merely followed the old man as he trailed along the maze of corridors, his demeanor showing a definite intent. He passed numerous closed doors and moved up a level, until coming to a closed door.

The companions held back, letting Doc enter the room on his own. They could hear the sounds of lockers being opened, the rustling of clothes and then silence.

Krysty moved forward silently, looking into the room. Doc was on his knees in front of a line of open lockers, among a pile of clothes. There were jackets, short skirts and buckskin boots. He took a yellow silk blouse and held it up to his nose, inhaling deeply before looking at Krysty with an almost infinite sadness.

"They don't even smell of her. They don't smell of anything at all. It's as though she never existed."

IT HAD BEEN A WHILE. Perhaps not that long, but it was hard to say. So much had happened to them since then that the passage of time seemed impossible to quantify. Finnegan and Hennings were gone. So were Okie and Hunnaker. Doc had been even more of an enigma. Mildred had still been frozen, and Jak still in the bayou. The corpses of Keeper Quint and his sister-wife Rachel were here somewhere, wherever they had dumped them after the firefight that had chilled them—Hunnaker, too. And Lori was lost to them. Quint's daughter—mebbe Rachel's, mebbe another chilled wife's, they'd never been able to work that one out—who had chosen them over the insanity of her inbred family existence and had become Doc's companion. The clean slate of her untutored mind provided a sounding board for the time-traveler's tortured psyche until she had been cruelly snatched from him.

The redoubt had continued to function without anyone to trouble its automated systems. Left to the efficiency of the old tech, it had continued to light and heat the underground warren and to maintain a level of operable capability. It hadn't changed since they had left it.

Which should have given them cause for celebration. The showers and baths still worked, the water was still hot. There were still plentiful supplies and the armory was as it had been left after they had plundered it last time. Even having taken all that they could carry, there was still far more that had been left behind. The size of the armory—indeed, the size of the redoubt as a whole—had been dictated by its proximity to the old Soviet Union, and even though that threat had long since been erased, the detritus of an ancient conflict still marked its passing.

The glittering mosaic floor of the stores still beckoned with operating old tech, clothes, vids and tapes of old shows and music the likes of which Mildred hadn't seen since her predark life.

It should have been a chance for them to rest up, knowing that they were alone and that there was little to disturb them beyond the sec doors to the outside world. They could relax and recuperate.

But it wasn't going to work that way.

The armory, for a start. If the remains of the twisted skeleton they had encountered on their last visit weren't enough, the distorted skeleton was now dust, disturbed from its years of rest, the warning scrawled in blood on the door now faded after being exposed to the touch of human flesh and sweat, they were soon reminded that the majority of the weaponry and ammo left in the armory was of little use to them. The blasters were too big or clumsy, or not makes and models in which any of them were proficient or comfortable. The ammo for the weapons they used was either cleaned out or not there in the first place, the only ordnance left suitable for the blasters they had dismissed.

Beyond the armory, there was enough old tech and cultural artifacts to keep them occupied for years. Except that Jak wasn't interested, Mildred found them reminders of her past that she would prefer to keep buried, and for the others they were reminders only of the previous visit and the disasters that had ensued.

Mildred, tired of being reminded of the world before the nukecaust, asked what had happened.

She listened while they told her and Jak of their previous visit to this redoubt and their encounter with the Keeper. How he had been desperate for new blood to provide for another Keeper to succeed him, and how he and his sister-wife Rachel had clung to the companions to give them that new blood, wanting to keep them here. About how, when they had then left the redoubt they had encountered the Russian bandits who had made their way across the wastelands separating the old United States from the old USSR in the snow-filled lands that had once been Alaska.

Jak nodded recognition when they spoke of the Russian Major, Zimyanin, who had led the Russian sec in pursuit of the bandits. The name was familiar to him from the time when the mat-trans had sent them to the old capital of the USSR, Moscow, and they had once more encountered the granite-faced sec man.

But even though he may have expected to have heard all about their previous encounter, he was astonished when the facts unfolded. The fact that they had broken a dam with an old missile and flooded part of the land in escaping from Zimyanin's arbitrary justice was something that had been unknown to him. Ryan's description of the expression on the Russian's face when the dam broke made Jak laugh, a short, loud bark that broke the silence. A noise he doubled when he heard how the man had been duped by another missile, this one a dummy.

It should have broken the tension, but it didn't. They were all still uneasy. There was little in the way of useful food supplies left from their previous stopover, so they would have to move soon anyway: jump to another location or walk out into a hostile and frozen environment that had been changed by the dam burst. If they jumped, it was possible that the new redoubt and its environs would be just as hostile.

As Ryan had once read in a predark book, better the devil you knew... They'd attempt to find more supplies in the frozen wasteland before attempting a jump.

'RECKON WE SHOULD MOVE as soon as possible," Ryan said to Krysty as they settled into the whirlpool bath that was still working perfectly. "Could make the food last a few days, but..."

Krysty shook her head, the long red tresses flowing freely over her shoulders. Despite the air of unease about the redoubt, there was no danger, and so her sentient hair remained at ease, despite the swirl of worry that surrounded her heart.

"It's going to be hard out there. Real hard. I remember what it was like from before. But it's got to be better than in here. It's like there are ghosts watching us, coming down and pressing us into the ground."

Ryan said nothing for a moment. Finally he broke the silence. "Shouldn't be that way. We've chilled our share—had to, before they chilled us. Quint and Rachel were just another two. No reason they should come back, not something stupe like ghosts, but the memory..."

Krysty reached out and stroked his face, tracing the line of his scar from the empty eye socket down to his jaw. "It isn't them," she said simply. "It's Hunnaker. It's Lori. It's being back where so much really started. And it's being able to relax for once. We know what's out there—more or less—and we know what's in here. There's nothing to keep on edge about. And when you do that, that's when the ghosts start to creep back and you have the time to think about all the things that you don't really want to think about."

"So mebbe the sooner we get on the move, the sooner we have things to deal with and the sooner this feeling will go."

"You got that, lover." She pulled him toward her. "But while we are here, do you remember what we did the last time we used this bath?" Her hands probed beneath the surface of the water, reaching for him. "Oh, yeah, I reckon you do." She smiled.

"Right…" Ryan moved in close, his hands reaching down under the water for her.

It wasn't just sex, it was making love, connecting in a way that they hadn't been able to for too long. They had the space, the privacy and the time. What was more, the intensity drove away the demons, banishing them to some area far away where they could no longer disturb or intrude.

It was only afterward, when they had finished, and had left the bath, that Ryan wandered into the gym that led off the bathroom. While the bath drained as noisily as it had on their previous visit, and Krysty dried herself off, there was some memory that had come back to Ryan and was bugging him. It was only when he looked over at the closed door and expected to see a length of green ribbon that he remembered: Quint had watched them when they were here before and had left the rib-

bon by accident. He wore it in his long, tangled beard.
Krysty had found the length that time. And now Ryan
had expected to see it once again, even though he knew
that was impossible.

He was still standing naked, staring at the door, when
she came out to him. Following the line of his gaze, she
knew what he was seeing in his mind's eye.

"Do you think Doc's right?" he asked simply. Then,
when he noticed Krysty's puzzled stare, he added:
"What he was saying in the chamber, about us repeat-
ing ourselves time and time again. Back here, waiting
for it to start over just like last time..."

"But it's not the same, is it? There's no Quint, no
Zimyanin, and the landscape outside is different after
the dam broke. We've got Jak and Mildred. So it's different. But there are some things that are the same, that
are always the same. There's always some bastard who
wants to stand in our way, or pick a fight with us. So
we fight. Either that or let them chill us, and I don't
know about you, but I don't want to buy the farm yet."

"True enough," Ryan agreed, putting his arm around
her and pulling her close so that he could feel her
warmth, reassure himself that she was real even if his
fears weren't. "But don't you remember that one time
we wanted to head to where Trader said there was a
place we could settle and build a life without having to
fight?"

"Yeah, and look how much we had to fight when we
were looking. No more or less than we have to fight
now. Mebbe it doesn't even exist. Mebbe it's like that
place Mildred told us about once, that was in an old
book. Erewhon. Even heard of that myself, back in Harmony. Supposed to be where everything was perfect."

"So where was it?"

Krysty fixed him with a stare. "Know what you get if you take the letters in Erewhon and put them in a reverse order? Nowhere, Ryan. And mebbe that's what Trader's place is—just somewhere in your head that you can try and make."

"But the disk. If we could ever have cracked that comp code, then—"

"Then mebbe it was only the plans for some so-called perfect place, like all the ideas that those stupes who started the nukecaust ever had. Plans, not a real place. And if it was a real place, mebbe it was standing then but not now."

"So there was no point in searching?"

She shrugged. "Depends what for. If it's for something solid and tangible, then mebbe not. But if it was for somewhere we could settle and make that place ourselves, then mebbe."

"Then every time we land somewhere, there's always a chance. If only it wasn't for those stupe bastards who just don't get it…"

IT SHOULD HAVE BEEN an opportunity for them to get some valuable sleep before they stepped out into the frozen wastes, but no one was in any mood to sleep easily in the redoubt that night. The sense of unease that had permeated the air like a poison gas got into their dreams, making them wake from nightmares. Some never got as far as the nightmares: Doc stayed awake all night, staring at the ceiling, trying to will himself into sleep but failing as the images tumbled around his head. Lori became mixed with Emily, Rachel and Jolyon. His love in the new century entangled with those of two hundred years before. All lost to him now, like everything. Like his very sanity. Even if only from the things he had witnessed since being shot forward into a post-nukecaust world. Let alone the horrors of being dragged from his own time, subjected to whitecoat experiment, then discarded like a broken doll.

By the time morning came, and most had groggily awakened from their disturbed slumbers, Doc was no longer sure if any of this was real. Was he really here or was he still in a cell, taunted and tortured for the benefit of a twisted science?

Even worse, was he still back in the nineteenth century, in a padded cell, raving and delusional while his beloved Emily wept for him?

For, if he were truly mad, how would he know?

Chapter Two

The sec code on the main door was still the same. Of course it was, there was no reason why it would change. The redoubt had been undisturbed since their last visit. That was, surely, part of the problem.

They stood at the entrance, waiting for the door to grind into motion and open. The extreme weather conditions in the wastelands beyond and the lack of anyone to maintain the system, except for those parts that were self-maintaining, had meant that the elements had taken their toll on both the door and its mechanism. Slowly it revealed the world beyond, from the first crack letting in the cold and driving winds, forcing back the constant warm air that had cosseted them since their arrival.

All were equipped for this: the food stores may have been low and next to useless, and the armory of little practical help following their previous incursion, but the mall-like storerooms still had treasures to give forth. They had arrived with clothes that had adequately seen them through warmer climes, but were ill-suited to the conditions they knew they were about to enter. Along the walls of the storerooms, and off in the walk-in compartments that littered the jeweled mosaic floor, they had found boxes and racks of furs and man-made fibers that insulated against the cold. One thing was for sure, the personnel who would have populated the redoubt in the days before the nukecaust, were prepared for the weather.

Krysty and Jak had both chosen furs—rabbit and fox—the pelts sewn together to form a muted pattern that would blend into a landscape less harsh than the one they were about to encounter. Out there, they would show up against the rock and snow. But camouflage wasn't a primary concern. Especially as the artificial fibers chosen by Mildred and J.B. were of brighter colors—orange and blue. These were designed specifically to stand out on the landscape, to make their wearers easy to track. That was irrelevant: what mattered was that both these three-quarter-length padded and insulated coats had a number of pockets, many of which had a depth of more than six inches, strewed about their person. Without such capacious storage, both would have had to keep their supplies swaddled in their usual clothing, tight beneath the outer layer and difficult to reach in times of emergency. It was impossible to carry all their supplies in their satchels.

Ryan had taken a full-length coat in artificial fiber, a Velcro fastening enabling it to be pulled open quickly. He still had his panga strapped to his thigh, and wanted to be sure he could reach it with ease and speed. For this very reason he, like the others, had eschewed the possibility of a full-body covering. In one of these, they would be completely insulated against the temperature drop: yet it would also make them slow and clumsy, their weapons having to be relocated on their bodies, leaving them unable to reach by instinct, and in a fraction of a second, their favored tools of slaughter. The moments spent fumbling in new places, remembering where they had relocated their weapons, would be minimal—yet could make the difference between chill or be chilled. He secured his scarf with its weighted ends around his neck.

Doc, who stood to the rear of the line, was in black. It suited his mood. He had taken a full-length fur that swamped his angular frame, bulking him out so that he was almost unrecognizable. He resembled nothing so much as the kind of trapper he would have been interested to encounter in the time of his birth. But it's doubtful if any trapper, no matter how long he had been alone in the backwoods, no matter how much cabin fever he had endured, would have had the unblinking intensity of stare with which Doc greeted the lifting of the main sec door and the harsh glare of the outside world.

As the door finally ground to a halt, the winds from outside swirled around and welcomed them in a cold embrace. The taint of sulfur in the air caught at their throats and made them choke and cough before they became used to breathing it in. Although it wasn't snowing, the air was still full of small flakes and particles of ice that had been chipped from the surrounding terrain by the strength of the winds. These stung on their exposed skin.

"Let's move it, people," Ryan said simply, leading the way out of the redoubt and into the frozen lands beyond.

Although they were alert for any threat that may be lurking around the mouth of the redoubt, all were still wrapped in their own thoughts, having barely communicated that morning.

Doc was last to leave. He tapped the sec code back

in to close the door, lingering as it ground slowly shut, taking a last look at the interior before it was finally cut off from view.

"Farewell, thou bitter friend," he muttered as the bland expanse of corridor lessened. It was a quote half remembered: where from, he couldn't recall. He could recall little with any clarity, these past few hours, and it was only when he had moments of such stark recognition that he realized what he had become. Old before his time and not even allowed to be within the constraints of that time. He was an exile. Something else came back to him. He said the words softly. "Home? I have no home. Driven out from those that I love, I—" He stopped, his brow furrowing as he sought the words that seemed to chase away in his mind. What was that, and where had he heard it?

Like everything, it was shrouded in a mist of confusion. Even his very being seemed to be nebulous, hidden even from himself. How did he know that everything he had seen and experienced had been true? He remembered his Descartes and the Frenchman's espousal of an idea that it was possible that all he saw was not true, just something placed in front of his eyes by an evil genius who sought to deceive him.

On first reading this, he had thought it a clever conceit and had argued with friends and colleagues on the inherent absurdity of the idea. But now he wasn't so sure. As the door finally closed, who was not to say that it wasn't merely another shutter in a long procession of such; a curtain brought down on a stage while the scenery was changed, ready for the next act.

"Doc, are you listening?"

The old man turned to find Mildred looking back at

him, her face almost obscured by the hood of her padded coat, the snorkel design taking it over her features and hiding her expression.

"Sorry, I—" Doc tried to make himself function, but all he could think was, What if she is not real? The ambiguity paralyzed him. He knew that if all this were genuine, then he had to move, keep up just to survive. But if not, then…

"What the hell is wrong with you? It's just as well I thought to look back, otherwise we would have lost you already. We haven't even got more than a hundred yards from the redoubt and you've already nearly vanished on us." Her tone was sharp, betraying her own unease and shortness of temper.

"My dear Doctor, I cannot apologize. I have not been myself." *Then who are you?* asked a voice in his head. "I shall try to, as you would say, snap out of it."

Mildred's expression, still partially obscured by her hood, softened. "We all felt weird in there, Doc. Even me, and I wasn't here before. It's okay, we can just walk away."

She beckoned to him and waited until Doc had walked a few steps toward her before turning and continuing after the others.

Doc Tanner followed, words and thoughts still racing in his mind, tumbling over one another. There may be situations you can walk away from, times and places. But if it is yourself from which you seek to escape? How can you ever walk away from yourself?

THE FROZEN WASTELAND was much as they remembered it, those who had been here before. The sky was tinged yellow with sulfur, the same that got down into their throats and lungs, making breathing difficult as it scraped at the membrane, making each of them want to choke. Breathing was best if taken in shallow gasps. Deep lungfuls of air made them cough, sucking in more air so that the urge to cough became greater, the circle harder to break. The chem clouds above them tinged the skies with yellow, the heavy banks of gray and yellow scudding across the expanse of sky with a rapidity that spoke of the intensity of the wind currents, the sudden changes in direction for the tumbling clouds making them all the more ominous, as though they were about to lose their abrasive contents upon the earth below.

The terrain was much as they remembered. Banks of snow, meters deep, were driven and formed against sheer rock by the force of the winds, the loose snow on top treacherous, the ice banked beneath waiting to trap them. Against this were the exposed walls and inclines of rock, slippery with long strings and trails of moss and lichen that had been allowed to grow and prosper as the snows were scoured from them. All around, the earth had been broken by the shifting of the rock beds, new inclines, small mountainous ranges and recently formed volcanoes spewing the sulfur into the air, peppering the landscape to the horizon.

It was a harsh terrain to cross and an even harsher environment in which to live. There was little sign of any life that made its home in this unwelcoming terrain, and yet Ryan clearly recalled being attacked by dwarf muties and encountering wild bears on his first excursion into the wastes. There had also been some small communities and isolated trappers who had fallen prey to the Russian bandits. It was doubtful whether their deserted settlements would have been reclaimed by others. Even so, Ryan was still intent on keeping his people focused for any dangers that may be lying in wait.

The floods caused by the breaking of the dam had done little to change this section of the Alaskan tundra. It would be another half-day's march through the oppressive weather conditions before they reached that spot. In the meantime, each could be lost in their own thoughts. Although they remained alert and aware, the atmosphere of the redoubt still weighed heavily on all of them.

MILDRED LOOKED BACK to check that Doc was still following. The black figure, stark against the landscape, trudged through the snow, head held erect against the winds, eyes seemingly—although surely this was a trick of the obscured light—unblinking and wide, regardless of the wind and ice.

Mildred was concerned about the old man. More than the others, she had some kind of grasp of what he had to be feeling. She, too, was out of time and in a world for which she had been ill-prepared. The others had been born to this, it was all that they had ever known. She, on the other hand, had been living in relative affluence and comfort in the late twentieth century before being put out for a routine operation. If all had been well, a few days and she would have been recuperating at home, catching up on soaps and developing couch potato habits, before resuming work. Instead she had awakened to a nightmare that was all the more terrifying for being real.

Since that first moment it had been fear, adrenaline, constant movement and action. Living on the brink of death. Perhaps life was always like that, but it wasn't something that the late 1990s had prepared her for; the stark choices of this new world were often not choices at all, but imperatives. Act first, ask questions later.

What had her life become? These people with whom she traveled were closer to her than anyone she had ever known. They had bonded with her in a way that no one else ever had. J.B., particularly. In many ways she knew them as well as she knew herself. Yet they were as alien to her as…as she was to them.

She frowned, keeping her eyes on the terrain, scanning constantly for any movement that might betoken danger. What the hell had made her feel that way? These were things she had never thought about before, and things that were, in many ways, pointless to consider. There had been downtime before, time in which they could stop and smell the roses—although, come to think of it, she couldn't remember the last time she'd seen anything resembling a rose—but it had never led to her feeling this way. It was something she had caught from the others; particularly from Doc. A kind of melancholy that had spread over them.

It was dangerous. If any of the others were still thinking like this, then they could be at less than triple red. God alone knew what could survive in conditions like this, but sure as hell something could. And it probably wouldn't like them intruding on its territory.

AS RYAN LED THE COMPANIONS, things nagged at him in a way they hadn't before. Since his early days in Front Royal, he had been brought up as befitted a baron's son, albeit not the firstborn. He had been taught to be a man of action, a man who could make snap decisions and be sure of his judgment. There were times when he had to think about what he was doing, when there were many arguments to weigh up, but for the most part he had to trust his gut instinct, honed by years of experience, and act accordingly.

But right now he wasn't sure what that instinct was telling him. A feeling of unease had settled over him like a shroud. Take what they were doing now. He knew, as most of them did, what the terrain and the weather conditions were like out here. In fact, they couldn't wait to get away last time they had landed in this pesthole. And yet, rather than jump immediately, he had decided to lead them out into the wasteland to try to head for the nearest settlement. Was he actually afraid of the mat-trans? The things that had flashed through his mind during the jump were little more than fleeting impressions, vanishing like dreams, like the tendrils of mist that remained after a jump. And yet they had triggered something within him. An unease at how much more of the mat-trans they could take. That had to have influenced his decision, as had the emotions stirred by landing back in a redoubt where they had experienced friends buying the farm.

The words exchanged with Krysty the night before also nagged at his mind. What were they doing this for? Where were they going? Were they cursed in some way to wander forever and never to find peace?

Ryan looked around him at the stark rocks, the deceptive snowbanks that looked solid yet could suck you in meters deep. No sign of wildlife yet, but that growling instinct deep inside told him it was here somewhere. He couldn't afford to let these things take over his mind.

Ryan looked back over his shoulder at the others as they followed. All seemed to be lost in their own thoughts.

All the more reason for him to stay on triple red.

JAK LOOKED UP as Ryan turned back, and for a moment the albino's red eyes flashed as they met with the single blue orb of the man at their head. Ryan never looked back; he was always focused entirely on keeping alert to their surroundings. The fact that he was acting out of character just confirmed what Jak had been thinking.

There was something very wrong with everyone. Something to do with landing in that particular mat-trans. Jak hadn't been to this place before, but it was too cold for his liking. The food in the redoubt had been poor and there hadn't been much of it. Plenty of everything else, but not of anything that really mattered. And there wasn't much out here. His finely honed senses told him that there was some wildlife, but it kept out of the harsh conditions as much as was possible, emerging only to forage for food. Difficult to tell anything from smell, as the rank odor of the sulfur from the volcanoes around them overlaid everything, making it hard to distinguish scents.

Jak could feel the air of gloom and despair that seemed to overlay everyone, but he didn't care. It would pass, like all things. Jak had seen those he cared about most taken from him and chilled. He had traveled forth in search of those who had perpetrated the deed and exacted revenge. And then it was gone. Yes, he remembered. And yes, it hurt. But it didn't matter. There was nothing he could do about it. The only important thing was to stay alive.

In many ways, Jak couldn't understand why the others seemed to be feeling and acting as they did. Things affected him, but he was always very sure of what was a priority. There was a time to think about such things, which was usually in the dark of the night. But not now. Not out here.

If everyone else was going to allow themselves to be distracted by what they had felt back at the redoubt, then Jak was going to have to keep himself on triple red. For the rest of them as much as for himself.

J.B. WAS UNEASY. He knew how everyone was feeling—he'd felt it himself—but now they were out in the wild and it was time to cut the crap and get with the plan. If they were going to reach the settlement called Ank Ridge, then they would have to set a strong pace. He looked up at the sky, pausing to wipe the ice from the lenses in his spectacles and to pull down the brim of his fedora. It would have made a little more sense to stow the hat away and use the hood on his coat—it had a snorkel like the one Mildred was wearing—but it would take a lot to dislodge the Armorer from his beloved hat. It was a part of him, and if you couldn't be yourself, then what was the point of going on?

Dark night, he couldn't believe that thought had just gone through his head. It was like some kind of mental virus that had spread through them, making them slack. They couldn't afford to be slack. Life was too precious, too easily snatched.

Looking up at the clouds, he could see no indication of which part of the sky held the sun. He had a rough idea of their location, but they hadn't made Ank Ridge last time they were here, and he really needed to get a reading so that they could plot a course. His hand went to the minisextant in one of his pockets, reassuringly feeling the contours. Once he could get a reading, then he would feel a little less anxious. The heavy clouds above them looked about ready to unleash a storm. Before that happened, he'd rather know exactly where he was.

Unusually he was in the center of the loose line. Another indication of how things had gone to shit this time out. They were in no fit condition to defend themselves if a danger arose, and this concerned him. But that wasn't all. It still rankled him that they had left so much behind in the armory. Blasters and ammo that weren't their usual weapons but could have been useful. It was a constant struggle to keep their supplies in any kind of firefight-ready state. A few more blasters wouldn't have gone amiss: but no one had been willing to consider that, wrapped up in the gloom of the redoubt and their memories.

For the most part J.B. didn't know what they had to worry about. Looking ahead to Krysty, Jak and Ryan, he felt they were all at the same point. They were alive, and nothing else mattered. He kind of figured Jak may feel that way, too.

But it was when he looked behind him, at Mildred and Doc, that he truly wondered. None of them could imagine what Millie or the old man had been through. None of them could know what was going on in their heads. They could only hope that they could keep it together.

TOGETHER. THAT WAS THE KEY. If they could keep together, they could get through this. Krysty was sensitive to other people's moods. It was a blessing and a curse. Right now, it felt like the latter. There was an oppressive weight—like the clouds above them, she thought with a wry grin—that hung over the group. It had begun when they had realized where they were, and had worsened as they had moped around the redoubt, letting the memories get to them, letting the lack of activity cause them to dwell on what had gone before. But Mother Sonja had taught her that regrets were useless. The only thing to do was to use the mistakes, to use the past to learn and move on.

At least they were moving physically. Mentally, she wasn't so sure. She could still feel the overall mood, and it was still dark. It affected the others as much as it affected her, she was sure. It was merely that they were unaware of the subtle way in which it permeated them.

It would pass. When something happened to jolt them from it, it would dissipate and they would be themselves once more. Most of them. Mebbe not Doc. Fragile at the best of times, coming back to where they had met Lori may be too much for him.

Doc worried her. She shivered from more than just the subzero temperature and pulled herself farther into the fur coat.

DOC KEPT PACE, but only physically. His eyes were staring ahead, but in truth he didn't see the people walking ahead of him as anything more than a series of shapes. They maintained their size as long as he kept equidistance: therefore he adjusted his pace accordingly to theirs. It was simple. It allowed his mind to wander.

Lori. So sweet. Beautiful and blond, with the most astoundingly long legs. Those eyes, always wide with amazement and wonder. He would talk to her, tell her things, and he was sure that she couldn't follow his discourse. Yet sometimes she would understand one thing, then a while after, another, and she would make the link between the two. The expression on her face: the joy of understanding, of having a point of communication between herself and the man who had become her protector. Those moments had been sublime. And they had been so few before she had been cruelly taken from him. As he had been cruelly taken from Emily.

As his life had been cruelly taken from him.

There was only cruelty. Nothing more. The rest was a pretence to lull him into a sense of security that was no longer justified.

There was— He stopped, looked up as a distant rumble was followed by a sudden flurry of snow and ice on the wind.

Storm.

Chapter Three

Within seconds the air around them became an impenetrable mass of ice and snow, whipped to a ferocious speed by the sudden squalls of wind. The lightly numbing sensation of ice on the skin became the pinprick whiplash of seemingly solid particles hurled against the face and hands with venom by the elements. Where they had been able to see in front, to the back and sides, to identify where the others stood, now they were all alone, each of them lost in the sudden blanket of white that the storm threw up around them.

Ryan cursed to himself, screwing up his good eye against the constant flurry of razor-sharp icicles that threatened to blind him, the empty socket of his rendered eye now gnawing with a dull ache as the cold penetrated through to the bone, bypassing even the flayed nerve-endings around the old wound. If they didn't find cover soon, then they would be lost forever. If they didn't find one another, then all hope should be abandoned now.

Taking a moment, dragging a breath as deep as he dare without taking the freezing snow into his lungs and turning them to ice, Ryan calmed himself. Panic was the real chiller in such situations. If he could keep calm, move with economy, then there was a chance.

He hadn't changed direction since the storm suddenly hit, so he knew roughly where the others had to be in relation to him. He could only hope that they, too, had been able to stay calm and not make any sudden, panicked movements. Normally he would stake his life on it, but since they had landed in the redoubt there had been a mood that made nothing as certain as it had been before. He knew how much he had been affected and had seen the others change similarly.

There was only one way to know for sure. In the pockets and concealed storage flaps on his coat, he had a length of nylon rope. Tough, fibrous and waxed to insure that it would run smoothly through the hands, it had lain unused since before skydark. What had made him pick it up, he couldn't say, but he was glad now that he had. He couldn't tell how long it was in total, so—unwilling to waste too much of the length—he opted to tie it around one sinewed wrist rather than his waist. Looping and tightening the knot, he payed out a short length and took slow, deliberate strides toward the last position he had seen Krysty.

He remained silent. There was no point shouting, as any cries would have been carried away on the winds, buried beneath the howling of the storm. To risk expelling air and inhaling the snows was another drawback. Better to try to use energy wisely.

Underfoot was becoming treacherous. They had been on a rock surface that grew slippery with the settling of the snow and ice. Ryan took each step carefully, trying to control the urge to move quickly lest he completely lose his way. The slow-motion feel was enhanced by the blanket of snow formed by the storm, making it seem as though he was standing still, even though he knew his feet were actually moving.

Then, so suddenly that it made him almost start in surprise, a shape loomed out of the white; a dark patch in the blizzard resolving itself into a head of wild red curls surmounting a heavy, snow-sodden fur. Krysty was looking around, wary, as though she were too cautious to move.

Without words, she moved toward Ryan. Although visibility was impaired by the whirling snow and ice, she could see the rope and she knew what she had to do. Tying herself on, she beckoned Ryan to the position where she had last seen Jak.

The albino was also noticeable by his fur, forming another dark shape that loomed out of the whiteness. He was waiting patiently, as though expecting them.

Forming a train, attached by the umbilical of the waxed rope, the three of them moved through the storm, trying to keep bearings on where their companions had been stationed when the storm descended. All could feel the cold begin to seep into their bones, aching that gave way to a comforting numbness, making them feel drowsy. Just lying down where they stood and falling into a deep sleep would feel so good—a sleep so deep that they knew, individually and without having to affirm this with the others, that they would never awaken.

Time was on a delicate balance. They had to find the others and then find some kind of shelter before the cold claimed them. One of the two was hard enough, given that they had to act swiftly and yet were hampered by conditions. To do both was almost asking the impossible. Yet they had no option: to think of either success or failure was to invite despair and to waste time. They could only act, not think.

Dogged movements through the opaque blanket of

white took them to J.B. The Armorer met them halfway, his own plan being to try to move toward them. His keen sense of direction had stood him in good stead among the whiteout chaos. Mildred was with him, having been close enough to catch up to him before the snows had become too obscuring.

Which left Doc.

THE WHITENESS. Comforting. Like the blankets that covered me when I was young. Perhaps I should lay down now and sleep as I once slept beneath a counterpane this hue. Feel cold and yet warm. The outside will try to suck the heat from within me. Who am I to resist? There is nothing now but the white: the blank sheet of my mind, wiped clear of all extraneous matter. This is the state to which I should aspire, the state from which all madness shall recede. I shall be whole again. To sleep perchance to dream. But what if I no longer wish to dream? What if I just wish to sleep and never wake? Or to sleep and then, when finally I am wrested from the arms of Morpheus to find myself back in the realms of sanity and the warm embrace of my beloved and our children?

Now there is little to do but sink into the embrace of the light. It keeps away the phantoms that have so tortured me, making it a matter of simply resting my weary bones before blessed oblivion...

MILDRED INDICATED where last she had seen Doc. Unwilling to say anything in the teeth of the gale, to waste breath and energy, she pointed to where the shambling figure of Doc had last been located.

Roped together, as quickly as they dared in the uncertain and treacherous conditions, the five of them moved in a close line through the blinding hail of ice and snow. Stumbling on the rock and ice beneath, one almost dragging the others down with every other step, they continued toward the area where Doc had last been seen.

Mildred let out an involuntary curse as her feet hit a soft yet unyielding object. There was nothing in front of her eyes except the white of the storm, and the sudden obstruction caused her to pitch forward, dragging J.B. behind her. Although Mildred went down, the Armorer struggled to keep his footing. The last thing they needed in such conditions was to tangle themselves by all hitting the ground. Feeling him pull on them, the others braced and held their footing until equilibrium was restored.

Mildred, meanwhile, had recovered herself enough to be in a kneeling position and to know that the obstruction that had caused her to fall was the prone body of Doc Tanner. He lay on his side, curled up in a fetal ball, eyes wide and unseeing. For a moment she feared that he might have bought the farm, but as she put her palm in front of his face she could feel the heat of his breath.

It was as though he had given up and lay down to die.

By this time, the others had gathered. Mildred looked up and from her expression they knew that he was alive, despite their first impression.

Now they were together; the first part of their task had been achieved. But with each passing second the blazing storm sucked the heat from them, despite the thickness of their garb. The snow and ice stung the skin, the constant wet and cold causing the skin to chafe and split on the faces, their eyes streaming as the water was driven relentlessly into the fragile membrane. Stiffness crept into their every limb, making movement harder with every moment.

They had to move, to find shelter. But where? Wordlessly, Ryan moved so that he could help Mildred lift Doc to his feet. The old man was unhelpful but not obstructive. It was as though he had no notion of what they were doing, his body a deadweight, a neutral presence.

Jak indicated that they should move to the left, and took the lead. Ryan had no idea where the albino was headed, but trusted the hunter's sharp instincts to have spotted some possible shelter before the storm had made the landscape a featureless blank.

Jak always kept himself open to the environment, no matter how it may be constituted, which was how he had managed to hone his hunting instincts in earlier days. It was how he was able to survive now. Even though thoughts other than the immediate surroundings had been racing through his mind while they had marched, still a part of his attention had been focused on the area through which they traveled, searching out any places where fresh game may be found and where dangers may lie. As a result, he had spotted an area almost hidden behind a snowbank, where the rock had risen from the earth and formed a shelf. The snow had banked and gathered beneath it, but at one end it tailed away. There seemed to be no apparent reason for this, and Jak had figured that some passing fauna had burrowed it out or else it had failed to take because of a vein of heat.

The nearest volcanic mass was about half-hour's march from where they now stood. That didn't mean that a shift in the earth and a fissure in the rock hadn't formed a tunnel through which some of the heat from the mass could escape.

Unerringly, not thinking but trusting to instincts that had rarely set him wrong, Jak led them toward the area where he had seen the break in the snowbank.

It was impossible to tell how near or far they may be until they were upon it. The ice beneath their feet grew less slippery, but the snows deeper, sucking at them with every step, trying to pull them down, making forward progress harder with every movement.

Breath came in short gasps, lactic acid building in muscle and making their limbs feel heavy and useless, stumbling and almost falling, dragging one another down. Ryan and Mildred suffered most, with Doc propped between them, his arms over their shoulders, their own supporting his weight. He moved his legs mechanically, almost as if unaware of what he was doing, his weight shifting unpredictably as his feet lost purchase and he slipped first one way, then another. It was difficult for Ryan and Mildred to keep him—and themselves—from falling face-first into the snowbank. Strength of will, stubbornness, a need to survive—those were the only things that could account for dragging one leaden foot after another, thigh muscles knotting in white-hot agony, so hot that they felt as though they could melt the snow and ice surrounding...

And then they were out of the storm. Without even realizing, they passed from light to dark, white to black. From numbing cold to something a little warmer that was at first ineffective, but gradually began to thaw the cold in their bones, the numbness turning to the pain of frozen skin and muscle before easing into something approaching normal. Pins and needles running through their extremities, a maddening itch inside their skin that couldn't be scratched.

The floor was solid rock, uneven and with a layer of moss that gave it an almost soft, carpeted feel. Inside their heavy clothing, even with the moisture the materials had absorbed, they felt circulation begin to return. They were thankful that Jak's ability to study and analyze his surroundings without even thinking about it had led him here. A thankfulness that they couldn't share with one another, as they gasped in the warm air, able now to breathe more easily without freezing their throats and lungs, yet still unable to speak.

After the bright white of the outside world, the cavern in which they found themselves was, at first, pitch-black. A little light filtered in from the narrow opening to the outside world, marked by some moisture where the storm intruded, the cold air battling in swirls with the warm air expelled from the cave. Gradually, as their eyes adjusted to the darkness, the light—such as it was—enabled them to discern dimly outlined shapes. Even Jak, whose red pigmentless eyes preferred the gloom to the brilliance of strong light, found the conditions hard to read.

They found themselves in a cavern that had a roof a little over ten feet in height. Recovered sufficiently to do more than hunker on his hands and knees gasping for breath and allowing his muscles to relax, for the seizing up of his body to gradually yield, Ryan withdrew a flashlight from one of his pockets and switched it on. The battery was still working, although not at full power. It barely illuminated the roof at the highest point, but showed the companions that they were in the cen-

ter of the largest section of the cavern. It was narrow at
the mouth through which they had passed, barely five
feet in height, and rose to the ten-foot limit at which
they found themselves, before sloping to less than the
circumference at the opening. Down to about four feet,
it seemed to tail off into an endless tunnel, the beam of
the flashlight not reaching far enough into the gloom to
make the far wall visible—if indeed, there was a far wall
and they were not at one end of an indefinite tunnel. The
constant flow of warm air made this likely.

"Thank heavens for that," Mildred gasped, the first
to speak. "I don't think any of us would have lasted
much longer out there."

"Some less than others," Krysty added, dragging
herself over to where Doc lay unmoving and seemingly
oblivious to his surroundings. "How's he doing?"

"Your guess is as good as mine." Mildred shrugged.
"It's more than just the blizzard that's got to him. The
physical symptoms I can treat, but the rest of it…" She
trailed off with a shrug.

"We'll worry about that later." Ryan spoke with a
note of concern in his voice. The flashlight was flickering, the beam failing. He hit the base, hoping that it
was a connection rather than the battery that was causing the problem. J.B. delved into his own supplies and
produced another.

"Always have a contingency plan," he commented
wryly as he handed it to Ryan. "Millie's got one, as
well, right?" he added, turning to her for confirmation.

Before answering, she rummaged through her own
storage capacity to check that it was still on her person.
"Check," she affirmed as she found it. "At least that
should keep us going for a while."

"Storm pass soon," Jak speculated, casting an eye at the mouth of the cave. "Too fierce last, mebbe blow out."

"Figure it might. If and when, we need to have some definite plan. We've been wandering like a bunch of stupes. Nearly bought us the farm...can't let that happen again." Ryan gasped between sentences, the warm air still hurting in lungs that had breathed too much ice to clear quickly.

"Soon as it passes, I'll work out exactly where we've ended up and head us toward Ank Ridge," J.B. stated. Ryan agreed. A glance at Krysty told him that she was agreeable.

"What Ank Ridge got?" Jak asked. It wasn't a question of dissent, rather one of curiosity.

"Didn't get there last time we were in these parts, but it's supposed to be the only ville in these Gaia-forsaken parts," Krysty explained. "Got to be better than what we've seen so far."

"Not hard." Jak shrugged.

Conversation fizzled out. They were too tired for anything other than basics. Mildred and Krysty tended to Doc. After a short while, he seemed to become a little more aware of his surroundings. Although still silent and staring unseeing around him, he responded to touch and allowed them to seat him upright to tend to the abrasions and cuts he had suffered during the flight from the storm.

Ryan, J.B. and Jak marked out territory, examining the mouth of the cave and venturing a few hundred yards down the dark abyss of the tunnel. It seemed to stay at a constant height after a certain point and showed no signs of harboring dangers.

"Where does it go?" J.B. asked. It was a rhetorical question, but Ryan answered, as much to confirm his ideas to himself as anything else.

"Figure it goes back to that big volcano we saw about two miles from here. When it got thrown up, I'd guess that this was formed by some kind of pressure blow-out, like a safety valve of some kind. That'd explain the hot air."

"Then let's just hope that the bastard doesn't want to blow itself before the storm blows out, otherwise we get boiled or frozen," J.B. muttered darkly.

Having marked out their parameters, the three men returned to where Doc was being tended by Krysty and Mildred.

"How's he doing?"

"Better physically, but as for the rest..." Mildred shook her head sadly. "Wherever he is, it sure isn't here."

They set camp where Doc was resting. With nothing in the cave to make a fire, they used some of the few self-heats they had left, some from the last remains of the food stores in the redoubt and some that they had been carrying with them. The food was foul-tasting, but had the necessary nutrition. They were all too exhausted to care about anything except restoring some nourishment and getting some sleep, eating in silence, Mildred feeding Doc. The old man took some of the food, but most of it dribbled down his slack chin, his eyes moving from side to side without seeing.

I. ONLY I. HOW CAN I be taking sustenance when there is nothing but myself, and I know that I am not the one feeding me. There is only one answer. Whoever is feed-

ing me does not exist, and I am not really eating. The food and the feeder are nothing more than mere illusions sent to torture me, to take me back to the hell from whence I have only recently managed to flee. But I shall not return. If that was sanity, then I wish nothing more than insanity. If it was insanity, then whatever truth sanity holds for me cannot surpass the horror of the mad places.

There is only I.

I... But who am I?

THEY TOOK TURNS SLEEPING, Ryan electing to take first watch as leader, allowing the others to rest. He kept one flashlight going, using the one that was beginning to fail until the flickering beam cast light no farther than a couple of yards past where they rested. He switched to the flashlight J.B. had given him, using it to sweep the area to the rear of the cave and to light the area at the mouth. All the same, he was careful to dip the beam so that it hit the rock immediately in front of the opening and didn't shine out into the wastes beyond. It was unlikely there was anything out there to notice a sudden sweep of light should it appear, but he sure wasn't about to take that chance.

A perverse aspect of this storm was that it seemed to have swept through them and burned out the melancholy and apathy that had permeated their bodies. Say what you like about the adrenaline rush of danger, and how much you'd like to avoid it, but it put things into perspective. Survival pissed all over introspection every time. It was just a shame that it had taken this storm and nearly buying the farm to wake them up.

Wake them up. Wake him up. Ryan was suddenly

aware that his reverie had been the beginning of a descent into sleep. Jerking his head up, blinking heavily, he realized that he hadn't been as aware as he would have liked. Outside, the sound of the howling wind had dropped and the snow shone white in the darkness of the night, the storm slowly subsiding and the blanket of white becoming a dappled curtain. Deceptively pretty to the eye, especially the eye that was trying to stay wakeful.

Ryan swept the area with the flashlight, the beam extending into the dark.

There was something that made him stop and flash back over the area he had already covered.

There was nothing. Something. Nothing... Was it his imagination, some hallucination brought on by his need to sleep?

"Ryan, what going on?" Jak raised his head, disturbed by the beam that had wavered and hit him as it passed over the ground. He was alert, having snapped into consciousness immediately. He frowned as he saw the torpor on Ryan's face.

"Not sure... Thought I saw something," Ryan said haltingly. "It was back there, but..."

Jak scrambled to his feet. He could see that Ryan was almost losing consciousness as he tried to speak. The one-eyed man had pushed himself to the limit and beyond, and it was now catching up with him.

Jak took the flashlight as Ryan let it droop. Now that Jak was awake, every fiber of his being was telling him he could rest, even though he was trying to will himself to stay conscious.

"Ryan, sleep now. Let me take over."

Ryan could hardly bring himself to assent before

letting his eye close and the warmth of sleep begin to
envelop him. Jak let him settle into a prone position before hunkering down to take over watch. He frowned
as he scanned the darkness beyond the scope of the
flashlight beam. There was nothing visible, but it wasn't
like Ryan to see things that weren't there—fatigue or
no fatigue. Yet he couldn't catch sight of anything.

That didn't mean it wasn't there.

Jak cast a glance toward the cave entrance. The storm
was subsiding, and perhaps by the time they had all
rested, and the daylight had come, they would be able
to move.

So why couldn't he shake the feeling that, despite the
evidence to the contrary, Ryan had been right when he
saw something in the dark maw of the tunnel?

Jak rose to his feet, moving a few yards into the
depths of the cave, throwing the flashlight beam farther
into the blackness that swallowed it up hungrily. He
wouldn't go farther, leave the sleeping companions un-
guarded, but he was torn. Something was nagging at
him. Something that had no reason but still irritated
like an unscratched itch.

Shaking his head, backing up to where they lay, he
settled down to keep watch. Eyeing the lightening sky
outside, he judged it only a few hours until daybreak.
They should be safe…should be.

JAK WAS STILL and silent. Nothing escaped him. Particularly the gradual change in temperature. From deep in
the caves the air began to heat up, the strength of the
current increasing exponentially. He looked toward the
mouth of the cave. The storm had almost subsided, the
darkness had almost broken into dawn. Yet it was still

night, there was still a squall, and the companions needed rest. Would fate allow them enough time to recover before the volcano a few miles away belched enough hot air—mebbe even lava—to engulf them and make staying here an impossibility?

It was a chance that they couldn't afford to take. Jak rose swiftly, moving to wake J.B. first, as the Armorer had rested longer than Ryan. It was as Jak crouched over J.B.'s supine form that he froze: there was something else on the air. The heat made the musk all the stronger and it was distant but growing closer with every breath. Dogs. Perhaps those that had strayed from settlements, been driven away from trappers when they had been decimated by nature or the Russians some time back. They'd be wild now, and presumably ended up in the caves seeking shelter from the storm, as had the companions, wandering farther down into the tunnels and caves, seeking the heat.

Now they were being driven back by that very heat as it intensified.

Jak shook J.B. roughly. The Armorer jolted awake, mumbling softly and fumbling for his spectacles.

"What—"

Jak silenced him with a hand across the mouth. "Trouble. Wild dogs. Near. Wake others." And before J.B. had a chance to fully take in what the albino was saying, he had moved on to Krysty, shaking her in a similar fashion.

There were times when Jak's use of words verged on the elliptical, but at least at this moment his meaning was clear. As was J.B.'s head, shaking it to clear the fug of sleep before he scrambled to his feet, reaching out to wake Mildred. He whispered a few words to her as she emerged from her slumber. It was as well that she slept lightly, needing as she did to think on her feet.

She had Doc to worry about. The old man was sleeping now, but in his current state there was little difference between Doc asleep and Doc awake. He was in no fit state to defend himself if trouble appeared. She moved over and shook him by the shoulder. His eyes snapped open instantly and he looked directly at her.

"I had hoped that you would have vanished and my terrible dreams would be at an end, but I can see that I am to be further tried by whatever agency deigns to—"

"Can it, Doc," she snapped, glad to see him less catatonic but in no mood to listen to one of his soliloquies. "Whatever you think I am, just know that you've got to defend yourself."

"I see, I—" This time he cut himself off, aware of the baying and skitter of claws on rock that began to reach the companions from deep in the tunnel. Because of the low roof, there was little echo to the sound and it was hard to tell if the animals were a few yards or a few hundred yards away. The only thing for sure was that the stench of their musk began to grow stronger, permeating their nostrils, lodging in their clothes and that they had to be prepared to fight within seconds.

Doc clammed up as though someone had clamped his jaw shut. Somewhere within his mind, an instinct for defense took over. Whatever space his head was inhabiting at this point in time, it had been pushed to one side by the will to survive.

While Doc was having no trouble adapting, Ryan was experiencing the opposite. Jak shook him hard, pounded at him, but the one-eyed man woke slowly. He had exhausted himself to such an extent that his aching limbs and weary muscles demanded respite, and the warm embrace of sleep refused to unclasp from around his mind. He opened his eye and saw Jak, lit from beneath by the flashlight he was holding so that his pale face looked all the more ghostly, but could not take in what the albino was saying. The words came as a jumble, even though they were sparing. Jak repeated himself, more urgently, but Ryan's attention was wandering and his eye roamed around the dark cavern, taking in that there was a lot of sudden movement, but not taking in why until he caught a flash of movement beyond the light, shapes shifting in the darkness that made the black move as a sentient beast. That and the smell that filled his lungs, the viscous smell of warm fur and sweating muscle.

That was when the instincts kicked in, the adrenaline flooded through him and, despite the fatigue that had been winning the battle only a few moments before, he scrambled to his feet, pushing Jak aside, reaching for the panga sheathed on his thigh. He had only one thing on his mind now—the shifting black was resolving itself into the shapes, sounds and smells of an attacking pack of wild dogs. Why now, why them? No time to think, only to act.

Ironic, then, that his sudden reaction to danger was to plunge them even further into trouble.

Not fully functioning, Ryan had moved too quickly, too rashly. As he came to his feet, fumbling for the panga sheath, he knocked Jak backward. The albino had excellent balance under usual circumstances, but the speed of Ryan's reaction, coming from a man who had been almost comatose only a few moments before, had taken him off guard. Jak slipped on the carpet of moss, only for a fraction of a second, but enough for him to shift his grip on the flashlight as he adjusted his balance. His thumb glanced over the switch and the flashlight was extinguished. The cavern was plunged into darkness.

The dogs were now upon them. Crazed with fear by whatever had driven them from the depths of the tunnels, they had no other desire than to escape and would rip to pieces anything that got in their way. Theirs wasn't the mien of creatures who were on the hunt. Deep within the tunnels and caves, where they had retreated for warmth and shelter, something was happening that had served to terrify them and to drive them out into the cold of the outside world. The sudden increase in the intensity of the air flow and the corresponding rise in heat from deep within the tunnel system suggested that the volcano had begun to spark into life.

The dogs were crazed with fear, every animal awareness telling them to flee. And now they were faced with a pack of hostile humans who blocked their way. Humans who were, for the most part, handicapped by the sudden loss of light.

The slavering dogs, dripping at the jaws from panic and the exertion of their flight, were guided more by their olfactory sense than by vision. They could smell the companions as they clustered in the center of the cavern, attempting to find their bearings by touch and smell alone, the sudden descent of the black curtain of darkness leaving them no time to adjust to any kind of wan light or moving shapes within the dark.

These creatures were in the way of the wild pack. They reeked of fear and confusion. They were easy meat.

Snarling and yelping, the dogs flew at the companions. Ryan had by now unsheathed his panga and J.B.'s hand had snaked toward his Tekna knife as soon as the light was extinguished. There was no way that anyone could risk blasterfire in this confined space, and with this lack of light, hand-to-hand combat was the only option...if hand-to-jaw fighting could be called as such.

Ryan and J.B. had weapons and Jak was quick to palm a leaf-bladed knife into each hand so that he could attack on two fronts. But Mildred, Krysty and Doc had no weapons to hand and their only chance was to make defensive moves, to try to prevent the animals from taking chunks from their flesh. Hard enough at the best of times, but made more difficult by the lack of any illumination. Only Jak had any degree of vision, his pigmentless red eyes better suited to the dark. But even he was no match for the wild dogs, guided by their noses rather than eyes.

The pack tore into the middle of the companions, scattering them across the floor of the cave, forcing them back against the walls. In a sense, this worked to their advantage, as their backs were now covered. But for those with weapons, it made it harder to thrust when their elbows were constricted by a sheer rock face, any force to their thrust and parry noticeably curtailed.

With no light, there were only the vaguest outlines of shapes, appearing and disappearing from their restricted lines of vision. A dark bulk would appear from nowhere, slamming into them or rising up above, the sudden flash of a wild yellow eye followed by fetid breath and sprays of rancid saliva. There was little or no indication from where the next shape would loom, and the snapping jaws and sharp claws gouged at any part of the body within reach, scratching and biting at exposed flesh, tearing cloth where the weaponless companions attempted to use their heavy clothing to block the attack.

For those with weapons, the indicator of a hit wasn't visual, but the jarring at the elbow when a blade stuck in flesh, grated against bone. The warm, sickly sweet smell of blood mixed with the musk of dog glands, yelping noises and cries of pain mixing with the exultation of the yowling attack, tempering the pack as some of their number slumped to the moss-covered floor. Underfoot, blood and urine—the ammonia stench mixing nauseously with the sweetness of the blood—swamped the moss and rock, making it treacherous. To move was to risk slipping, falling beneath the wild animals and leaving yourself open to a chilling attack.

Ryan and J.B. were hitting with roughly every third strike, feeling skin rip and flesh score beneath their blades, smelling the blood flow. Jak was more efficient, almost every strike hitting home, helped by the fact that his vision was slightly better, his aim unimpeded by the lack of light. But was it making the creatures wilder and angrier, feeding a ravenous desire to attack more? Or was it keeping them at bay? It was a difficult call, and there was little the companions could do except to keep striking out.

Ryan cursed heavily when he heard a human scream in among the animals. It was Doc. The voice was unmistakable. One of the creatures had got through the old man's guard and taken a chunk from him. Would he be able to stay on his feet or would the wound cause him to stumble and fall? There was nothing the one-eyed man could do to expedite the situation. He just had to hope for the best, hope that the spreading pools of blood and urine, the stench of this mixed with fear and confusion in the wounded animals, would persuade the pack to retreat.

In the end, it was something else that forced their hand. From deep within the caves, there was a low rumble and a violent blast of hot air that singed hair and skin, the force of it almost knocking the companions from their feet. Volcanic activity, perhaps the precursor to the main stack blowing.

It was decisive. The heat and noise spread panic among the pack, distracting them from their task. Yelping in fear, the dogs retreated from the fray, heading for the mouth of the cave and the relative safety of the outside world.

So hard was it for the companions to keep upright and overcome heat so strong that none realized, for a moment, that their attackers had fled. Then the blast of hot air, stinking of sulfur strong enough to obscure the blood and urine, dissipated, dropping to a gentle waft of air, the heat becoming more bearable.

Jak realized that the pack had fled before anyone else, and groped among the shapes on the floor for the flashlight, finding it slick with blood. It took three attempts to hit the switch, so slippery was the surface, and he had to clean the bulb of splattered blood, which gave the light a reddish tinge.

Casting the beam around the floor of the cavern, he was able to assess the extent of the carnage. The floor was awash with a lake of fluid, mixed equally of blood and urine. Five dogs lay within it, staring lifelessly, their throats, stomachs and forequarters covered in deep cuts. They were still seeping their precious fluids into the lake. Some looked like huskies, others had a more mixed lineage. If there were five chilled, Jak wondered how many others had limped out with wounds that would later claim them. The mouth of the cave, as he cast the beam farther afield, showed trails of blood that staggered out into the snow beyond. There were at least six of these, maybe more. They were so confused that it was hard to tell. He wondered how large the pack had been, but that no longer mattered. They were gone, and from the blast that had driven them out, it was a safe bet that the companions should follow swiftly.

Throwing the beam around the cavern walls, he could see that Ryan and J.B. were breathing heavily, spattered in blood that wasn't their own. Both men did, however, have some contusions. Their blades drooped limply in their hands, slick liquid dripping from the tip of each. Seeing their superficial wounds, Jak was aware of a slight stinging on his own face and arms where he had been caught. Best to get these dressed soon, before they became infected.

As for Krysty and Mildred, they seemed to have fared better, in some ways, than the armed members of the party. Keeping their movements to the defensive and not having to expose themselves by attacking, they had escaped anything but the most minor grazes, although the clothing they had wrapped around their forearms to block the dog attacks had been ripped to shreds.

But it was Doc who caused the most concern. The old man was slumped against the wall of the cavern, sunk to his haunches. His hair hung around a face whose ashen pallor it matched. It was as though the blood seeping from the wounds on his right arm and ribs had drained straight from his shocked, expressionless features. No sooner had Jak's flashlight highlighted his plight than Mildred was beside him, reaching into a pocket to find something among her medical supplies that would staunch the bleeding.

"Fireblast and fuck it." Ryan spit. "That was one thing we didn't need."

"You mean, the volcano, the dogs or Doc getting bitten?" J.B. asked dryly.

"Shit, all of them," Ryan muttered, casting a glance toward the dark maw of the tunnel. "Can't hang around here waiting for that bastard to blow and fry us. We're gonna have to move out."

"Not before I've treated Doc," Mildred said over her shoulder, pulling Doc's frock coat and shirt away from the bite wounds. She examined them, squinting in the half light. "Jak, bring that damn flashlight over where I can see something," she yelled. As Jak complied, it became obvious that the wounds seemed worse than they really were. Although Doc was bleeding freely, the flesh hadn't been scored that deeply and some bandaging would staunch the flow. She set about the task while the others cleaned themselves off as best as they could and prepared to leave.

"Anyone else?" she questioned as she slipped a needle from a vacupack and injected the old man with antibiotics. The prepacked and loaded hypos had been in the redoubt's med bay for more than a century, but there was no reason to believe that they had been tampered with or contaminated in any way. Biggest risk was that the serum within had lost its potency, the chemical makeup breaking down. If that was so, she would have to watch Doc for the first signs of a fever and hit him with another.

Quickly and efficiently she dressed the minor abrasions and contusions that the others had suffered, all the while casting a glance back to Doc, who sat slumped on the floor, seemingly unaware of anything that was going on around him.

Ryan could see that the dawn was breaking beyond the mouth of the cave. Krysty followed his gaze.

"Let's hope the pack hasn't decided to stick around to see if they can pick us off when we come out," she murmured.

"It's not likely. They were more scared of the heat than pissed at us, and from the look of those, they've been feeding well of late," he added, indicating the corpses on the cave floor. "They'll be well away from here. Our problem's gonna be the cold and finding a ville, because I'm wondering just what they've been feeding on lately."

Krysty followed his eye down to the dog carrion. The creatures were well-muscled and their fur, though matted by blood now, showed signs of having been in good condition. So where, in this wasteland, had they found a rich source of food?

The temperature within the cave was rising and deep rumblings from far off suggested that a second expulsion of heat and pressure wasn't far away. It would be best if they moved sooner rather than later.

"Is Doc ready to go?" Ryan asked Mildred.

"As he'll ever be." She helped Doc to his feet. He looked around him, eyes staring but unseeing. He seemed confused, but at least he was able to move under his own propulsion. That would make things easier. "Doc, I hope you can take some of this in, you old buzzard. We've got to leave now. Stick close, just keep walking, and tell me if you think you're running a temperature. You got that?"

He failed to respond, seeming to stare right through her.

"Do you think he understood any of that?" Krysty asked.

"I don't know," Mildred replied, shaking her head. "Even if only part of it made sense, that's better than nothing. We're just gonna have to keep a real close eye on the old bastard."

Gathering themselves together, they headed out into the early morning light, the cold hitting them like a hammer as they stepped beyond the bounds of the cave, slipping and sliding their way down the snowbank to the rock beneath. The trail of blood left by the dog pack became less visible on the moss and lichen, petering away to nothing. There was no sign of the animals within view. They had either gone to ground somewhere else or made their way off around the rock ledge and were headed in a direction obscured by the outcrops. Whatever the answer, it left the companions free of at least one worry.

J.B. looked up at the sun. The sky was almost clear of cloud right now, only a few wisps of yellow-tinged cumulus disturbing the purple-tinged blue. The cold was crisp, so much so that it almost froze the breath from their mouths. The winds had dropped in the post-storm lull so that there was no ice or snow swirling around them.

Perfect conditions for the Armorer to determine their position. Taking the minisextant from one of his pockets, he took readings that enabled him to pinpoint where they were currently and where the settlement of Ank

Ridge lay in relation to their position. He worked quickly, aware that the sooner they got moving, the quicker they would reach their destination and the sooner they would start to generate some warmth through activity.

"It's got to be that way, due east," he said finally, pointing across the plains of rock and ice, away from the volcanic activity. "Hell of a trek by the look of it. Land's so flat I figure we can see a good ten miles with the naked eye. No sign of anything there, so it's got to be beyond."

Mildred sighed. "If that's the way that it's got to be, then that's the way it's got to be. Sooner we get going, the sooner we find some kind of life, right?"

Ryan shrugged. "If there was a better way…"

Falling into formation, they began to march, not wanting to waste energy on further words. Their options were limited, and the only thing to do was to march and hope, a steady pace to keep warm and make progress, not fast enough to exhaust them but not too slow to arrest that very progress.

As they marched—Ryan at point, J.B. at the rear, with Jak following Ryan, Mildred and Krysty flanking Doc—each had time for his or her own thoughts once more. But unlike their march from the redoubt, there was determination and purpose here. The morbid introspection and melancholy that had run through them like a virus in the redoubt had been banished by the need to focus. Whatever psychological infection had swept through them had been wiped out by the urge to survive.

Across the lichen-covered rock and patches of ice they made good time, keeping a steady pace. There was nothing to distract them. Nothing outside. The only distraction that could possibly cause delay would be internal—and none would fall prey to that.

Except perhaps Doc.

I ALONE. I alone yet tired. If there truly is nothing beyond my own self, then what am I doing to cause myself so much pain? Phantoms that appear as wild beasts. Phantoms that appear as those who have populated my dreams once before. The beasts that tear my flesh as they tear my soul. Yet these people who are my dream companions seek to help me. I know not why, yet feel that if I am to understand why I am dreaming this madness I must follow them. They are my guides.

Perhaps, if I follow, they will reveal the purpose of my dream. Perhaps they are here to lead me from the madness and back to the real world.

If this is a test, from a deity or from some evil genius who seeks to test me for their own end, then I must stay the course. But every step becomes so hard. It is so cold, and yet I feel so hot, as though the very blood that courses through my veins is liquid fire.

THEY HAD BEEN MARCHING for hours, thinking of nothing but the task at hand. Krysty and Mildred had stayed close to Doc. He remained silent, distant from them. There was little indication that he could even acknowledge their existence. But he was still marching, keeping pace. Something was driving him onward.

Mildred frowned as she looked back at him. Was she wrong, or were there red patches flaring over his cheekbones, barely visible against the pallor of his gaunt visage? Was his gait getting a little stiff compared to when she had looked back a few minutes before?

She dropped back, so that she could keep pace beside him.

"Doc. Doc, can you hear me?" she asked gently. He showed no signs of registering her words.

She took his wrist and felt his pulse. He didn't seem to notice her do this. It was fast. Even allowing for the pace they were setting, it was still a little more than she would expect. She put her hand up to his forehead, half expecting him to brush it away.

"Mildred, what's wrong?" Krysty asked from just behind them.

Mildred withdrew her hand in surprise. Doc's forehead was slick with sweat, his skin burning beneath the veneer of perspiration.

This was just what she had feared.

Chapter Four

"We can't stop now—look around you. There's no shelter, the cold is starting to bite into me just like it is you, and we need to find food and shelter before the next storm blows up."

"So that's a no, then," Mildred said quietly.

Ryan failed to respond. "I can't see why we can't just rig something to carry Doc. It won't be the first time. There's no immediate danger."

"I'm not saying we can't do that, just that we need to stop awhile. I need to examine him properly, see if his wounds are infected, or if this is something in his blood. I can't give him another shot until I know what's going on with him. It won't take that long, Ryan."

She looked back to where Krysty was helping the old man along. His gait was stiffer than before and he was trembling. There was little doubt that it would only be a matter of half an hour—perhaps not even that—before they had to carry him. But if she waited until that was forced on them, it could make all the difference between treating his fever successfully or leaving him too far down the road to the farm.

Ryan kept walking, narrowing his eye to take in the horizon. At the edge there were a few objects that may be croppings or may be the first signs of a settlement. Maybe another hour's march if they could force the pace. But Ryan felt the ice seep into his marrow, was still tired from lack of sleep and exertion; the only thing keeping him going was sheer will. He was scared. If he stopped, would he be able to start again?

Then he looked back for the first time. Resolutely he had kept his eyes ahead while they marched, not wanting to turn back to check Doc when Mildred caught up to him. He knew that if he did, he would probably agree with her assessment. That was something he didn't want to do. He wanted to press on, for his own sake, but knew that his sense of duty to those he led would make him stop.

As it did when he saw the condition that Doc was now in. The old man had never looked so frail. Ryan didn't even want to consider what the fever was doing to his already fractured mind.

Wearily, and with a sense of resignation that he could not hide, he slowed and held up his hand. "Okay, okay, we stop and check Doc. But you'd better make it quick for his sake as much as ours. There isn't much shelter out here, and we can't make much."

"I don't need long, believe me," Mildred said, hurrying back to where Krysty had gently lowered Doc onto the cold rock floor of the plain. He was unresponsive, lost in his own world.

Needing no direction, Jak and J.B. joined Ryan in using what they could spare of their own outer clothing to form an improvised barrier against the winds that blew around the prone figure. They had traveled light and there was nothing across this arid expanse of rock and ice to use as a windbreak. Shedding an outer layer meant exposure to the elements themselves, but it was playing percentages. If Mildred could be as quick as she had said, then they may just avoid exposure.

Working quickly, Mildred was on her knees. Krysty pulled away Doc's fur coat, the frock coat beneath and the tattered remnants of his shirt, the bloodied edges of which had already been trimmed to allow Mildred access to his wounds in the cave. The Titian-haired woman also maneuvered her body so that it formed an extra barrier between the prone Doc and the direction of the winds.

Mildred knew that she could count in seconds, rather than minutes, the time she would have to make her examination before Doc's exposed flesh wound succumbed to the elements and before those who had sacrificed their own warmth to provide cover would begin, equally, to succumb.

The area uncovered was around his ribs. The wounds on the arm could be dealt with swiftly and would not need him to be so protected. But the torso was another matter. Krysty had contrived to expose as little of the old man as possible, and Mildred had just enough area in which to work. She removed the dressings she had placed earlier and could see that the wounds showed no signs of infection. The flesh was healthy, if still raw.

Fumbling with the cold, she redressed the wound and Krysty dextrously reclothed Doc while Mildred looked up at the men standing over them.

"You can get covered again, guys. There's enough slack to just roll up his sleeve."

While J.B., Ryan and Jak gratefully replaced their heavy coats and hugged themselves into the materials to try to suck warmth from them, Mildred jacked up the layers of sleeve on Doc's arm, thanking whatever deity she thought may still exist that the old man's wounds had been on the forearm. It saved a whole lot of hassle.

Having to strip him to examine the upper arm would have taken precious time and probably finish him off by itself.

Removing the dressings and checking the wounds, she could see that these, too, were clean.

Replacing the dressing, her mind raced. No infection visible, so it had to be something that acted quickly in the bloodstream. Why hadn't that antibiotic shot worked? No one else who had needed a shot was feverish…but then, their wounds had been the lesser. It had to be that just one of the hypos was a dud. She'd have to try another and hope that it worked.

"I'm going to give him another shot and hope it works. Meantime, we're going to have to help him until we can find some shelter, because he won't be strong enough to stand alone until we can get some rest."

"No problem. We'll take it in turns. I'll take first—"

"No." Mildred cut him off. "You don't look so hot yourself. Let me or John do it."

Ryan looked her in the eye. He could see that she had been studying him as they had marched and knew that he had his own battle with fatigue. He nodded briefly. "Okay."

Pulling Doc to his feet, Mildred and J.B. supported him between them. Jak took the rear defensive position in line and Krysty dropped in behind Ryan.

"Fifteen minutes, then we swap," Ryan said, checking his wrist chron. "That way we try to stay fresh."

"Yeah, sounds good to me," Mildred muttered, feeling Doc's weight sag in time with each step.

They would be slower now, but as Ryan fixed his gaze on the shapes littering the horizon, he felt that they could still make the settlement within a couple of hours. Assuming that those shapes were buildings. Assuming they could withstand the bone-chilling cold. Assuming that no storms blew up from nowhere.

Best not to think. Best to just concentrate on putting one foot in front of another, on ignoring the stench of sulfur searing their lungs with every breath, the jarring of foot on rock that made the ankles turn to jelly with every step.

There was little they could do until they reached shelter. And if the distant shapes didn't represent that shelter, then they would just have to hope....

THE PHANTOMS now lift me up like angels, e'en though they may be devils of the foulest kind. They support me so that I am as light as air.

They take me toward the horizon, as though in search of something. But does not the horizon retreat in proportion to the distance you travel? Better to travel hopefully than to arrive... Why does that come to mind, where have I heard it before?

I can see them all now, as though I am on a procession. A parade, like those on Independence Day, when the children played in the fields and bobbed for apples while we drank beer and brandy, and talked of the wonders of the age. Then to return to our frame houses where, by the light of the oil lamp, Emily would lay our children down to rest before coming to me, disrobing and joining me in the conjugal bed. I miss the smell of her hair, the touch of her skin. Perhaps, when I have shed this madness and I once more can take my place in the world, I will feel, smell and taste her once again.

But there is another... She comes toward me now.

Golden hair flowing like the corn in summer over her shoulders. Long, lean limbs that stretch to infinity and beyond. Eyes wide open and innocent, trusting of me and asking only that I trust her in return. Of course I do, my love. You and Emily are equal in my heart. You always will be. You showed me that there could be a path to goodness in this bedlam of the soul.

She holds out her hand. There is a reason why I have returned to this place of other dreams, other times. I have purpose.

Tell me, Lori, tell me...

She holds out her hand. I want to take it, but I am constrained by those who would wish to be my protectors.

"It's okay, Doc. You can do it. You can do anything here."

She is right. I am the I who controls my own dreams. I disentangle my arms from those who support me and step out of myself to walk toward her. I reach out and take her hand, pulling her to me. We embrace and once more I feel the warmth of another being close to me.

"You have to listen, Doc. I can't be here long, but I have something to tell you."

"No, you must stay. You cannot leave me again, not after so long."

She steps back, smiles. Those eyes light with joy, pull me into her very being.

"I wish I could stay, or take you with me. I can't. Got to tell you this. You must know. You have been chosen. You have followed the others for too long. They lead you in circles that take you nowhere. If you are ever to escape this place, then you must assert your right to lead. The chance will come to you soon. You must take it.

Seize the day and you will be free once more. Stay silent and you will be trapped forever."

I consider her words. But while I do she begins to slip away from me. I want to call out to her, but I know she must go, and there is nothing I can do to prevent her taking her leave. Sadly I watch her recede into the distance, just as I feel myself drawn back to the arms of those angels who support me, stop me falling to the ground once more.

Sweet, sweet Lori. So wise. So true.

I must wait, bide my time, take my chance...

'DON'T STOP NOW, Ryan. We're so close that I can manage a little longer," Krysty said as the one-eyed man dropped back to take his turn at assisting Doc. He smiled gratefully. Truth to tell, he was about ready to drop just carrying himself. If Krysty and Jak could take the burden just a little longer, he was in no condition to complain.

Turning back, he could see what had once been indistinct shapes had now resolved themselves into identifiable blocks of huts and shacks, log cabins and metal-sheeted shelters from the weather.

Yet it was too quiet. The hairs at the base of his neck prickled.

"Something's not right. Triple red, people," he said softly, bringing a blaster to hand for the first time since leaving the cave.

"There should be more signs of life when weather's this stable. Where the hell are all the people?"

Chapter Five

Carnage. That was the only way to describe what they had stumbled into: the result of a bitter battle.

The buildings were empty. The windows in most had been shattered, allowing the elements to rend what had been within. Snow and ice covered clothing, tables, bed and chairs that had had been ripped, smashed and scattered by the winds and by some other agency. Doors hung open, some almost ripped from their hinges, others broken as though rammed. Wood had been splintered by the violence of battle, and those walls that were of corrugated metal, or reinforced by sheeting, showed signs of being bent out of shape. The few that were of cinder block remained intact apart from shattered windows, their lack of damage delineating the limits of the violence. The snow had fallen and settled on the paths between the huts, a light covering that obscured some of what lay beneath. But there were patches of ice, clear enough to show the blood and the churned mud beneath the glassy surface.

And there were the remains. Nothing more than carrion now. Shreds of clothing identifying them as people, but little else that could act as an indicator. There were detached limbs, torsos and crushed bone that may have once been skull. Whatever had whipped through the settlement like a hurricane of violence had made good work of the people living here. Stripped of most of the flesh, no skin remaining with only a few red lumps of flesh and gristle hanging on what had once been rib cages, and mauled out of shape, these were the few remnants of what had once been a community.

"Dark night, what could have done this?" J.B. whispered as he bent to examine something that looked as though it may have been a pelvis. Nearby, a hank of hair with some scalp still attached lay discarded in the mud.

That was odd: mud. The Armorer rose to his feet and walked along the path, noting the churned-up patches under ice. There was little in the way of soil in these parts, little more than rock and ice. Any soil that did manage to exist lay on the upland rock formations to the west.

Around back of one of the cinder block huts he found an answer: log troughs that had held earth two feet deep had been torn apart, the splintered wood littering the immediate area, the remains of some vegetable matter coaxed from the unyielding earth crushed underfoot. Tarpaulins, ripped into shreds, were scattered farther afield.

He heard a noise behind him and whirled, bringing up his mini-Uzi, trigger finger flexing minutely as his nerves tightened.

"There's nobody here but us chickens, John. Relax." Mildred stepped around the back of the cinder block building to join him, surveying the decimated troughs. "Crops? Out here?"

J.B. scratched his forehead, pushing back his fedora. "Strange one. Mebbe they couldn't find as much wildlife as they needed to trap. Must've had some kind of trading route set up, though. No way they went and got this much soil for themselves, not as far as it is to the nearest supply. Must have bartered it for something."

"So, other communities hereabouts," Mildred concluded.

J.B. nodded. "Which means we can't be all that far from them. Mebbe press on a little."

"Not stay here, rest up?" she questioned.

J.B. shrugged. "Depends if we want to stick around to see if whoever or whatever did this turns up again," he said mildly.

"Not likely. Everyone here bought the farm at least a week back, by the look of what's left. And most of the damage to that has come from critters making the most of an easy meal."

"Okay. Figure Doc needs to rest up and Ryan looks like he could do with some, too. Hasn't had the chance while the rest of us have been grabbing some sleep. Let's get back and clue them in. And one more thing."

"What's that?"

J.B. grinned. "Don't sneak up behind me like that again. I'm getting more and more jumpy as I get older."

Mildred raised an eyebrow. "I'll remember that."

THE OTHERS WERE WAITING for them a quarter mile off, having found some scant cover among rock formations that had been chipped away by the settlement dwellers for their own use. Where rock had been taken to build walls and reinforce hut defenses, a hollow had been made in which Krysty and Jak had been able to secure Doc. Ryan waited with them, feeling relieved that they had been able to help Doc walk and not have to rig up some kind of carrier, after all. This cover was scant enough, without the extra space a stretcher would demand. That, at least, was one small piece of luck. Maybe there would be others. Nonetheless, he felt uneasy the whole time that Mildred and J.B. were gone. He should be taking the chances, scouting the area. That was part of his responsibility. Besides which, movement would keep him warmer than he felt right now.

"That Ank Ridge you talk about?" Jak murmured, indicating the settlement as they watched J.B. and Mildred approach, spread out and with weapons to hand. They had to approach head-on, with no cover to make use of, and Ryan was too distracted to initially assimilate Jak's question. It was only when the albino repeated himself that Ryan realized what had been said.

"Can't be," he answered tersely. "Ank Ridge was a port, as far as we could make out. End of the river we opened up again when we blew the dam. This is just a little ville that—I hope—is on the way."

"Why we not follow river when leave redoubt?" Jak asked with a frown.

"Set off in the wrong direction. No reason why we shouldn't have gone that route. Everything was wrong when we got out of there, and by the time J.B. took direction and set us right, we'd somehow ended up wide of the river." He shook his head. "Dammit, should have got that right."

"Shit happens," Krysty said softly. "None of us were thinking right in that place, it was bound to screw us up. Thing to do is not let it screw us up any more."

Ryan agreed. "Shitload of things to put right, though. First thing is to see if we can get some proper rest and see to Doc. Fireblast, what's taking them so long?"

He felt impatient waiting for J.B. and Mildred to reappear. Part of him nagged that he should be doing it. There was something wrong with the settlement. It shouldn't be that quiet unless it was deserted, and if it was, then why? He wasn't used to having to sit around doing nothing. It rankled, made him feel irritable.

So it was with a sense of relief that he saw J.B. and Mildred come into view as they trekked back the quarter mile to where the others lay in wait. From the ease with which they traversed the distance, he could see that there was little danger. But what had they found?

When they reached the spot where the other companions were hidden, J.B. told Ryan of everything they had discovered while Mildred checked Doc. He hadn't deteriorated, but at the same time any progress was being checked by the conditions. She looked up to the sky. Clouds were beginning to gather again, giving the light a yellow tinge. The sooner they could move, the better.

J.B. finished his report. Ryan looked at the others. "Sounds safe enough if we get there quickly, secure one of the huts for ourselves. Whatever hit them will do us more damage out here if it catches us than if we've got some kind of cover. And whatever wildlife stripped those carcasses will find us easier pickings here than behind wood or cinder block."

"You won't find any complaints from me on that," Mildred asserted. "And we really need to get Doc under cover."

With Ryan and J.B. taking their turn in supporting the ailing Doc, the companions came out of cover and headed for the settlement. They made rapid progress, knowing that—at least for now—the territory was safe, and within half an hour had selected one of the cinder block huts as their shelter. Dragging the least-damaged bedding from the other huts, Krysty and Jak cleared out the selected hut and put the bedding down. There was a wood-burning stove set in the middle of the hut, its metal piping chimney into the roof still intact. They selected the driest wood they could find from the damage caused in the settlement, selecting some debris from the troughs and from wooden huts as well as the driest of the wood from the stores that had been ripped open, their contents strewed, at the back of the cinder block hut. The windows had been smashed, so Jak and Ryan foraged for metal sheeting or wooden shutters intact enough to be taken from other huts and placed over the glassless gaps.

While they did this, Mildred settled Doc into one corner of the room and went in search of blankets and clothing that was salvageable from the wreckage of the settlement. She came back with very little, but enough to give Doc a few extra layers of warmth. Searching through her med supplies, she was able to find some sedatives to calm him while the fever raged.

On her search, she also looked for food and water. There were still some water supplies left—each home in the settlement having its own supply tanks which had to have been refilled regularly by the inhabitants—but, as she had suspected, any food had been scavenged by the predators who had stripped the corpses. She reported this to the others when they had completed their tasks and were miserably forcing down more of the self-heats, thus depleting their own supplies, while warming in front of the stove.

"How many huts did you count?" she asked when she had finished detailing her findings.

"Not sure—eight, mebbe nine." Ryan frowned.

"There are eleven. I counted as I searched them," Mildred affirmed. "Most of them looked like they had at least two people in them, so there were about twenty-five, thirty people here."

"Okay," Ryan said slowly. "So whatever came through here had enough force to take on that many people. We need to be triple red on this, but—"

Mildred shook her head. "That's not really the point I wanted to make. I know the carrion out there was pretty badly mauled, but how many actual people do you reckon there were scattered around?"

"Hard to say," Ryan mused. "They were ripped up, scattered about, stripped—"

"But not enough to be all," Jak interjected, nodding slowly to himself. "Few bones, even if some taken by animals."

"So what happened to the rest of them?" Millie asked rhetorically. "Whatever hit this ville, it took a lot of them away, live or chilled. What the fuck does that, and why?"

There was a silence while they all considered this. Finally, Jak spoke. "Not matter. If comes back, be ready fight. If doesn't, then not matter."

The albino teen made sense. To worry over the unknown would do them no good. All they could do was mount a guard through the night and try to rest up before moving on to the next ville. Maybe do some hunting along the way. At least they knew there was game in the area, thanks to the dogs.

Ryan organized a guard, with Jak and J.B. taking first watch, before gratefully sinking into sleep. Mildred stayed by Doc. His fever showed signs of peaking and the sedatives at least enabled him to get some rest. But she wanted to be close in case it worsened and he needed immediate attention. Krysty curled up near Ryan, but found it hard to sleep. She knew she had to, as she was on next watch and it would be advisable to grab some rest now. But something was worrying her. Her hair rustled and moved of its own volition as she tossed and turned. It was nothing immediate; all the same, she knew that whatever had decimated this settlement was out there somewhere and there was a good chance they would walk right into it.

The cinder block hut was lit by a small oil lamp that Mildred had found in one of the buildings. As with everything else, most of the lighting had been smashed during whatever battle had taken place. Only this one item had survived, along with just enough tallow oil to run it for the night. It meant that they could save the batteries on the remaining working flashlights they carried, although the glow it cast was small and the smell of the oil was caustic if any were fool enough to stand too close.

Most of the hut was in shadow. The lamp illuminated the area where the sentry stood his or her guard, the rest of the hut in a pleasant semidarkness to facilitate sleep. As the others settled, some less easily than others, Jak and J.B. stood silently, occasionally moving from one covered window to another to check the outside.

The hut had four windows: two at the front on either side of the entrance and two at the back, evenly spaced. These were the long walls on the rectangular building, with the shorter walls being devoid of space. And there was only the single door. It had the advantage that there were only five entry points to guard, and the corresponding disadvantage that there were, equally, only the five exit points should they need to evacuate quickly.

When they had reinforced the hut's security for the night, they had made sure that one window on each side of the hut had a shutter that could be opened from the inside to facilitate the need to survey the area. Added to this, one of the two on watch would patrol the outside, returning at intervals, signaling to be admitted and then replaced by the other. The night temperature was bitingly cold, so it was advisable to spend as little time as possible on the outside.

A simple sec system, and one that worked well for the first hour of watch, with no event. But as they slipped into the second hour, things began to change. It was J.B. who first noticed, on his third stint on patrol.

As the Armorer was admitted after rapping out the prearranged tattoo, Jak could see from his expression that all was not well.

"Something coming down from cover, up a mile or so where the rocks rise."

Jak nodded. It hadn't escaped his notice that the area to the west, where the beginnings of the volcanic regions housed some growth of flora in the otherwise barren rocks, would provide cover for anyone—or anything—that would care to bide its time before attack.

J.B. continued. "Ain't people…animals of some kind, moving pretty quick, too. About a dozen, mebbe more. Look like bears to me, though all I could see were big bastard shapes moving onto the plain."

"Take look," Jak murmured. "How big?"

"Big—five-hundred-pounders to show at that distance."

Jak's impassive visage showed nothing, but the Ar-

morer knew what was running through his mind. If a
pack of bears in search of food had come across this settlement before, then that could account for what had
happened. And from the havoc they had found here, it
could mean big trouble.

Jak indicated to J.B. that he would be back soon and
slipped out the door.

THREE QUARTER MOON. No surprise that J.B. had been able
to make such a good assessment, as the sky was devoid
of cloud and the light from the wan, yellow-tinged satel-
lite spread over the bare expanse of rock, showing the
crops of moss and lichens as black against the slate gray
of the plain. To the west, the rising lands with ash, soil
and small gatherings of shrub and forestation showed as
indistinguishable shapes that took on a malevolent mien
with the knowledge of that which they had sheltered.

But not, perhaps, as malevolent as the shuffling pack
of dark shapes that moved across the gray rocks. Jak
judged the distance. At their current speed, it would take
them about fifteen to twenty minutes to traverse the
distance to the settlement. Their ambling gait was deceptive. They were moving at a rapid rate, knowing
that now was the time to hunt. Jak wondered if they had
got the scent of fresh prey across such a great distance,
borne on the winds, or if they were only returning to
scavenge what little carrion was left.

They were moving as a tight pack, making it hard to
pick off individuals as they moved, one obscuring another so that you found it hard to tell if two were three,
or three were four. Jak figured that J.B.'s initial assessment was about right. But it wouldn't do any harm to
take a closer look.

The albino youth moved out to meet the pack, moving across the plain, using whatever cover he could find. There was little, but that didn't really matter. The bears knew he was there, just as he knew they were. All he needed was a clearer look before racing back to prepare a defense.

One of the creatures at the front of the pack got wind of him, perhaps sight, but more likely smell. It rose on its hind legs and roared: a warning to him, a rallying call to its fellows. If J.B. hadn't already awakened the others, this would sure as hell suffice. Meanwhile, Jak assessed the creature.

J.B. was wide of the mark. This evil-looking bastard was at least six, maybe seven hundred pounds. Its fur was matted and bare in some places, dark markings on its skin under the moon glow looking like sores or scars. Even in the pale, yellow-tinged light it was possible to see the strings of mucus and saliva that extended the length of the jaws, dangling off the sharp incisors and catching the light to gleam dully their threat. The tiny eyes, buried in the folds of muscle and fur, were dark specks that betrayed no hint of what may be going through that primeval mind.

Jak was pretty sure, though. He had slipped his Colt Python into his palm as he made his way forward. But even the briefest of visual assessments told him that the weapon would be next to useless unless he could get a direct hit in a vulnerable area. For a .357 Magnum bullet to be so ineffective meant that they would have to use some serious blasterfire against this pack.

Jak turned and ran, knowing that the movement would cause the bears to increase their own speed, to give chase, but knowing that he had the speed and head start to get back to the cinder block hut with time to spare.

As he approached, J.B. threw the door open. The Armorer had been watching and was ready.

As were the others. Ryan, Mildred and Krysty were on their feet. Only Doc remained supine. He was awake, but weak—in passing, Jak noted that Doc was looking around him and seemed to be aware of his surroundings, which was an improvement on before, though was still too ill to join them.

"More than twelve, and more than five hundred pounds. Need gren take 'em out," Jak gasped as he entered the hut.

J.B. turned to Mildred. "How good's your throwing arm, Millie?"

"I used to pitch in the junior leagues." She shrugged, adding, when she saw his blank expression, "I can throw pretty good, though it's been a while."

"You've got a good eye, that's what matters. Come with me." He glanced across at Ryan, knowing that he had assumed command of the situation without deferring to the head man.

Ryan nodded briefly. "You go and do it. We'll get this place secured."

J.B. and Mildred slipped out into the night, while Ryan took a look around. There was nothing in the cinder-block hut to use to shore up the windows and door. They would have to rely on standing guard and using their blasters to keep the bears at bay, maybe pick them off. The walls of the hut had withstood the previous attack, but the windows and door had been damaged. Dammit, he wished they had something solid to reinforce those vulnerable spots…

Doc was out of the picture. There were five vantage points, and five of them when—if—Mildred and J.B. returned. He assigned Jak and Krysty a window on each side. One with a shutter so that they could keep a lookout on the action and be prepared. He would take the door.

"Check your blasters, and remember we need to make every shot count if we're to stand a chance."

Grimly they checked their weapons, making sure they were fully loaded and spare ammo was easily to hand for swift reloading. Jak had his Colt Python, Krysty her Smith & Wesson .38 Model 640. Both were good handblasters, but would need real accuracy on a vulnerable spot to make a hole in the enemy forces. Ryan favored his Steyr. Its range and accuracy as a rifle would also help him provide covering fire, to try to pick off the bears as Mildred and J.B. made their way back to the hut.

He opened the door a crack and looked out. Under the moon, he could see the duo advance on the bears, J.B. handed Mildred a clutch of grens, then the two of them part in separate directions to get a better angle of throw.

Showtime.

J.B. COUNTED THE FRAG GRENS he carried with him as he and Mildred made their way forward at the double. Enough for four each. At this distance—even getting a little closer—it was a matter of balancing the damage against wasting precious weapons.

"You head to the left, I'll go to the right. Take it about twenty yards, count ten, then aim for the center of the pack. When they scatter, try and pick at groups with the other three grens. Now go."

Mildred needed no second bidding. Her heart raced, feeling as though it was going to burst through her rib cage. And despite the cold, she was covered in a film of sweat. She could see her breath frosting on the night air, but it seemed incongruous to her. She ran steadily, judging twenty yards, then turning. She hadn't dared look at the pack as she ran, concentrating instead on keeping her footing on the treacherous rock surface. A quick glance told her where the pack was and J.B.'s position. He, too, had reached his goal. She counted to ten, then pulled the pin on the first gren, letting go of the spoon and arcing the deadly pitch high into the center of the pack.

It was a fine judgment call. The pack was still advancing and some of the bears were interested in breaking off and following the prey in their eyeline. As such, the grens failed to fall exactly in the middle, landing at the rear of the pack.

But it was close enough to inflict severe damage. The two grens exploded almost simultaneously, sounding as one long roar, drowning out the cries of anger and pain from those bears in line for the fragments of white-hot metal that were scattered in the wake of detonation.

Three were hit full-on by the double blast. Their fur, flesh and a shower of blood splattered over the rock floor and over the other bears. One was severed, the front half mewling in agony as the blood and intestines imploded under a hail of metal, its life ending less than a heartbeat later as its organs were pulped by hot metal. The other two were reduced to a steaming mass of fur and splintered bone, not even knowing what hit them.

Their mass absorbed the brunt of the blast, protecting those in front of them to a degree. There were fewer fragments and their speed was impaired, but they still managed to rip into at least four of the other bears, lacerating flesh and scorching fur, causing the creatures to rear up in agony. They were confused, lashing out in blind terror and fury, their razored claws scratching at the animals in front of them.

For a second, it seemed as though the bears would turn on one another, fighting among themselves and forgetting their prey, clustering in a way that would make them an easy target.

But it wasn't to be that simple. As both J.B. and Mildred prepared for a second throw, a brace of the creatures broke away. One headed toward J.B., but at an angle that would take him past the Armorer and away from the settlement. The other turned and headed straight for Mildred, though it was doubtful that it registered her presence at that moment. Not that she was going to take the chance. Judging her pitch, she pulled the pin on another gren and threw the bomb in a curve that would take it almost level to the head of the charging bear. Instinctively as the gren flew toward it, the bear raised its head, opened its jaws and lifted itself to catch the gren, as though it were a bird in flight that would provide a light repast.

Mildred hit the ground as the great jaws snapped shut. She didn't see the gren explode, the bear's head suddenly disappearing in a riotous explosion of bone, brain and fur. But she felt the jellied fragments of the bear's head as the outer edges of the resultant rain hit her, carrying with them fragments from the gren that were, thankfully, now dissipated of lethal force.

While this was happening, J.B. opted to deal with his own runaway. The reasoning was simple: the others were still clustered in a group, occupied with themselves. This gave a few moments" respite before they demanded attention. He pulled the pin, let loose the spoon and arced the gren in the direction of the runaway. It hit the bear on the side, rebounding a couple of feet from the soft fur before detonating, the force of the blast driving the creature sideways while obliterating one side of fur, flesh, blood and bone.

J.B. hit the ground to shield himself from the outer reaches of the blast. Only to find, when he scrambled once more to his feet, that the double blast had stopped the bears from fighting among themselves and called their attention to the direction of the source.

Already, the bears were almost on them. To stay and throw more grens would be to risk getting caught by the angered animals. J.B. yelled something incoherent at Mildred and she needed no explanation.

They turned tail and raced for the cinder-block hut as fast as they could run.

RYAN SWORE SOFTLY as he saw them approach. They were making good progress, but the bears' loping gait was taking them a greater distance with each stride. It would be close, but there was something they could do to help. He directed Jak and Krysty to fire over J.B. and Mildred, toward the oncoming creatures.

At that distance, in the pale light of the moon, there was little chance of the accuracy required to take out any of the opposition. The ammo, even from the Colt Python, would be little more than an irritation. But even if it was this, and slowed them, then it would buy valuable time for J.B. and Mildred.

Ryan pulled the door wide, trying to sight the Steyr

so that he could take advantage of its greater accuracy over distance. As Mildred and J.B. were stumbling toward him, he squeezed the trigger, focused only on the bear in his sights. He felt the recoil, didn't notice his companions fall past him into the hut, and saw only the leading creature stop and fall sideways, one eye popped by the Steyr shell as it bored through the eyeball and into the slow brain, snuffing out one threat.

Stepping back, Ryan slammed the door shut and secured it. They had five people against seven or eight wild animals, at least two of which were beginning to lag and tire, falling behind the others as their wounds began to take a toll. Not good odds, especially as they were now too close to use any more grens and the only reliable firepower against seven hundred pounds of fur and muscle was J.B.'s M-4000. The shot charge of Doc's LeMat may also be useful, and Ryan directed Mildred to take it from the still-confused Doc, who watched her with a puzzled frown as she extracted the percussion pistol from his clothing.

The hut shook as the creatures reached the front and threw themselves at the opening into which they had seen their prey disappear. Their roars filled the night air and the side walls began to shake as the bears flung themselves against the whole of the building in fury, hunger and pain. The door bulged and the shutters creaked, but they held firm. Inside, buffeted by this sound and fury, it was almost impossible to decide on a course of action. If they waited for the bears to break through, then there was every chance that the resulting wreckage would obscure a clear shot or possibly injure them before they had a chance to fire. If they opened up the shutters to fire, they again risked being hit by a furious creature before they could discharge a weapon. If they tried to sit it out, they risked the former; if they seized the initiative, they risked the latter.

The noise from outside showed no signs of abating. Dust fell from the ceiling of the hut as it was rocked by the vibrations of impact.

"Let me blast one," J.B. yelled over the noise. "Might drive 'em back."

Ryan looked up, to be showered with a fine rain of dust. They had to do something.

"Okay. Wait till one of the bastards is hammering at the shutter, then I'll open it, you fire, and I'll slam it shut as quickly as possible, hope for the best. It's not much of a plan, but it'll have to do."

J.B. agreed. There was a shutter front and back, but most of the bears' attention was focused on the front and sides of the hut, so they opted for the front shutter. Ryan aligned himself to the side, ready to open and close quickly. J.B. raised the M-4000, and they waited for one of the creatures to hit the right spot.

The bears seemed to do everything but pick that one area. Four times Ryan steeled himself, only for the expected battering to fail to materialize. He was keyed to the point where he could feel his nerves so taut that they were singing under the pressure.

So keyed that he almost missed the moment. The wall shook at his shoulder, the shutter bulged under the pressure of seven-hundred-plus pounds of wild animal. Ryan yelled a signal to J.B. and pulled open the shutter. The Armorer settled the M-4000 into his shoulder and squeezed as the shutter flew back. By the time it was fully extended, his finger had tightened enough to pressure the trigger, loosing a load of barbed-metal flé-

chettes into the ravenous maw of a wild bear. He barely
saw the result before Ryan had slammed and secured
the shutter once more, but that fragmentary image was
imprinted on his retina. He could see the face of the
bear—the impassive, glittering eyes, the slavering jaws
and sharp incisors, the distended snout—suddenly tear
itself apart in a hundred directions as the load hit home,
shredding bone and pulping flesh, rendering the brain
and eye mush into nothing more than a fine spray that
spurted backward from the bear's suddenly imploding
skull, landing on the rock and ice beyond.

For a few minutes it seemed to have the opposite effect to that intended, as the attack redoubled in fury, the
bears making every effort to barge their way past the
cinder block to get at their prey. The walls shook and it
seemed as though they had to surely crumble under the
assault, the structure groaning and cracking under the
continued pressure. Whichever way the companions
turned, responding to the sounds from outside, expecting each to be the breach of their defenses, then there
was another sound from the opposite direction that
seemed to spell the same message.

The air was thick with dust from the crumbling hut,
making it hard to breathe, catching in their throats and
making their eyes water, obscuring their vision. But
still the cinder block held firm.

Gradually the attacks began to subside, the constant
waves of battering becoming less and less frequent, the
yowling of the bears still outside losing its anger, becoming more and more a howl of frustration and fatigue.

As daylight began to creep into the cracks at the
windows, and through the cracks in the roof where the

structure had been moved by the attack, they heard the bears begin to retreat. Still howling, the sounds grew more distant with each plaintive cry.

"Figure it's safe to take a look?" Krysty asked.

"With caution," Ryan agreed. He and J.B. moved to the door, the Armorer keeping the M-4000 poised. Ryan opened it to let the daylight flood in, blinding them after the low level light of the oil lamp.

The two men stepped outside. It was quiet around the hut, although there were signs of frantic activity earlier, and the front was awash with semifrozen pools of blood. The corpse of the headless bear lay sprawled under one window, a viscous mess spread around the body all that remained of the head.

Looking away toward the west, Ryan and J.B. could see the remnants of the bear pack wearily wandering back toward their dens. There were only five left, now. One lay under the window, two were scattered where they had fled the night before, and three were clustered in a mess of fur and blood where the initial gren blast had hit. There were three others who had bought the farm on the way back, just falling in their stride as the effect of their wounds and loss of blood had finally taken its toll.

"Got lucky," J.B. said shortly. "We need to get the hell away from here."

"Agreed," Ryan replied. "We know where Ank Ridge is, and we know that there must be some kind of trade trail. We hit that, and we should be headed right. Question is, how far have we got to go?"

"As far as we have to," J.B. answered, as though it were a question not worth asking.

Ryan fixed his friend with a stare. "It's not that simple, is it? Doc's still screwed, everyone else is strung out—me included—and we don't have much in the way of food or warm clothing after the last couple of days. We need the next ville to be close…real close."

J.B. nodded, then added something that Ryan had already been thinking. "That's not all, is it? Look at the way those buildings were ripped apart. Those critters were hammerin' at us all night and couldn't get in. Whatever chilled everyone in the ville and tore shit out of it, it wasn't those bears. They were just there for the pickings."

Ryan nodded. "So just who or what did do that? And where the fuck are they now?"

Chapter Six

Exhilaration. Expectation. A sense of anticipation.

No way around it. He shouldn't feel his good, but he did. Ryan looked to the horizon and relished the chance to walk on and tread the path toward the ville they knew as Ank Ridge. Coming out of the ruins where they had spent the night, and surveying the remains of the enemy they had vanquished despite their strung-out condition, Ryan felt a burst of fire explode within his soul. Yes, they knew there was another enemy out there—one that caused the ruins before the bears came scavenging. Yes, they knew that the enemy was probably out there somewhere, and there was every chance that they would encounter it if they followed the trading trail between here and Ank Ridge. But wasn't that exactly what they did?

Meet a problem head-on and blow the bastard out of the water. Ryan wasn't a stupe. If there was a way to solve a problem without risking life and limb in a firefight, then they'd go for that option first. Truth was, though, that often the other side of the fight didn't want to know about anything other than hand-to-hand, blaster-to-blaster confrontation. So, if that was what they wanted, then give it to them. It wasn't necessarily the best way, but it was often the only way. And it became a habit that was hard to break, an adrenaline fix that made them feel alive.

What was it that Mildred said occasionally? Some old predark expression that Ryan was sure he had seen or heard somewhere before, but not really understood. Something about stopping to smell the roses. Fireblast, the only thing that roses smelled of in this world was the shit that made them grow. There was nothing here to stop and look at, nothing that was worth it. So maybe that's what they were doing: fighting on until they found something. And maybe the fighting was like jolt, something that took over and became the most important thing of all.

One thing was for sure—as they began to move out from the ruins toward the next settlement on the trail, and the eventual destination of Ank Ridge, Ryan could only think of one thing. Whatever was out there, bring it on: let them see what it could do.

J.B.'s minisextant readings and their own sparse knowledge of the territory had given them a destination. It led them across the rock and snow-strewed plains toward the upland ridges around the base of the volcanic region. Those who had regularly forged paths between the settlements and individual huts to trade—or just for the occasional human contact in the case of those who lived and hunted out in the wild—had chosen to make their trail in the relative shelter of the scrub growth and stunted trees that clustered at the base of volcanic activity, given warmth and some topsoil as a result of the churning rocks below.

It took three hours for the companions to reach this relative shelter, and such were the conditions they traversed that it seemed almost like a tropical forest as they reached the first trees. They had little in the way of supplies—water they had been able to replenish at the ruined settlement—but they were running low on the self-heats, and although these did provide the basic nutrients, they were often hard to force down. And the cold seemed to wrap around their bones like an ice shroud. The winds were strong and consistent, howling across the emptiness of the plain, with little except the occasional crop of rock or man-made huts to break them. Even though they had been fortunate enough to encounter only the one storm, there were still ice and snow particles constantly in the air, soured by the ever present sulfur from volcanic activity. It caught in the throat and lungs, making communication—even breathing—hard. The stench worsened as they moved closer to the uplands, but faced with a choice of freezing to death or choking on some sulfur fumes, there was really no contest. They had taken warm outer clothing from the redoubt, but that had been severely damaged during the encounter with the dog pack, leaving them with, in relative terms, some rags that didn't fulfill their function. The cold seeped in through the cracks, leaving them at the mercy of the elements.

The trek across the plain was made bearable by the knowledge that they would soon be able to find a little shelter from the harshest excesses of the environment. Furthermore, there would be the chance to hunt for some fresh game that was able to survive and make its home in the sparse forestation. With a grim-set determination that ran throughout the group, they marched on, each lost in his or her thoughts, and the majority of those thoughts concerned with shutting out the cold and just putting one foot in front of another until they were in less stringent climes.

For nearly all of them, these thoughts ran along similar lines to Ryan's: life in the Deathlands was about the adrenaline rush of survival. There was nothing more than dreams to dwell on when that rush was absent, and all those dreams told you was that the reality sucked. Better to live for the instant, to live in that rush, than to acknowledge the apparent futility of striving to survive. They would each have articulated this in a different way, but for all of them it was a feeling shared. Ryan's sense of exhilaration had spread throughout them, and their progress was steady, if at times slowed by the exegeses of the climate.

Their pace began to pick up as they neared relative shelter. There was little sign of a trail across the plain: some worn rock, some signs of activity across the barren land; but as they neared the lower slopes, the rock broke down into a rough, gravely soil, segueing into the kind of loam in which plantlife could take root. Within this, snaking through the trees and shrubs that doggedly withstood the icy blasts, there were signs of a trail. Dogs had trodden this flat, compacted beneath their heavy paws and flattened further by the runners of the sleds they pulled.

With a trail to follow, and some shelter now provided by the environment, they could begin to think about a faster progress. There was the possibility of hostile wildlife, such as the bears they had fought off the previous night, but equally there would be smaller mammals to supplement their diet.

On balance, it was a better place to be, and the grim determination that hung over them was replaced by an optimism. Here was something with which they could work.

Meanwhile, Doc walked with them, but was not of

them. His fever having passed the crisis, he was now a little better, and although Krysty and Mildred had taken turns to hang back with him, he was able to keep pace. His eyes were clear, if faraway, and he was able to conduct brief conversations with them as he marched, informing them that, despite their worries, he was now perfectly all right and they could leave him be.

But inside his head, there was turmoil.

WHAT IS THIS THAT STANDS before me? Is this the extent of my world, or the extent of my imaginings? Or are they, indeed, much the same thing?

I can recall little of the last day or so. I remember Lori coming to me from out of the mists of time and space to tell me of my mission. Yet that mission is lost to me. I shall recall it, I know, for things come back to me at the strangest of times. And yet I wonder if it shall appear to me in the same manner. Will she come to me again?

I remember their names—Krysty and Mildred. The man with one eye is Ryan; the one with spectacles, John Barrymore, and the albino is named Jak. I remember things we have experienced together, matters in which it seemed all was lost and yet we still managed to come out attached to our hides. And yet, for all that these things seem so real, I wonder if they were. I remember the whitecoats who took me from my home and into another time. I remember the things they did to me. Were these real? It seems so improbable that I quail before the fact that it may be truth. If so, then there is no sanity in the world and it is this, and not myself, that is at fault.

I saw them as angels, come to carry me from the seas

*of madness and return me to the isle of sanity. But these
are not angels. Neither am I insane…at least, I assume
not. Perhaps the whitecoats were true, and the arcane
and bizarre technology—I can think of no other way to
describe it—that they used to trap me is now being used
to feed this into my mind, to make of me an experiment,
and see how I act within the parameters of their fictions.*

*But I am not a rat in a maze. And these are not an-
gels. Neither are they devils. They do not exist. I will play
the whitecoat games until I am ready to break free. If it
again makes me mad, then what is that? Am I not mad
already? They underestimate me on this score. I have
nothing to lose, and they have their precious experi-
ments.*

We shall see who is the wilier, the smarter.

I just have to bide my time. And of that, I have plenty.

"DOC—YOU OKAY?"

The old man snapped out of his trance to see J.B. Dix
in front of his face, a look of confusion crossing the
man's thin, weather-beaten face.

"I—I'm sorry, I fear I was miles away," Doc mumbled, suppressing the urge to smile now that he was sure
this was nothing more than a drug or electronically in-
duced illusion.

"Well, good. Me and Jak are going to hunt, see if we
can get something other than these shitty self-heats to
eat. Can you help the others get some shelter together?"

Doc nodded. "You can rely on me, my dear John
Barrymore," he said. He knew that he always addressed
J.B. thus, and the satisfied flicker that crossed the man's
face told him that he had hit the right buttons.

Let them think I am well again, back to my "old

self," and that all is well. The Tanner philosophy for the moment...

Doc watched J.B. and Jak disappear into the denser parts of the woodlands, then glanced up at the sky. There was cloud cover, but not so dense that he was unable to place the sun. A brighter patch of cloud where it tried to shine through told him that it was now late afternoon. They had been marching for hours and it had seemed to pass in the blinking of an eye.

Looking around him, Doc could see that the other three companions were gathering brush and rocks to build both a shelter and a fire. Mildred placed the rocks in a circle, clearing the space within before starting to build the fire. She worked meticulously and fast, touching a match to the outer edge, using drier wood to spark the rest, nursing the sparks until the fire took and began to send sweet smoke upward to counter the ever present sulfur. While she did this, Ryan and Krysty worked quickly and tirelessly, despite the rigors of the day, to build a shelter from branches and foliage that would at least cut down the wind chill that swept from the plain. And despite the fact that the smoke would attract any predators by smell, they wanted to cut out the light from the surrounding area, making their camp harder to find. The pack that had attacked them the previous night was still roaming, and there may be other dangers...specifically, whatever had reduced the settlement to a ruin.

Doc took part. He dragged branches, wove foliage into a protective cover, and responded to any questions about how he felt with politeness and an ambivalence he hoped flew over their heads.

Bide your time, Theophilus Tanner. Bide your time.

JAK AND J.B. HAD BEEN making their own progress while
the others had been making camp. As they traversed farther into the woodland, they found that the cold became
more bearable. Without the wind-chill factor, which
had been neutralized by the forestation, the cold became
manageable and the canopy of foliage over their heads
held the snows at bay. Beneath, there was a layer of
moss and lichens that mingled with bracken and the
hard-packed soil. There were spores for bear, as well as
more obvious signs of their passing, such as broken
branches and trampled bracken, but also spores for the
smaller mammals that eked out an existence in the harsh
weather. Squirrels and rabbits for sure, and some larger
mammals to judge by what they left in their wake.

Both men would use blades and snares for hunting.
Jak had an accuracy with the leaf-bladed knives that was
uncanny, and J.B. constructed a wire snare with which
he was able to trap rabbits.

Moving slowly and as quietly as possible, breathing
shallow and waiting frozen until their muscles cramped
in the cold, they managed to catch enough game for a
good meal. Water to supplement that which they carried
with them was also available from a small stream that
flowed from farther up the ridge.

J.B. took some of the water in the palm of his hand
and lifted it to his lips. He grimaced as the bitter taste
caught the back of his throat.

"Drinkable, but not what you'd call sweet," he said
to Jak. "I just hope that there were some water purify-
ing tablets in the haul Millie took back at the redoubt."
He used his canteen to gather some of the bitter fluid.

The two men returned to their camp to find the fire
taking and their companions able to rest up. They joined

them, Jak and J.B. continuing where they left off by skinning their prey before setting it to roast over the flames. The meat tasted sweet after the foul slop of the self-heats, and they all ate until full. J.B. and Jak had been so successful that there was even some food left for the next morning, a rarity that would be enjoyed.

Watch assigned, Ryan settled down to sleep before he was called, Krysty moving up close to him.

"Think we're out of the rough yet?" she asked.

"Not until we find people, another ville. We need to know we're headed the right way, and that whatever took out that settlement hasn't got to the others before us. We might be able to let up a little then, as we'll have a source of food and water. But right now..."

"It's better, though. At least we've been able to eat properly and we can organize a proper rest. And it's not so damned cold."

"Still be better to be in a warm hut with a blazing stove." He grinned. "We could always try to make a little more heat."

"Lover, you get it out in this and it'll break off with frostbite." She laughed.

"Mebbe... Sure you don't want to try?"

"Sure you do?" she countered.

But they didn't. Fatigue took its toll and the next thing Ryan knew Jak was waking him a few hours later to take over watch. Krysty was still huddled against him and he carefully disentangled himself before standing and stretching while Jak reported. There was nothing happening around them that suggested any danger. If the bears had emerged from licking their wounds, they had headed back to the settlement, drawn by the possibility that there was still some carrion. Other wildlife had emerged, but it was smaller, and discretion had dictated it give the intruders in its midst as wide a berth as possible.

Ryan took his watch before waking Mildred for her turn. He, too, had little to report. It was as quiet and restful a night as they could have wished for in such conditions. Certainly more so than the previous evening.

By the time day broke, Ryan had returned to his rest and was woken to the daylight by Krysty bearing water and some of the food left from the previous meal.

"Time to kick over the traces, lover. We've still got a long way to go until Ank Ridge, and the weather feels like its gonna be stable today."

WITHIN AN HOUR they had struck camp and hit the trade trail once more. It moved up into the warmer areas of the volcanic ridge where there was a denser growth of foliage. The canopy provided protection from the harsher outside elements, allowing the flora and fauna to flourish to a degree that would have been impossible lower down. And although the air got thinner, and a little harsher with the sulfur fumes, the trail became more pronounced where it cut through the growth. As such, it made their progress easier: follow the trail and there was no battle with nature.

On each side of them, the green of the leaves contrasted with the vibrant colors that flowered from the plants: oranges, purples and varied shades of red spotted the trail, while creepers with white blooms snaked onto the well-trodden path. They could hear the scuttling movements and cries of animals, while a few birds fluted and fluttered through the trees, audible but staying out of view.

Strung out in line, with J.B. ahead at point, then

Ryan, Krysty, Mildred and Jak, Doc unusually was bringing up the rear. He had seemed so much his old self, conversing in a lucid and coherent manner, and appearing to be fit enough physically to last the pace, that Mildred had fallen into leaving the old man to make his own way. She had her own concerns. They had taken a battering, and some of them were still showing signs of the wounds sustained in recent combat. They had lost their edge, both in speed and mobility, and it hadn't escaped her attention that J.B. and Ryan both walked a little stiffly, as though troubled by leg strains and injuries. For her own part, she was aware that her right arm ached where she had wrenched it two nights before when battling the wild bears. She was right-handed and if it came to a firefight at some point in the near future, she wanted to be sure that it wouldn't let her—or the others—down.

Dropping behind the others, Doc was lost in a world that was all of his own making. Partly believing that this was all an illusion, partly that it was a test from a higher power, and partly that it was in his own mind and an examination of his own sanity, he had managed to keep enough cunning and lucidity together to construct an outward persona that seemed to be the old Doc—eccentric and unfathomable, but still a functioning and valuable member of a team.

Inside his own head, it was all a little different. Things there were confused, following only the kind of logic that is found in dreams.

THESE SURROUNDINGS DRAW *me into them. Somehow, I recognize them as though more phantoms from my past come back to haunt me. The legends of the lost cities of gold—El Dorado—and the jungles that have drawn man into themselves since the beginning of time. For do not the interior hells of a jungle match the interior hell of a man's mind? Is that what is happening here? Has my mind created this jungle for me as an exteriorization of the labyrinthine hot spots of my own psyche?*

It would, of course, make sense. For is not the idea of a city of gold, held at the center of a jungle, merely an allegory for the greater learning and understanding of what it is to be human that can be found at the center of each mind?

Perhaps that is my purpose at this point in the journey? Could it be that I am sticking too closely to the well-worn paths of thought and that is why I cannot find the lost city of gold? What if I were to just step off the path and into the wilderness? Would I then find the treasure of enlightenment?

But it would mean leaving my companions behind. Ah, yes, but if they are the figments of my imaginings that I assume them to be, then surely they represent things I must let go to find the truth? If so, then they will find me again when I find myself...the city itself.

So if I just step off the path and into the wilderness, then I have taken the all-important first step: the plunge into the abyss without which true discovery cannot come.

"DOC? FUCK IT, where has the stupe old bastard gone?" Mildred's voice was, despite her words, racked with anxiety as she realized that the old man had disappeared.

Up ahead, J.B. and Ryan stopped and looked back at her cry, while Jak and Krysty were already past her, searching the immediate area on each side of the trail to see if they could find any indication of what had happened or where he had gone.

"Here," Jak called, indicating an area where the foliage had been beaten down recently. As the others approached, they could see that the path he made was soon lost in the thick undergrowth, any disturbance made by his passing obscured by the sheer volume.

"Doesn't look like it was against his will," Krysty commented. "It's not messed up enough for a struggle, and besides which we would have heard that."

"Old buzzard's finally flipped, gone off like an elephant to die," Mildred said, finding it hard to believe that even someone as crazy as Doc would just wander off in the wilderness. She picked up something in the foliage that caught her eye. "I guess he just doesn't care any more," she whispered, handling the silver lion's-head sword stick that the old man habitually carried.

"Mebbe he figures he wouldn't want that anymore," Krysty said softly, adding when Mildred looked puzzled. "He got it from the redoubt first time we were here. Mebbe it meant something he wanted to let go."

"And mebbe he just dropped it," J.B. snapped. "The longer we stand around acting like he's bought the farm, the more likely that he will."

"Mebbe we should leave him," Ryan said softly, explaining, "If Doc's finally snapped, then nothing's going to bring him back. And look at us. We need to press on—and face it, people, we aren't in too good shape."

"We can't just leave him," Mildred said, as though it needed no justification.

"I've got to think of all of us. I've seen you looking

at us in turn, Mildred, I know you know what kind of shape we're in. Risk it all chasing Doc or make sure we survive. What's the better bet?"

Mildred shook her head, glaring at Ryan. "That doesn't matter, and you know it. Yeah, we're tired and carrying injuries. But next time we fight, how are we going to be able to trust one another knowing we left one of our own without even looking for him?"

Ryan tightened about the jaw, his eye blazing. There was no way he would leave any of them out of hand, but with Doc the way he was, and the rest of them carrying their own problems… In his heart, though, he knew she was right.

"Okay, we search, but try to follow his path, and we only spread out a little. Keep in visual contact."

A delicate balance between searching for Doc and keeping their own security, but one he felt they could maintain. As it proved to be: although it was at first difficult to keep one another in sight as they moved through the dense forestation, moving back down the slopes on a sometimes treacherous incline, it became easier as they got closer to the foot and the trees thinned out.

But none of them expected what they saw when, after a quarter of an hour battling the incline and increasingly harsh winds, they broke cover to find Doc standing near the base of the upland ridge, conversing with an armed hunting party. They could see that he was talking to the group, even though his words were whipped away by the winds. Ryan cursed the fact that all sound had been lost to them, and they were caught unawares and breaking cover, unable to easily track back on the slopes.

Doc turned to them at the sound of the crashing trees, raising his voice as he called across the driving wind.

"Ah, I was just this minute saying that you probably weren't that far behind me. Just as well, it saves us having to look for you.'

Chapter Seven

Doc's tone may have been welcoming and pleasant—despite having to yell over the crosswind to be heard—but the demeanor of his new companions gave lie to his optimism. They were clustered around the old man and had been trying to understand who he was and where he had come from when the companions burst from cover.

Although their faces were set as if in stone, betraying nothing, the manner in which their hands tightened around their blasters, ready to use them at a moment's notice, showed that beneath the impassive exterior they were on edge.

Ryan skidded to a halt, about thirty yards from where Doc stood. He had no weapon in his hands and neither—he was sure—did the others. He heard the others also slither and slide to a halt on either side of him, and he risked a look to see if they had all emerged. If one had been able to stay in cover, alerted by the sudden cessation of movement, then they may have an edge.

Slowly, Ryan turned his head so that he could see to his right. J.B., Krysty, Mildred, Jak…all of them were in the open, frozen as much by the sight of the group in front of them as by the temperatures. Ryan swore under his breath. This was what came of not being triple red all the time; this was the result of fatigue and the inability to find a place where they could rest up and recoup themselves.

Doc—the same Doc who had led them into this mess—had once used the word "ennui," and told the one-eyed man that it came from a place called France, and that explaining it in English was hard. But he'd tried, at Ryan's behest. Not that his explanation had made a whole lot of sense; Doc groping for words was even more confusing than Doc in full flow, never at a loss for them. But the gist of his explanation was this: the word meant that feeling when you couldn't be bothered to go on, when it all seemed drab and pointless, and when you felt detached, as though watching yourself in a story but not really being part of the action.

So, ennui: a good term for how they'd been since landing back in this pesthole of a region. A reason for why they had stumbled from one disaster to another. An explanation for why they were in so much trouble now, lined up against a fully armed group of hunters without a single blaster to hand.

They'd be damned lucky if they didn't buy the farm. Ryan had felt that they were sharpening up after they left the ruined settlement. How wrong he'd been. But if they got out of this… Fireblast, sharp wouldn't even begin to explain how they were going to be.

Bizarrely, as it was his own actions that had gotten them into this predicament, it was Doc who managed to extract them.

The old man had been experiencing everything in a heightened manner since his return from the frontiers of madness to something that meant he could absorb his everyday surroundings. It was as if his nerve endings now jangled to the slightest stimulus, each one setting off chains of thought and association in his head.

As he saw his erstwhile friends and companions break from cover, he could feel from them their concern for his safety, and his heart was glad. Even if this was all a construct of his own mind, at least his imagination had made people who cared for him. At the same time, he could feel the mood of the hunting party change. They had looked upon him with curiosity when he'd emerged from the trees, his ripped fur billowing around him, his hair whipping across his face. He was unarmed, alone, and had to have looked as though he were half-crazed—perhaps he was, but no matter for the moment—more importantly, he presented no threat.

He had walked down to them, talking all the while, asking who they were and where they came from, then telling them who he was and the mission he was engaged upon…on reflection, it was little surprise that they had failed to reply to any of his questions. He hadn't given them the space in which to speak and his crazed monologue had seemingly silenced them with bemusement.

Curiosity, confusion, amusement—all these he could read in their attitude, if not their immobile faces. But that had changed when the others had burst from the trees. Tightening of muscles, setting of jaws. Doc could feel a sea of change. And he could see that his erstwhile friends were unarmed and at the mercy of the hunters.

Doc took decisive action. He stepped back and around so that he stood in the area between the hunters and the companions, facing the former. He flung his arms into the air and intoned, "These people mean you no harm. They have arms, but do not bear them for you.

They have only come looking for me, to assist me when I am lost. I beg of you, spare them."

Ryan had singled out one hunter as the head of the group. He saw the man's eyes flicker—the only sign of life in an otherwise still body—from Doc to Ryan, then along the line.

"You got blasters?" the leader said finally, his lips barely moving and his voice hard to understand beneath a burring accent that seemed to twist the words out of shape.

Ryan nodded. "Yeah. All of us. But we can't reach them before you can chill us, so you've got all the aces."

"Let's keep it that way for now. This bastard always this crazy, or you people just been out here too long?"

"Something of both," Ryan said carefully. "Get even crazier if we have to stand here like this. So you figure on trying to chill us, or you figure on letting us be?"

"Neither. Got some questions you might like to answer," the leader said slowly, in a tone of voice that told Ryan this was not an optional question but a statement.

"Talking isn't going to chill us, so that sounds good to me. Figure we all agree on that."

The leader grunted, nodded and stepped forward. "Then you follow us."

THE COMPANIONS FELL IN with the hunting party, and walked with them. It gave each group a better chance to examine the other.

As far as Ryan was concerned, the strangest thing was that the hunters didn't choose to disarm his people. It couldn't be that they were too stupe to do that. No one would survive long without acquiring such skills in this world. It seemed to imply more that the hunters were confident that they could strike down the companions before they posed a threat. Maybe they were right. Either way, it gave Ryan an uneasy feeling. It went with the air that the party carried with them anyway. They seemed to be at one with their surroundings and relaxed in a way that suggested they had long since established themselves as top of the chain. With that assurance came a feeling that anyone they picked up could be discarded with ease. Not a good feeling when you were walking with them to their ville.

There were seven of them, and the things they shared in common were their facial characteristics and body shape. They had flat, broad faces, with noses that were also flat, spread with wide nostrils. Thin, tight lips and dark eyes that were buried beneath protective layers of fat around their brows. All were fairly short and squat, with the bulk appearing to be muscle as much as fat.

Ryan had read in some old books once about the people who lived in these ice-covered regions. Their overall name was Inuit, although there were several different tribes within this grouping. They had adapted and developed over the years to cope with the harsh conditions.

They were still a very adaptable people, for their shape and facial characteristics were all they had in common.

The nukecaust and their isolation had hit their gene pool hard. Some had obvious signs of mutation and inbreeding. such as eyes that were weeping and sore. One of them had a lipless hole where his mouth should be, with no teeth and a truncated jawline that suggested he was unable to speak. Not that this was a problem, as they seemed a taciturn people, none other than the leader speaking to the companions, and even his few words having ceased.

Others walked with a peculiar gait that suggested they may have all their limbs, but perhaps they had something else amiss on their torso, hidden beneath the layers of clothing. These layers were composed of old rags and materials woven and stitched into furs in such a way as to make it hard to tell where one piece ended and another began. Their feet were encased in bound layers of cloth and fur, worn in places to show heavy boots underneath.

They all carried blasters. Some were Lee Enfield .303s, there were a couple of Sharps rifles, and the leader of the pack carried a Steyr much like Ryan's. From some of the bulges on their layers of clothing, it was probable that they also carried handblasters and almost certainly blades for skinning prey, if little else.

As they walked, there was an almost casual air about them that made them seem all the more dangerous. This was their land, and no one could best them on it.

Looking at the others, Ryan could see that they felt ill at ease to be joining the hunting party so casually. Jak's face, as ever betrayed nothing, but his hands hovered expectantly, ready to reach for his concealed blades; J.B.'s eyes flickered behind his spectacles, taking in all that was around him; Mildred was impassive, but her stiff gait betrayed her tension, and Krysty walked as though nothing was amiss, but her hair had tightened protectively to coil around her head and neck, betraying her true feelings. Only Doc seemed unconcerned. If anything, the old man carried with him an air of casual fascination, as though curious and expectant for what should happen next.

Come to that, Ryan was feeling a similar expectancy, although his was tinged with apprehension.

The hunting party took them into the forested areas on the uplands. If they had been returning from an expedition, then it had been empty-handed. If they had been setting forth, then they'd considered the intrusion of the companions enough of a reason to turn back without accomplishing their mission. Either way, it was another little thing that made all the companions—with the notable exception of Doc—feel uneasy.

They took the trail for the first quarter mile, then veered off into the scrub. There appeared to be nothing in front of them but foliage, thick and impossible to pass, but this was illusory. The growth of bushes and small trees shadowed by the larger trunks had been carefully arranged to disguise another trail, this one more narrow, less well-trodden than the one they had left. It snaked away at an angle and took them deep into the forest.

Perhaps these Inuit just liked to keep to themselves—they certainly didn't seem to be overly sociable types—but maybe there was another reason they hid themselves off the trail taken by those trading between the scattered settlements.

They walked for just over half an hour at a steady but not taxing pace. Suddenly, turning a corner, they reached the Inuit ville. It was silent and disguised, and the first view was shocking to the companions. Shocking because it seemed to appear from nowhere, with no clue, and shocking because of its composition.

Wood-and-log huts, sheet-metal-covered constructions and cinder-block huts—much like the ville they had stumbled across down on the plain—were arranged around a central point, a piece of round, open space that was scuffed and churned as though in constant use. The dwellings all faced the center, and were populated by men and women who barely looked up from their everyday tasks as the hunting party entered. The stoops of the huts saw people wash clothes, sew, butcher meat for salting and storage, and clean blasters—all without paying heed to the strangers in their midst.

Except for one man, who detached himself from a group of others who were rendering the remains of what could once have been a deer for fat and bone, and walked across with a peculiar shuffle to where the hunting party was now standing.

"Strange quarry," he said elliptically to the hunt leader, ignoring the companions.

"Found 'em wandering about, lost. Seem friendly enough—not so stupe as to try to draw on us, anyway. Came from up there," he added, gesturing toward the distant volcano, away up the slopes.

The Inuit chief—for surely he had to be, such was the quiet authority he seemed to have over the others—sniffed back a string of mucus that started to drip from his nose and gave the companions a long perusal. He was the same height as the others, perhaps a little rounder and certainly older. The lines around his eyes seemed to form caverns around the dark orbs that called attention to the depths. The rest of his skin was like leather, toughened by the elements and tanned by the harsh suns of too many summers that were cold yet bright. He held up a hand in greeting. When he spoke, he shared the same rich burr as the hunt leader. It was an accent the likes of which they hadn't heard before and, as with the huntsman, it took no little concentration to understand what he said.

"I don't know how long you've been out here, or what you've been doing, but you don't look as though you could do it for much longer."

As a greeting, it was hardly fulsome. It was, however, an accurate summation of how the companions both looked and felt.

"We've been traveling a long time, and we got ourselves a little lost. Found a ruined ville back along the way, and were heading for somewhere a little more hospitable," Ryan told him, choosing his words carefully.

The Inuit chief looked at the hunt leader. There seemed to be an unspoken question that passed between them, at which the hunt leader shrugged.

The chief fixed Ryan with a glare. His eyes narrowed. "You're on foot? Where d'you come from that you got this far on foot?"

Krysty broke in before Ryan had a chance to answer. "We had a wag at one time, but the axle got broken on some ice. We had to leave it, but thought we were nearer Ank Ridge than we were."

"Looks like you people are just real shit at directions. Lack of sense in that direction ain't going to get you nothing but chilled around here. Maybe you struck lucky running into my people."

"I hope so," Ryan said pointedly.

The Inuit chief stayed silent, his eyes locked with Ryan's singular orb. Both men were trying to see into the other, to judge what they really meant by their statements. Finally the Inuit spoke.

"Okay, here's the deal. You can stay here and rest up before heading to Ank Ridge. We'll put you in the right direction. But you earn your keep while you're here.

You hunt with us, work with us. You don't stay long, and you don't make trouble. Then everything's good."

"You want our weapons?" Ryan asked. Then, when the Inuit shook his head shortly, asked, "Why not?"

"We're quicker, tougher than you."

"How do you know that?" Ryan tried to keep his voice neutral, to not make it sound like a challenge.

The Inuit shrugged. "You're tired. And I know how good my people are."

AT THE DIRECTION of the Inuit chief, the hunt leader and one of the women—who were almost indistinguishable from the men in build and dress—took the companions to one of the huts.

"If you want to eat, meal is at sundown. We eat together here. Need to chop wood and clean livestock before then. Maybe you start earning by helping then," the leader said brusquely. His tone left no doubt that this wasn't a request.

As the door closed on the companions, they found themselves alone in a log hut that had mattresses on the floor and blankets piled in one corner. The blankets and mattresses were clean, and the floor had been swept. A wood-burning stove, run from logs and tallow to fire it, was in one corner. There was nothing else. One window, to the left of the door, supplied the only light and the only way of observing what was going on outside. J.B. walked over to the window and watched the Inuit go about their everyday tasks.

"Dark night, these people have been on their own too long," he muttered. It was an observation prompted by the sight of the dwellers. Some were like the hunt party, but others had more severe mutations. There were those who had no arms, just vestigial flippers; others had more severe facial distortions, with flaps of skin where nose or mouth should be. Others were without legs, propelling themselves on sleds or carts with wheels attached. But despite this, they all seemed to be strong, and all were working. It was clear that this was a society where only the strong and adaptable survived, and all were geared toward working for a common cause, making them strong as a group as well as individuals.

And yet the taciturn nature seemed to spread throughout that group, as they went about their tasks without much need or, indeed, desire for conversation.

"These people put the fear in me," J.B. said simply. "I don't trust them."

"You and me both," Ryan agreed, joining the Armorer at the window.

"Then why are we here?"

"You tell me what option we had?" Ryan countered. "They had the drop on us, and they offered us shelter when we're in unknown territory and in need of rest."

Mildred, like the others, had been listening, and took it upon herself to speak. "There are a few other things that are bugging me about these people—like how come they're all so in-bred when there are other communities around? They must have come across them in the course of hunting and trading, so why haven't they mixed it up a little to stop all those mutations? And how come they've hidden themselves away here, with no way of seeing where they are from the main trail?"

"Could be that they want to keep to themselves because that's what they believe," Krysty pondered. "You know, like some communities believe that in trying to keep their people free of outside taint? Not necessarily right, but it might explain it."

"Not why hide," Jak countered. "Only hide trail when don't want be found."

"Exactly," Mildred affirmed. "They've covered their tracks for a reason, and I've got an idea why that might be."

"Which is?" Ryan asked.

"Come on, Ryan, are you telling me you didn't notice it, too? The homesteads in this ville, look at the way they're constructed."

"Like the ville we left behind." J.B. frowned. "But that's the way they all are around here, right?"

"Mebbe, but where we stayed last night hadn't just been smashed. There were some parts that had been taken. Mebbe as replacements for what these people needed on their own buildings."

"Come on, you've no grounds for saying that other than paranoia," Krysty reasoned.

"No? Mebbe paranoia's not such a bad thing. That ville was ripped to shreds, and this one's untouched—"

"But it was out in the open, and this one is hidden," Krysty interjected.

"Which brings me back to Jak's point—why? Why 'hide' where you are if you trade with the other villes and are part of the chain between here and Ank Ridge? Why be the only ville that hasn't been ripped apart?"

"We don't know what the other villes on the route are like, Millie," J.B. pointed out. "And we won't until we reach them. And mebbe part of the reason for this place being hidden is to avoid being attacked by whatever's doing it."

"Anyway, we don't even know for sure that this trail is all the way to Ank Ridge, or used for trade," Krysty added mildly. "There's a lot of mebbes and ifs in there, Millie."

Mildred sighed and rubbed at her face, revealing the extent of her tiredness. "Yeah, you might be right. But it just doesn't feel right, and I guess I was trying to look for reasons why."

"Now *that* I will agree with you," Krysty murmured, trying to tease out Titian locks that remained almost painfully tight. "This feels real bad."

"Anything we did would be bad at this point," Ryan said, trying to calm his people. "We've just got to try to pick our way through the minefield and hope we don't blow a leg off. At least we've got some shelter, we'll have food and rest, and we'll be ready for trouble if it comes. Yeah, at least we'll know what direction it's gonna come from."

It wasn't a sentiment with which any of the companions felt reassured, but there was sense to it: better to know your enemy than to be caught from behind.

There was one other thing, which had occurred to Jak if not to the others, and which he refrained from speaking of until he knew more. Why had the hunt party, which had picked them up, been returning from the plains, when any wildlife they would wish to hunt would be more likely to be in the territory immediately surrounding their settlement?

OPTING TO GO ALONG with things until they could get a better idea of what was actually happening within the ville, they emerged from their cabin as the light began to fade. There was still enough time for them to join their hosts in feeding the livestock and preparing supplies of firewood for the stoves that heated the buildings. They worked mostly in silence, unwilling to talk too much among themselves, and coming up, once more, against the wall of taciturn silence that they had experienced on first entering the community.

The work was hard. The Inuit drove at a hard pace and expected the same from their "guests." Instructions were barked in that same burr that was shared, seemingly, by all the dwellers and made them hard to understand. Nonetheless, the companions were able to fulfill their tasks and join the ville dwellers as they queued to receive their food from the communal kitchen cabin that seemingly serviced the whole community.

"Why don't people cook in their own huts? Why do you eat like this?" Ryan asked of the chief. He was only partly interested, figuring that it was also a good way to draw the man into conversation.

"Food's sometimes scarce. It helps if we keep it all in one place, cook it all in one place. Means no one hoards, and we all share and share alike. That's the way it's always been, and the only way that's right."

As he left the cookhouse, he beckoned to Ryan to follow him to his own cabin. Ryan gave him a questioning glance and the chief then beckoned to the other companions. As they followed, each figured that they were about to learn something of the community. Why else would such a taciturn man want their company?

When they had settled in his cabin—as sparse as their own, except for a framed print of an old map behind grimy glass that rendered it almost opaque, hanging from one wall, and an iron chest on the far side of the room—they waited for revelation. Except conversation didn't come easily to these people and it was actually Doc who broke the silence…with a comment that seemed, at first hearing, cryptic.

"Scots—I do believe I finally have it!" he exclaimed, seemingly out of the blue. "Tell me, dear sir, what is your name? I don't believe you have graced us with as of yet."

The Inuit chief gave Doc a long, hard stare. It was as though he were trying to figure out if Doc was being funny or was just plain crazy. Finally he said, "Thompson. John Thompson."

"I knew it!" Doc exclaimed, thumping the table so that their plates rattled. "I knew I'd heard that accent before, and it all started to fall into place…of course, there were stories about remote camps and expeditions where the locals and the pioneers fused in such a way, but with no media to really reinforce…quite impossible to verify. But then again, by the time there were such means, the possibility of such a thing had been decreased by…McLuan, MacLyon, something like that? He was a Marshal, though how a lawman found time to study such a subject in depth did not bode well for the people he was supposed to protect. Anyway, the concept of the Global Village, something that I always thought—"

"Doc! Shut up," Ryan yelled, getting to his feet. The old man stopped dead and looked up at the one-eyed man in astonishment. Inside Doc's head, he was stunned that a figment of his imagination should be able to talk to him in this way. Outside of that head, it appeared as though Ryan were asserting his authority over the group.

Thompson seemed impassive, but his eyes flickered

across the companions. This was an interesting test of group strength and loyalty. Would they stick up for the mad one, assuming he was talking garbage, or would they follow the one-eye?

"I—I do apologize," Doc stammered softly. "I do not know what came over me there. I think perhaps excitement that, after recent events, I found it easy to follow a train of thought. I did not mean…"

"It's okay, Doc," Ryan said gently. "You've been through a lot of crap, and it's kinda good to have you back to talking shit like usual. But mebbe this isn't the time."

Mildred had been thinking about what Doc had said, and decided that it may be the right time to reinforce some of the old man's words—because it would do him good to know he had been doing more than merely ranting and because it may clear up a few things about their hosts.

"MacLuhan, Doc. Marshall MacLuhan. You remembered it well, but it was his name, not his rank. And he was right. Things were going toward a Global Village before the villagers squabbled and blew it up. Hell of a memory you've got rattling around in there," she added, declining to note that MacLuhan's theories had come along in the time between Doc being trawled and then ending up at the end of the twentieth century. He had to have had some time to do a lot of reading while he was being used as a lab rat. Leaving that for another time or place, she went back on tack. "And you're right about the accent, too. I wouldn't have placed it as well."

"Ah, of course, that explains everything," Doc said. "What a silly mistake to make, a little like Wyatt Earp discovering the secret of quantum mechanics before polishing off the Dalton boys." He chuckled to himself, not noticing that Thompson was staring up and down the table, his expression no longer inscrutable.

Instead he was barely suppressing his excitement. Although, given the normal stony-faced expression of his people, this was admittedly barely visible. Only if you subjected him to the close scrutiny that Krysty observed. It made her spine tingle, her hair tighten so that it pulled on her scalp.

Thompson rose from the table and went over to the framed map.

"See this? Many years before skydark, men and women come from across the big seas. You're right—Scotland. A place called Ireland, too. They were escaping lack of jack, lack of food. They found people like me. They found we had the same problem. Out of the pan and into the flame, as they said. But they had the Almighty, and the Almighty would send something."

"They brought you religion instead of bread? Very big of them," Doc muttered.

Thompson was across the table before anyone had the chance to move. For one so bulky, he moved at an incredible pace. He lunged for Doc before the other companions had a chance to move, and stopped inches short of the old man's face. Doc could taste his sour breath.

"No, you old fool, you don't understand. You say smart things then be so stupid—how does that work, eh? Listen to me. The Almighty had guided them from starving in their lands, brought them safely across the big seas and landed them here. Sure, we all starved together to begin with, but the Almighty works with mystery. That's what they said. No one understands, but it works. Faith and trust. We had things to teach them, they had things to teach us. Things that made the hunting better, the living better. And they and we became one. That's why we have their names, their voice. They gave us the Almighty, showed us the way. And through the way, the light and the truth. And now we live better than others out here because we work together, use everything, make it work, have faith."

He pulled back and walked over to the map, taking the frame from the wall and placing it in the middle of the table. He seemed oblivious to the stunned silence around him. If he did notice it, he didn't let it show. Hoicking up, he spit onto the frame and cleaned off some of the dust and dirt from the glass, revealing underneath a map of how the Alaskan regions had once looked. The map was yellowed and stained, even under glass, and bore a date in one corner: 1879.

"This was what it was like before skydark," he began simply. "The travelers came over these plains of ice and around these coastal areas, moving toward the port Ank Ridge." He spoke as though it was something he had learned by heart: certainly, it would have been simple to do this, as his finger followed a thinly traced, dotted line that wove across the face of the paper, taking the travelers across the continent on a hesitant path until they reached the far coast, then upward to the point marked "Anchorage." The fact that he mispronounced the name gave away the fact that he couldn't read and was reciting from memory.

"Here they settled," he said, indicating an area some thirty miles inland—a fraction of an inch on the map's surface scale. "Then skydark came and things changed. Our old homes destroyed, the land reaching up to the

skies and spitting fire back at the heavens before settling down once more. Most who still lived made villes
back on the ice and rock, but we came up here."

"Why? Why did they do that?" Ryan asked.

"Rocks still spit fire, but down there is safer from the
hot seas. Animals, too—bear, wolf—all move to
warmer region. They don't have huts to save if the rocks
spit again, they just run," he explained, a smile
momentarily cracking his face. "The others don't want
to have to build again. And they're scared of the wildlife
chilling them. But it's warmer here, and the rocks don't
spit that much, and the closer the wildlife, the easier the
hunting."

"So why hunt party on rock and ice when find us?"
Jak asked.

Ryan shot him a glare. They were learning something, and the one-eyed man thought Jak's question
would make Thompson clam up.

He was wrong. Thompson shrugged. "Sometimes
we can track bear or wolf down onto the plain. That's
where they go to hunt, and if we follow, then it's more
open. Depends on the trail we pick up."

It seemed, on the face of it, a reasonable answer. But
there was something that didn't ring true to the albino.
He would let it lie, for now. Leave any further questions
until later.

Ryan returned to the subject of the map. Indicating
the coast around Ank Ridge, he asked, "This is all still
like it is here?"

Thompson shrugged. "Mostly. Some of it fell off
during the rock shifting after skydark, some of it was
hit by nukes, they say. But Ank Ridge still there. And
now a trail that runs from here to here." He indicated a

point that was near the redoubt, tracing past its location and past the ransacked ville they had encountered. The trail then continued up and around until it snaked its way into Ank Ridge.

"How many villes along that route?" Ryan asked.

Thompson shrugged. "Hard to say. Some are villes, some no more than one, maybe two huts where trappers try to stay alive. Maybe eight, ten in all."

"We stayed in one last night. It had been ripped to shreds by something. What was that?" J.B. asked bluntly.

Thompson paused. For a moment it seemed as though he would refuse to answer. As though each word had to be considered carefully before he was ready to speak. Finally he said, "We don't have that much to do with the villes on the trail. Lazy fuckers who want something for nothing. Don't realize you have to work for everything in this life. They only want to take. So we don't mix with 'em, not unless we've got something we really want to trade. Some of the trappers, they know what work is, they're okay. But the villes… Dunno what could be giving them trouble. Maybe they're just fighting with each other. It wouldn't be the first time that it's happened."

It sounded reasonable, plausible, even. But there was something a little too contrived about the answer. All of the companions felt the same thing, as one: by asking the question, J.B. had taken them from safe to stormy waters. They would have to be careful now.

As if to emphasize this, Thompson put the map back on the wall and brought the meal to an abrupt close.

"Best if you return to your hut now. Tomorrow you go out with the hunt party, catch food for yourself and us. Starts at sunup, so you need to rest. You catch nothing, you eat nothing. That's the way it is with us."

As they returned to their hut, across the dark and quiet ville, with every inhabitant inside their own dwelling, shored up against the night, they could only wonder if the hunt party would turn them into the prey. Had they asked too much of the chief? Enough to make themselves a danger?

Only the cessation of an uneasy night's sleep would bring an answer.

EARLY NEXT MORNING found them standing in the center of the ville, faced with a group of hunters. The hunt leader who had found them the day before was leading the new party, and he introduced the six hunters—including himself—to the companions.

They were a motley crew. Apart from the hunt leader, who was named McIndoe, there were three who had either withered arms or limps, and two who had missing limbs. One had only one arm and the other had no legs but highly developed arm muscles to propel himself on a sled.

"This is Connelly, Quinn, Ferguson, McHugh, and Taggart," McIndoe said shortly, indicating each briefly in turn. The man on the sled was Taggart, and it was hard for any of them to take their eyes from him. The idea that he could be a good hunter was something that was difficult to assimilate. Yet he had to be, for the Inuit had no time or space for those who couldn't contribute.

"Don't worry about him," McIndoe said, noting their stares. "Worry about yourselves. You don't get nothing, you don't eat nothing."

"I was just wondering," Doc said distantly, "I note

that you all have Irish- or Scots-derived names. Do any of you have any native names at all?"

McIndoe looked at Doc strangely, like Thompson the day before. Was the old man trying to be funny or was he just crazy? The other Inuit betrayed little, but a few swift exchanges of expression warned the companions that Doc was on thin ice, thinner than they would have to traverse this day.

"These are our native names. We get two—one for our fathers, and one for the Almighty, just as it was handed down to us."

"Ah…" Doc nodded and tapped his nose. "I think I begin to see."

Taggart hoicked a phlegm ball, which landed at Doc's feet. "Can we get goin' before I freeze my balls off?" he growled.

McIndoe nodded and, with no further words wasted, indicated that they move out.

The companions fell in with the hunting party. There was no conversation among the hunters, and so the companions likewise declined to talk—either to their hosts or among themselves. What could they say to one another that may not give something away to the hunters? What could they say that may not cause offense and put them in danger? What, indeed, could they say without the very silence being broken and construed as an insult?

So they walked in silence. The hunting party led them through the short trail to the concealed exit that lay on the wider trading trail that ran through the forest. Without a word, the party led the companions farther along the trail than they had progressed before Doc's detour, and they were surprised to find that the trail began to wind back down toward the icy plains. Although it was still bitingly cold at this level, the increased foliage and the fact that they were on the lower slopes of volcanic activity warmed the area in relation to the plains, and they couldn't understand why the trail didn't proceed through the seemingly more inviting forested areas.

Jak suddenly stopped. Ryan and J.B., noticing this, also held back, attracting the attention of Mildred and Krysty. Only Doc continued with the Inuit, seemingly in a world of his own making. It was only when McIndoe held up his hand to halt them that Doc looked back with astonishment on his face.

The Inuit hunt leader also looked back and nodded with satisfaction. "Hear it, too?" he asked simply.

Jak nodded. "Three or four, tracking us. Stopped now. Will they attack?"

McIndoe shook his head. "Not in daylight. Probably coming back from hunting themselves, maybe tired. Could take us, but the odds not good. Won't say bears are clever, but learn to be cunning. If we were a smaller group…"

"We take them?" Jak asked.

Again, the hunt leader shook his head. "Not if we can't see 'em. Go in there to get 'em and we get separated, make easy meat. We wait, see who moves first."

"Mexican standoff," Doc muttered.

The Inuit looked baffled—or, at least, as baffled as their bland expressions would allow.

"What's a 'Mexican,' some kind of bear we ain't seen before?" McIndoe asked.

"Just an expression, dear boy, meaning that neither of us wishes to be the first to move," Doc explained.

McIndoe didn't reply. He just gave a brief nod, with the kind of expression that suggested all his suspicions about Doc had just been confirmed.

They stood on the exposed path, following the sounds of the bears as they moved through the undergrowth. Ryan was sure he caught sight of a patch of fur through the green, but he might have been mistaken. Like the others, he had withdrawn a weapon, pulling the Steyr and gently racking a shell.

The noise grew fainter.

"Must be well-fed and tired," McIndoe commented, adding, "Bastards…"

"So that's why the trading trail doesn't make more use of the slope for warmth and windbreak?" Mildred questioned.

The hunt leader graced her with the faint ghost of a smile. "Might be colder down there, but at least you can see what's coming at you," he commented.

They continued on in silence until they moved through the sparsest clumps of tree and brush, down onto the flat of the plain where all was rock and ice, and the trail became fainter, harder to follow.

McIndoe stopped and looked around him, ignoring the screaming winds that battered them from all sides now that they were in the open.

"Thing is," he yelled over the noise of the wind, "up there the game can hide from you, and a lot of it's got a hell of a punch if it decides to fight back. Less if it down here, but easier to see, and less chance of it getting you first. Our ancestors found that out the hard way."

"Sounds right to me," Ryan agreed, "you can't argue with experience."

Experience may have been correct, but it was not necessarily the easiest route. The enlarged hunting party continued on across the plain, following the trade trail that was just visible in the conditions. There was no snow falling, but the clouds had settled heavy overhead and the winds were blowing in from the volcanoes in the distance, making the stench of sulfur stronger than ever in the already sour air. The ground was hard beneath their feet, each footstep jolting up to the knee joint as heels hit solid rock and ice. As they moved farther from the forest, there were banks of snow blown up against the sudden upward thrusts of rock wrenched from the earth by the post-skydark upheavals. Some may have hidden caves like the one they had stumbled into. It seemed like years before, though it was only a matter of days.

And all the while, the Inuit stayed silent, padding across the plains, Taggart propelling himself on the icy rock with more ease than the others, his sled taking to the conditions. There was no sign of any game.

Nor was there any sign of another dwelling or settlement.

"McIndoe, tell me something," Ryan yelled over the crosswinds. "How far is it to the next ville from here?"

"No ville for a good few hours, maybe more—next stop is a fur trapper, just two huts. Used to live there with his wife, two kids."

"Used?"

McIndoe shrugged. "Something come and rip shit out of them, just like the last place on the trail."

"But it hasn't got your ville."

McIndoe fixed Ryan with a glare. "We ain't on the trail, and we keep ourselves hidden. You having trouble figuring why with all your stupid questions?"

Ryan bit back an answer, choked on the desire to lash out. He wasn't the sort of man to take such an insult, yet he could see why the Inuit had spoken thusly. The questions were stupe: deliberately so, as he wished to probe without seeming too obvious. Guess he'd failed there. Maybe he'd need to keep his eye out to watch his back.

"There—over north northeast," Quinn yelled, gesturing with a misshapen hand. "Deer."

The companions followed the hunter's indication. About half a mile away, but moving slowly toward them, was a herd of twenty deer. They looked fatigued, slow and hungry. From their height, they should have been carrying more bulk, but they would still supply the ville with a good source of meat if they could be mowed down.

The Inuit snapped into a practiced maneuver, spreading out and moving swiftly across the packed ice and rock. They made no allowance for the companions having little knowledge of their hunting methods, so Ryan decided that his people would best act as an independent hunt party from this point onward.

The deer were headed for the shelter and comparative warmth of the uplands, and rather than head back to the wastes and a lingering chill, were attempting to reach safety by outrunning the hunters coming toward them, their desire to survive directing their choices.

The Inuit each chose a deer, or a pair if they ran together, and closed in across the plain. They shot on the run, raising their rifles as their fur-wrapped feet pounded across the slippery plain. Taggart grunted heavily as he thrust himself forward with one gigantic push, angling his sled so he headed for his appointed target with a clear and flat run, pulling his Sharps from his shoulder as he glided across the surface, drawing a bead and firing, bringing down one of the deer with a clean shot that drilled through its skull.

Others weren't such good shots, taking wild aim and firing over and above the deer as well as wounding them. The injured creatures squealed, throwing terror into the herd, scattering them even more across the plain as they slipped on a cocktail of ice and their own warm blood.

The companions moved more methodically, using their skills to head off running deer and pick them off with single shots. Doc, however, got carried away at the noise and sounds of battle around him and loosed the charge from his LeMat toward one unfortunate creature, its middle dissolving into a soup of blood, offal and bone. He cackled wildly as it flew sideways into another deer, for a moment all reason once more extinguished in his mind.

Taggart set his sled on course for another brace of deer, propelling himself on a long slide and leveling his rifle. It was risky, as it took him across the path of a wounded deer that was galloping in wildly varying directions, blinded by fear and pain.

It was as he snapped off the second shot, taking his eye from the rogue beast for the second it took, that it occurred. The creature stumbled into his sled, catching the back with a force that sent it spinning, picking up pace as it hit an ice patch. Thrown off balance, it was all Taggart could do to stay on the sled. Perhaps he would have been better to have taken the fall. As he battled to regain control, the sled careered into a snowbank, coming to a sudden halt. His momentum threw him from the sled, flailing helplessly for a second in the air before hitting the rocks with a sickening crunch, taking the full impact on his left shoulder. He screamed with the pain, high and keening.

The hunt was almost complete. A dozen of the deer were down, and the hunters were beginning to round up the corpses, dragging them together across the ice. Even though the creatures were malnourished, they were still relatively heavy, and as he and J.B. hauled on a carcass, Ryan was glad that the ice covering the rock would assist them to drag the spoils partway back to the ville.

"What do we do when we get off the plain?" Ryan yelled to McIndoe.

"I send someone ahead. Others will come to help us haul it home," he returned. "I must see to Taggart."

Without another word he set off toward the snow-bank where the stricken hunter lay. Ryan watched him, and then some instinct told him to follow. He chased after the hunt leader and was close enough to hear the following exchange across the wastes.

"... shattered. Hurts like hell. Useless after this, and what use is that?"

"Sure? If there's any chance that you could—"

"I'll be a burden. You know that can't happen. Better it happens here. You know what to do."

Ryan arrived in time to see McIndoe retrieve Taggart's Sharps and chamber a shell.

"What the fuck—"

"This doesn't concern you," McIndoe said sharply, turning to face the one-eyed man. "Don't mess with something that has nothing to do with you."

"He's right," Taggart snapped. "You may have your

ways, but we have ours. I'm useless now, and there's only one thing to be done."

"Just chill you?" Ryan asked. He could see the reasoning, but had his own reasons for confirming this.

"You think I like this?" McIndoe snapped. "Taggart and me grew up together."

"Just do it, for fuck's sake," Taggart yelled with anguish.

McIndoe raised the Sharps and put the barrel to the prone hunter's temple. "Goodbye, friend," he said simply before squeezing the trigger and snuffing out Taggart's life. He turned away, face impassive but body language tight and tense.

Ryan pondered on what he had seen. It wasn't shocking. He could see why they did this. But if their people were that easily dispensable, then he was damn sure that his own people were equally disposable.

They'd have to be triple red careful from now on….

Chapter Eight

In the days following the first hunting party, the companions tried to keep to themselves as much as possible. Something that was made considerably easier to achieve by the attitude of the Inuit toward them. The natives of the settlement went about their daily business with a reserve toward one another that seemed exaggerated to ridiculous extremes when it came to their guests. It was usual for the inhabitants of a ville to be curious about strangers. Be they friendly or hostile, the native dwellers usually had some desire to know about the strangers who had landed in their midst, an attitude that was driven by survival, at either extreme. Curiosity brought questions, brought answers, brought information: a simple chain of cause and effect that would inform whatever action the dwellers would take against the interlopers.

A simple piece of human behavior that drove so much interaction, and which time and the ravages of the nukecaust had done nothing to change.

Except here, in this ville for which they didn't even have a name. For it was true that Thompson had been so reluctant to converse in any sense other than the strictly necessary with Ryan that he hadn't even told them if the ville had a name. It was possible to specu-

late that it retained some old predark name as a last ves-
tige of the links with the Scots and Irish settlers who
had integrated with the Inuit. But that was all it could
be, mere speculation.

For several days the companions joined with the
Inuit to take their food from the cookhouse that served
the whole settlement. Not a word was said by any of the
natives, not the most casual of inquiries nor even the
simplest gesture of acknowledgment. It was as though
the companions had always been there and were not
even of the slightest interest.

That did not, however, mean that they were to be left
to their own devices. Thompson had been exact in his
terms of their stay. The Inuit worked hard to survive in
the climate, and the fact that they were well-fed and
their dwellings well-maintained was owed to hard work.

Regular hunting parties set off each day to track for
food, and for skins and furs that could be stripped,
cleaned, cured and used for both clothing and bedding.
They had little in the way of woven materials. Old wool-
ens, cottons and some man-made fabrics that had lasted
since the predark days were now at the end of any life
that could be wrung from them, requiring a return to old
traditions. When the hunting parties returned, and the
carcasses had been dragged up onto the slopes and into
the ville, teams of Inuit would set to work bleeding and
skinning the carcasses before they were quartered, some
of the meat being used for fresh, the rest salted to be
preserved. The hides and pelt were then taken by other
members of the tribe, and the processes of curing and
cleaning begun before the prepared hide and pelt were
worked into clothing and blankets. It was a well-orga-
nized production line, and worked in speed and silence.

While this went on, there were other activities. A small herd of livestock was kept for milk, and a constant guard, with teams working in rotation, kept the herd safe from wolf and bear. Sec patrols also circled the forested areas at regular intervals for both human and animal intrusion.

There were some attempts to grow vegetables using the trough methods that J.B. and Mildred had seen back in the ruined ville on the plain. The sight of these was something that gave the Armorer pause for thought. Had the Inuit taken the idea by force when attacking the ville? Something that troubled at the corners of his mind, for there was no real evidence that the Inuit were interested in taking on other villes in combat. Indeed, their existence seemed to revolve around maintaining a certain isolation.

Meanwhile, while the hunting and sec parties made their rounds, within the settlement each had their appointed tasks. The gathering and preparation of wood to fuel their stoves; the rendering of tallow of use in lamps and stoves; the maintenance of the huts and cabins; the preparation of food and drink; the cleaning of the dwellings. Each of these tasks was the duty of a small group of Inuit, who would set about each day with methodical stoicism. There was no rush, but neither was there any sense of complacency. The whole tribe worked as one unit and seemed to operate without the need for any obvious communication.

"How the hell do they ever reproduce?" Krysty asked Ryan as they were resting in their hut. Despite the fact that there was no apparent surveillance, she still kept her voice low.

"Same as everyone else, I guess," Ryan replied, "except for the fact that there are so many muties that it must be getting harder for some of the women to bear children."

"That's not what I meant," Krysty said. "I mean, how does one of them ever know if the other wants to have sex? They don't look like they'd ask."

Ryan stifled a laugh. "Mebbe they have that organized like everything else, and it happens once a year, between harvesting the crop and skinning the deer."

Doc had been lying in the dark, listening, and felt it incumbent upon himself to speak. "It is so easy to mock, my dear Ryan, but who are we to poke fun at the way they live? Does it not strike you that they have a system appropriate to the environment in which they are forced, by chance, to live?"

"I wasn't dismissing them, Doc," Ryan answered. "They get by pretty well, especially as keeping themselves isolated means they're chilling themselves in the long run. Have you noticed many kids running around? It's getting harder for them to reproduce because they're too damn inbred, and mebbe too strict. You saw how they treated that guy Taggart a couple of days back. And they haven't been exactly friendly toward us."

Mildred had risen from her bed and was now looking out the window. It was a clear night and there was enough moonlight to illuminate the sleeping settlement.

"I don't like it here," she said as she watched a group of sec men shuffle out of the settlement and into the cover of the woods. "Yet the weirdest thing is that I couldn't tell you why. It's not like they've done anything to threaten us, and they don't seem to care whether we're here or not, as long as we work with them...but maybe that's it. Why don't they care? They've made no effort to try to find out if we're going to do them harm, or if we want to stay. It's like we're invisible to them."

"Perhaps that is because they have no concern about us, consider us no threat," Doc said quietly. "Is that not really the thing that unsettles you the most? They aren't wary. You have no power."

"Hey, make that 'we' have no power, or are you bailing out on us?" Mildred said angrily, turning to face Doc. "Maybe you're right—but what's wrong with that? The only thing we have going for us in a situation like this is that we don't look like a pushover. If we come across like the kind of pussies who can be walked on easily, then we'll buy the farm in no time."

"My dear Doctor, pray do not allow your paranoia to boil over. Has it not occurred to you that the 'problem,' as you see it, has nothing to do with our little group per se? This is not about how we appear to them, it is about how they are. We do not threaten them because we have assimilated into their system, and they have not become friendly on our terms because, to them, such a thing is alien and does not, in fact, exist."

Mildred shook her head. "I can't believe you're arguing philosophy with me on this. Perception and—"

"And bullshit," Jak blurted. "Mebbe you know what say, but not me. Don't care. Something here not right. J.B. tell about the crop?"

"Yeah," Ryan stated. "Crop cultivation exactly the way they were doing it in the ville we found."

"Come, sir," Doc frowned, "you cannot suggest that a method of cultivation constitutes grounds for suspicion."

"It does when it's a method we've never seen before and the wood on the troughs they've got here has been freshly cut," J.B. commented darkly. "It looks like a new idea for them, and it's just a little suspicious that they started using it so soon after the other ville got wrecked."

"Are you sure that your fears are based on nothing more than that they are different to us?" Doc reiterated.

"Mebbe," Ryan admitted, "but you've gotta admit, Doc, it's what's kept us alive up to now. Gut instinct has saved us more than reasoning."

"Has it? Has it really? I wonder…" the old man mused.

"Stayed too long already. Best go Ank Ridge." Jak interjected.

"He's right, lover," Krysty said quietly. "No matter how much we argue about this, the fact is that they haven't welcomed us, and they haven't been hostile. It's not going to stay that way forever. Sooner or later, they're going to want us to either do more or stop using their resources. Mebbe the time to go is now, before they reach that point."

"What about the wrecked ville?" J.B. asked. "If they did that, then they may have attacked others—"

"That's not really our concern," Ryan snapped, cutting him off. "It only becomes our problem if they make it ours by attacking us. If they don't, they can do what the hell they want to other people."

"You haven't seen it that way before," Krysty said, a little bemused by the one-eyed man's definite stance.

"Mebbe I've not been this cold, this pissed off, and this willing to get the hell out of the north," Ryan answered.

A silence fell across the cabin. It was eventually broken by Jak, the albino, as ever, wasting few words.

"So go tomorrow, get away from this place and feeling, yeah?"

Ryan nodded firmly. "Yeah. Hell, yeah."

MORNING COULDN'T BREAK quickly enough. Knowing that they would be on the move, none of the companions could get much rest, but for differing reasons. Jak and J.B. would have been glad to get out of the ville that night, not risking any kind of confrontation over their choice to leave. Mildred and Krysty were, in their own ways, concerned over Ryan's attitude. The man who assumed the mantle of leadership seemed, for the first time they could remember, uneasy with it. Which didn't bode well, for any group needs a strong leader in times of trouble, when decisions need making fast and debate wasn't an option. As for Doc, he, too, was pondering Ryan's state of mind, but for a different reason. Did this mean that his time to rise from the ashes was coming near? He would have to watch and wait.

Ryan, for his part, wasn't content with his state of mind, nor his behavior. He thought he'd shaken it off with the coming of action, but since the hunting party and his witnessing of Taggart's death, the uncertainty had returned. Possibly the inertia of the past couple of days had contributed. They had taken part in the ville's activities, but these had been matters of routine, with too much time for his brooding mood to settle once more. Try as he might, the nagging fear that they were doing nothing more than treading water wouldn't go away. As long as they were on the move, and in some kind of action, then he was able to keep these fears at bay. But one moment's respite and they would creep around the corners of his consciousness.

Maybe that was to be his fate: to keep moving, almost literally running away from his fears.

As the companions emerged from their cabin into the

chill morning air, the Inuit were already about their tasks and paid the companions the same attention as for the past three days: none at all. The six of them went and collected their morning meal and ate it in almost total silence. This wasn't to be deemed unusual, as it seemed that the Inuit behaved in much the same way and merely assumed—if at all—that the companions were falling in with their ways.

After they had eaten, Ryan searched out Thompson while the others waited in the center of the ville. The fact that they weren't joining any of the parties of workers, as they had on the two previous mornings, should have delineated that something unusual was to occur. Yet even with this possibility, they were spared no more than the occasional half glance.

Ryan found Thompson in his cabin. When Ryan entered, the chief was seated alone and seemed to be doing nothing more than staring into space. He had to have been doing something before the one-eyed man entered, and yet it appeared to Ryan as though the Inuit chief could have been in the same position all night and could continue to sit in this manner all day.

"I wanted to tell you that we're moving on," Ryan began. He paused, waiting for an answer, but there was none forthcoming. The only thing that could be remotely construed as an acknowledgment was a barely perceptible nod. Ryan continued. "It's not that we don't appreciate your letting us stay here, and it's not that we're not prepared to work. But we feel that we should be moving on to where we were headed before we first ran into your hunters."

"If you must go, you must go. You have given as well as taken, so we have no problem with you."

Ryan waited, wondering if there was to be anything beyond this gnomic utterance. But Thompson fell silent again, leaving Ryan feeling as though he had to explain: "We're ready to go now. We'll head back to the bottom of the slopes and out across the plain, on the Ank Ridge trail."

Thompson didn't, seemingly, acknowledge this last statement. So Ryan turned and left the chief's cabin.

"We go now?" Jak asked as Ryan approached.

The one-eyed man nodded. "They don't seem to care one way or the other, but keep it triple red, just in case."

"You don't trust them?" Krysty asked in a whisper.

Ryan shook his head. "I don't trust myself. I've just got a weird feeling that this is too easy."

Without a backward glance they left the center of the ville. They left the huts and cabins behind and they plunged through the undergrowth until they reached the concealed exit to the trading trail. In an uneasy silence they made their way along the trail as it snaked first upward, then back down toward the plains, echoing the route of the hunting party from a few days previously.

It seemed as though their passing hadn't even been noted by the inhabitants of the ville. Only a few of those working around the huts had raised their heads as the companions left; and there were none to watch them pass on the trail.

But they were only too well aware that appearance can be deceptive.

Chapter Nine

It began when they hit the plains. As the lower slopes of the volcanic region filtered their sparse growth of tree and foliage into the icy rock and snowdrifts of the wastes, so the weather began to bite harder. Without the warm channels of lava infusing heat into the ground, the air around them grew harsher; without the shelter of the trees, the winds were unbroken, strong and stinging as they bit into exposed flesh.

Taking the march in line, keeping a steady pace, they found themselves unconsciously slowing as soon as they were out of shelter. The rocks were slippery underfoot, the freezing air filled with ice and snow, the sulfurous smell catching at the backs of their throats, making breathing hard and unpleasant.

At the head, Ryan found himself wondering why they had set out now. The conditions back in the ville were much more clement. Yet something was tugging at the corners of his consciousness, making his gut turn as he thought about the Inuit. Like Mildred and Jak, he had a feeling that was hard to articulate, but that screamed at him that it was time to leave. He hoped that the others felt the same.

Behind him, J.B. and Jak were thinking much the same, in their own ways. Both men huddled into their thick outer coverings, trying to keep as much warmth as possible within the fur and fabric. As both were slight of build, wiry but thin, they lost more heat than the others, who had a little more body fat. Even Doc, for all his ranginess, was better equipped for the cold. Movement generated warmth, but was no substitute for the upward flow of volcanically heated air they had left behind. Jak wondered if they would be able to hunt before long. A good supply of food would be imperative. J.B. wondered if the next ville or settlement was more than half a day's march. What would they do if they hadn't come upon somewhere by nightfall?

Mildred and Krysty were also wondering such things, but in the Titian-haired woman's mind was something else: a growing feeling that there was danger, and not even as far as on the horizon. The Inuit had seemed indifferent to their going, and the bears and wolves were, generally, nocturnal. So what was the source of the feeling that hugged itself to her, a black void that drained her spirit? She wanted to say something, but was too cold to speak unless she could articulate clearly and simply, not wasting breath.

Mildred was worrying about Doc. The old man seemed to be okay, and although he was vague, that was no different to usual. All the same, there was something odd about him that she couldn't quite identify. Whereas once, whatever the madness in him, they could see the real Doc shining through, this time there was no real Doc. He seemed to be acting normally, but it was only surface: a bland exterior masking…what? That was the worrying thing. She had no idea what was beneath and what—or even why—had changed.

Doc, for his part, put one foot in front of another and kept walking, lost in his own world of dreams.

THE TRADING TRAIL HUGGED the lower slopes, winding between crops of rock that clustered malevolently at the base of the volcanic surge. Beyond, there was little except flat rock, bleached white by sun and wind building layers of ice to reflect the light with a blinding intensity. The wind swept across the barren landscape, driving ice and snow almost horizontal against whoever or whatever should be in its path. Yet, for all the hostility of this environment, it was free of the lurking dangers that the lower slopes held. There was no cover out there for any predators to conceal themselves, ready to strike. No bear or wolf that could hide until you were upon it, with no time to defend yourself.

As such, it was obvious that, as the trail wound down from the tree line, it would be a virtual admission of buying the farm to strike out across the icy plain. The settlers who had forged the trail had opted to try to tread as safe a path as possible among the crops of rock that littered the base of the downward slope and would provide enough cover to keep the worst excesses of the weather from them, but not enough to enable the predators to lie in wait.

The trail itself was a treacherous combination of some loose topsoil that was trodden flat and hard by generations of wags and feet, iced solid and then thawed during volcanic activity before being frozen over once more; and rock from beneath the thin crust that poked through, hard and treacherous on the ankles if caught. It was barely twelve feet wide as it snaked in and out of the taller rocks, with some towering up to twenty feet over the companions as they walked. The majority of the rock crop was between five and ten feet in height, but the shadows cast by the taller formations were ominous. To their left as they marched, the rocks were almost continuous, but to the right there were breaks, eroded by the conditions, that gave out onto the empty and desolate plain, allowing the howling gales to drive ice and snow through the gaps. There were places where snowbanks had been made, spilling over and narrowing the trail, threatening collapse on those who dared to pass.

Krysty's feeling of foreboding increased, but she put it down to the weather. The gales presaged a gathering storm, and it seemed likely that the gaps in the trail would turn the passage into a wind tunnel, with possibly fatal results. She knew that the rock passage would have to eventually give way to more open territory, and at least there they wouldn't be trapped in a bottleneck when the storm broke.

Jak, too, had feelings of imminent danger, but his were based on more than a doomie feeling. Since they had left the forest and the heat behind, he had been aware that they were being followed. Whoever, or whatever, was tracking them was expert, but few were as expert in the arts of hunting and concealment as Jak Lauren. The albino could hear movement coming from behind the crops of rock that comprised the broken walls of the passage. There were no voices, no vocal sounds at all, just the movement of feet on ice and snow, the occasional disturbance of gravel and small rocks that barely registered over the screaming of the gales, but could reach his highly attuned ears.

He wasn't sure if they were human or animal sounds,

but he knew that they had started to track the companions once they had left the sanctity of the woodland slopes. They were bargaining on the fact that the noise of the winds, amplified by the natural acoustics of the passage, would make them completely inaudible. They had been getting closer for the past half hour, taking their time in gaining ground, choosing patience over speed so that they wouldn't reveal themselves. But now they were right on top of the companions and it was time to act.

To avoid suspicion—lest their predators be human rather than animal—Jak chose to move slowly, overtaking J.B. and moving up to confer with Ryan. He was almost level with the one-eyed man and about to speak when all hell broke loose.

Dimly, at the back of his mind, Jak would wonder if his actions had precipitated events. But in real time, as it happened, there was no chance for him to do anything other than react.

Above the noise of the winds he heard a rumbling that echoed along the passage before being whipped away on the air. It was enough for both Jak and Ryan to look up at the same moment to see a shower of rocks tumble from the peak of one crop, rushing toward them. The rocks appeared to move in slow motion, falling from the peak with almost agonizing slowness, as though the force of the gales was keeping them aloft. But when they parted company with the rest of the rock face, they raced down, growing larger within a second and seeming to fill the whole of Ryan's vision. He felt a shove in his side and found himself tumbling to the left, catching his ankle and feeling it turn, thrusting out a hand to find the far wall that would stop him falling prone or hitting the rock wall with his unprotected head. He almost felt the rush of air as the rocks missed him by inches, crashing and splintering on the icy trail.

Jak pushed Ryan, then threw himself to the right, narrowly avoiding being hit by flying boulders. He cannoned into J.B., who managed to catch him.

"What—" the Armorer began before Jak cut him short.

"Get Ryan—under attack," he gasped, trying to catch his breath.

J.B. left Jak and hurried to Ryan, who was scrambling to his feet, having landed on one knee. His combat pants were ripped and blood seeped from a superficial wound just below the kneecap. It hurt like hell now, and he knew it would soon stiffen up, but he had to keep going.

"No accident," he yelled at J.B. as the Armorer helped him to his feet.

There was little need for any other comment: events were making such speculation redundant. The rock fall hadn't blocked the trail, but up ahead a snowbank had been dislodged, and the white death poured down, blocking the way with a wall some eight or nine feet deep.

"What the hell—" Mildred muttered.

"Being hunted—with us some way," Jak yelled over the noise, the need for discretion now gone.

"Why didn't they take us when we were in their ville?" Krysty asked. It was a reasonable question. Why would the Inuit wait?

"Who says it's them? Mebbe it's someone else," J.B. answered.

"Doesn't matter who the fuck it is," Ryan snapped.

"They've got us trapped while we're in here. We need to get the hell out."

Looking back along the way they had already traveled, it became clear that their only option would be to head for a gap in the outcrops that led onto the plain. But that wasn't inviting. Suddenly it became clear why whoever was hunting them had chosen that moment to begin the attack. Outside the passage, the plain was a churning maelstrom of ice and snow plucked from the surface, visibly tracing the conflicting currents of the crosswinds. The sky was heavy and dark with clouds that were about to burst and loose their sulfurous rains and snows upon the plain, a vicious storm that would give them no place to hide.

"Fireblast, we can't risk going out there. We're gonna have to backtrack," Ryan yelled.

"But that's exactly what they want!" Mildred exclaimed. "Why else take out the trail in front of us?"

"Yeah, mebbe, but we don't have a lot of choice," Ryan yelled. "So we don't go back like bastard animals to slaughter. We go back to hunt them down and chill them."

"Sounds good to me," J.B. agreed.

Ryan barked directions into the howling mouth of the encroaching storm, shouting himself hoarse to be heard as the conditions suddenly dipped. He and Jak would try to get up into the outcrops to track down the hunters responsible for the rock and snowfall while the rest of the companions would start to backtrack. They knew that moving out onto the plain was impossible now that the storm had arrived, but they were reluctant to go back as far as the forested areas, with their resultant threats, until they knew who was trying to direct them.

J.B. and Krysty led the charge back along the trail, with Mildred lagging behind to make sure that Doc followed. The old man seemed to be taking in what was happening, but the beatific smile that now seemed ever present on his face did little more than mask whatever may or may not be going on inside his head.

Jak and Ryan began to scale the rock walls. Each handhold was like clutching ice, their skin sticking to the cold surface. Their fingers were numbed by the ice and wind, the toes of their boots slipping on the treacherous surfaces. It was difficult enough to ascend to the top, without the added burden of having to watch for any attack that may come from above.

The fact that they were able to reach the top without confrontation was a sure sign that their unseen enemy had retreated. As they both stumbled onto the uneven surface that plateaued across the outcrops, they could see no one. The clear area in front of them was empty, but as Jak squinted into the swirling snows, he was sure that he could detect some movement on the lower levels of the foliage as the bushes and grasses were disturbed by their opponents. He directed Ryan's attention with an outstretched arm, not wasting breath on words.

Ryan acknowledged, and indicated that they should move toward the area, circling it so that they could come upon their attackers from the rear. Without a word, both men set off across the plateau as quickly as possible.

Below, in the channel formed by the rocks, the other four companions were making their way back. J.B. had the mini-Uzi ready, set on rapid fire, and Krysty held her Smith & Wesson Model 640; but Mildred didn't bother to unsheathe her ZKR. It was a precision weapon, and these were no conditions for her to fire; besides which, she had Doc to contend with. The old man was moving fairly quickly, but seemingly without a sense of urgency. Frankly, she didn't want him to unsheathe his LeMat, as he was completely unpredictable in this state and there was no telling at who, or at what imaginings he may be tempted to fire. She hung back to guide him, and he seemed to be only too pleased to accept this. But they were falling behind Krysty and J.B., and she urged him to increase his pace.

Ahead, the Armorer was squinting against the storm, wincing as the blasts of air and snow hit him broadside when he passed an opening onto the plains. Whoever was against them had timed their move to perfection, he had to admit. The only way for them to go now was back toward the relative shelter and safety of the lower slopes, which offered their trackers plenty of cover.

It was obvious that this was where they would go, and it was obvious that they now knew they were being tracked. From here on in, it was a matter of cat-and-mouse, and J.B. had an unpleasant feeling that he was one of the rodents.

Back up on the plateau of rock that bled slowly into the lower slopes of the volcanic region, both Jak and Ryan were moving swiftly toward cover. They had no idea if they were being watched, but suspected that the tracking party's attention would be focused on guiding the group in the passage exactly where they wanted them. They would notice two of the companions were missing, but could they afford the manpower to send back trackers to find them? Ryan was betting that they couldn't.

Both men felt a palpable relief when they crashed

into the cover of trees and shrubs that started to pepper the lower slopes, their feet all the more sure as they hit earth rather than icy rock. The biting edge was taken off the cold, the winds broken by the canopy of foliage, enabling them to breathe a little more easily, to see a little more clearly.

"Which way?" Ryan snapped as they came to a halt.

Jak paused, his impassive face refusing to betray the intensity of his concentration. There was no movement to the north or west, but he could hear movement, detect the faintest of scents that told him that the trackers had moved through here recently, moving south and east, moving to intersect with the other companions as they reached the mouth of the passage where the trail led back into the tree line of the slopes.

"There…there…" he said simply, indicating the direction. Ryan knew what the albino was thinking: it was an obvious move. These people either credited them with no intelligence, or had an innate confidence in the conditions leaving them with little option.

"Let's do it," Ryan stated. "I'll go clockwise, you counterclockwise. See how many there are, and how they're spread, then meet at the mouth of the passage, fill in the others."

"What if they not want us meet up?" Jak asked.

Ryan grinned. It was cold and without mirth. "They'll want that. Right now they're wondering where the fuck we are. They'll be so relieved we've turned up and they've got us all in one place that they won't wonder what we've been doing until it's too late."

Something that may have been a smile, but more resembled a death's-head grin, cut briefly across the albino's face before he left Ryan and set off on the trek that would take him around the enemy, leaving Ryan to—for the briefest second—watch him go before taking off on his own course.

This far down the slopes the covering foliage was much more sparse than he would have liked. It enabled him to move swiftly and with ease, but it also made it harder for him to conceal his considerable muscular bulk. Jak was more wiry than the Inuit—and Ryan was almost certain that these were their trackers—and of the same height. It would be relatively easy for him to conceal himself. Ryan, on the other hand, was taller and broader, and the lower slopes weren't ideal conditions for stealth.

The ground beneath him was sure of foot and he moved from scrub to scrub keeping close to the ground, the ferns and mosses disguising his footfalls, the low cover just about keeping him from view. He stopped periodically to take stock of his surroundings. He could hear very little above the howl of the wind—still incredibly loud, if reduced by cover—and his own labored breathing. There was no sign of Jak and certainly no sign of any trackers. From his vantage point he had an interrupted view of the passage shaped by the rock formations. It was easy to see the four companions moving backward toward the point where the passage bled into the forest trail, and he now understood how simple their progress had been for the trackers to follow.

So what if they were already at the mouth of the passage? They had to know that was where the others were headed.

Why were they doing this? It nagged at him. It would have been easy to mount an attack and chill the companions as they traversed the trail. It would be easy to do this when they reached the mouth. And yet chilling them didn't seem to be the objective. They were being directed. But where, and why? He had a notion that it was back to the Inuit settlement. In which case, why had Thompson and his people allowed them to leave in the first place?

The whole thing made no sense as yet. But what did sense matter when the first priority was to get the drop on their opponents and to assume the superior position, to be in control instead of being directed.

Ryan took to his toes once more, careering through the sparse undergrowth, the Steyr in his hands, primed to fire. He didn't want to initiate a firefight—not before the safety of the others had been secured—but he was ready if the trackers had other ideas.

Jak, meanwhile, had made a much swifter progress, even though he had a greater distance to cover. The small, wiry albino youth found cover easily and skipped over tracts of open space without a thought. He treated this as though it were a hunt and the opponents were animal rather than human. Unconsciously clicking into the frame of mind that had made him such a good hunter, he stopped thinking and acted on his instinct and his senses. Picking out small sounds from the maelstrom of noise that constituted a storm, even in this relatively protected area, he could tell that the tracking party wasn't near. Therefore he could move freely for the moment, exercising speed over caution. He had no scent of human that he could pick from the animal musk around: human smell was sharper, more pungent than that of other mammals, sweat trapped in the clothing souring over time and making it penetrate the sense more than the free-flowing odors of wolf or bear.

As with Ryan, Jak was able to see how clearly they

had been exposed as they'd followed the trade trail. Part of his mind was appalled at how open they had been, a lesson to be digested later. But right now he had to insure that there was to be a later. He slowed as he hit a denser growth of forest. Partly because he would have to exercise caution now to insure that he stayed silent and betrayed no sign of his presence. Partly because he had picked up the slightest change in the makeup of the surrounding noise, the constitution of the forest smell. There were people around here, well-concealed but not so much that they could deceive him.

Jak slowed to a crawl. He knew he was approaching the intersection of the forest trail and the beginnings of the rock passage. Now he would be the hunter and their hunters become the hunted.

He caught his first glimpse of their trackers: two men swathed in fur and hide, conferring by gesture as they overlooked the four companions making their way back along the path. He recognized one of them as McIndoe, the Inuit hunter they had journeyed out with. He was seemingly in charge of this expedition, as well, as he dismissed the other with a final gesture and sent him scurrying off to his destination.

Jak considered chilling the bastard. His hand was stayed by the knowledge that one small noise, one notion that the hunters were under attack, and the four companions were a sitting target. Besides which, the Inuit didn't seem as though they had, at this stage, a hostile intent. McIndoe had his Sharps over his shoulder, and the man he had sent away was also carrying just the one blaster, and this over his shoulder.

Maybe Ryan was right. Maybe they should just go along with this for now, see what it meant.

McIndoe had no notion of how close he had come to buying the farm as Jak left him, following the other Inuit hunter at a distance. The man was a messenger of sorts, as he traveled back along the parallel to the rock-enclosed trail, alerting four of his fellows that they should pull back. Jak returned with them. They had no idea he was here, and he could have easily taken them out before they had a chance to react or to locate the source of the attack. But once again he stayed his hand. He would play the long game, this time.

Ryan had, by this time, located some Inuit of his own, his suspicions confirmed. He had almost run into the messenger who scouted this area of the hunting party, only just avoiding a collision that would have given the game away. Both men were too stealthy for their own good, but fortunately the one-eyed warrior had been that bit more alert. The Inuit hunter had no notion there was anyone else in the forest, and had been too relaxed to hear the sounds of movement. Ryan watched him pass from cover, before following as the messenger rounded up the rest of the party. They were headed back to the intersection of rock wall and forest.

Would this be the moment when they chose to attack?

Ryan followed at a distance and watched as the Inuit party made its rendezvous, assembling on either side of the forest trail. They were about three hundred yards into the forest, and as he looked back he could see the four companions coming close to the mouth of the rock passage.

The Inuit had to know that he and Jak were missing from the party, so why hadn't they tried to do anything about it? None of it made sense to him, but he knew that their options were limited. The best he could do for now was to go along with what was happening and get back to his people.

Jak had obviously had the same idea, for as Ryan dropped onto the trail, J.B. whirling and very nearly loosing a hail of Uzi fire at him, Jak appeared at his back.

"Dark night," the Armorer cursed, "you should have called, Ryan. I nearly—"

"But you didn't," Ryan interrupted. "Listen, there's something strange going on here." He filled in the four companions on what had occurred since he had left them, and then listened while Jak told a similar story. The six of them had halted just short of the intersection and yet they had drawn no fire—or even interest—from those who had directed them back to this point.

"What the hell do we do now?" J.B. asked. "We can't try to go back."

"Back which way?" Mildred queried. "We either walk into their trap or we try to get back through the storm and the crap on the trail, and they put us through this all over again."

"Only one thing we can do," Krysty muttered. "Call their bluff."

Ryan agreed and indicated that his people follow him. He led them past the intersection and about two hundred yards into the forest. The snow and ice still blew here, stinging their eyes and skin, but a greater tension meant that they no longer noticed the raging storm.

"McIndoe," Ryan yelled, hoping his voice would carry above the roaring gales, "we know you're there. You must know that, too. So come out and either fight or tell us what you want."

There was a pause. The companions focused their attention on the area ahead, all with blasters to hand except Doc, who blandly looked around as though not caring what would happen. It was obvious that, in his current state, he had little—if any—conception of danger.

Jak jerked his head in the direction of small noises that alerted him to movement. The Inuit party was spreading down the area to the sides of the trail, moving toward the exposed party. Ryan noted Jak's motion.

"Come on, man, we know what you're doing. Come out and fight, or we'll come in after you. We're like rats in a barrel out here, so we've got shit to lose."

There was a pause that seemed to reach to infinity, their nerves stretched taut and jangling as they watched and listened for the slightest sign of activity. They were more than on edge. They were tipped over into the abyss. So much so that when they heard the rustle of foliage as McIndoe stepped out of cover, five of them snapped their blasters in his direction, only their instincts stopping them from firing immediately, wasting him and starting a firefight they would be sure to lose. Only Doc refrained, seemingly oblivious.

The Inuit hunter had his Sharps still flung across his back, and his arms were raised from his body as far as the bulk of fur and hide would allow. He had to have been sweating to see five blasters trained on him, but his flat features betrayed no signs of emotion.

Gradually muscles relaxed, tautness subsided and blasters were lowered. Ryan tried to speak, but his voice came out harsh and cracked, his throat dry and tight with the tension.

"You're a lucky man." His voice grated.

"You chill me, it's my problem. I got it wrong. But I'd buy the farm knowing you were following close behind." The Inuit shrugged.

"So why haven't you chilled us?" Ryan continued, ignoring the hunter's words.

"Not my job. My job to take you back to the ville."

"Then why not just take us by force, why all this?" Ryan asked, gesturing behind to the blocked trail.

"Try to force you, then it's a firefight and some of you get chilled. Some of us get chilled. No good to anyone that way. Better to give you no option than to go back."

"But why?"

"Come back and you see," McIndoe suggested.

Ryan looked to his people, seeing mirrored in their expressions his own confusion and bafflement. If there had been a reason to keep them there, then why let them leave? And if it were hostile, why not chill them now? And if not hostile, then what was the point of all this? There was only one way to find out.

Ryan dropped his Steyr. Following his lead, the others let their blasters fall.

"Okay, we'll go with it. Doesn't seem much choice, anyway. Take us back, let's see what the hell this is all about."

At a signal from the hunt leader, the rest of his men came out of cover. All had their blasters secured, but the manner in which they clustered around the companions suggested that deviation from the intended route wouldn't be tolerated. Following suit, and Ryan's lead, blasters were secured and the bizarre party began its trek back to the ville.

It was certainly more pleasant to be going back into

the warmer climes of the volcanic regions, where the foliage broke the winds and provided a canopy from the worst of the storm, and where the bitter edge was taken off the cold. They traversed the trading trail until they reached the point where the hidden access to the ville was located and plunged through into the forest. In a short time, they arrived at their destination to find things were not as they had been just a few hours before.

The center of the ville was no longer an empty space. A canvas canopy, much patched and repaired, had been laid over the area, suspended on poles eight feet high, pitched one in each corner of the clearing. Beneath the canopy were six tables: rough wood, with four legs and crosspieces to insure that they could bear a large amount of weight. Each table had been daubed. At first it was hard to see with what, but as they approached, even under the dimmed illumination of the canvas covering, it was apparent that there were symbols painted in red and yellow, each table the same in those markings.

There was no sign of any life. Usually, there were people carrying out their work on the stoops of the huts and cabins or going about their business. Now it was empty.

McIndoe brought his party to a halt, holding out an arm to prevent the companions taking another step into the center of the ville.

"Are you going to tell us what this is all about?" Ryan asked softly.

"I think we may have already guessed," Krysty added under her breath.

"Not my place. Wait," McIndoe replied.

The door to Thompson's hut opened and he emerged, as though he had been waiting for them. Possibly he had. He was followed by a heavily limping man that they had seen around the ville. He was older and stouter than the Inuit chief and his impassive face was heavily lined. As opposed to the skins and furs they had seen him wear before, he was now in a ceremonial costume of dyed black hide with a white yolk, with a headdress of small animal bones around a broad-brimmed hide hat.

"Are you going to tell me, then?" Ryan asked without ceremony.

"Figure you'd be a fool if you hadn't already worked it out." Thompson shrugged.

"So why did you let us leave?"

The faintest trace of a smile crossed the chief's face. "Couldn't very well get this prepared while you watched—you would have figured out what was going on and tried to blast your way out."

"And we're not going to do that now?" Mildred growled.

"You could try, but you're surrounded and heavily outnumbered, plus we're prepared for you. No, my friends, it was less trouble to let you think you could go, then guide you back here. Avoided unnecessary waste of ammo, gave us time to prepare and meant you're all here in one piece. Not harmed, or less than whole. And that's important."

"Important for who?"

"For us. In case you hadn't noticed, we're having a few problems here. Skydark was a judgment on the ways of the world, but the Lord was a little amiss. His own people got some shit, as well. Lot of us born with problems, and now a lot less of us born. A lot of barren women, and babies that don't last more than a few weeks or months. Those that survive can adapt—that's the way of the world—but ain't no good if there aren't any being born."

"And you think we can bring new blood to you?" Ryan said.

Thompson looked shocked. "Hell, no! We don't want outsiders among us. Hellfire and brimstone, boy, if that was the case, don't you think we would have mixed a little more with those on the trail?" He shook his head. "Knew you wouldn't get it. See, when our two tribes mixed, the ones from overseas—the ones you call Scots and Irish—they brought us the Almighty, our Lord. And they brought us other ways that worked for them on the islands they came from. Ways that had worked for centuries. Blood for boon."

"Ah," Doc muttered, almost inaudibly, "the old ways. Pagan sacrifice to the moon and sun for bounty. Bound to be confused with Christianity in those outposts of civilization."

But no one was listening. They'd got the gist and didn't care about the history.

"So you sacrifice us? What makes you think we'll just lie down and take it?" Ryan snarled.

Thompson sighed. "Look around."

They did so, to find that the huts and cabins were discharging the entire population of the ville, all armed.

The chief continued. "You either chill in a firefight, maybe slowly and painfully, or you let us take your lives for the glory of the greater good and the Almighty. It'll be quick, I promise you that. We don't mean to make you suffer, it's just that we need your blood for the Lord, so he'll shine on us. We've tried the others, but they were too intrinsically evil. You came out of nowhere. You were sent."

The companions looked around at the Inuit as they closed ranks, coming closer to the companions. So that was the idea: a human sacrifice to appease their gods and banish the taint that was making them barren. And not the first. The condition of the ruined ville they had first encountered now made sense. How many others on the route to Ank Ridge had also been decimated in this cause?

"You need us whole, do you?" Ryan asked calmly, drawing his SIG-Sauer. "So I guess that means you can't chill us yet, or even blast us. One wrong move and your sacrifice is fucked, right? So if we try to do that, you can't fire on us without ruining your plans. Mebbe you aren't as on top of this as you'd like us to think."

He looked back over his shoulder at the others and could see the situation becoming as clear to them as it had to him. With the exception of the still-distant Doc, who was amiably smiling at their foes, the others began to reach for their previously secured blasters.

Mildred grinned. "I do love it when you get logical, boss man," she said, withdrawing her ZKR as the Inuit closed in on them. "Looks like it's time to cut loose a little."

Chapter Ten

"Call 'em off, Thompson, or we'll start blasting," Ryan said calmly, assessing the situation. In truth, it didn't look good. The inhabitants of the ville were closing fast, and soon any kind of blasterfire would be as dangerous to his own people as to their opponents in such an enclosed space. J.B., having already realized this, had cast aside the M-4000 and the mini-Uzi, unsheathing his Tekna knife. Both the shotgun and the SMG would run too great a risk of taking out his own at these close quarters.

Jak had also eschewed the use of his Colt Python. The .357 Magnum handblaster was too powerful to use in a combat area that was rapidly becoming as closed down as the center of the ville. He palmed two of his leaf-bladed throwing knives from their concealed sheathing in his patched camou jacket. Even impeded by the bulk of the fur he wore over it, the speed of the hand was greater than that of the eye.

Mildred and Krysty had to rely on their handblasters, as they had no blades to substitute. Hand-to-hand combat would have to suffice when the distance was too small to risk shots.

But as of yet, there was no initiation of fire. The Inuit kept coming and Ryan held his people back. Casting his eye over the crowd, he could see that they were at least twenty deep on all sides. Everyone who lived in the settlement had come back in for this moment. There were no hunters on expedition, no sec out on patrol. The odds were heavily stacked against the companions, and their only hope would be that Thompson would not wish any more of his people to be unnecessarily chilled.

But then again, that depended on how you defined "unnecessary." If it was for the greater good of the tribe, then Ryan had seen—with the sacrifice of the hunter Taggart—that none of the Inuit had any qualms about themselves or others buying the farm.

It was as if Thompson could hear Ryan's thoughts. The Inuit chief fixed the one-eyed warrior with a stare.

"You won't stop us. We won't back down."

Ryan shrugged. If that was so, there was nothing to lose. If they were going to be taken down, they may as well go down fighting. He raised the SIG-Sauer and fired directly into the face of an approaching Inuit male. A neat round hole appeared in his forehead, and those who followed in his wake found themselves showered with blood, brain and bone fragments from the larger exit wound in the back of his skull. His otherwise impassive visage registered the vaguest shock before he crumpled to the dirt.

It made no difference. Those behind him either stepped on, over or around his inert form. Those covered with the viscous fluid from his skull cavity, which steamed lightly in the freezing air, wiped it from their faces as they continued.

"We aren't going to stop them," Mildred said with an air of weary resignation, "but we might even the odds if we take a few of 'em with us."

Before the last syllable had died, its echo was drowned by the crack of the ZKR. Her first shot hit an Inuit woman full in the face, shattered septum traveling up and out at velocity to pierce her frontal lobes as the shell from the target pistol was deflected downward through her palate, sheering flesh as it ripped into her throat before tearing a hole in the carotid artery as it exited her body. Although her brain function was now virtually nonexistent, there was enough motor function left to carry her forward a few stumbling steps, the blood rhythmically pulsing from the hole in the side of her neck, a steaming claret spray that showered over those who advanced beside her. The smell of fresh warm blood carried on the cold winds, drifting across the center of the ville.

It was as though this, not the visual or aural signs of violence, was the trigger for an increase in action. From their slow, silent march toward their prey, the Inuit surrounding the companions suddenly snapped into faster, harder action. It was as if they had been held back by some invisible force that had curtailed their action, and now that this was lifted they found themselves propelled forward with a sudden and violent sense of momentum.

Still eerily silent, they rushed upon the six people in their midst. Doc was the first to fall. The old man hadn't even bothered to draw his LeMat, which, in the circumstances, was a good thing. However, neither had he unsheathed the silver lion's-head sword stick, which may have offered him some protection. In his mind, he wasn't looking for protection, he was looking to observe dispassionately, to see what happened next in this strange world that was of his own imaginings.

What happened was simply that he was swept up by the onrush of human flesh, knocked from his feet, pummeled by fists and nicked time and again by sharp blades that made him bleed from superficial lacerations, energy draining with the sharp, nagging little pains and the loss of blood that resulted. Feet clad in skins and heavy boots thudded against him, some accidentally and some in deliberately placed kicks. The force of the feet was dissipated somewhat, cushioned by the fur and skins wrapped around them, but still enough to drive the breath from him.

He rode these blows, allowing himself to be carried along with the flow of the hand-to-hand fighting. He was curious only to discover what would happen next.

His companions weren't so accommodating.

As the wave of Inuit swept toward them from all sides, closing them in, they began to fight. They knew that the Inuit didn't care about themselves and would gladly go to buy the farm to overpower their opponents. They also knew that the Inuit wanted them alive and not harmed in any major way. They had to be whole for the sacrifice, and to accidentally chill them before any ritual would be a pointless waste of a sacrificial lamb. So maybe they had an edge. If they could keep fighting and make their way through the crowds to the edge of the clearing, then they could attempt to escape into the upland slopes of the volcanic region, losing their opponents in the undergrowth.

To say that this was a long shot would be an understatement: but it was something, no matter how slight, to which they could cling. Any hope was better than none and would fuel a seemingly hopeless fight.

Mildred, Ryan and Krysty all fired into the oncoming crowd, each with a vague notion of clearing a path with their fire. In front of them, Inuit men and women too slow to move—either because of deformities that limited their movement or because of the density of the crowd surrounding them—were drilled with shells from the SIG-Sauer, the ZKR and the Smith & Wesson, each one doing enough damage to remove one opponent from the pay permanently.

Yet none of these shots made any real impact on the advance. For each Inuit that fell, there were many others to step into the gap their chilling caused. And once all three blasters were empty, there was no time to reload with the enemy in such close proximity. Ryan was able to snatch his panga from the sheath on his thigh, but for Mildred and Krysty it came down to trying to defend themselves with hands and feet.

Jak and J.B. had made better progress. Working only with blades from the first, both had decided that the only way to make any kind of dent on the enemy would be to take an offensive rather than defensive stance—to take the game to them from the off. To this end, both men had moved toward the oncoming crowd, Jak becoming a whirling blur of arms as he twirled the knives, the razor-sharp blades cutting through hide, fur and skin with ease. He was the first to elicit any kind of vocal response from their enemies, his slashing motion drawing yelps of pain and screams of agony as easily as it drew blood. He cut an immediate swath through the mass of Inuit flesh, carving himself a small path. But it wasn't to be easy for anyone to follow. No sooner had he made inroads than the gap closed behind him, sealing him into a pocket of the enemy, with no way to reach his compatriots, or for them to reach him should he need their assistance. All he had succeeded in doing was isolating himself.

He fought harder, his arms never tiring as he thrust and parried with the knives, deflecting blows and scoring through the flesh of his enemies. Yet they kept coming, wave after wave, with an increasing determination. No matter that he deflected two with cuts that took them out of the action. Four would take their place. Fists and feet lashed out at him. Some he could skip over, shimmy and feint around. Others struck home. Not blows that were damaging by themselves, but with a continuing cumulative effect that bruised his flesh, drove breath from his body, caught him on an intake of air, stopping it short... Blows that, by their very persistence, were wearing him down. Short, jabbing motions from knives held by the Inuit, motions designed to lacerate and eviscerate rather than chill, became harder to avoid as he grew more and more tired. The sharpness of a sudden pain slicing across his skin became more frequent. More: more of everything against him, and less of his own blows hitting home. He could avoid so much, but not everything, and as he became exhausted, so the ratio shrunk until he was admitting more blows than he was able to repel.

While Jak was succumbing to the continued onslaught, J.B. attempted to put up as much of a fight as possible. On drawing the Tekna, he had also taken the precaution of wrapping part of his coat around his free arm. The skirt of the long, man-made fiber jacket was already ripped from previous adventuring, so to slice it cleanly away was the work of a second. Gripped and wrapped around his free wrist and forearm, it would act as kind of shield against attack. The thickness would stop any real damage from blades, although it would do little to cushion any hard blows from blunt objects. It was, however, better than nothing. Indeed, it soon proved its worth when the Inuit closed on the group and the Armorer was able to stop several jabs from Inuit hunting knives while, at the same time, striking back with jabbing blows of his own from the Tekna.

The problem was that he could do little more than adopt defensive measures. Their strength lay in staying together. Jak's sudden isolation only proved this. Yet if they did this, they were static in the center of the ville. It was a seemingly insurmountable problem, and one to which he could give no thought while wave upon wave of Inuit crashed upon him, drowning him in pummeling fists, sharp and sly knife thrusts, and a wall of flesh and fur that seemed as though, on sheer weight alone, it would drive him to the ground.

Still he fought on, not knowing how to give in, even if common sense had told him to accept his fate. He scored through hide and fur, felt flesh snag and tear, smelled blood and fear as he continued to fight. But the fists began to wear him down, the feet caught at his knees, the kicks making his calves and knee joints sore and jittery, threatening to give way at the next assault. There was no respite, and every time he felt he may be making some progress, there was a fresh wave of Inuit flowing over him. They didn't care how badly any of them were hurt; they only cared that they take him down without chilling him or causing him serious physical harm. Their stoic persistence would, inevitably, outlast his own through sheer strength of numbers.

The wrapping around his free arm was heavy with soaked-in blood, both his own and that of his opponents;

his knife hand was slippery, slick with that same blood. One last kick behind his knee connected well enough for his joint to give way and he was down.

Ryan was roaring with sheer frustration and fury, yelling so that his lungs were filled with the scent of blood and the stench of sulfur as he lashed out with his free hand, the scarred and brawny fist and forearm a club that was seemingly oblivious to the cuts inflicted, the blood streaming down it as it cut through the air, scattering Inuit tribesmen. With his other hand, he used the panga to cut through the air, the blade cutting into anything that got in the way of its momentum. He sliced into arms, faces and torsos, no longer seeing anything but the red mist in front of his eye, tugging the blade free of anything in which it was stuck.

But still they kept coming. Nothing could stop the onslaught of Inuit. Slowly they wore him down, the fists and feet, the sly knives, all taking their toll. In some ways, the one-eyed warrior was easier to fight than any of the others. His anger had blinded him to anything except his own bloodlust, and they were able to avoid his blows and his swinging blade with a greater ease than was possible with any of the others, who had a more considered approach to the current combat. Ryan was exhausting himself, and making of himself an easier target for the Inuit tactics, slowly chipping away at his strength, bringing him down by degrees. Slowly, but inexorably.

For Mildred and Krysty, capitulation came much more quickly and at a greater price. Once they had discharged their weapons, before there was a chance to reload, they were under a hail of bodies, fists and feet, knives prodding at them, probing and cutting, blood endlessly flowing in small rivulets from nicks and tears that accumulated in such a way that the blood loss began to tell. Smaller and lighter than Ryan, but not armed with blades like the slight forms of J.B. and Jak, they were by far the most vulnerable targets after Doc. And the ville dwellers took full advantage of this. They were relentless in their attack, swarming over the two women, not giving them even the room to form blows against their foe. Battered by fists that came from nowhere, feet that hacked at their shins and knees to take them off balance and put them down on the cold earth, there was little they could do to fight back in any manner that could be construed as constructive.

Mildred had wondered why they had been left with their weapons when they were directed back toward the settlement, and more particularly after McIndoe had revealed his party to them. Surely it would have made sense to disarm them, even if at the risk of a firefight on the lower slopes? More particularly, it would have prevented the chilling of some of the Inuit in this fight… But then she realized that it didn't matter. If things were for the greater good, then the Inuit would have just kept coming, relentlessly, regardless of any defense that the companions could form. A few chilled men and women were nothing next to the ritual that they felt sure would save their ville from sterility. A small price for the greater good. It was a way of looking at things that hadn't occurred to her before this moment. An alien perspective on events. And even now it only occurred to her in that brief moment before consciousness was lost.

Krysty fought on a little longer. The unremitting attack took a great toll on her, and in part she wanted to call on the Gaia power that she could use in emergencies to give her greater strength. Yet was this the right time? To harness that force would leave her so drained. The chances of laying waste to the entire tribe and saving her friends was remote. All she would do would be to write off a few more of the Inuit and then find herself devoid of energy at a crucial moment. Best to go down fighting now and save that force for if and when it could do some real damage. They were needed alive and whole for a ritual. Perhaps that would be the time to call upon Mother Earth.

Although she kept fighting, the rain of blows and the sly jabbing of the knives were taking their toll. She grew weary, light-headed, and eventually slipped to the floor, the feet and fists pummeling her even when she could no longer feel them.

SHE WAS THE FIRST to regain consciousness, aware at first of little more than the unpleasant sensation of being probed. Fingers searched her body, pulling apart the scabbed cuts, pressuring bruised areas to determine the damage that may lay beneath. Her genitals were probed with an infinite delicacy, yet there was nothing sexual about the examination. It was impersonal, brisk, perfunctory. She was being checked for damage. She tried to move her feet, bring her legs closer together; she tried to reach down and cover herself, offer some kind of protection. It was at those moments that she realized her hands and feet had been secured, and that she was lying prone, vulnerable to any attack that may be made upon her person.

She also became aware of the temperature. One part of her was icy cold, the other flushed and hot.

Forcing her eyes open, taking a few moments to

focus and assimilate what she saw, Krysty was astounded. She could still turn her head one hundred and eighty degrees, feeling the hard wood beneath her skull, painful as she moved. Part of her vision at each end of the turn was obscured by her own arms as they lay, pinned above her head. There was, however, enough in her field of vision to explain what she could feel.

She was on her back, under the canvas tarpaulin, tied to one of the painted tables. The extreme heat she could feel on one side was provided by a blazing fire that had been laid just beyond the reach of the tarpaulin, to prevent it catching from the flames that licked the cold air, smoke spiraling upward on the conflicting currents of air. There were four of these that had been fired since she had lost consciousness, one on each corner of the space delineated by the canvas covering. The nearest heated one side of her body, the other side froze in the cold air that still blew through the center of the ville. She was so cold simply because she was naked. If her shivering skin hadn't told her that, then the sight of her blue-tinged, pimpled flesh at the extremities of her vision would have informed her of the fact.

She wasn't alone. Each of the six tables they had seen in the center of the ville was occupied by one of the companions, each in a similar state of nakedness, each secured in the same manner. The others appeared to still be in a state of unconsciousness, and they were being left alone. She looked down the length of her body. Thompson and the bizarrely attired man who had followed him from his hut were bending over her lower body, their attention focused on their task. The old man standing on the opposite side of the table to Thompson was conducting the examination. He had finished with her genitals and was now examining her thighs, working down toward her knees.

Thompson looked up and around, his eye catching hers.

"You're awake. That's good. Just checking to see if you're all in one piece. Can't have you harmed…yet."

Without another word, he returned his attention to the task being completed by the old man, who had by now reached as far as her ankles and feet. She felt his touch skim across the soles of her feet, the pressure light yet firm, making her twitch and try to pull her feet away from him. He ignored her and looked at Thompson, nodding and grunting.

The Inuit chief seemed pleased, and he returned the nod before the two men moved across to the next table, where Jak lay secured.

Krysty tried to ignore the cold that pierced and numbed one side of her body, working its way into the core of her being before hitting the wall of heat that penetrated from the other side, scorched by the fire. She followed their progress as they began to conduct a similar examination on the albino teen, their touch making him stir from his unconsciousness and thrash wildly as he tried to loosen himself. The two men stepped back and waited for him to exhaust himself before calmly resuming with their examination.

Looking around as much as she could, Krysty was astounded to see that the fringes of the clearing, where not blocked by the fires, were filled with the Inuit, who stood calmly and silently, watching the progress of the examination.

Jak finished with, the two men continued on, turning next to Ryan. What was it that Thompson had said?

Something about being all in one piece...for now. Krysty's mind was still fogged by the torpor of her recent blackout, but she worked to clear it, to try to focus on what was occurring. They were to be sacrificed in some kind of ritual and, for it to be effective, they had to be whole. The small cuts and bruises they had suffered were nothing: everyday contusions. The check was obviously to see if any major damage had occurred or if they were lacking in any way from encounters in the past.

So were they to be sacrificed immediately? She doubted it. They had been stripped for the examination, but they hadn't been prepared in any other way. The fact that the tables on which they were secured had been painted with so many symbols, and that the old man was dressed as though for a ceremony, suggested to her that there was a high level of ritual involved. A perfunctory examination and then a quick chill wouldn't fit with the rest of the picture.

The Inuit chief and the old man were now checking Doc. The old man was mumbling incoherently, shouting and mouthing formless words as he rose up out of the sea of unconscious, the anguished tone of his voice enough to cut through Krysty's sensibilities and make her cringe at the pain contained within. Yet, despite the vocal protestations, he succumbed easily to their probing fingers, and subsided into a kind of sleep once they had finished, moving on to Mildred.

Krysty moved her head and tried to alter the position of her arm so that she could see what they did to Mildred. It was of little use, as her biceps blocked a view of their examination of the woman. But there was no escaping the curses that rained from Mildred's lips as she came around to find their fingers invading her body. Curses that didn't subside as they moved back into Krysty's line of vision, finishing their task with an examination of J.B. She could see the Armorer go rigid as he regained consciousness at their probing, his back arching off the table and every sinew and muscle standing out on his wiry body. There was nothing he could do to stop them, and he stoically stayed silent, but his attitude was betrayed by the mute screams of his body.

Finally, Thompson and the old man had completed their task. Every one of the companions had been examined, and they were now conscious.

"Glad you're all awake," Thompson said simply, moving among them. "Makes it easier to tell you all what's going to happen. We've just been checking you over to see that you're right for sacrifice. You have to be whole—the Almighty demands that, and if we sent you to him when you were damaged in some way, then he'd get real mad and bring it all down on us. Which is the last thing we want from him.

"Wish you hadn't been so damn stupid and put up a fight. Could have saved yourselves a lot of pain and hardship if you'd let us take you without any problems. Face it, there was no way you were ever going to get out of here in one piece, so you may as well have taken the easy route.

"Now, to be a good sacrifice, you have to be in good condition. The Lord wants you whole, and he wants you healthy. It's that energy that means so much to him. So we're going to feed you up for a couple of days, get you ready for the rituals that precede the sacrifice. Paying homage to the Almighty, that's what it is. And you need to be good and ready for it. So you eat what's coming around now, and then you'll eat some more later, build up that strength."

From outside the area covered by canvas, Inuit men and women moved forward with platters that contained strips of cooked meat, garnished and covered with a glaze that contained herbs. A sweet smell wafted across the space, carried by the wind currents, and despite themselves and their situation, the six captives found their mouths watering. As they lay back on the tables, unable to move more than a couple of inches, the platters were held in front of them and their carriers lifted strips of meat from off the plates, holding them above the mouths of the captives, gently lowering them in and allowing the companions to nibble at the sweet meat. Their mouths filled with an infusion that was like roasted pork glazed with honey, smothered in basil and thyme, with something else that was indefinable but encouraged—compelled—them to eat more as it was offered. The meat was warm, but had obviously been prepared for some time. Despite this, there was a heat in the glaze that warmed their throats as it slipped down.

They continued to eat until the meat was gone, each platter now containing nothing more than the sticky remnants of the glaze that had covered the meat. Each of them now felt relaxed, warmed through, and perhaps distant from the events that were going on around them. They were aware of little except for the fact that their desire to break their bonds had subsided and that they were no longer feeling the extremes of heat and cold from the fires and the atmosphere.

Thompson waited until the Inuit had withdrawn with the platters, then stepped forward into the middle of the tarpaulined area once again, accompanied by the strangely dressed old man. Krysty caught sight of them as they passed her—she couldn't be bothered to strain her neck to try to get a good look at them as they stood in the center—and of a sudden it struck her that the old man was dressed halfway between a priest from old religions predark and a shaman from the much older traditions that had been carried on after the nukecaust, and which she had heard spoken of in Harmony when she was young. If that was the case…

She groaned, almost inaudibly, realizing why the meat had been so sweet, why it had demanded of them the compulsion to eat more. If the old man was an Inuit medicine man, and they were to be a sacrifice, then the meat had been laced with herbs that would drug them, make them compliant and susceptible to whatever was suggested. It would take from them the desire to escape and make of them little more than puppets. In short, put them right where the Inuit wanted them.

As this realization hit her, Thompson began to speak—to the Inuit, rather than to their captives.

"People, they have eaten of the flesh and they have taken the herbs that will make them do as we desire. They will be taken from here to huts where they will regain their strength for the rituals leading to their sacrifice. They will have no wish to run, and will realize that they are to be part of the greater good. We will let them rest for at least one day before assessing whether or not they are ready to begin. Before they are taken from here, Reverend McPhee will bless us all, particularly those who will give their lives for us, as decreed by the Almighty."

The old man moved between the tables, anointing the prone companions with oils that smelled as sweet as the meat. They received three dabs of oil: one on the forehead, one on the chest, one on the genitals. Each dab of oil seemed to sink into them like lead, warming through the area on which it landed. It felt sticky, viscous and warm against the skin, and seemed to make perfect sense of the words that he spoke.

"Great Father in the heavens, for whom thine is the power and the glory, we commend unto you these souls that will soon depart to join you on the celestial trail. We beseech that you grant them speed in their passing and that you accept their lives in the spirit in which they are offered—as a sign to you that you are the leader of our people and that we wish to ask of you that you save us from extinction. We have always followed your teachings, and all we ask is that subsequent generations be offered the chance to also pay homage to you."

Krysty, by now trying desperately to cling to the knowledge that she had been drugged in the hope that it would help her fight against the effects, marveled at his words. Anointing them with oil and seemingly making up his address as he spoke, his words were a bizarre mix of the mundane, something taken from old religious texts. But it was as nothing compared to his next action.

Lifting her head as much as she could to get a better view of what was occurring, Krysty was astounded to see the old man begin to whirl and dance to a rhythm only he could hear. As he did so, he began to chant words and syllables that were in a language she didn't understand. He moved slowly because of his age, yet at the same time there was an undeniable grace to his ritual dance. The words continued as long as he moved, until he suddenly stopped, lifting his head and his arms toward the heavens in supplication, finishing his ceremony in English.

"For thine is the kingdom, the power and the glory. Forever and ever. Amen."

The Inuit all chanted the single word "Amen" before the medicine man dropped his arms and moved out of the tarpaulined area.

The ceremony was now obviously at a close, as the Inuit swarmed into the area, buzzing around the tables. The drugged meat was beginning to take a greater effect and Krysty felt her head become heavy, her hearing and vision blurring at the edges. She felt her bonds being untied and she was lifted from the table. Furs and skins were wrapped around her and she shivered not from the cold, but from the sudden realization that she had been almost frozen as the skins and furs warmed her, the feeling beginning to seep back into her bones beside the artificial heat of the drug.

She tried to look around, but her head was slow to react to the signals from her brain, her neck twisting slowly. She could see the bland faces of the Inuit all around her, coming in and out of focus as she was passed over their heads, bobbing up and down on a sea of hands. She caught glimpses of the others as the same happened to them.

She was moved out from under the tarpaulin, the darkening skies above her betraying the passing of time. She could feel the Inuit swarming beneath her, but it became harder to keep a grasp on reality. The swarm beneath her was like a sea of flesh that swept her along. The tide carried her toward three huts, all of which were fenced off from the rest of the ville in a way that she hadn't seen before. Each had wire and wooden fence posts to isolate it from the other dwellings. But surely they did not expect anyone to try to escape? That was what the drugs were for…unless it was to keep the Inuit out?

She couldn't tell, and thinking was becoming harder. Her head lolled on her shoulders and, with no support beneath her for her skull, she kept dropping her head so that the world turned upside down.

But she could keep herself alert enough to see that they were being taken to the huts: two per dwelling. Mildred was being carried ahead of her, taken into the hut that Krysty felt herself being swept to by the tide of the Inuit. How come she was being swept while Mildred was carried? Or was it just a trick of perception, caused by the drugs?

It became harder to tell what was real and what wasn't. She could see the others being paired off into the other two huts. They were carried one moment, moving on a tide the next.

Krysty saw the black maw of the hut doorway closing in on her. It caught her on the head, her reactions too slow to duck in time, and the world went blissfully black.

Chapter Eleven

They lay in the huts, the drugged meat making them sluggish and torpid. Stripped of their clothes, stripped of their weapons and, more importantly, stripped of the will to fight back, each of them began to warm through in the log cabins, the tallow and wood-burning stoves filling the air with the thick, sweet smell of wood smoke. Most was funneled efficiently through the chimney stacks attached to the stove that ascended through the roof, but as with all such ageing dwellings, there was enough give in the stack to allow a little of the smoke to escape.

It was a soothing odor, overpowering the sour smells of their own sweat and the stench of fear. Because each of them was now afraid.

Fear wasn't a terrible thing. If it wasn't kept in check, it could overpower a fighter, prevent him or her from performing to his or her full capacity, ruin timing. It could stop a person attacking at the right moment, from defending successfully. But in essence, fear was a good thing. A healthy dose of it was a remarkably efficient early warning system. Fear was that nagging in the gut that forced a person to act, that put a person on the defensive when danger was near.

For each of them, individually, fear was something

that they lived with every day and that they welcomed as a friend. It had kept them alive and ahead of the game this far, and there had been no reason to suppose that it would continue doing so for some time to come...until now.

The lack of clothes and the lack of weapons was a problem, but hardly an insurmountable one. They had faced such obstacles many times before. At least they were warm, and were given a day's grace in which to rest and recover. In previous experience, that had been enough for them to formulate some kind of plan, either as a group or individually. And at least they were two to a hut, meaning that some kind of team work could be used.

But not this time. This time they lacked something that worked in conjunction with the fear to drive them on, spur them to action. This time, they were lacking the will to act.

They knew this. Their fear knew this. And instead of nagging them to action, it did little other than gnaw at their vitals. A kind of hopeless despair started to seep through the velvet blanket of torpor, invading the darker recesses of the mind. This perfidious drug that they had been fed in the meat had now left them without the will to survive.

And without that, they would surely buy the farm.

KRYSTY AND MILDRED were in one hut, Jak and J.B. in another, with the third containing Doc and Ryan. It was to this hut that Thompson and McPhee, the medicine man, went first.

Ryan huddled into the blankets and furs that covered him as the door to the hut swung open briefly, admitting the two Inuit before slamming behind them. Open only for a brief moment, but enough for him to note that the huts were guarded, a dour Inuit with a Sharps standing by.

Thompson said nothing, indicating with the briefest movement of his head that McPhee should conduct an examination. It would seem that the old man was part-doctor, part-priest, for he moved forward and began to check Ryan in a business-like, brisk manner. The one-eyed warrior wanted to push him away, to assert himself against the shaman, yet he found that the will to do so was sapped, and he meekly let the old man push him around. Although he wanted to bridle with anger at the way in which he was being treated, he could muster nothing more than apathy.

McPhee grunted to himself as he prodded at the superficial wounds on the muscled torso, probing for breaks in the skin, pressuring bruises to assess their depth. He moved down to Ryan's legs, the iron-hard pressure of his grip causing the one-eyed man's muscles to cramp. He winced, and the shaman could feel the tightening of the muscle. The degree of pressure changed and he soothed the cramp from the limbs.

Ryan hated himself at that moment. He felt gratitude toward the old man wash through him at the release from pain, and at the same moment he felt contempt for the gratitude. How could he be feeling this way toward a man who had drugged him and would most likely be the one to chill him on the morrow?

McPhee had, by this time, worked his way on to Doc. The old man lay among the huddle of blankets and furs, and hadn't spoken since they had been taken into the hut. Ryan had crawled across to him, but had been alarmed to see Doc staring ahead, unblinking, unresponsive to any stimulus—speech, touch, all had proved fruitless. Ryan wanted to tell Thompson and the shaman about this, but found he could not even muster the will to speak.

McPhee examined Doc thoroughly, standing back with a flicker of puzzlement passing across his stoic, bland countenance.

"Well?" Thompson asked.

McPhee shrugged. "He's okay," he began, indicating Ryan. "But he worries me," he added, gesturing toward Doc.

"Is he whole?"

"Depends what you mean." McPhee shrugged again. Anywhere else, such limited and minimal means of expression would have brought an explosive response, but all it elicited from Thompson was a grunt.

There was a long silence before the Inuit chief spoke again.

"Is there any damage to his body that would prevent him from being one of the offerings? It's vital we do not anger the Almighty."

"Hell, his body's fine," McPhee said off-handedly. "That's not the problem."

"Then what is?" Thompson prompted after it was clear that the medicine man had once more lapsed into silence.

"Not his body. Don't know what's going on in his head, though. Seems like he's just shut down. Burning up, too. Guess the initiation was too much for him. Should burn out the fever for tomorrow, but…"

"But what?" Thompson asked, for the first time a hint of worry cracking his otherwise impassive tone.

McPhee shook his head slowly, as if to emphasize each word. "His head. If he's gone... I mean, got the snow blindness and no longer sees us as we see him, then I'm not sure how the Lord stands on the mad. He's whole in body, but would the madness be an insult?"

Ryan couldn't quite believe what he was hearing. Doc had always been flaky, but this trip seemed to have been the thing that had finally severed whatever links the old man could claim with sanity. Somehow, that wasn't really surprising. There had been something about the whole expedition that had seemed doomed. Landing in the redoubt that held so many memories had been the trigger, and since then it had been one disaster after another, a series of blows that had left them reeling and from which it had been hard to regain equilibrium, so that each successive blow had been another hit to drive them further and further into the dirt.

No wonder Doc had finally decided to cut loose that last tie to the real world. In some ways, Ryan envied him as he lay here, unable to muster the fight to even make a token show of resistance. If the herbs coursing through his blood did not subside before the morrow—and given the intelligence of Thompson and McPhee, that was unlikely—then he would go meekly to his demise, as would they all. At least Doc would be spared the humiliation.

Meanwhile, Thompson had been carefully mulling over McPhee's words.

"What do the teachings tell us? As I was told, it has to be whole in body. There's nothing about the mind of the offering."

"Just my point," McPhee concurred. "Nothing against it, but nothing for it, either. What if the Lord gets real pissed at us sending a loony to him? He'll think it was an insult, and then where will we be?"

Thompson said nothing for what seemed to be an eternity. The oppressive heat and smoke seemed to overwhelm Ryan as he strained to hear what the Inuit chief would say.

Finally the chief spoke. "Hell, it doesn't say no, does it? The way I see it, the teachings are about offering whole bodies for their strength. What they think and feel don't come into it. If anything, the fact that they're offering themselves, going willingly with the help of the herbs, makes them acceptable to the Almighty."

McPhee shrugged once more. His stock response to any problem about which he wished to remain noncommittal, it seemed.

"You're the chief," he said simply.

The two men left without any ceremony and without another glance at either Doc or Ryan.

The one-eyed man was gratified that he had managed to catch so much of their conversation. He had been right to assume that the feeling of torpor and helplessness was caused by the drugged meat. The lassitude that swept over him was from an outside agency and not from himself. That scrap of knowledge was something he could use to battle against what was now in him.

Maybe they had been doomed, maybe not. What had seemed helpless a short while before now had a glimmering of hope. It wasn't Ryan's own despair. It was thrust on him by an outside agency. There was, deep within, the rumbling of an anger that his fight had been taken from him. And that may just be the thorn with which he could nag at himself and bring back that fight that would enable him to, at the very least, go down fighting rather than go placidly to his demise.

But as he looked at the blank staring eyes of Doc, bulging out from beneath a sweat-spangled brow, he wondered if he would be alone in his fight.

HE STANDS OVER ME and talks as though I were insensible. I feel insulted by his ignorance, and yet at the same time I know that he is doing well by me. Treat me as a simpleton, you old fool. Underestimate me, and allow me the opportunity to beat you by your own stupidity.

So hot in this room. But soon the time will come when I will rise again. Perhaps the heat is like a simple incubation chamber, allowing me to shed my old skin like the snake, hatch from the egg, emerge from the chrysalis. Transformation. Reconfiguration.

This ceremony of which the old fool speaks shall be a sacrifice of sorts. But it shall not be myself that is sent to their false god. It will be the last vestiges of the old me traveling on to the next plane, while the new me shall rise triumphant to lead them on to glory. I shall be the God on Earth, the saviour... They are my destiny, whether they are real or some illusory analogy. Even if this is nothing more than a play, it is a play in which I must act my part. Ritual that shall lead to eventual enlightenment.

Now I feel my limbs rigid, burning. Poisons drain into my muscles before being dispersed. The moment of crisis, the moment of truth. Soon I shall know.

I, always I. Ego. Ego sum. I am. But am I? I wonder if I shall know me after the changes are complete? Shall I have an inkling of who or what I was, or will that all be wiped from my mind? If the "me" who I know now is not the real me, but only he who stands in wait of the true arrival, then will I retain any semblance of that he?

I do not know. I will find out. And if it is not so, then I will have no recollection of these times before. So it will not, I suppose, matter very much. Nonetheless, I shall be sad to lose me...

THOMPSON AND McPhee proceeded, little knowing the turmoil in which they had left both Ryan and Doc. Blissfully unaware, they next turned to the hut where Krysty and Mildred were huddled, slowly thawing. Krysty still felt concussed from the blow she had taken on the head when being carried into the hut. She sat by the stove, her head still clouded, her vision blurred. She saw two doors open, four men enter. She wanted to shake her head to clear it, but knew that if she did, the pain would be greater.

Thus she was compliant when the medicine man walked over to her and pulled the furs from around her body, running his hands over her to check her contusions. He took her chin between thumb and forefinger, tilting her head so that he could get a good view of her eyes.

"She took a hell of a knock on the head, but it should clear by morning," he told the chief, rummaging in a pouch he kept secure in his clothing. He produced something between his other finger and thumb. Moving her head toward him, he pressured gently on her chin as an indication for her to open wide. She complied, without even knowing why. He popped the object into her mouth with the command, "Chew." Krysty did so, only a very dim part of her—past the drug and past the concussion—marveling at how malleable she was. Her mouth went numb as whatever was contained within the bitter leaf she tasted began to seep out. Her woolly head began to clear and her vision sharpened.

"Good, yes?" McPhee asked. She could do little more than nod like a stupe. A rare smile cracked the stoic face of the shaman. "She'll be fine," he said to his chief.

"Okay. But what about her?" Thompson asked.

The medicine man turned to find Mildred huddled under a pile of blankets and furs. She had backed herself up into a corner of the hut and, although the fury in her eyes was dulled by the drug she had been fed, there was enough fire to make the medicine man pause.

"Well? Aren't you going to make the examination?" Thompson asked in a tone of voice that suggested he did not want to be the first to approach Mildred.

The medicine man said nothing, but approached Mildred with caution. She backed up against the wall so far that she was driving herself up into a standing position. Her nostrils flared and her teeth bared like a frightened animal. It was obvious that the drug had affected her adversely. McPhee rummaged around in his pouch and came up with another leaf-wrapped package, which he held out to her.

"Eat. It will make you feel better," he said in soothing tones, trusting that there would be enough of the drug in her system to make her comply with his softly spoken command.

Mildred watched his hand as it came toward her, palm up, the leaf capsule on display. She snatched at it, crammed it in her mouth. It tasted bitter from the leaf, then sweet and minty from within. A warmth encircled her brain and she sank back toward the floor.

Tranquilized sufficiently not to care if she was man-handled, it was simple enough for McPhee to carry out his examination.

"She's the fittest yet—her and the one-eyed man are the strongest."

"Good. Are you sure he's all right to use?" Thompson asked in tones that suggested this had been worrying him for some time.

McPhee sighed. "Once again, think back to your teachings. Someone is not whole when they have a limb missing, or are injured in such a way that they will chill without the need for sacrifice. Fingers, toes, senses such as hearing and blindness—these are not major enough. They have to be fit enough to be of service. You can do that without a toe, but not without a leg. Without an eye, but not without a head."

Thompson chewed on his lip. True, there were few among those living in these times that were completely whole, without some kind of minor loss. But it did worry the chief that whole meant whole, meant without any kind of loss. Having all your arms and legs, and not having blaster holes in your chest leaking your life away were obvious insults to the Almighty. But how did he stand on eyes, fingers and not being able to hear the prayers before you were chilled?

Perhaps these would seem to be childish, ridiculous considerations. But Thompson took his position as chief seriously. The attempt to find a good sacrifice had taken time, and it was imperative that it be successful. He didn't want to leave anything to chance, to cover all the possibilities. He didn't want to be the chief who had condemned his tribe to a slow chill.

"Okay," he said doubtfully, "I just hope you're right."

They left the hut, with both Mildred and Krysty in ecstatic states from the herbs contained in the leaf capsules fed them by the shaman. They would be quiet and compliant, lost in their own small worlds, for a few hours more.

Outside, in the chill air, the chief was having his doubts about the planned sacrifice.

"What if we're wrong?" he said suddenly. "What if they're not whole enough—the one-eyed man and the lunatic—what if all they do is bring down the wrath of the Almighty?"

McPhee stopped and faced his chief. In a low tone, so that they could not be overheard, he said, "What does it matter? The way things are, we're doomed in two or three generations at most. We have the choice of doing nothing and seeing it all go to shit, or trying this and maybe—just maybe—making it work. Now I don't know about you, but I don't really see that as a choice after all. Do you?"

Thompson pondered that for a moment.

"No," he said finally. "No choice at all."

The Inuit continued to the final hut, where J.B. and Jak were waiting. Both had shown remarkable powers of recovery and were sitting upright around the stove, warming themselves and muttering to each other in terse undertones. They stopped abruptly when the door was flung open and the Inuit entered. Thompson and McPhee found themselves faced by hostile, blank stares emanating from the angular, otherwise expressionless duo.

"Interesting," McPhee murmured. "They ate as much as the others, but seem a whole lot brighter. Hasn't stayed in their systems for as long."

"That important?" Thompson returned.

"Maybe," the medicine man replied enigmatically.

Leaving his chief to ponder this how he may, McPhee made his way across the bare wooden floor until he reached the oasis of skins, blankets and furs the two men had made around the stove.

"If you two gentlemen don't mind, I'm going to examine you."

"And if we do?" J.B. returned, keeping his voice neutral.

"Then I call for assistance and we beat the fuck out of you until you give in. Long as we don't rupture an organ or rip off an arm, you can have as many bruises as you like."

"Like that, not seem choice," Jak stated, unconsciously echoing the Inuit conversation outside their hut.

With ill-concealed bad grace the two men allowed the Inuit medicine man to examine them. He was swift, efficient, and for the most part painless. Both men winced as his firm pressure probed into tissue areas that were still damaged and blood-engorged, but other than the humiliation of having their balls tweaked by a complete stranger, there was nothing that they could seriously object to in their current situation.

Nonetheless, McPhee was quick enough to step back after finishing his examination, just in case they should decide to exact some revenge. He glanced across at his chief and gave a brief nod. Thompson returned this, and the two men left the hut. Jak and J.B. waited, listening to their footfalls on the earth outside as they receded into the distance, before speaking.

"Need clothes, weapons. No plan," Jak muttered,

sniffing back a stream of mucus from his nose. "Need move before becomes fever," he added.

"We could try to break for it, but where have they stashed our clothes and supplies? Even if we can't get at them, how the hell we gonna get more than a hundred yards like this, even assuming we could whack a guard and steal his clothes and blasters? Keeping all this around us to keep warm takes both hands, and without it we'll freeze in seconds," he added, clutching the furs to him for emphasis.

Jak was silent. He knew J.B. was right, but he felt helpless. As though he had to wait for the Inuit to make the next move. Jak was an expert at waiting for prey, but this time he was the prey, and he found he had no patience when the situation was reversed.

"Besides," J.B. continued after a pause, "we've got fuck-all idea where the others are, or even how they are."

It was another frustrating nail in the wall for Jak. Action without the knowledge of the others could endanger them all the more. But as things stood, they had no way of finding out what was happening to their companions, and any move they may make could do little more than endanger them.

It was going to be a hell of a wait to see what happened next.

NOTHING. FOR THE REST of that day, and into the night, nothing happened. In the three huts, the six companions rested or fretted, endlessly went over possible escape plans or drifted into dreams inspired by madness or fatigue. There was nothing else they could do except to lose themselves in their own interiors. It wasn't something that they often had the opportunity to indulge, and for most, they would have preferred action.

But not Doc. He was getting all too familiar with his interior landscape, and, ironically enough, with its propensity for almost constant change.

DARKNESS DRAWS DOWN upon the land, just as it draws down upon my mind. Yet are they not the same thing out here? I am the emperor of all creation, and this is the world that I, myself, have defined. Darkness that is always greatest before the dawn: the concrete realization of a metaphor that is the signal for my own rebirth.

Of course, it all makes sense: since the dawn of time—the dawn of light, if I may delight myself with yet another parallel—there have been rituals that describe the process of transformation from one state of awareness to another. Is that not, after all, what religion may be? So it makes sense that, to make the transformation in my own skull real, it becomes necessary to externalize that in the form of a ritual. Even if, as I believe, the world in which I currently move is entirely inside my own head and therefore internalized. Is it possible for me to externalize while internalizing? How paradoxical: the mind is nothing more than a maze that plays the most appallingly complex games with itself, twisting inside and out until there is little that makes sense. Yet everything makes sense.

I feel that if the new me that emerges at the end of this understands anything because of the confusion of torturous tautologies that now beset me, then it will have been worthwhile.

Hark, what light through yonder window breaks—it is the sun... No, that is not right. Correction, not accu-

rate. But right. For it is the sun that breaks with the
dawn, and the light that will fill my head will be greater
than a thousand suns at the glory of rebirth.

MORNING BROUGHT a sudden flurry of activity. As the
day grew brighter, the chem clouds that had gathered
so heavily for storms over the preceding days once
more giving way to icy azure-blue tinged with cyan, so
the Inuit emerged en masse from their dwellings, eating hurriedly before preparing the center of the ville for
the rituals that were about to begin.

The tarpaulin covering the center was taken down,
so that the ceremonial tables faced the empty sky. The
tables were washed down, their markings repainted
afresh by a team of artists who knew exactly what
should be inscribed. The bonfires on the corners of the
center were once more restoked and rebuilt, fired up so
that they began to smolder and grow in intensity for the
day ahead.

McPhee, in his hut, carefully brushed his ceremonial
robes and hat, so that he would be presenting himself
to the Almighty in his best aspect. This finished, he left
the hut and stood on his stoop, watching the tribe go
about the business of preparing the ville for the sacrifice. The fires were burning well. The tables were
painted well.

Looking over to the far side of the ville, he could see
one of the Inuit carefully whetting the ceremonial
knives that would be used to cut the beating hearts from
the sacrificial victims. The long, curved daggers had
originated long before skydark, and the blades were
now thin with repeated blunting and whetting, the
stocks oft-repaired, tied with strips of hide. They didn't

look as fine as once they had. No matter, they had a sacred purpose and couldn't be replaced. On the opposite side of the ville to this activity, food and drink was being prepared. Not the usual fare of the ville, but dishes and beverages that were laced with herbs and plant extract as dictated by McPhee, handed down to him from other medicine men, that would lift the celebrants into an ecstatic state that would bring them nearer to the Lord.

He looked upon his work, and he was pleased. Stepping down, he walked across to Thompson's dwelling, acknowledging the greetings of the Inuit as he passed. They were almost as taciturn and silent as ever, yet there was something about their demeanor that had altered. In just the slightest manner, they were lifted. The dwindling birth rate among them, and the subsequent slow chill of their society, had been casting a long shadow over their lives. This would reverse that trend. And if it didn't? By the time the success or the failure of the sacrifice had been determined, McPhee would probably have long ago bought the farm. He was no longer young, and the years became harder. He gave them faith because that was his role; but could he be certain? He was at an age where he no longer believed in certainty. All he could do was have a greater faith than those he served.

By this time, he had reached Thompson's hut and had banged on the door. A surly grunt from within told him that the chief beckoned him to enter. Inside, the Inuit chief was wearing his own ceremonial suit, made of dyed skins stitched together to emulate an old Inuit costume from before the settlers arrived. This mixture of the old heathen and the old Christian gave the faith of the Inuit a fervor that few could match. A fervor that the chief did not, at this moment, seem to share.

"What's eating you?" McPhee said without preamble.

Thompson looked at him, his eyes narrow. "This isn't going to work. We're going to chill them for no reason."

"How do you know it won't work?"

"It hasn't before," Thompson replied. "We've done it, and for what…nothing."

"Maybe the sacrifices haven't been right," McPhee reasoned.

"Maybe there isn't an Almighty," Thompson snapped back.

McPhee moved with a surprising speed for one so old and stout. Before the Inuit chief had even the time to blink, the medicine man was on him and had him by the throat.

"Don't you ever say that," McPhee growled. "Even if you think it's true, don't ever say it. You've got fears? I've got fears—shit, we've all got fears, man…but you're the leader of this tribe and it's up to you to lead us by example. That means that you keep whatever you've got to worry you in here." He emphasized his statement by beating his own chest. "And you don't let anyone else see that it's worrying you. You keep firm, you keep sure. You do, and I do. It's the only way to keep the people together. And even if we ain't got a future—more so if we ain't—that's what matters. Do you understand that?"

Thompson was silent. There was a pause before he nodded slowly. He'd never heard the medicine man talk in this way, and had no idea that was how he felt. It didn't make things better, but it did help him in a way: to know that he wasn't alone in his fears was something. And yes, McPhee was right. They had to stand firm, stand together. It was the only way to keep the tribe going, no matter what.

And maybe this time the Lord would smile on them and these strangers would be who they had spent so long searching for…they would bring absolution and the mercy of the Almighty.

"Let's do this," he said with a brief nod.

A grin cracked the medicine man's weathered visage. "Yeah, let's."

The two men walked out of the hut and into the cold morning sun. The preparations were almost complete, with the sacrificial knives and tables prepared and the sacrificial feast readied. The people of the tribe had, for the most part, completed their tasks in contribution to what was about to occur. They were now milling around, looking expectant. There was an undercurrent of excitement and hope that carried itself across to the chief and the medicine man as they strode across the center of the ville. If they needed reminding why they had to do this, then the eyes of the people upon them was reminder enough.

McPhee examined the tables, then beckoned to one of the Inuit to bring him the sacrificial knives. He examined these, feeling the edges. They were sharp enough to cut his skin with only the slightest pressure. When the moment came, he knew that the fatal wounds could be delivered swiftly and mercifully, for he had no real desire to cause pain. To him, this wasn't about sadism, it was about pure function. As the hunters were content to leave behind those who fell by the wayside, so he saw the sacrifice as something that was necessary. Quick, clean, and with no malice. Besides which, it would please the Lord all the more if the sacrificial lambs reached him in a beatific state, without the anguish of pain and fear to tarnish their souls.

To this end, not only did he wish the chilling to be swift, he had also arranged for the victims to be fed another concoction of herbs that would anesthetize their pain and awareness.

He took a deep breath, turned to the chief and gave the smallest inclination of the head.

Thompson raised his arms. "It begins," he intoned solemnly.

This was the cue the Inuit had been waiting for. Now that he had spoken, they began to act. The majority gathered in a circle around the now exposed clearing, separating only where the heat and flames of the now roaring fires kept them apart. Twelve of the Inuit peeled off toward the huts that housed the victims, four per shack. The inhabitants had already been fed that morning, their meal laced with the drug. It was unlikely that they would present any problem; regardless, they were to be well guarded.

As the eyes of the settlement rested upon them, the companions were led from the huts, bleary and confused. The herbs had done their job well, and they would be presenting little problem to anyone. Jak and J.B. had debated leaving their meal, perhaps concealing the evidence lest it be discovered and forced upon them. They didn't know that it was laced with herbs to pacify them, but were too cautious and long in the tooth to trust the Inuit on this, of all mornings. But their hunger had overtaken them and they had wolfed down

the food. Ryan had felt the same, separated from them
as he was, but once again his ravenous appetite had got
the better of reason. Doc had calmly partaken of the
meal and seemed not to care. Mildred and Krysty were
still dazed from their infusions of the evening before
and so had succumbed without opposition to the meal
placed in front of them.

They were led through the silent crowd, the only
one seeming to take in what was happening being Doc.
Even then, it seemed that he had to be a fool to those
who watched, as he smiled benignly upon them, ap-
parently little realizing that he was being led to his own
chilling.

The companions were laid on the sacrificial tables,
so placid and compliant that they didn't need to be secured in any way, which was exactly how the medicine
man wanted it. They had to go willingly to meet the Almighty, not trussed like livestock awaiting slaughter,
squealing in fear.

The medicine man moved between them, chanting
softly and anointing them with the heavy, aromatic oil
that he had used on them previously. Content with this,
he then stepped across to take one of the ceremonial
knives, raising it above his head.

"Our Lord, who is in the skies, bring to us this day
our sustenance. Forgive us our misdeeds, as we will forgive those who attempt to offend against us. Lead us into
glory, for yours is the everlasting land of light. Amen."

The Inuit joined him on the last word of the chant,
signaling his next action. Slowly he moved among the
companions, using the knife to score a thin line on each
foot, taking their arms and turning them so that he
opened each palm and made a small incision therein.

All the while, with each cut, he said softly, "The scars of the Lord, to make you one with him."

When this was done, and the blood was drying on the small cuts that were intended to identify the sacrifice with the deity to which they were offered, the Inuit lined up to partake of the food and drink prepared specially for the sacrifice. They moved forward slowly to meet the shaman, one by one. As each stood in front of him, he gave them a small oatcake that they ate before sipping from a cup he constantly refilled from the brew by his side. While Thompson looked on, McPhee said to each one, "The fruits of the Lord made food and water."

To service the entire ville in such a manner took some time. This, however, was part of the plan. While they were partaking of the offering, the wounds on the sacrificial victims were closing and beginning to scar.

As the last Inuit moved away from the shaman and he took the sacrificial dagger offered to him in readiness to begin the business of chilling, he was surprised to hear a voice issuing from the area of the sacrificial tables. Surprised because it wasn't a voice familiar to him. Not one of the Inuit, nor of those who lay prone on the tables. It was rich and resonant, with a thick Scots burr to it.

"What is this? Am I to be dispatched from this world before I have even had a chance to sample it? Is this how ye treat one who returns after so long?"

McPhee was bewildered. He looked at his chief. Thompson's face was no longer its usual impassive mask. Instead his jaw had dropped, his eyes widened in amazement.

"Come, are ye not going to speak to me after I have come so far to be with ye?"

That voice again. There was something familiar, but yet... McPhee turned to face the same direction as his chief—and, indeed, of the vast majority of the Inuit—and was astounded at the sight that greeted him.

Doc Tanner was sitting upright, his eyes no longer staring unseeingly. His face no longer the bland rictus of an insane smile. Instead it seemed to be full of a life that they hadn't seen from him before.

"What do I have to say to stir some action from ye? Am I to freeze before someone offers me a coat?"

The voice—the voice that was of a stranger—was issuing from his mouth...

Chapter Twelve

Thompson and McPhee exchanged glances. Even with the naturally stoic and impassive set of the Inuit features, it was obvious that both men were both astounded and confused. The mad old man who had said so little during the past several days was now speaking in a completely different voice and acting in a manner contrary to his previous behavior.

"Well, am I to stand here freezing my balls off, or do I get some proper clothes?" Doc roared, frustrated by their sudden inaction. "Ye were keen enough to drive a blade through me a few minutes ago, so why are ye like a pack of statues right now?"

Thompson was looking to McPhee for guidance. He was, after all, the medicine man. He should know how to deal with these things. But McPhee looked just as floored by events as his chief. As for the rest of the Inuit, they were silent. Not their usual silence, but a kind of awed hush. They were all aware that something strange, and possibly momentous, had occurred in front of them, and the thrill of it ran through them like a lightning bolt. Yet they had no real idea what had transpired or what it may mean. For that, they, too, were awaiting a cue from McPhee.

The shaman was frozen. He'd followed the rituals,

said the prayers, blended his herbs. Yet, after so long, it was only in the latter that he had any real faith. The rest was just for show, they were just words. The Almighty had taken so long to shine upon them that the shaman half suspected that he was nothing more than a palliative to get them through the long, harsh winters.

But now… It seemed to him as though a spirit had been sent down to them. One of their ancestors—he spoke, after all, with the voice—had entered into the empty vessel of the mad old man. The Almighty had sent a messenger down to them. And all he—McPhee—could do was stand with his mouth open catching stray flakes of snow and ice, not believing that, after all these years, there may actually be an Almighty after all.

He was nudged from his reverie by Thompson, who knocked him on the arm and whispered harshly, "What the fuck is going on?"

"I don't know," the shaman answered without thinking. "I really don't know." Although his tone held an awe that suggested he had a good idea and wasn't quite ready to accept it.

The few words, in almost an undertone, were enough to break the blanket of inaction that had fallen over the assembled throng. From the crowd surrounding the central area, several Inuit rushed forward, taking a layer of skins and fur from their backs and wrapping them around the seminaked figure of Doc Tanner.

"That's better," he stated, adding, "Not just me, ye dolts. My friends need to be warmed, as well. D'ye want them to perish because of frostbite?"

Without looking to their chief or the shaman, the Inuit followed the directions of Doc. There was something about the accent and the hint of authority in his voice that made them respond immediately, without recourse to their leader. While Thompson and McPhee watched, astounded, the Inuit freed the rest of the companions from the tables, wrapped them in furs and skins ripped from their own backs.

The companions were still under the effects of the drugs they had been fed earlier, and so responded passively to whatever was being done to them. They allowed themselves to be lifted up and clothed, without any kind of response beyond blank, confused stares. For their part, the Inuit were under the influence of the herbs in their ritual feast, and so were in a state of rapture at what, in predark days, would have been called a miracle.

"Good, good, now take them where they can rest and be warm," Doc said in his rich Scots voice. "Put them together in one of those huts," he added, gesturing to where they had spent the previous twenty-four hours. Then he set his vision grimly on the still inert, still stunned figures of Thompson and McPhee. "I've got a few things that need to be said to yon chief."

Responding to Doc as though he had been their leader for many years, the Inuit bore the companions away to one of the huts, putting them together in the one building and firing the stove. Even in their state of rapture, the Inuit were still eerily silent, only a few words being exchanged about the strange events. Those who did speak felt that the event was a miracle, a sign from the Lord that he didn't wish these people to be sacrificed and had sent them to assist the tribe in its quest... Why else would one of them arise and speak in the voice of the ancestors?

Befuddled as they were by the drugs that coursed

through their systems, a rough idea of what had occurred seeped through the bewildered consciousness of each of the companions. Somehow it seemed as though Doc's madness had saved them at the last, before they were about to be chilled. Yet how long would this reprieve last—and more importantly, perhaps—what was going on in the old man's head?

As the Inuit left them alone, Ryan tried to speak. His mouth felt dry and furred, and although his brain shaped words, his mouth refused to respond. Jak tried to get to his feet, but found he could not stay upright, the world spinning out of control even as he tried to anchor himself.

"Leave…wait wear off…" Mildred managed to mutter as she saw Jak slump down once more. "Strong… can't…" The few words that she managed to mushmouth were barely audible or comprehensible, but they made enough sense to the others for them to realize that they had no option but to wait until the effects of the drug had subsided before they could say, let alone do, anything constructive.

In the meantime, they could only wonder what the hell Doc was doing.

WATCHING THE PEOPLE he knew were his friends carried off, he felt a sense of achievement that he had secured their safety. He didn't know their names, but had a deep gut instinct that they had traveled with him for a long time and that to save their skins was to repay many a kindness, many a debt.

He turned to where the Inuit chief and the shaman were standing. "Ye two, I'm wanting a few words with ye," he bellowed, striding toward them. "There's a lot for us to talk over."

As he approached, he could see a flicker of fear in the eye of the chief, but in the shaman's face was something else. Something like awe, yet also a hint of disbelief. Why not? He was as astounded about this turn of events as anyone. He looked down at the weather-beaten body and made a mental note to check a mirror. He wondered if his face resembled anyone he had known, or if it would be strange to him—as strange as the knowledge that only an hour ago he had been someone else, someone he could no longer remember. Not even his name.

"Are ye who I think ye are?" the shaman asked him as he neared them.

"That depends who ye think I might be," he replied with a wide grin. "So why don't ye start by telling me that?"

"A messenger," McPhee said slowly, shrewdly eyeing the figure of Doc Tanner. "A messenger from the Lord."

A frown creased the brow of the old man standing in front of the shaman. "Y'know, I'm not sure. Maybe I am, at that. It hadn't occurred to me. Just that I was back where I belong, and that I had a new body."

"What?" Thompson's first word to the "stranger" standing in front of him was uttered in a strangled croak, as though forced out against his will.

"Have ye never heard of the concept of transmigration of the soul?" he said with a grin spreading across his face. "Surely your Almighty, my Lord, tells you of that." He looked around and took in a deep breath, then wrinkled his nose at the smell of sulfur. "Aye, things have changed, but I was here before. A long time ago, by the looks of it, but I was here. I recognize the way ye look, although ye never spoke like that when I knew ye. Now ye speak like me, which is a strange idea. And this has changed—aye, changed a lot," he said almost to himself as he cast a glance around. Coming back to the two men standing in front of him, he could see from their faces that they needed further explanation.

"I was here a long, long time ago. It was 1865, and we were a party of twelve making our way from the south toward Anchorage, where we sought to sell the pelts we had spent time trapping. It was freezing, and there were storms—big, strong ones that ripped through our party, scattering us across the wastes. Somehow we always managed to find our way back to one another, to stick together somehow... Aye, it takes a lot to keep us down when we've got the bit between our teeth. And we found ourselves shelter eventually, with people like ye. Although ye didn't have these kinds of houses, and there was no trees like this. And the air didn't stink like it does now. But it was around here, I can feel it.

"We were tired and weary. Hungry, too. All our food was either eaten or lost, and we couldn't hunt because the weather made it hard enough just to stay alive. Well, we stumbled into your people and thought that we would be slaughtered, that ye wouldn't want us intruding on your land. Used, we were, to people out here in this godforsaken land being hostile to strangers. We left the homelands to get away from those who were hostile to us because of our beliefs, and we made homes here, but it was still the same. People are people are people, I'm supposing. The good Lord made us all the same in his eyes, but then maybe we don't see through those eyes like we should.

"Anyhow, I'm getting away from what I should be

saying to ye. We found your people, and ye weren't un-
kind to us. Rather than try to wipe us out, ye took us in
and tried to nurse us back to health. For make no mistake, we were in a bad way by then. The weather had
taken its toll and many of us had fevers. When the fever
takes ye, ye see things that are not there and imagine
that people talk to ye who are not really there. It's a
strange thing, not knowing anymore what is real and
what is not.

"I had the fever worse than many, and I knew after a
while that I would not pull through. It's the strangest
feeling, knowing that your time is up and that it will not
be long before ye meet your maker. I could feel myself
slipping away, the light getting brighter, like I was racing toward the end of a long tunnel. I'd heard many say
that before, and never believed them. But they were
right. The only thing I really wanted was to see my children and my wife once more, back where I had left
them. But I knew that the chance was gone and that I
would see them no more in this world. I prayed to the
Almighty to keep my soul safe, and if he could give me
just one more chance. If I had the chance to redeem myself in his eyes, then I begged him to spare my life.

"At the last, when I felt sure that my life was about
to end, I moved toward the light with a rapidity that star-
tled me. I felt as though my very being was being ripped
into a thousand shreds then put back together again. I
opened my eyes, and I was here.

"D'ye not see what this means? I have been spared
by the Lord to do his work. My soul has been taken from
where I was before and brought to here, wherever this
may be. I'm guessing it's later than when I was last

alive, but other than that the only thing I know for sure is that ye need help and that the Lord sent me here to help ye. It's my chance to redeem myself, and the poor soul who was last in this body—and didn't take great care of it, by the looks of things—has gone to a better place."

His oration finished, the man who was Doc Tanner stood silent, waiting for Thompson and McPhee to respond. The two Inuit looked at each other and then at the stranger in front of them.

"I don't know if I should believe you," Thompson said slowly. "It could be some kind of trick."

"I can understand your caution," the stranger replied. "If I was ye, I wouldnae believe me. Come to that, I don't know if I believe me, or what I'm seeing," he replied disingenuously.

"This is no trick," McPhee breathed. "It can't be. There's no way… Lord help me, I'd almost given up faith in the Almighty without realizing. It's been so long since there was any kind of a sign." The shaman fell to his knees. "I just hope the good Lord can forgive me for my doubts, but I now know they were wrong. You are proof of that."

The stranger stretched out his hand. "I know how ye feel. Did I not feel that way myself before this happened? But it's never too late."

His hand touched McPhee's head and the medicine man raised his face so that his eyes met with those that had once belonged to Doc Tanner. Whereas previously the old man's had only ever seemed empty and blank, now they seemed imbued with strength and life.

Thompson was aware of the rest of the tribe. Some had stayed around the edges while the others had taken the companions to their rest. These few had heard everything, and in whispers were revealing details to those who had now returned. The chief was aware that his people were watching him, expectant and waiting. But what could he tell them? In truth, he had barely managed to assimilate what was going on for himself.

He stepped away from the stranger and McPhee to address his tribe.

"People, there are strange things afoot. This man—who was to be one of the sacrifices—is no longer the same man he was an hour ago. The Lord has emptied him and filled the empty vessel with one who has been here before. One of our ancestors, who has come to guide us in our hour of need. Myself and McPhee must speak with him alone, but we will soon be able to tell you of the Almighty's plans for us. While he reveals his purpose to us, you must go about your daily tasks. Have patience, people. All will be soon made clear. First, I have to get it clear."

He dismissed the Inuit with a gesture. Although confused by what had occurred in the past hour, the tribe trusted its chief implicitly, and he had never before been found wanting. There was no reason to believe that what he now said was untrue. Without a murmur, the tribe began to put out the bonfires and take down the sacrificial tables.

"As for you," Thompson said, turning and directing his remarks to the stranger and McPhee in such a way that neither was too sure to whom he spoke, "you've got some explaining to do."

INSIDE THEIR HUT, the companions were slowly beginning to return to a normal state. The drugs had scrambled their sense in such a way that they couldn't be sure of what had occurred on the outside. Gradually they pieced together enough recollections between them to make a picture. It wasn't, however, one that made a lot of sense.

"The old buzzard's finally flipped, and this time it might be for good and all," Mildred muttered at the conclusion. "If he's adopted a whole new personality, then that's the mind completely retreating in on itself and making up the new personality to protect the real one. Maybe he's gone for good, and this shield will be all we ever see of him from now on."

"Can't be sad—stopped us getting chilled," Jak commented.

"There is that to it," Krysty said slowly. "But… No, it's too ridiculous, but—"

"But what if something really has happened and Doc has been taken over by someone else?" Ryan finished for her.

"That's impossible," J.B. snorted.

"Is it?" Krysty asked softly. "I wouldn't be too surprised at anything. Think of all the weird shit we've seen."

"But ghosts—that's just stupe," J.B. said with a shake of his head.

"Is it?" Krysty persisted. "Religious ceremonies, and leaves and herbs that give you hallucinations, alter your mind—they do some strange things that you can't explain. Mebbe Mildred's right, but is that any weirder than what I'm saying might—and only might, mind you—have happened?"

"You put it like that and even I might agree with you," Mildred replied. "I don't know, I'm only guessing, like you are… The only thing we know for sure is that Doc sure as shit isn't himself right now, and that as long as he's got Thompson's ear, we've got a better than even chance of making it through this in one piece."

"Better chance than we had when the sun came up," Ryan agreed. "Right now, there's not a damn thing we can do either way. Just got to wait and see what happens."

"Must be more," Jak muttered irritably.

"Like what?" Ryan questioned. "Yeah, those fire-blasted drugs are wearing off, but we've got no clothes and no weapons, and we don't know where they're keeping them. In a lot of ways we're not better or worse off than we were this time yesterday—except for the fact that Doc seems to be someone else."

"That makes me feel a whole lot better," J.B. murmured laconically. "All we can do is sit this one out, then."

Ryan agreed. "Looks that way," he said, trying but failing to keep the note of helplessness from his voice.

THOMPSON AND MCPHEE took their guest into the chief's hut after he had dispatched one of his men to get Doc's clothes.

"Sit down," the chief said, indicating a chair. "Get your clothes, then we can talk a bit more."

"We?" The stranger laughed. "Listen, I have no idea quite where or when I am, so I think it may be for the best if ye fill me in a little on what's going on around here, and why ye were ready to drive a dagger into my heart, and those of the people who were—I guess—my friends."

The two Inuit exchanged puzzled glances. Where to start with such explanations? Hesitating, almost stammering over his words, Thompson began to tell the stranger about the nukecaust and the problems the Inuit were having with keeping up the numbers in their tribe. He explained about the previous attempts at sacrifice that yielded little result, and how the companions—including the subject of his lecture—had come to be in the settlement. He stopped only when a tribesman entered with Doc's clothes, including his lion's-head silver sword stick and the LeMat, and continued once the man had left, stopping only at the point where Doc had risen up and spoken to them.

The stranger looked at them with a twinkle in his eye—one that widened as he regarded himself in his new apparel.

"Well, I don't seem to be that much of an offering to the Lord myself, by the look of me," he said with a humorous edge to his voice. This became more guarded as he continued. "So why were ye thinking that the Almighty would like to see these good people sacrificed to him?"

"Because that was what your people taught us when they first came among us," McPhee answered. "They came from their old countries and they mixed with us, and they gave us some of their old ways. Some of them were older even than when they first heard of the Almighty."

The medicine man paused, unwilling to go further. If this man was truly who he said, and not some clever ruse by the insane one to try to save himself—a lurking doubt of that McPhee still harbored in the depths of his mind—then he would know of the old ways.

McPhee wasn't to be disappointed. The stranger looked at him with a faraway glint in his eyes.

"Aye, I know that. Back in the day, before our religious beliefs saw us driven from our own shores to find solace and a new life out here, we used to worship the Almighty, but we also knew that he gave us Mother Earth, and the seasons had their own demands. Sometimes we would have bad harvests that decimated the lands, blight that meant no food for our children. We would pray to the Lord, but we also knew that what we take from the land we must give back. To insure that the land would give us food, we had to feed it by returning one of our own to it. Their blood, the ashes of their flesh and bones, these are the things that would nourish the spirit of the earth and encourage it to give forth to us once more."

"Ashes?" McPhee asked, silencing his chief with a gesture as Thompson was about to speak.

"Aye, ashes. Surely ye must know, must ye not, that to sacrifice in the way ye intended is not the proscribed manner of the old ways?"

McPhee agreed. "That's something we can't do here. The rituals had to be adapted from their old form…" He trailed off expectantly.

Catching his drift, the stranger smiled. "I see. Ye do not trust me entirely, and think that I may be in some manner shamming for ye." He nodded slowly to himself. "Aye, aye, I can see where this idea comes from. It must be as hard for ye to accept as it is for myself. But if I have to tell ye this to prove myself, then tell ye I must…

"In the old lands, we would build a giant made of wicker. The sacrifice would be led willingly to it in a procession, and there—along with animals, birds and whatever pitiful crops had been yielded—he would be offered up, put into the wicker giant and set afire. He—for it was always a man, which may be, if I may be so bold, where ye have been going wrong—would go willingly, with no drugs to quell him. He would be a warrior, offering himself in the battle against nature, and he would go with pride and honor that so befits going to die in battle."

McPhee nodded gravely. This fitted in with old legends to which only the shamen of the tribe were privy. There was no way that the mad old man would have known any of this.

The stranger could see that the medicine man was being won over, and so decided to share some more history with which the shaman may be familiar.

"So ye know about how we came to be here?" he asked.

"You told us outside," the medicine man remarked blandly. Thompson, eyes going from one to the other, decided to stay quiet and let the two men battle this one out between them: the medicine man had been passed on stories about the tribe and its origins that were purely the preserve of the shaman. If this was genuine, then he would know. For his own part, Thompson was convinced. This was something big.

"Ah, that was just how we came to be here, in this place," the stranger replied easily. "There was more to it than that. Ye will be knowing, I presume, that we came from the old lands of Hibernia—what they used to call Scotland and Ireland, though what they call them now I have no idea. Perhaps they no longer even exist after these things ye speak of. We lived in hard, cold lands, where the living was difficult. Up to the north of our country, some of us lived on islands that were barely big enough to support our communities. We were tied together by our belief in God and the way in which we worshiped the Almighty. By the sounds of things, ye don't have to worry about such things now as the idea of a God is an alien one in your world; but back then, people would have wars not over whether or not they believed in God, but in how they worshiped him. Who was right and who was wrong. It all seems a little pointless now, but back then it seemed important to be able to worship how ye wished. So we set off for what was called the new world, where we were told that life would be easier, there would be better places to farm and we would be free to worship how we wished. That was how it had been for over a hundred years before.

"All lies, of course. It's true that there were less people to fight over ways of worship, and it's true that there was better land to farm if ye wished, but that was because it was a bigger land and the people were farther apart. So was the good land. And there were no maps to help ye find your way around. Ye just started out in any direction and kept going until ye found somewhere, which is how we ended up trying to trap furs in a land that was harder and colder than the one we had left. But we had not the money or the wagons to go back, so we had to stay and try to make the best we could of things. Which is how come ye found us, and how I came to see the light and so…" He finished with a shrug.

"You could have picked that up from things we told you about when you were first here," the medicine man said in a deceptively offhand manner. "Maybe if there were details that—"

"Ye still doubt me?" the stranger interrupted. "After the things I've said? I suppose your suspicion does ye credit. It would be a great shame if ye were willing to hand over the running of your wee town so easily."

"What?" Thompson sat forward, alarm obvious in his voice, even if he managed to keep it from his face.

The stranger grinned. "Aye, ye heard right enough. D'ye think that I was sent here by the Almighty just to sit around and do nothing? If I have any task at all, it's to save ye from the mess ye've gotten yourselves into. But I'll prove who I am. I came from a place known as Fairbanks, which was on the mouth of the river Clyde back in Scotland. We were on the same river as the city of Glasgow, but we had none of their wealth and only a fraction of their size. Years of famine in the 1860s led to me and many others emigrating with our families. We took the *Pride Of Liverpool* from that very port in July 1868, having traveled down over a period of weeks by foot, saving money by walking and doing odd jobs along the way to earn extra silver. Not that we were welcomed anywhere, only by a few who knew what Christian charity truly was. We were at sea for nearly three months and landed in Boston. From there we made our way across and up the Americas, somehow losing ourselves in the vast spaces, wandering ever farther north as well as west, before hitting these lands over a year later, in November 1869. It was during that month that ye found us, and that I saw the light. Ye can, of course, verify this. We were not the sort of people who didn't keep records."

The stranger looked from one to the other. Thompson was nervous. Like nearly all the tribe, he couldn't read, even though he had maps and books that had been passed down through the generations, surviving sky-dark. McPhee, on the other hand, was able to read. It was something that was handed down from shaman to shaman. It was a skill that he hadn't had to use for a long time, but he was ready for the challenge. He indicated this with an inclination of his head.

Thompson reluctantly rose and walked over to the far side of the room, where an iron chest lay against the wall, covered with an old, supple hide. It was the only piece of furniture in the room that seemed to have no purpose. However, it held the key to the stranger's assertions.

Thompson uncovered the chest, unlocked it with a key kept around his neck on an old chain, and extracted from its depths a crumbling book. With infinite care he took this across to the table, and laid it down, inviting the shaman to open it.

With the stranger looking over his shoulder, McPhee delicately turned the crumbling pages until he came to the relevant year. He was rusty, not having had to use the skill for some years, but with a hesitating voice he read out the entry in the history of the tribe relating to the time that the Scots first came among them.

It was as the stranger had said. The archivist who had started the record had faithfully transcribed the detail of how the Scots and Irish came to be traveling through the wastes of icy lands and how they had stumbled upon the Inuit. Some of the initial party had passed away, the cold and exposure being too much for them. But those who had survived had left the Inuit temporarily, fetching their families to join the tribe and begin a joint quest for survival that had seen them settle into a hunting and trapping existence that remained largely undisturbed until the coming of the nukecaust.

Thompson watched the shaman carefully as he read, then their eyes met as the medicine man gently closed the tome.

"I have no more doubts," McPhee said softly. "The mad old man could not have seen the book. And yet everything he says now is true. I believe that the Almighty has sent him to guide us."

"Now isn't that just that I've been trying to tell ye?" the stranger said heartily, clapping both men on their backs. "And if we're trying to get somewhere, the first thing we need to do is forget about sacrificing the people I came here with."

"Why?" Thompson asked, failing to keep the suspicion from his voice.

"Because they have two women, and women are not good sacrifices. They must be men, unafraid to go to their deaths. And I traveled with them in this body, e'en though it was not me who walked their paths. I owe them that much, for in loyalty given is loyalty returned in times of trouble.

"Furthermore, we shall need their skills to help us find greater sacrifices. Tell me, is there still a big town near here?"

"Ank Ridge lies away on the coast, if that's what you mean," Thompson replied.

"Fairbanks is nearer," the medicine man cut in. "Not a big ville these days, but it must have been when you were first here—and it must have been named for your home ville."

"That's the one I mean," the stranger replied. "No doubt it has changed much over the years, but if they are of the old stock, then they will know something of the old ways like yourselves. We take them by force, and they will understand the nobility of their demise."

McPhee looked at Thompson. Fairbanks was the next substantial stop on the trading trail to Ank Ridge and the inhabitants outnumbered the Inuit by at least two to one. It would be a hard firefight if they were to go. The stranger caught their mood and laughed.

"Come now, ye are not the sort to be that easily deterred, are ye? We shall fight them and win. I've never lost a battle yet, and I don't intend to start. After all, I'm here, am I not? Look—" He took the book and flipped the crumbling pages to the point where McPhee had been reading. "There I am," he said triumphantly, pointing at a list of those lost during the hunting trip that first crossed the Inuit settlement. "It says I died, but yet I am risen and still here…it'll take more than a few men with rifles to kill Joseph Jordan a second time around!"

Chapter Thirteen

By the time that darkness had descended on the day they were supposed to buy the farm, the companions were actually alive, well, and returning to their former selves. Although still far from a hundred percent physically—strains and contusions still making muscles ache when moved too swiftly, stretched too far—the herbs that had clouded their senses were now beginning to clear from their systems, and they found themselves able to think more quickly and clearly, and to react with greater clarity to what was said and done around them.

Not that, in truth, this amounted to much. For several hours, measured only by the lazy manner in which the sun made its way across the relatively clear chem-tinged sky, they had little to do except talk idly among themselves and to try to clear the confusion that clouded their minds and the situation in which they now found themselves.

But without full possession of the facts, they could do little about either, giving up when discussion took them full circle time and time again, always arriving at the same point, from which they would then, in confusion, have to depart.

The salient facts were these: they were supposed to have been sacrificed; they had been saved by Doc; Doc appeared to have a new personality, either assumed or the result of insanity.

That was all that they knew for sure, and it was very little from which to attempt a construction of the truth. Their hut was guarded by a lone Inuit with a Sharps rifle who stood at the gap between the fencing that delineated their prison. Beyond him, they could see that the sacrificial and ritual area in the center of the ville was being deconstructed, torn down and left as it had been a few days before, as little more than an empty space. The Inuit moved swiftly and with a sense of purpose. Their deportment suggested that the sudden cessation of the sacrifice hadn't downcast them in any way. To the contrary, it seemed that the events that had led to the cancellation of the sacrifice had imbued them with a new sense of hope and purpose.

What that could be was a complete mystery to the five inhabitants of the guarded hut. The only thing they could conclude with any sense of certainty was that this was, in some way, down to Doc Tanner…or to what Doc now was.

For a long time the old man hadn't been visible. After disappearing into the chief's hut with Thompson and McPhee, there had been plenty of activity going on in the ville, but no sign of the three men. Although they had still been partially immobilized by the effects of the herbs they had ingested, the companions had been just about aware enough to mount a watch at the window, so that at least they would have some idea of what was going on. J.B. had drawn the short straw and had spent most of his time glued to the filthy pane, trying to link up what was occurring from seemingly random events.

At one point he saw an Inuit rush to one of the huts

near those they had vacated, entering and then emerging again quickly, bearing what looked like clothing across to the chief's hut. He disappeared inside, then emerged a few moments later empty-handed. That one wasn't too difficult to work out. Doc, in his new persona, had demanded his clothes. What's more, he'd received them on the double, which suggested that—whatever he was saying—it was more than impressive to Thompson and McPhee.

As nothing else happened for some while, J.B. had gazed down at his own naked body, covered haphazardly by the skins and furs, idly wondering in his still partially drugged state if Doc would be able to get them back their own clothes. Glancing across to the others, huddling by the stove, he was sure they felt the same way.

The Armorer had iron determination and he returned his attention to the outside world. He would make sense of what was happening out there, even if it took forever.

It seemed that long, but in truth it was only an hour or two before he saw the door of the chief's hut open and the two Inuit emerge, with Doc in the vanguard. Except that it wasn't Doc. At first appearances, the old man was unchanged, especially now that he was in his usual clothes, with the long fur he had taken from the redoubt stores flapping around him as he gesticulated across the width of the ville and out to the wastelands beyond the slopes. All the while, he was talking. J.B. could see his lips move, although not well enough to pick out anything he said. Certainly, sound didn't carry across the ville well enough, and the thickness of the glass and the wood surrounding it made any attempts to try to define what was being said nothing more than futile.

At first appearances… But there were things that seemed strange and set off alarms in the Armorer's rapidly clearing mind.

Doc had weapons. Certainly he carried the silver lion's-head sword stick, with which he gestured broadly. Not, however, with his usual Tanner-like flourish. And J.B. was sure that he got a glimpse of the LeMat stuffed into Doc's waistband when his coat swirled around him during one particularly broad gesture. Again, a gesture very unlike Doc; as was the location of the LeMat.

Why had he been given back his weapons, seemingly without any qualms? What kind of bargain had he struck?

The other thing, which was a little less definable but—perhaps because of this—all the more eerie, was that Doc didn't seem to be moving like Doc. It was the bearing of the man, the way he held himself and the way he moved. The gestures and posture were so unlike Doc that it seemed strange to be watching him strike them. It was as though someone who bore a resemblance to Doc had been dressed up in the same clothes and made up to look exactly like him, but hadn't been briefed in how the man moved or acted, so that to those who knew Doc only too well—such as the watching J.B.—the result was strangely disorienting. It looked like Doc, but yet acted like someone else, creating a bizarre impression.

The gesturing figure that looked like Doc pointed over at the hut where the companions were being kept—almost as though he could read the Armorer's thoughts and wanted to let him know this—and made some emphatic arm movements. What his meaning was, J.B.

could only guess, but he figured it meant that they would soon be brought back into the fray, in one way or another.

J.B. withdrew from the window.

"What is it, John?" Mildred asked. The Armorer was glad to hear that her voice was returning to its old, sharp tones, the muzziness of the drugs now clearing. He wanted her to be sharp, because he wasn't too sure of how any of them would take what he was about to run by them. As succinctly as possible, he reviewed what had happened while he was at the window, and apprehensively relayed to them his impressions of the "new" Doc.

"So he look you and you draw back?" Jak asked when J.B. had finished. When the Armorer nodded, Jak continued. "Maybe he not know you looking, but got hunter instinct for being watched and just turn."

"Which doesn't sound like Doc, right?" J.B. questioned.

Jak nodded. "Whatever else, Doc no hunter."

"So this new personality that has overtaken him has that kind of instinct," Mildred mused. "I don't like the sound of that. If he was making a new him to protect the old Doc, then it's not likely to have traits that he never had before."

"Sounds to me like you're coming 'round to the idea of him being taken over by someone else," Krysty said, unable to keep the surprise out of her voice.

"I'm not exactly saying that." Mildred smiled. "I'm just going to keep my options open on this."

"Right now, it doesn't matter which of us is right about who or what Doc's become," Ryan interjected. "It's more a matter of what he's going to do now that he is someone else. That's what's going to shape the next few hours. If he's had them take down the tables and the cover, then they sure as shit aren't going to chill us."

"Which is something to be thankful for," Krysty added.

"Right," Ryan agreed. "But the bigger question is, what does he have in mind for us now? And how long before we find out?"

Mildred mused on that. "The longer we have to wait, the longer it gives our systems to clear out the shit they fed us to make us pliable. Assuming that you guys feel the way that I do, I'd say that it's clearing rapidly. It didn't need to be long-lasting, as we should have all bought the farm by now." She paused, noticing from the set of their faces that this previously unspoken thought had not escaped any of them. "And the sooner it's completely expunged from our bodies, the sooner we're a hundred percent in terms of thought and reflex. Physically it's a little different. I'd guess we're all a little stiff, and mebbe we should work on that. Assuming that they feed and water us soon, so that we don't lose strength through thirst or hunger—and that the food and water is not tainted by more herbs—then we'll be as ready for them as we ever could be."

"So it may benefit us to be caged like this a bit longer?" J.B. questioned, one eye still on the window.

Mildred agreed. "Assuming food and water, then the longer we're here the sharper we can get, and the more we can work on our physical problems."

"Biggest problem this," Jak muttered, proffering a handful of skin and fur.

"Exactly," Krysty said thoughtfully. "We could be

here for weeks, getting stronger, but it doesn't matter shit if we don't have clothes and weapons. Clothes alone, even. No way we could fight effectively and try to keep these damn things around us," she added, gesturing to the skins wrapped around her body.

"Doc's got his clothes back, mebbe he'll get us ours," J.B. mused. "If he does have plans for us, then it figures that he'll need us covered and able to move about in the cold."

"Kinda depends on what his new plans are," Mildred murmured, "and just how we fit into them."

"CAN'T BE SERIOUS," Thompson yelled, shaking his head. "Can't trust them just like that. For the Lord's sake, we were about to offer them up to the Almighty and chill them. No way would they trust us."

Doc smiled. To those who knew him, it would seem strange. Rather than the open beam that had been his usual mode of smiling, he now affected a sly grin that tugged at the edges of his mouth in a wolfish fashion.

"Since when did I mention trust?" he asked in a low voice.

"Listen to me, son. There are some advantages to being resurrected in a strange man's body, no matter how old and frail it may feel to me. I know things— don't ask me how, 'cause I don't know how, I just know," he said to McPhee, before continuing to the chief. "Point is, I know about those people ye got holed up in that hut. I know that they're hunters and fighters. And, maybe more importantly, they're survivors. They'll do what needs to be done. What my old ma used to call pragmatic. Ye offer them the chance to live, and they'll take that rather than the alternative, no matter what. Maybe ye can't trust them like ye'd trust your own people, but ye can rely on them not to sign their own death warrant."

Thompson looked at McPhee, puzzled. The medicine man returned the look twofold, shrugging his own confusion.

Doc sighed. "I mean that they're not gonna risk their own lives if ye offer them a chance of prolonging them by doing this. It's what they do anyway."

Thompson nodded. He still wasn't too sure of what the Lord's messenger Joseph Jordan was actually saying some of the time, but he figured that he was getting the general idea.

"Okay, if you say that they'll go along with this, then we'll include them. The Lord alone knows that we'll be outnumbered, so any extra warriors will be useful."

"But don't give 'em their blasters until we're on the trail," McPhee counseled. "Just to be sure."

"Do ye not trust what I say, despite it all?" Doc asked, eyes narrowing dangerously.

"I say we shouldn't trust them," McPhee said firmly, meeting Doc's gaze. Their eyes locked for a few moments before the old man nodded and grunted.

"Fair enough, ye may be right at that," he agreed. "The first thing to do is get them their clothes, and then get across to talk to them."

"Better to talk first, then give them back their clothes if they agree," Thompson said.

Doc shook his head. "Would ye agree to anything if ye had to stand naked before those who would ask ye?"

McPhee gave a short, barking laugh. "He's right about that, all right." He snorted.

Reluctantly—almost as though he felt he were in some way handing over all his power in acquiescing on just this one small point—Thompson agreed and called for one of his sec guards.

The Inuit warrior, having been thus detailed, hurried to where the one-time sacrifices' clothes were being stored and retrieved them, hurrying from that hut to the nearby dwelling where they were incarcerated.

As this happened and Doc watched him through the open doorway of the chief's hut, he consulted the chron he kept on a chain in his vest pocket. Considering the lives these people seemed to lead, he marveled that it was still operational.

"Give them a little time to get dressed, regain their dignity, and then we'll head over and talk to them," he said over his shoulder. All the while his eyes were focused on the guarded hut. He caught sight of a man in spectacles staring out at him, and their eyes met over the distance.

Doc grinned. It was completely unlike any gesture he had made in his previous existence.

The face at the window disappeared.

"DARK NIGHT, he scares the shit out of me," J.B. exclaimed, pulling back from the window.

"What?" Mildred was at his side in an instant. The Armorer was shivering as though they had just pushed him out of the hut with no skins or furs.

"Doc. He's up to something over there, ordering them about as though he runs the ville. He looked right over at me as I was watching him and his eyes seemed to go right through me. Except that they weren't Doc's eyes. It was his face, but a stranger looking at me."

"But what's he up to?" Ryan mused. "Does he even know who we are anymore?"

Krysty was about to speak, but held back as she heard the sound of feet approaching the hut before there was a scuffling at the door and it was opened, the lock having been released. An Inuit tribesman stumbled over the threshold, almost obscured by the piles of clothing he carried in his arms, his short stature making it difficult for him to see over the top of the pile. He dumped the clothes in the middle of the hut and backed out warily, little more than this showing in his expression. From the door, he was covered by the guard with the Sharps.

Not wanting to risk anything at this stage, the companions held back until the door had been secured once more. Once they were locked in, Ryan moved forward to poke at the pile of clothes.

"All ours, and all here," he commented. "But just the clothes. Everything else has been stripped—blasters, ammo, med supplies, food and water. Guess they want us to cover up for something, but they don't trust us any more than that."

"Guess we'd do the same if we were them," Krysty said philosophically. "Might as well go ahead. I reckon we won't learn anything about their plans—or about just what has happened to Doc—until we're ready to face them."

Ryan indicated his agreement and gestured to the others that they should pick their own clothes from the pile and once more get dressed. Jak pulled out his patched camou jacket and slipped his hands expertly into all the hidden places where he had secreted his small, leaf-bladed knives. Every last one had been found and removed.

"Fuckers smart for own good," he mumbled to himself.

"Say that again," Ryan agreed, overhearing the albino's muttered imprecation. "They've kept my scarf." This seemingly innocuous item of apparel, made dangerous by the weights sewn into the ends that enabled it to be used for a number of offensive purposes, had been retained by the Inuit along with Jak's concealed weapons and their more overt hardware.

The Inuit may want them for something, but they were obviously taking no chances until they had obtained agreement.

"So what do we say to them?" Mildred asked.

"Yes," Ryan replied simply. "Whatever the hell it is, we don't have a choice at this moment, so short of agreeing to cut our own throats, we just smile and nod and say yes until we figure a way out of it."

"Trouble is, if Doc is carrying any kind of memory of what he was, then he'll have already told them that," Krysty said.

"Yeah, that could be a problem," Ryan agreed with a wry grin. It was, in many ways, a lose-lose situation no matter what the Inuit wanted from them.

They settled to wait. Once more, the feeling of being in a position where they had to be reactive rather active, almost passive in the face of a potential danger, weighed heavily upon each of them. Krysty and Mildred were better equipped to internalize than Ryan, Jak or J.B., yet even they were finding the waiting hard. What could they expect? Would the Inuit and Doc come to them, or would they be summoned? Was there a chance that their weaponry would be restored? What would their captors now demand of them, or would Doc—even though hidden behind some new persona—have parlayed some kind of freedom for them?

Introspection ill befitted any of them, but it was all they had in the few minutes between finishing reclothing themselves and the beginning of any action. Minutes that hung heavily for that reason, the worst fears and best hopes racing jumbled through each person's mind, each differing slightly according to their personality and ability to see the best and worst in any situation. To discuss them would have taken forever and would have been fruitless. Instead, a sour silence descended on them and marked the slow passing of the chron.

Then, just when it seemed that the tension of waiting would snap nerves that were already frayed to the point of ultimate tension, they heard footsteps approaching the hut. Deliberately, none had wished to watch from the window. They faced the door, spread out across the floor of the hut, all on their feet: it was a defensive position, making it hard for a single attack to take them out, and something that they had fallen into without having to discuss the matter.

But now there were the footsteps. The moment for action was at its cusp. Should they take the front foot and move on the Inuit as soon as the door opened, or should they take the back foot and wait until the purpose of their captors had been revealed?

From the sounds emanating from the exterior, they could tell that there were three people approaching the hut. The footsteps halted. They heard the scrabbling of the lock and the door was flung open to reveal Thompson, McPhee, and—taking center stage—Doc Tanner.

Yet this impression that it was Doc was soon dispelled. The way the man strode into the center of the room, stopped dead with his hands on his hips and lazily looked around him, revealed that the character of the figure facing them had changed, seemingly irrevocably.

There was a light in the eyes that showed a shrewd, native intelligence that would not be given to the reams of verbiage Doc inflicted upon them. The ways the eyes narrowed as he surveyed the interior of the hut also revealed that here was a man less open, more guarded and dangerous that the Doc they had known. His stance was easy, but held that hint of coiled danger, like a sleeping snake that could strike before there was a chance to move. It was the same shell as Doc, but a man of a very different hue inside.

Which was nothing as to the shock they received when they heard him speak. Although he had declaimed loudly when they were on the sacrificial tables, the herbs had taken the edge off perception, and although they had each known that there was something different about his voice, none had been truly able to take in the change. Now, at closer quarters and in a fully conscious state, the difference in timbre and tone was astounding. The voice seemed almost an octave deeper, and the heavy Scots burr—so hard to understand in the Inuit—was even harder when coming from someone so unexpected.

"I'm expecting ye'll be a little shocked to hear me talk like this," he began. "Not, perhaps, as shocked as I was myself to be here." Briefly he retold for them the tale he had unfolded in front of Thompson and McPhee, noting the looks of incredulity that spread across the expression of both Mildred and Krysty, and the studied inscrutability of J.B. and Jak. Ryan, however, seemed quizzical. When Joseph Jordan had revealed his identity, Ryan spoke up.

"And we're supposed to believe you? Just like that? And they're supposed to believe you, too?" he added, indicating the Inuit chief and his medicine man.

"Ye can believe what ye like," Jordan flashed angrily. "I don't ask ye to believe anything. I'm telling ye what I know to be true. Ye can either accept it or not…"

"There are things he knows about our history that are known only to the few," McPhee said softly. "Things that are only passed down to the medicine man…and the chief," he added as an afterthought, noticing the look Thompson threw at him. "Things that he couldn't have known unless what he says is the truth."

Ryan wasn't so sure. He had heard Doc outline a brief history of migration in the region to the Inuit chief only a few evenings previously. They didn't know the true history of the man. If they had, they would never believe it over the truth to which they chose to subscribe. The times the man claiming to be Joseph Jordan spoke of were before Doc had been trawled for the first time by the Chronos project; such events could have made the newspapers of the day, been talked of and written about widely. A man of Doc's erudite nature could easily have come across them during his first lifetime in the predark era.

If this were the case, then given the circumstances it wasn't impossible to imagine that Doc had retreated so far into his madness that he would construct a new persona that called on things that could defend him in the current situation. The things Mildred had told them about the way men's minds worked would make this feasible. Certainly, Ryan found it a whole lot more believable than transmigration of the soul.

More importantly, if this were the case, then the real Doc was still in there and could come back to them; was, perhaps, even now finding some hidden way in which to assist them. After all, it didn't sound as though they were about to buy the farm.

This spun through his mind in the seconds after McPhee had spoken. It was crucial, now, to win the trust of the Inuit.

"Okay," Ryan said with a brief nod, "I guess that kinda convinces me."

"Good, good," Jordan said, nodding in emphasis with the repetition. "Look, will ye all look a little less like we're gonna gut ye like fish. Relax a little, I've got something to say to ye."

Warily, casting looks to one another, the companions reached an unspoken consensus to uncoil and listen to what the man had to say. Krysty was the first to sit, and Jordan followed suit. Within seconds, they were all seated on the floor and the tension in the atmosphere had eased. Even the two Inuit seemed to be a little less reserved and on edge than before. Correspondingly, Jordan's tone eased and became more confidential as he began.

"Ye are not to be the sacrifice. There's something not right about it, and that's why I was sent to these people. To stop it—"

It seemed to occur to neither Jordan nor the Inuit that this may have been something to do with Doc Tanner, still lurking, a prisoner within his own body. It didn't, however, escape the listening companions. But now wasn't the time to raise the matter. Instead they continued to listen in silence.

"—and to make something better happen. Something that would serve the purpose of these people, and prove to them that the good Lord has not deserted them. He needs a sign from them of their obedience and servitude before he will deign to help, and in an act of good faith for their faith, he has sent me…" Jordan was beginning to ramble; it was, perhaps, a sign of Doc trying to break through. Jordan shook his head violently, as though clearing it of clouded thought, before continuing. "This sacrifice was wrong. It would not have appeased him and would not have brought good fortune to the tribe. He demands of them something greater, something that befits their debt to him as their creator, and he has sent me to guide them on this. It is a great task, and I would ask for your help in fulfilling it, as we will need all those who can fight."

"Wouldn't it anger the Almighty if outsiders were to assist?" Krysty asked. "Wouldn't it sully the purity of the sacrifice?"

Thompson looked across to McPhee. "That's true," he said. "Why would the Almighty—"

"Because he would not have sent me in the first place unless he felt ye needed help," Jordan thundered, punching his fist into the floor of the hut to emphasize his point. It was a sudden explosion, and took the Inuit by surprise.

Not the companions. If this was a soul in possession of Doc Tanner, then it seemed as though Doc were still in there somewhere. If it was an alternate personality created by a shattered Doc, then the real Tanner was still influencing the surrogate.

Jordan continued in a milder tone, seemingly as shocked by his outburst as the two Inuit men.

"I am from the original stock of this village. It was my people who came to this land and brought the Lord to these people, joining with them to make the tribe that we see today. That is why I was sent. In the same way, the Lord has sent ye here so that ye may become one with the tribe and join in the fight. Ye will become servants of the Lord, as we are. Ye—" he turned to McPhee "—will attend to this. It will happen soon. For we must move soon, before the storms worsen and the seasons change once more."

He turned his attention back to the five people who sat in a semicircle in front of him.

"There is a large ville on the trail between here and Anchorage—Ank Ridge, as ye now call it in these days—which was known in my day as Fairbanks, and is still. Back in the day, it was a place where trappers and traders would meet to sell their wares and to drink and whore. From what I hear, it has changed little, e'en though the world has much. It will be no great shame to wipe the godless pit of hell from the face of the earth.

"These are souls who should welcome the embrace of the Lord, and should be grateful to be offered to him. But I doubt if they will. They are many, and we are few. More, if ye are with us. We must trek to their settlement and purge them with the fires of righteousness, sacrificing them so that Lord's servants may have greater longitude."

"What you mean is, we get in a firefight where we're outnumbered so that we can chill a few unsuspecting trappers for your purpose," Mildred said coldly.

Jordan fixed her with a baleful glare. "Ye can choose to look on it in that way if ye wish," he said softly. "Ye would be wrong, but ye could see it in that manner." He paused, then shrugged. "Can ye honestly say that ye have never done the same or any the less?"

A sobering thought. Mildred cast her mind back over the things that had happened to her since she had been unfrozen. It seemed like decades. During that period there had been many occasions when she had been forced to choose between the lesser of two evils; times when even that had been denied her and she knew that she was doing something of which she may not be proud. But better to know that than to buy the farm, which was the only alternative.

Was Jordan presenting her with a case that was, in essence, any different? Knowing this, there was little opposition that she could offer. Looking at her compatriots, she could see that Krysty felt the same way. For Jak, these distinctions didn't apply. Unless you were granted the luxury, then survival would win out every time. J.B.'s stony expression told the same story. There were times when, despite the closeness that had arisen between them, she felt that J.B. was a stranger to her, an unknown territory whose thoughts were forever closed. Which left Ryan. The one-eyed man had a sense of conscience that sometimes troubled him. He tried not to let it show, but she could see that the sense of responsibility he felt as leader sometimes clashed with the equally strong sense of right and wrong that he carried in his head. Pragmatism would emerge triumphant.

As, in truth, it would for her. Despite the morality she carried in her head and heart; despite the ideals for which she would have fought and argued in the days before skydark; despite all of these, she didn't give a damn about the greater good right now. All she really cared about was staying alive and keeping her friends and fellow travelers alive. No matter what it took.

A sobering thought, indeed. Something about herself that she had, perhaps, never truly had the time to dwell on before. Not something about herself with which she felt at ease. But something that was there, regardless.

"No, I guess you're right," she said softly.

"Good. I'm glad ye agree. For if ye did not agree, then ye would be against us, and if that were the case, then I can't guarantee it would be worth keeping ye."

The inference was clear. From now on, they would have to follow what Jordan said or risk being chilled before there was a chance of escape.

Jordan got to his feet, Doc's tender bones betraying him, making the rise a little more difficult than he would have liked. "It would have been better if the Almighty had given me a better body to work with," he moaned, stretching and clutching at his back. "But it will have to do."

"Doc Tanner was a good and wise man. A brave one, too. You could have done a lot worse," Mildred said, shrewdly eyeing the stranger in Doc's body as she spoke. If the real Doc was in there somewhere, she wanted to do everything she could to encourage him.

"I shall take your word for that. I shall have to," Jordan said.

He turned to the Inuit. "How long before they can be received into the faith?"

"I can do it tomorrow morning, as soon as the sun rises," McPhee answered. "It's late now, the dark will soon descend. And there is some preparation I must do. In the meantime, we can make plans so that we have an attack ready to unveil to them and to our people."

Jordan's eyes narrowed. The medicine man was still seated and the stranger towered over him. "Aye, that sounds a good idea. But don't be taking too much upon yourself, man—ye are, after all, only the medicine man."

For the briefest moment, anger flashed across McPhee's face, so swiftly that it was possible to believe that it was imagined. They all saw it and noted the pause before the medicine man, keeping control of his voice, replied, "Of course."

Was Thompson aware of the sudden clash between the stranger and the shaman? It was hard for them to tell, as his face remained as blank as ever. But if he hadn't registered what had just occurred, then it could mean a complication that lay ahead…in a situation that was already fraught.

The two Inuit rose effortlessly to their feet and left without a word. Jordan paused at the door and looked back over the assembly. "I'll be seeing ye," he said simply before closing the door in his wake.

Was there something in the way he said that? Did it suggest that there was something of Doc in there, struggling to make its way to the surface?

There was a silence that hung over them like a pall when they were left alone. It had been a confusing meeting: from being sacrifices to the Inuit religion they were now to be inducted into that same religion and used as sec men in an attack on another ville to make replacement sacrifices.

That was one hell of a turnaround in less than a day.

"What do you think?" Krysty asked Ryan eventually, as much to break the oppressive silence as for anything else.

"About what?" the one-eyed man replied. "Do I think Doc's finally left this world behind? Do I think we should get ourselves into some kind of stupe religion? Do I think we should go and virtually chill ourselves attacking a ville bigger than this just because of a madman's vision?"

"Guess that about covers everything," J.B. commented wryly.

Ryan shook his head. "Fireblast, you might as well ask me if I figure we have any choice. 'Cause that's all that it comes down to."

Krysty finished the sentence for him. "And the answer is no."

Chapter Fourteen

Doc, in his new persona of Joseph Jordan, returned to them once more that night. It had been dark for several hours and the outside was lit only by the glow of lamps that gave away the location of the Inuit huts and cabins. Some had shielded windows, but most were secure in their cover among the woods of the downlands slopes and couldn't be bothered to blacken their lights. A hollow glow fell over the earth that had been their place of sacrifice only a few hours before and was nothing more than a patch of fallow land.

Clothed, alert, and still a little confused over what had happened during the preceding day, they were now waiting with strained nerves for what would happen next. More than that, they were kept awake by the gnawing in their guts and their parched throats. The herbs in the sacrificial meal that had earlier been forced upon them had eased through their systems and had left behind an almost maddening desire to eat and drink. Yet they had not been fed, nor given water, since Doc had entered with Thompson and McPhee.

"How they expect us to fight when starving?" Jak grumbled, hunkering down and hugging himself, as though he could make the pangs subside by squeezing them from his body.

"An army marches on its stomach," Mildred said absently. Then, noticing the stares of bemusement she received, explained, "Napoleon was supposed to have said it. Hell of a sec chief in his day."

"He wouldn't have reckoned much to this, then," J.B. drawled laconically.

They subsided into a pained silence that was broken when Krysty beckoned them to the window.

"Doc may not be Doc, but it looks like he still wants to look after us."

The man now known as Joseph Jordan was striding across the center of the ville from the direction of the cookhouse. He was at the head of three Inuit women: one carrying a steaming pot, another with plates and cups and a third with a pitcher of fluid. What it might be was unclear, but it was steaming as gently as the pot carried ahead of it.

They heard a scrabbling as the lock on the cabin door was freed and the door swung open to reveal a smiling Doc.

"Bet ye thought we'd forgotten ye," he said in his deep Scots burr. "How could we expect ye to join with us and fight if ye didnea have food in your bellies?"

He stood to one side and ushered the three women into the hut. The pot was a deer stew with stodgy dumplings that bubbled on the surface before turning and sinking into the morass. There were vegetables and vegetable matter of an indeterminate origin floating in the stew, which smelled slightly rank, as though the meat had been left just a little too long before being thrown into the pot.

The pitcher had a herb infusion that smelled sweet. It was light brown in color and the warmth almost radiated from the surface toward them.

The Inuit women put the pot, the pitcher and the plates and cups in the center of the room.

"Come, enjoy." Jordan gestured toward the meal. A frown of puzzlement momentarily crossed his brow when they held back, until the realization hit him. "Of course, of course," he muttered, almost to himself. "Ye'd be stupid to just take it after what's been done to ye before."

Jordan took a plate and cup from the pile. He helped himself to some of the stew and took a few mouthfuls, washing it down with the herbal tea.

"Does that, perhaps, reassure ye?" he asked, wiping the sleeve of his frock coat across his mouth in a gesture that seemed alien coming from the body of Doc Tanner.

"Only if you stay here and we see what it does or doesn't do to you," Ryan answered. "Be too easy to go outside and puke it right now, before it had any effect."

A sly grin crossed Jordan's face. "I like the cut of your jib, son. It's a fair point. I'll stay awhile and talk. Ye can go—hist!" he added, directing his attention to the three Inuit women and driving them out of the hut. When they had gone, he turned a shrewd eye on Ryan. "Now, I'm thinking that perhaps there was more reason to ye wanting me to stay than just to test your meal."

"You're right about that," Ryan agreed. "I'm not going to bullshit you. There's a few things I need to know."

"Need? Ye think you're in a position to demand?"

"Mebbe not, but it won't stop me asking."

"Fair, fair." Jordan shrugged. "Go ahead, then."

Ryan looked at the others. They were torn between the need to know and the need to fill their aching bellies, even the rank smell of the stewed deer meat enough to get their juices flowing.

"Why do you think we'll come with you and fight in a firefight that isn't ours?" he began, approaching his object circumspectly.

"Because ye have little choice. It's the only way ye'll get your weapons back, and where else are ye going to go?" But even as he said it, Jordan frowned, as though there was something pricking at the edge of his consciousness. Something he couldn't quite identify, but that niggled at him.

"Mebbe we would have somewhere, mebbe not. But what's to stop us going anyway? Mebbe we'd rather take our chances than take part in someone else's firefight," Ryan continued.

Jordan screwed up his face, as though trying to mentally dig out some piece of vital information. "No, not ye. I know that ye all are fighters, good ones at that. I know that ye have a sense of right and wrong, and that ye can be relied upon to back each other up. And I know that I'm included in that, for the man who was in this shell before me." He stopped, bewilderment crossing his face. "How would I know that? Why is that still there? Shouldn't…" His voiced wavered, and for a moment—for only a few syllables—the Scots burr fell away and the familiar tones of Doc broke through. "Shouldn't that be something that did not remain, that went with the man who…" He shook his head. "Lord, these are demons sent to tempt me from my past, a test perhaps from the Almighty to prove my faith."

Ryan pressed home what little advantage he could see. "So you wouldn't come with us if we were to make a break for it when our blasters are back with us? Break for the redoubt and get the hell out of here?"

"The what? What is this of which ye speak?" Jordan put his hand to his temple, as though pressure were building. The gentle touch became a grinding knuckle, skin whitening at the temple around the area of pressure. "No, I must do the Lord's work. Lori? I have purpose, reborn like the phoenix… A test, don't ye see?"

Mildred seized the opportunity. "Doc, Doc, it's me. Think about who you are, where you came from. How you got here. Remember that you are Doctor Theophilus Tanner, from—"

"No!" Jordan roared, shaking his head to clear it. "Ye are not going to trap me with your cleverness. I am Joseph Jordan, and I have been sent to do the Lord's work and redeem these people who are descended from my kith and kin. This is all still strange to me and I will not allow ye to make the strange seem even stranger. Your food and drink is good, as ye can see from the way in which I still stand before ye. Now eat and drink, for tomorrow we begin our assault on Fairbanks. Now I bid ye good-night until the morrow."

Holding himself unnaturally erect, as though every movement had to be forced from his body, Jordan turned and stormed to the door, slamming it behind him and securing the lock before walking heavily into the night. They could hear his pounding feet punctuating his low mutterings as he crossed the center of the ville.

"Well, what do you make of that?" Mildred said softly.

"Whatever it is, possession or madness, I don't care," J.B. answered. "Doc's in there somewhere. Just for a moment…"

"Yeah, I thought he was coming back to us," Ryan commented. "But whatever it is, it's keeping the real Doc clamped down. Which means we can't leave the old bastard to these people, and it's sure as shit he won't come with us if we make a break. Even if we force him, he'd be wanting to get away and back to them."

"So what do? Just walk into chill for them?" Jak asked. His tone was neutral, but his words betrayed his displeasure.

"We make sure that we aren't walking into anything," Ryan replied. "We bide our time, we go along with them, and we see how Doc's doing. When the time is right, then we take him with us."

"Even if it means getting into a bloodbath?" Krysty asked.

Ryan nodded slowly. "Even that, I guess. We do it and make sure that every other bastard gets chilled other than us."

"That's not going to be easy, even assuming they give us all our hardware back, and not just some of it," J.B. pointed out.

"Fireblast and fuck it, when has it ever been easy?" Ryan countered. "Best thing we can do is actually fill our bellies, quench our thirst and wait for the morning, see where it takes us."

THOMPSON AND MCPHEE had been arguing since sunup. The shaman had been waiting for the Inuit chief when he came out of his cabin.

"Not like you to be up and working so early," the chief said pointedly.

"Never mind that shit. I've got something to talk to

you about," McPhee said urgently, taking the chief by the arm and leading him away from the cabin. He spoke in low tones, and it didn't take Thompson much to guess that this was because the stranger Jordan had been sleeping at the chief's. Whatever was itching at the medicine man, he didn't want to risk Jordan catching wind of it.

"Don't take much to guess what it's about," Thompson said softly. "Don't want someone to hear, eh? Figure you were the one told me he was the real deal, so—"

"It's not about him...not really," McPhee cut in, picking carefully at his words. "Him I don't doubt, but... Tell me, Chief, do you feel good about him wanting the others to take part in this?"

"He says that he remembers them being good fighters, from the time before he came into that body. Shit, we know they are, anyway. And he figures that they'll go along with him because of who he used to be."

"That's just it, though," McPhee mused.

"What?" The Inuit chief looked genuinely puzzled.

"Well, he ain't who he used to be, is he? He might have some memories left in his brain from that time, but he ain't the mad old coot they brought with them. So why would they stick with someone who, when you think about it, they don't actually know? Don't say that hasn't crossed your mind. You'd have to be pretty stupid not to think about it, and if you're anything, you ain't that."

"I hope you mean that," Thompson said coldly. Then, after a pause while he waited for the import of his word to sink in, he continued. "Jordan told me that he spoke to them last night, and that they agreed to come with us and fight. Even if we leave hardly anyone here to look after the ville while we're gone, we still don't number that many. Not against the size of Fairbanks. We need them."

"Do we? You think I'm going to be the only one who's not sure about them being involved. Fuck's sake, we were ready to carve them up this time yesterday, and now we're supposed to think that they'll go along with us just like that?"

"You got a better idea?" Thompson countered. "Jordan wants them. We need them. He's been sent to us. You put it together and see what else you can make from it. Only fits one way."

McPhee shrugged. "Have it your way. You're chief, and there ain't shit I can say to change your mind if that's how you really want it. But don't expect everyone to accept it that easily. I trust Jordan, but not the others. There are some who may find it hard to even trust him if they're part of the deal. Gotta think about that— d'you really want to send us into a firefight where not everyone'll be totally committed?"

"They will be because I tell them. I have the power, and they accept that. They'll have to trust me."

McPhee studied his chief closely. The Inuit's bland features betrayed no flicker of doubt, but the shaman wondered if, behind the impassive facade, the chief was as confident of his power of the people as he claimed. McPhee hoped so. He would find out soon enough, at any rate.

As the sun rose higher, more of the Inuit began to emerge from their dwellings to go about their early morning chores, with the smell of food coming from the cookhouse, carried on wafts of steam. The chief stood at the middle of the ville, watching them, McPhee at his side. The medicine man's body language betrayed his current ambivalence and was soon noted by a people whose communication was based on more than their verbal reticence.

It was obvious from the respective postures of both chief and shaman that something was about to happen, and an air of expectation swept through the ville. It increased when Jordan emerged from the chief's cabin and strode over to where the two Inuit elders stood. He exchanged a few words of greeting, and noted the ambivalence of the shaman: something he figured he may need to get to the bottom of before too long. But right now, there was serious business to attend to. As he watched, Thompson beckoned McIndoe over to him. The hunter and sec man was one of Thompson's most trusted warriors, and he entrusted to him the task of bringing the companions into the center of the ville while some of his men rounded up the tribe.

The hunter moved swiftly, detailing his men to fetch the tribe members from their chores and assemble them in the center. A few words passed around were enough to bring the curious and expectant Inuit into the rapidly filling open space. Meanwhile, McIndoe sent one of his men to gather the weaponry taken from the companions, now stored in the ville's armory. This done, he went across to the hut where they had passed the night.

Inside, Jak had been watching the Inuit elders and had reported what appeared to be some kind of disagreement with them. He had continued to observe while McIndoe was called to them, and the sec man had instituted the gathering of the tribe. Thus it was no surprise when the sec man came up to their hut and loosed the door.

"Chief wants you now, in the middle. Everyone gathering. Guess it's something big." His manner was bizarrely offhand, as though these were people with whom he had been carousing the night before, rather than those he—with the rest of the tribe—had been ready to sacrifice.

Without waiting for them, he turned and walked away, leaving the door gaping wide.

Krysty gave Ryan a puzzled glance. "Guess we're back in favor. Think Doc's said anything?"

"Can't see how he could have got the word across to them, but mebbe it don't matter. If Thompson says something, then they all jump."

Mildred grimaced. "I'll believe that when I see it, but I guess we should just roll with it for now."

The one-eyed man nodded. "Just take it as it comes."

Ryan led them out of the hut and toward the gathering of the tribe. They walked slowly, cautiously, not sure of how they would be received. Those Inuit who were in their path parted to let them through, and from the expressions on their faces—those that could be read— it seemed that they felt much the same.

When they reached the center, Thompson and McPhee greeted them with a nod and Jordan spared them a few words of greeting; but only a few. It seemed that the personality in Doc Tanner's body lacked the garrulous qualities of the previous inhabitant and so was loathe to waste words at this juncture.

It was only when the chief was sure that the whole of the tribe was assembled—waiting for word from McIndoe that his men had made sure all were present—that he began. In a few words, he told them of what he had discussed with Jordan the night before and how they had to make a greater, purer sacrifice to appease the Almighty: a sacrifice that would mean an assault on the ville of Fairbanks.

"… you know that we have tried to find suitable offerings in the smaller villes and failed. When there are more people, then we are more certain of making it right. Friend Jordan will guide us, as he has been sent to do, and in order to assist us these warriors will join us."

While the companions knew that this was coming, it was doubtful that it could be anything other than a complete surprise to the Inuit. The hushed murmurings that swept through the otherwise silent throng were an indication of their depth of feeling. Any kind of verbal communication was at a premium, so the intensity of emotion that had to have been passing through the assembled tribe was obvious. Ryan took in the Inuit with a sweeping eye: some of them were as inscrutable as ever, but others evinced a certain hostility that he feared could presage nothing but trouble.

Thompson raised a hand to silence them. "I know you must be wondering why we need outsiders to help us with our sacred task. But think on this. They came with friend Jordan, who was sent to us by the Almighty. They are part of the same gift from the Lord, proving to us that he is taking our offerings seriously and is giving us the chance to redeem ourselves in his eyes and make the great sacrifice that will save our people."

It occurred to Mildred that Doc's garrulousness had to be catching. She couldn't imagine the Inuit chief ever having to make a speech that long before. He seemed uncomfortable with the words and they came haltingly from his mouth. Perhaps it was because of this that they seemed to carry with them a tone of sincerity that appeared to strike directly into the hearts of his people. Like Ryan, she could see the hostility in some faces, but she could also see that the majority of the Inuit were thinking about what he said, and that some of those who had been opposed were coming 'round to his view, the minute changes on expression indicating the mental tumult that went on beneath the calm exterior.

"Think they want skin us alive?" Jak mumbled.

"Think it's closer than I'd like it to be," J.B. returned wryly.

"Shut it," Krysty murmured. "I think the old bastard is actually convincing them that chilling us might not be their best option."

McPhee coughed. A throat-clearing hawk that was ended with a hoicked phlegm ball into the earth. It was designed to quell the comparative row of the Inuit dissensions, and it worked. All eyes turned to him as he spoke, haltingly, and seemingly with little conviction for his words.

"The old ones used to have a saying—the Lord works in mysterious ways, and sometimes it's a wonder that he performs at all. I guess this is one of those occasions," he continued, with a sideways glance at Jordan. "One thing I do know is that sometimes I don't know what the hell is going on myself, and I talk to the Lord for you. We have to trust. Faith. This is one of those times."

He shook his head, as though running out of words, and stepped back to allow Jordan and Thompson center stage. The chief frowned. McPhee had been the one to convince him that Jordan should be listened to, and yet now he seemed to be having doubts. His seeming reluctance to speak only added to the dissension he had shown earlier. It wouldn't do to have a medicine man who was openly falling out with his leader over something that was so related to his own area of expertise. The chief knew that he would have to discuss this with the shaman; but not now, and not here.

Meanwhile the stranger had taken it upon himself to speak.

"Friends, this is a glorious chance for us to forge a path ahead. Do not be afraid of these outsiders. If not for them, I would not have been granted a vessel by our Lord with which to come and join with ye. I know that these people are good fighters, and ye know this as ye have seen them partake in a hunt..."

Ryan caught this reference, and it set alarm bells ringing in his mind. Their participation in a hunt had occurred before Doc had been possessed by the personality of Jordan—did this mean that some semblance of Doc was still in there, struggling to surface as before? Was it in greater touch with the whole of the new persona than they could have suspected from his performance back in the cabin?

No matter now, Jordan was still in flight. "—and ye know their capabilities. We will be outnumbered, and if we are to do the Lord's work, then we will need allies who will assist us in our hour of need, and upon whom we can rely. I can vouch for the integrity of these folk, and I know that they will not be found wanting."

It was a strange speech and yet it seemed to strike the right note with the assembled tribe. There seemed to be a wave of acceptance that washed over them: some, perhaps, accepting this more grudgingly than

others, but nonetheless acquiescing to the man they had
been told was their savior.

Thompson felt it was time for him to assume the
upper hand as chief once more. Stepping forward, he
told the tribe to return to their dwellings and make ready
to leave within the hour. As the Inuit turned to leave,
Thompson strode forward so that he was only a few feet
from the companions, who were holding their ground,
unsure of what was now demanded from them. He
beckoned, and McIndoe came forward from the edge
of the crowd, laden with hardware. At a gesture from
his chief he laid the weaponry down in front of them
and stepped back. His face was set, but his eyes were
glittering as he stared at them, betraying that he was one
of the few who still felt ill at ease with the concept of
the companions joining forces with the tribe. Ryan met
his gaze and could see from the unflinching way in
which McIndoe refused to back down that he—and
others who still felt like him—would have to be
watched.

Thompson, who either ignored or didn't notice this
exchange, gestured at the pile of weaponry and ammo
at their feet.

"You see—I give this back to you in good faith. You
will need arms to join us, but I could just as easily have
kept you weapon-less until we neared the ville of Fairbanks. You would have been less danger, would have
had less temptation that way…but I trust you because
Jordan says that I should. And I trust him as he was sent
from the Almighty." He paused. "Can I trust you?"

"I think your mission is folly, and we must be triple
stupe to just walk into a firefight that isn't our own. But
we want our freedom, and joining arms with you will

help that. It's a trade-off, and we'll keep to our side of the trade."

Thompson considered this before finally assenting with a brief nod. "You make no bones about our pre-sumed folly, so I can see no reason why you would lie about joining us. Why be honest on the one hand, then lie on the other? Your trade is a bargain, then." He gestured to the weapons. "Take them. Be ready within the hour to move out."

He turned to McIndoe, his business now done. "Assemble the hunters. We must form parties of no more than ten to move in formation..." His words trailed off as his voice dropped, and he moved away across the center of the ville toward his own cabin talking in low and urgent tones to his sec chief.

The companions were left alone in the ville's open center, all around them the tribe engaged in preparing for departure. It was as though they were the calm center of the storm that raged around. Thompson was now engrossed in planning tactics with his sec chief. The companions' concerns were now discarded from his mind, and he left them alone with an implicit trust that they would be as good as their word.

It was a strange attitude. Ryan would have expected the Inuit to watch them closely, having at least some suspicion that they would be waiting for the first opportunity to break. And yet, despite the minority of the tribe still having obvious doubts, they placed enough faith and obedience in the chief—and he in the assumed messenger of the Almighty, Joseph Jordan—to dismiss their doubts and place trust in his judgment.

"So what the hell do we do now?" Mildred asked.

"Guess we prepare ourselves to leave," J.B. said,

crouching over the pile of hardware and collection of ammo to sort through it. Jak joined him, rooting through the pile to recover his knives, hurrying to secrete them in his camou jacket—only when they were in place would he feel secure, knowing that he was protected once more. J.B., meanwhile, kissed his teeth as he separated the weapons. "And another thing," he added. "I hope they look after their own blasters better than they've looked after ours." He held up his mini-Uzi to demonstrate. The usually immaculate weapon now carried a patina of dust and grime. "Who knows what the hell the rest of them are like. We need to get these stripped and cleaned if we're gonna feel safe with them."

It was something with which Ryan could only agree. At his direction, the companions returned to the hut where they had previously been held captive. As everyone else in the ville appeared to have retreated to their own abodes to make ready for the trek, it seemed only right that they take advantage of the last few hours' warmth and shelter provided by the hut before beginning the journey to Fairbanks across the harsh, frozen wastes.

It was good to be in the warmth again, and they also took the opportunity to finish what remained of the stew and the herb tea that had been provided earlier in the day. As they ate and drank, they stripped their blasters to clean and oil them before reloading and making sure that they each carried adequate supplies of ammo about their person, supplied from the canvas bag J.B. carried along with his grens and plas-ex. They were running low on hardware, and as he doled out the right ammo to each member of the group, it crossed his mind that if the firefight at Fairbanks carried on too long, or they became too embroiled in it, then they were running a very real risk of running out completely, leaving them exposed.

It was not a position in which he wished to find himself. Rummaging through the supplies he had, he outlined the position to the others.

"Way I see it, we go with them until they begin this attack on Fairbanks, and then in the confusion we see if we can get the hell away without getting our asses kicked. From that old map Thompson showed us the first night, there isn't that big a hike from Fairbanks to Ank Ridge. If we can hit the trail and get a clean run at it, then that's our best bet of finding some kind of shelter, mebbe pick up some work and food before making our next move."

"Sounds good, but is that with or without Doc?" Krysty questioned.

Ryan paused before answering, considering what he had to say. "I'd like it to be with the old bastard, but if he's still thinking that he's this guy Jordan, there may be little we can do other than leave him behind."

It was a prospect that held little appeal for any of them. Doc was a part of their lives, and any prime directive would include taking him with them; but if he was in the vanguard of the Inuit action, still believing himself to be a two-hundred-year-old Scots trapper, there may be little they could do to fulfill this directive.

Ryan filled the silence. "We do what we can to make sure he comes along with us—and that's all we can do, right?"

There was a silence that hung over the room like a fog. So much that needed to be said, yet was not worth the bother of articulation. They were all only too well aware of how they felt. None of them would wish to leave Doc behind if they had the chance to break for Ank Ridge, yet at the same time they knew that the good of the group had to, ultimately, count for more than the concerns of one man. Ryan had articulated this as well as any of them could. All they could do right now was wait until that moment came, and wait for how the cards would fall.

They continued their preparations in silence and it was in this way that they were found by McIndoe when the sec chief came to tell them it was time for the war party to depart.

THE CENTER OF THE VILLE was an awesome sight. Only a handful of the Inuit women and the few children that had survived beyond infancy in recent generations were to stay behind and maintain the ville. The remainder of the population was gathered, ready to depart. With their lack of height and their body shapes distorted both by their mutations and the bulk of their furs and skins, it was hard to differentiate male from female: something that was exacerbated by the hard set of grim determination that now shaped most of their faces.

Thompson stood apart from them, flanked by McPhee and Jordan. Although all three were also dressed in bulky furs and skins, there was something about the quality of the skin and fur that swathed the two Inuit that set them apart—Jordan was noticeable for Doc's height and mane of hair.

"I'm glad ye are joining us," Jordan commented. "As ye can see, we are ready to depart, and I wouldn't have liked to have left without ye."

Ryan looked around at the massed ranks of the Inuit, who seemed prepared to make the long trek by foot, and the few ponies and mules that they had with them—scrawny creatures, laden with pack—as well as the sleds with supplies that were pulled by dogs of indeterminate breed, seemingly rickety enough to fall apart when they hit the first pothole on track. He gazed upon this and wondered how the Inuit had a hope of taking on an entire ville at the end of a long, exhausting trek. Then he remembered the stubborn and ruthless manner in which they had tackled the hunt and suddenly he realized that it didn't matter what the result of the trek may be. They had set their mind to the assault and would stop at nothing short of all buying the farm to realize their objective.

Suddenly the idea of being able to slip away from these relentless warriors in the heat of a firefight seemed an impossibility.

Thompson raised a hand when he saw the companions join the pack and indicated the path leading through the woodlands and toward the trade trail through the volcanic downland slopes. McIndoe responded to the gesture with hand movements of his own, which were perfectly understood by his men. The tribe began their exodus in a procession that was headed by a detachment of hunters who set forth to work their way down to the trail. A bottleneck formed behind them as the tribe narrowed into a line that could safely pass through the narrow track.

It took some time for the Inuit to filter out of the ville and onto the track. It seemed impossibly slow, but this was illusory, caused by the fact that the hidden trail was, by its nature, not designed to accommodate such a large body of warriors. It seemed to the companions that nothing was happening for a great amount of time, considering this was an army on its way to a great battle—indeed, a crucial one—in its history. Yet the Inuit showed no signs of impatience. Indeed, their stoic acceptance in the light of such conditions said more about the way in which they were focused.

Finally, after what seemed like an eternity, the companions joined those who were among the last to filter through the path and down to the main trade trail. Once they had reached this point, the pace of the party began to pick up. Soon they were treading the trade trail itself, headed in the direction they had taken—was it only a few days before? Whereas the trail had seemed long, winding and capable of hiding a multitude of dangers back then, now it seemed to be too small and insignificant to take the vast party that crammed its boundaries, moving at a brisk pace.

The Inuit kept close together, clustering in a main body with a sec patrol at point to scout in advance when they reached harsher regions and a party at rear to insure the pace was kept and also to watch for wildlife approaching from the shelter of the woodlands at their backs.

The path wound down toward the sheltered rock in which the companions had been trapped and turned back so recently. Perhaps it was because they were so familiar with the terrain this time around that it didn't seem to take up such a distance as before. It wasn't too long before they were overshadowed by the rock walls, the front section of the party emerging onto the frozen wastes. Already, as they traversed beyond the warm streams of air fed by the outlying pockets of volcanic activity, they noticed the way in which the icy winds began to bite, making them huddle into their furs. It was a crisp, clear day, with no visible signs to betray a chance of storm and snow, and little ice circulating in the air. But what there was still constituted enough to chill the air in their lungs and freeze their breath as it emerged from their mouths and nostrils in streams of steam.

The walls of rock narrowed into an overhang that seemed to dangle oppressively, as though at any moment it would collapse in upon them and solve their problems for once and all. But before this gloomy atmosphere could overtake them, the walls came to a sudden halt, widening briefly before leading out onto the vast expanse of ice and rock that stretched to the horizon, with little to break the monotony other than the occasional outcrop and banked snow.

From their position at the rear of the caravan, they could see the ranks of the Inuit stretch in front of them. Their pace was steady, but surprisingly brisk for all that. Fairbanks was some distance away, and the trail was across harshly exposed terrain, marked now by the warriors as they began to spread out a little on a winding path that picked its way between deceptively jagged rock and ice, and potholes that harbored potentially deadly pockets of ice and snow that would entrap like quicksand. Although there was no glacial activity that could be defined, these isolated spots operated in much the same deadly manner.

The companions stayed to the rear of the war party, not wanting to work their way up—partly to conserve energy and partly because it was useful to them to stay at the rear. Jordan—Doc—was at the head, with

Thompson and McPhee, and so out of reach. It would have been preferable if the old buzzard had been within easy reach, but it was more important to try to keep as distanced as possible from the beginnings of any action. Their priorities were clear. Stay alive and try to extricate Doc from any mess he may get them into while he was still Joseph Jordan. The two may actually turn out to be exclusive. Hanging back at the rear of the caravan could give them the chance to make a break for freedom if an opportunity arose.

This, however, looked far from likely. There were sec men at their rear who occasionally came up close, their demeanor suggesting that they wouldn't hesitate to shoot first and ask questions after. There was little chance of dropping back farther from the caravan.

Those Inuit who were closest to them also cast disapproving glances in their direction. It was pretty clear that a good proportion of the tribe found it hard to trust them. Which meant, in turn, that they were under close surveillance.

It was going to be a long haul to Fairbanks.

TWO DAYS OF MARCHING across terrain that was unwelcoming and unforgiving. The clear skies of their departure gave way to chem clouds that turned the skies a yellow-gray, the stench of sulfur trapped beneath their oppressive weight. The strength of the winds, unbroken by any land mass, began to increase, and within a few hours the first storm had broken. Nowhere near the force of other storms previously encountered, no one sought shelter. Jordan, Thompson and McPhee were driven men, forcing their charges to proceed along the trail, fighting against the horizontal rain and snow that whipped in the darkened air.

The terrified whining of the animals could be heard, straining to break through the howling winds, and the tribesmen in front of the companions became nothing more than a vague blur. The caravan had stayed close together to facilitate such action during a storm, but nonetheless the range of vision grew smaller with each passing minute.

At the rear, this made the companions more determined to keep the caravan in sight. Although the storm would give them cover in which to slip away, where would they go? Right now, they needed the protection and sense of direction the caravan could bring.

Speech was useless, words whipped away by the storm before they had a chance to travel to their intended target. Instead, they used gestures to communicate. The five closed up, Ryan leading them nearer to the Inuit pack a few yards in front.

It was as he moved forward that he caught the slightest glimpse of a small figure moving swiftly from the side—his blind side, so he caught it too late to react quickly enough. Launching itself forward, the figure cannoned into him, knocking him off balance on the slippery, icy rock of the trail. Letting out a yell that was lost in the storm, Ryan fell sideways, thrusting an arm out to try to break his fall. He felt the bones in his wrist and forearm jar heavily when they hit the rock, the shock catching a nerve and numbing the arm from the elbow down.

The figure was heavy on him and difficult to come to grips with. The skins and furs swathed the figure so well that it was hard to tell where the Inuit ended and the swaddling clothes began. Ryan felt the cold seep through into his back as he grappled with the figure atop him. In the poor visibility, even at such close range, it was hard to see what kind of weapon the Inuit held. A cold, metallic clang on the rock by his head and the sparks from steel on stone told him that it was a blade. The figure had masked its face, so he wouldn't be able to identify it; more importantly, unless he fought off the tribesman, he wouldn't be in a position to even attempt this. One-armed, it was all he could do to keep the Inuit from chilling him, using his working arm to fend off the blows. There was little chance of him having the luxury of reaching for a weapon.

There was only one chance to get the little bastard off him and try to get things back on an equal footing. Shifting so that the bulk of his attacker's weight settled on his lower body, Ryan thrust upward with his hips. The sudden movement pushed the Inuit warrior upward, relieving Ryan of his weight. With his legs momentarily freed, Ryan braced his feet and pushed up harder, the increased momentum propelling the tribesman up and over his head to land on the rock with a sickening crunch.

Ryan was scrambling to his feet when he felt rather than heard or saw someone at his side.

"Me, Ryan," Jak whispered in his ear before the one-eyed man answered the instinctive urge to strike out. "What happen?"

Ryan, one arm still numbed, fumbled the panga from its sheath with his good hand as he spoke. "Some little bastard just tried to chill me. He's..." His voice trailed off. There was no sign of his attacker where he had heard the tribesman hit the rock. No sign of any kind that he had been attacked.

The other companions had now clustered around, but before they had a chance to ask further questions, they were on the sharp end of Lee Enfield .303 barrels as the sec men closed on them.

"Keep moving—mustn't lose sight of the others," one of the sec men snapped.

In the storm, there was no chance to discuss or to explain. Seeing that the retreating caravan was almost out of vision, the companions moved on, some not even aware of the attack on Ryan, but feeling nonetheless uneasy about what had occurred.

At the end of the second day, the storms began to abate. As darkness closed on them, the skies began to clear. The crescent moon and some constellations were visible through the heavy, chem-tinged atmosphere, and their faint light cast an unearthly glow over the flattened landscape, the banks of snow showing blue against black stretches of rock.

The caravan stopped to pitch camp and Ryan spoke hurriedly and in hushed tones as he relayed to the others what had happened to him.

"Not just you," Krysty said firmly when he had finished. She noted the questioning looks she received from the others and continued, keeping her tones as low as Ryan's. "During the storm, I was attacked. Not directly, not like you were. Mebbe it was the same person, which would figure if it was one of the sec behind us, but…" She shook her head, aware that she was getting off the point. "I saw someone moving past me and then they seemed to drop back a little. I never heard the shot, but I felt the slug go past me—so close that I could feel how damn hot it was. It made me pull up quickly, but…I dunno, I couldn't quite believe it,

thought I might have been mistaken. I think I'd probably still be thinking that if you hadn't just told us what
you have," she finished, looking at Ryan.

"Dark night, we're gonna have to be triple red from
now on," J.B. muttered. "Some of these bastards might
be okay with us tagging along, but others are gonna be
direct about showing how they don't like it."

Ryan looked around. The Inuit had made camp for
the night out on the trail. The sleds driven by dogs had
carried tents that were pitched and weighted to act as
windbreaks on the vast expanse of wasteland. Behind
these, groups of Inuit huddled together under extra skins
and furs while the dogs hunkered down close to them.
Allocated sec patrols were visible, carrying lamps and
blasters, scouting the surrounding area.

The companions had their own windbreak, and gave
themselves some distance. Jordan was out of sight, but
the prime objective now was to stay alive during the
night. They divided into watches of their own and got
an uneasy night's rest, unwilling to trust to the sec patrols of the Inuit.

As Ryan took watch, he looked to the horizon. In the
direction they were headed, there was a small ville
within view, laying about five hundred yards from the
path of the trading trail. He figured they had probably
passed one during the storm, as well. No signs of life
from either. The Inuit had acted as though it was a direct route to Fairbanks, with no problems en route, and
he could see why. They had already laid waste to anything that may lay between the volcanic region and
their destination.

How many of the bastards wanted to lay waste to
them, as well?

It was only when morning came that he felt he could relax, which wasn't a good thing. How could they stay on top of the game if they had to keep awake while the Inuit slept, and then tried to keep pace with the caravan? They would need their wits about them when they hit Fairbanks, but another day of this and they would be operating below their best.

No time to consider this as they set off across the wastes once more, the windbreaks and extra furs stowed on the sleds, the dogs and packhorses setting pace with the leading Inuit.

It came to the point where all attention was focused on putting one foot in front of the other. At least the day was clear of storms. The winds still blew strong, but only carried residual particles of ice. The clouds scudded across the skies, too fast to settle and dump their loads on the caravan below.

At least they were making rapid progress, so much so that they had arrived at the deserted ville before the sun was halfway across the sky. Consisting of little more than a few log and cinder-block huts, it had an air of desolation, as though it had been deserted for some time. As they neared it, the companions could see that the caravan had halted on the trail. Jordan was conferring with Thompson, and both men were gesturing toward the deserted ville. The chief beckoned McIndoe over to him, and after a few brief words the sec chief began to make his way to the rear of the caravan.

"What's going on?" J.B. queried.

"Something I'm betting we're not gonna like," Mildred replied wryly.

The sec chief approached them. "We're checking that ville—see if anyone's still around."

"I'm guessing that you could just as easily tell that from here," Ryan replied.

McIndoe made no indication of his feelings, just shrugged. "Not my job to say, just to do."

"So why are you telling us?" Ryan continued.

"Because the old man wants you to come with us, see what's there," McIndoe answered.

Ryan exchanged puzzled glances with the rest of the companions. Why would Jordan want to send them into an empty ville, unless it was to prove their loyalty to the cause? It wasn't a prospect that held much appeal. To be in a deserted ville with plenty of cover for any Inuit who chose to take a shot at them? On the other hand, who would be so stupe as to do that in front of the whole caravan? While it would be useful to know who they were up against when the firefight started at Fairbanks, it would only expose their enemies to the wrath of the Inuit chief and shaman.

In the end, they had no real choice in the matter. They had to prove Jordan's faith in them, or else the whole of the community, including the chief and shaman, would turn against them.

While the caravan waited, strung out along the trail, half a dozen Inuit sec, along with the companions, walked in silence the five hundred yards to the outskirts of the ville. In truth, the settlement was so small that it was almost an exaggeration to call it such.

As they approached, all they could hear over the constant sounds of the windswept landscape was the banging of doors and window shutters, random and seemingly at the mercy of wind currents that constantly changed on this flat plain.

"Sure as hell sounds empty to me," Mildred murmured.

"Yeah, but it ain't whoever lived there that we've got to worry about," Krysty returned.

"Got that right."

McIndoe directed his men so that they spread and combed the ville. He gestured to Ryan that he should do the same with his people. Reluctantly, as he was unwilling to separate them in the maze that the settlement represented, Ryan followed suit, directing his people to follow the Inuit sec into the ville.

The settlement had been evacuated quickly and violently. Ryan frowned as he saw doors ripped from the fronts of cabins and shattered windows. There were dark patches in the clustered ice around the tracks that snaked between the huts and some remnants of bone. It was an almost identical scene to the ville they had encountered before stumbling into the Inuit hunting party, and the sudden recall made the one-eyed warrior recoil slightly.

The huts were empty, their contents nothing more than a mass of broken wood and ripped-up material.

Mildred turned a corner and came fact-to-face with McIndoe as he stepped out of a hut.

"Shit, you frightened me," she gasped.

"Just making sure," the Inuit replied.

"Making sure of what?" Mildred questioned, but the sec man didn't reply, turning and walking away without a sound.

The two parties met up at the edge of the settlement that led back to the trading trail.

"Anything?" the sec chief asked simply. His men didn't speak, merely inclined their heads to indicate that nothing had been found. He looked at Ryan questioningly.

"Empty," the one-eyed man replied. "Not sure what the hell we were supposed to find anyway."

The two parties began to make their way back to the trail, where the caravan waited patiently for them. As they walked across the plain, there was a sound from the settlement. A dull whump, as though something had fallen over heavily onto a bank of snow. Except that there was no snow.

"What—" Ryan whirled, to see a plume of smoke rise from the far side of the settlement.

"You said you found nothing," McIndoe yelled, his voice suddenly louder than any of the companions had heard before. "You didn't look. Go back, dammit!"

Ryan felt his guts churn in warning. McIndoe was one of those who were set against them. It had to be. He had deliberately raised his voice and chosen his words so that they would carry to Thompson, McPhee and Jordan. If the companions refused to go back and search the ville once more, then they would look like cowards and incapable in the eyes of the caravan. If they did, then there was a trap waiting for them. And if McIndoe was against them, it was safe to assume that the majority of the sec would follow him.

They had no choice.

"Let's go back," Ryan said through gritted teeth.

Realizing the position they were in, the companions turned and jogged toward the ville. They had their blasters to hand, but knew that they were unlikely to face a living enemy. Smoke was now rising from one hut within the cluster of the settlement, and Mildred knew it was the one she had seen McIndoe exit from. She relayed this as they ran.

"Triple red, you don't know what that bastard has

laid in there," Ryan said. "Fan out, approach with extreme caution."

The companions spread out, each taking a separate route into the settlement. J.B. opted for the most direct. The Armorer had an idea of the kind of trap McIndoe might lay, and wanted to be first on the scene.

As he approached the hut that had been fired, the smoke was beginning to billow out in waves that threatened to stop him getting closer. But why would they be sent back to a building that was too fired to entrap them?

It was obvious, but he needed to make sure. Choking back the smoke, ignoring the way in which his eyes were streaming, J.B. forged ahead into the doorway of the cabin. The fire had been set in the far corner, but why? J.B. scanned the room through the thick smoke and caught sight of what he was after: a large block of plas-ex in the near corner, with a fuse attached...a fuse that was attached to a tallow wick to fire it. The flames from the fire were closing on the wick.

A block that size would take out half the ville. He had to move quickly. J.B., coughing heavily and spitting phlegm, pulled himself away from the cabin and began to run, yelling loudly to get the hell back. Despite the maze-like design of the settlement and the winds, he was able to make his voice heard, and in turn each of the companions turned and backtracked. They trusted J.B. implicitly and knew that if it was that urgent, then they had to move.

Straggling out in a line, they traveled two hundred yards when the plas-ex went up. The force threw them forward onto the rock, showered with debris. The caravan scattered before regrouping in the stillness that followed the explosion.

Ryan raised his head. The caravan was in confusion,

and all his people were out of the danger zone, but he noted the way in which McIndoe and several other Inuit were staring at them.

Fairbanks couldn't come soon enough.

Chapter Fifteen

Still another day until they reached the ville of Fairbanks: a day of marching in wind-driven conditions that took on an atmosphere of suspicion and indecision. The companions kept to the rear of the caravan, as before, trying to keep themselves apart from the horde of the Inuit. They were, however, not allowed to fall too far behind. McIndoe may have made it obvious to them that he was one of the tribe who felt hostility at their presence—indeed, as sec chief he was able to cause a lot of trouble for them if he wished—but he kept his own counsel after the explosion in the deserted ville.

He may wish to be rid of them himself, but he also knew that Thompson and McPhee were in thrall to Jordan, and that they had trust in the stranger's judgment. If he wanted to be rid of the outsiders, then he would have to wait until such time as he was able to dispose of them in an inconspicuous manner: perhaps a few misplaced shots in the heat of a firefight. Meanwhile, knowing that they would hang back and perhaps make a break for it if circumstances allowed, the sec chief detailed a larger unit of men to drop back and keep the rear of the caravan guarded.

The more that Ryan tried to retreat his group from the main body for their own protection, the more they had sec men snapping at their heels like rabid dogs, driving them closer to the tribe.

"You think either of the main men is in on this?" Krysty whispered to Ryan after their pace had once again been forced by an Inuit with a Sharps rifle coming up behind them to hustle them closer to the pack.

Ryan gave her a short shake of the head. "Thompson believes totally in Doc. He's virtually given up being baron to let Doc run the show. McPhee, though... There's something not quite right, there. It's like he believes, but doesn't want to."

"Mebbe he finds the idea of Doc being inhabited by a two-hundred-year-old spirit as crazy as I do," Mildred murmured, keeping an eye on the Inuit sec around her. "He may be the medicine man, but he's not stupid."

"That's a pretty reasonable assumption," Ryan conceded. "I dunno if he'd really go against the chief, though. I can't see him having the balls to do it."

"Which leaves us with laughing boy of the sec force leading the charge," Mildred concluded.

Ryan agreed. "As much as anyone's leading it, he is. I don't think there's really an organized campaign to get us. They haven't had time to get that together. But those who don't want us around can spot the like-minded, and they're loosely allied, if only by an unspoken agreement."

"So what you're saying is that we've got to watch our backs 'cause we could get shot at from anywhere at any time, right?" Krysty questioned.

"That's about it," Ryan agreed. "Can't pin it down to more than that."

"I feel so much better knowing that," Mildred commented bitterly.

An Inuit sec man ran up to them. Without speaking, he prodded Krysty with the barrel of his rifle and gestured that they should hurry, and also that they should shut up.

"Yeah, so much better," Mildred added under her breath as they upped their pace to move closer to the main caravan.

CLIMACTIC CONDITIONS were holding well for them. One brief flurry of storm was all that they had so far encountered. The skies were still heavy with the yellow-tinged chem clouds, but the ominous scudding of the roaring crosscurrents prevented the dark belly of the sky from opening and unleashing its hail of liquid cold upon the caravan.

The trading trail wound across the plain, passing crops of exposed rock and blanks of snow hardened into ice that was almost as hard. The horizon stretched endlessly in front of them as they trudged, the only sound being their marching feet and the yelping of the dogs as they pulled on the heavy supply sleds, mixed with the occasional whine from an exhausted pack animal forced to keep pace despite its load.

They rested three times during the day. Each was timed by wrist chron so that it came at a regular interval. At each break, there was no time to set up camp, so the Inuit hunkered down together, using their own body heat trapped in their furs and skins, magnified by their mass, for warmth. Water and food was taken to replenish them for the next stage of the journey. There was a sense of function rather than enjoyment about the repasts, as though they were essential and necessary rather than enjoyable. This was most definitely a peo-

ple on a mission, who almost found it an irritation to
waste their time seated when they could be eating up
more miles on the route to Fairbanks.

When these breaks came, Ryan and his people sat
apart from the mass. They felt safer, though it was
doubtful any attempt to attack them would be made in
full view of the chief, the medicine man and Jordan. It
wasn't this that was getting under their skins. It was the
sense of not knowing, the living every second on a knife
edge of expectation and looking at every impassive
Inuit face, wondering if it was friend or foe.

They were as glad as the Inuit when the time came
to stop resting and to continue marching…albeit for
very different reasons.

THERE WERE NO MORE villes between here and Fairbanks. This much Ryan knew from the map he had seen
in Thompson's cabin the first day they had arrived at the
settlement. But he figured that there may be a few more
far-flung cabins along the route. Something other than
the geology of the land had to account for the way in
which the trading trail altered direction from time to
time. The vast plain was treacherous, sure: shelf rock
gave way to hidden ice and snow that could suck you
in without warning. But there was more to the detours
that this. He whispered to J.B., who had been reckon-
ing their direction by the minisextant that he habitually
carried.

"Weird thing is that it feels like we're turning almost
in the opposite direction to Fairbanks at times," he murmured in reply. "I can't figure out why, unless…"

"Unless what?" Ryan queried.

"Unless this trail was made not to drive as straight a

track as possible between two points, but was intended to take in any hunters and trappers along the way."

"Y'know, I was wondering about the same thing myself," Ryan answered. "It'd make sense to link up everyone between here and Ank Ridge, right?"

"Right. Question is, what are the trappers gonna think when they see us bearing down on them?" the Armorer mused.

"If I was them, I'd be inclined to wonder what we were up to and how long it was gonna be before I shit myself, knowing I was outnumbered so heavily," Ryan muttered darkly.

"Yeah, or just mebbe I'd hightail it to Fairbanks, where I'd feel a whole lot safer, and try to warn the bigger numbers what was coming so that they'd be prepared."

"Sure as shit what I'd do," Ryan agreed.

The Armorer and Ryan fell silent, both lost in thoughts that ran along similar lines. They had assumed that the Inuit caravan would bear down on their target without much chance of being seen until they were too close for the dwellers of Fairbanks to have time to prepare a defense. This assumption had been based on the Inuit having already attacked and decimated the smaller villes en route, but if the trail took them past lone trappers, or small groups of hunters and trappers, then these would have represented too small a target for the previous war parties. And there was no way you could hide a caravan this big.

A few men and women could travel faster than a force this large. Moreover, the smaller groups—or individuals—would see the Inuit approaching from some distance and would run like hell, giving them a good head start.

Which meant that there was a strong likelihood that

the residents of Fairbanks would be ready and waiting when the holy-rolling caravan of Inuit warriors approached. Something that would make an already difficult firefight seem all the harder. Given the fact that they knew some of the Inuit would also waste no time in adding them to the numbers chilled, it made for a very uncomfortable situation.

Watching carefully to see that their sec guard was far enough away, and keeping his voice low so that it wouldn't travel, Ryan briefly outlined his concerns to the others. As he suspected, J.B.'s mind had been working along similar lines. As for Jak, Mildred and Krysty, before he had even finished outlining the situation, they knew exactly where he was going.

It wasn't an enticing thought. They were in the middle of a frozen wasteland with a war party, at least some of whom, perhaps even a majority, were against them. They were crisscrossing this wasteland in following a trail that was, although forged for the most practical of reasons, disorienting to those who were unfamiliar with it. Along the way, they were likely to provide a distant early warning to their enemies.

And there seemed to be no way out: to turn back would invite the wrath of the Inuit, who outnumbered them. To go on was to walk into a bloodbath. The best they could hope for was to try to extract themselves— and hopefully the deluded Doc—from the mess that would be Fairbanks, then head maybe for Ank Ridge, maybe back to the redoubt to jump the hell out of here... Not much of a plan, and not much of a prospect.

Meanwhile, there was the weather. Bitter cold, ice and snow blowing constantly against any exposed areas of skin, gales that cut through the layers of fur and skin, no matter how well you tried to wrap yourself up in them, and the heavy, oppressive clouds that thundered across the skies. They seemed so low that you could almost reach up and touch them, puncturing the gray-yellow membrane that seemed to breath in rhythm with the winds, loosing the chem-stained contents down on the land below. The clouds formed a ceiling that seemed to lower with almost every hour, pushing them closer and closer to the ground, making the icy air thicker so that it was like breathing iced water, sucking it into your lungs and hawking up phlegm as the stench of sulfur irritated your trachea, clogged up your lungs and seared your throat.

The clouds bore down on everyone, at times seeming to slow the pace of progress to a crawl, the objective moving farther and farther from reach until it became nothing more than a distantly grasped dream.

The skies lowered until they seemed to blot out the horizon. What had stretched for miles now appeared so close that you could hold out a hand and grab at it. Visibility, despite the fact that it was still ostensibly daylight, decreased. The previously endless expanses of rock and ice became a smaller pallet on which was imposed the straggling line of the caravan. It became harder to look back to see where they had been; harder still to see what lay in front of them.

It was when an irregular shape appeared through the gloom that Ryan knew the moment of truth was upon them.

THOMPSON HALTED the caravan when they were within five hundred yards of the shape, which had resolved itself into a cluster of three huts: two were log cabins with sheets of metal hammered into them, and the third was a cinder-block building, smaller than the other two, which seemed to be more of a storage block than the others, which were definitely dwellings.

The chief and Jordan sent word back through the caravan that the companions should join them at the head. Making their way to the front, they were only too aware that they were the subject of intense scrutiny, just as they were only too aware that they were to be placed directly in the firing line once more.

"Are ye willing to undertake a reconnaissance?" Jordan asked as they approached, adding, "Especially in view of what happened to ye the last time?"

Was the old man testing them or giving them a way out that wouldn't lose face with the tribe? Ryan tried to judge from the look in the old man's eye, but it was still so strange to see another light in Doc's eyes that he couldn't tell.

"The last time was just a piece of bad luck. For someone," Ryan said carefully, scanning the crowd that watched them, catching sight of the ever-impassive McIndoe to one side of that crowd. The sec chief gave nothing away.

"Aye, for ye, but not for us," Jordan continued. "At least we now know that these deserted places are likely to harbor traps."

Ryan frowned. He didn't know if Jordan was deliberately ignoring his inference or that he simply did not realize what was being said. The latter seemed likely, as the old man seemed lost in thought, continuing with his musing in a way that reminded Ryan of Doc's ability to ramble—perhaps there was more of Doc creeping through than they dared hope.

"I'm wondering if they just leave these traps when they evacuate to spoil anyone who mayhap stumble upon their settlement, or if it be directed solely against us...but if so, how would they know that we were following on their trail?"

Jordan was so deeply lost in thought that his attitude caused Thompson to look to McPhee. The medicine man shrugged. He was still wavering in his faith, and if the chief wished to defer to this stranger, he would go along with it. That didn't necessarily mean that he was wholehearted in his devotions. Let Thompson assume the full responsibility lest there be trouble.

It was a brief silence, an even briefer stumble in the wall of authority that emanated from the caravan's leading trio, but it was enough to enable Ryan to jump into the breach and seize the initiative.

"Can I suggest that my people go and look over the huts by ourselves? That way, none of your people will be at risk. Perhaps we can offer you some answers, if only in the way we buy the farm."

Thompson was suspicious. Why would anyone willingly walk into a trap? Yet he didn't understand Ryan's reasoning. He had no idea that the previous explosion had been down to his own men, even though at least half the tribe had guessed as much. The chief had become so swept up in the messianic fervor stirred by Jordan that he couldn't conceive of his own people going against the word of the stranger.

McPhee, on the other hand, was determined to keep to himself and see how things panned out before committing himself. He allowed the ghost of a smile to flicker across his lips as he watched the one-eyed man carefully phrase his request, and immediately understood Ryan's position. He wasn't so blinded by the stranger as to see the hostility the outsiders had provoked among certain sections of the tribe. And he had his suspicions about McIndoe…

"That's an excellent idea," he said to Thompson and Jordan, adding, "You were right about the courage shown by these warriors."

Jordan, snapped from his reverie by this praise for his acumen, responded almost without thinking. "Aye, they are noble fighters, indeed. Aye, Ryan Cawdor, ye must undertake the mission as ye requested."

Ryan assented and indicated to his people that they should move toward the three-hut settlement at speed: partly for the reason that anyone still within the cabins would know they were coming and therefore speed was of the essence; and partly to prevent any of the Inuit stopping them, or attempting to join them. Although they would, as ever, exercise caution, they knew that the real danger lay to their rear rather than in front of them.

Ryan indicated that they spread out, making themselves harder targets to hit with one burst. There was little to no cover between the point on the trail where the caravan waited and the area taken up by the three huts.

They traveled swiftly over the rock and ice, weapons to hand even though all were sure that the cabins were deserted. There was a stillness about them that betrayed their desolation. Still, triple red and no chances taken was the only way to keep from buying the farm.

They fanned out so that they approached the settlement in a semicircle, with Jak and J.B. on each extremity, circling around to cover the rear as much as possible. Ryan was in the middle, forging a path to the center of their target, flanked by Krysty and Mildred.

Jak relaxed as he rounded the outside of the triangle formed by the huts. Whatever life he could smell was stale: old scents left by those—human and animal—that had departed. All he could hear was the sound of his own breathing, slow and steady. There were no other noises from within the cluster of wood, cinder-block and metal that comprised the three huts. Yet, even though he relaxed, he still kept his .357 Magnum Colt Python tight in his grasp. His instincts had never led him wrong before, but it would take only one, all-too rare occasion to wipe him from the face of the earth. If that was going to be now, then at least he would be prepared and go down fighting.

It was an attitude that was shared by his fellows. To a lesser degree than the albino hunter, they had all developed and honed instincts that told them when danger threatened. Without these, they would long ago have been chilled. Right now, those instincts were telling them that the settlement was deserted. But caution was an instinct that had grown as strong and served them as well.

From a distance, as the Inuit watched them, it seemed to Thompson that they were taking an inordinate amount of time. Doubts about their abilities, given such apparent overcaution, plagued him. But how to phrase them without appearing to cross the stranger?

"Place seems empty," he began haltingly, "but I guess they have to be that careful, don't they?"

Jordan eyed him with a sly grin. "Do not worry yourself, my friend. They are true warriors, and they know that whatever the situation, the one without caution is the one who doesn't come back. Trust in them."

Easier said than done, thought the medicine man as

he watched his chief nod stupidly to the stranger. Although he believed that Jordan had come to guide them, sent by the Almighty, there was still that element of skepticism and caution in his mind that warned him not to follow slavishly. The man may have been sent by the Lord, but that didn't mean that he knew shit about fighting in this world.

Unaware of the exchanges that continued to their rear, Ryan's companions had fanned out and surrounded the three huts. The absolute still of the settlement told them that it was deserted. From their points around the settlement they could clearly see one another—indeed, they could have clearly been seen from inside the cabins and would surely have been attacked by now if the settlement was populated—and Ryan indicated that they close in.

In a tightening circle, they moved toward the cabins. The cinder-block hut to one side was open to the elements and had obviously been used to house dogs. The inside was clearly visible, the pen door thrust wide and the smell from within confirmation of its purpose. That was now out of the running. There were just the two cabins, the windows of which were intact and blankly staring out at them. The doors were closed. As with most of the cabins they had seen on this trek, the design was simple and functional: two windows for light and a view of the outside; a solid wooden door; the remainder built firm, with no other ingress or egress, designed solely to combat the elements and reduce the heat loss from within.

It meant that whoever may be within was trapped, yet at the same time secure as there were only three spots to defend from attack.

The only way to tackle these cabins was full-on: Ryan, Mildred and Krysty took one; Jak and J.B. the other. One member of the party attacked the door, while the others flanked them, ready to provide cover if necessary.

It was over in a second. The two men taking the entrance to each hut tried the doors. They were unlocked, opening outward. Pulled to their fullest extent, they allowed a wide-angled view of the interior while also framing their target in the portal. Ryan and Jak both went low as they pulled at the doors, making themselves as small as possible and scanning for any enemy within.

There was none. As their instincts had told them, the cabins were long since deserted.

J.B. joined Jak in his cabin, shouldering the M-4000 he had been ready to use in this instance. A spreading load of barbed-metal fléchettes from the weapon would have been the simplest and most effective one-shot within such an enclosed space.

"Looks like they left in a hurry, but of their own accord," he noted, taking in the contents of the cabin.

Jak agreed, his eyes roaming the interior. There were three beds in the cabin, each covered in filthy blankets and furs. A small table stood near the stove and on it were plates covered in scraps of food that had congealed. The floor was scattered with clothes and stray shells, as though spilled from a pack. It looked as though the contents had been packed in a hurry, but there was no sign of destruction or forced entry as there had been in the small villes they had seen along the trail.

Jak leaned over the plates and sniffed them, then tentatively felt the stove. Frowning, he opened the door to the grate and sifted the ashes gathered.

"Mebbe twenty hours since went—mebbe less," he said, ruminatively rubbing the powdered ash between his fingers.

"So where would they go in such a hurry?" J.B. queried.

"Or why?" Jak returned.

In truth, both men suspected the answer. They left the cabin and walked over to its adjacent companion, where Ryan, Mildred and Krysty were inside.

In essence, this cabin was the same as its partner. It had been stripped of most things, and seemingly in a hurry. There were two beds here, and a larger table that had a battered and rusting tin chest beneath it. As Jak and J.B. entered, Ryan had just pulled the chest from beneath the table and was opening it.

"Looks like they shot through in a panic," Mildred remarked to the two newcomers, indicating the surrounding area. The beds were covered in disheveled furs, with a couple of empty plates lying on top. There were a few clothes also heaped on the bed, as though discarded at the last moment, and a wooden box that had a stenciled reference on the side. J.B. recognized it immediately as a predark case that would have contained ammo for a Heckler & Koch MP-5, the boxes of ammo cased in the wooden container for easy transport. At a guess, there had been little left in the case; whoever had fled the cabin had decided it would be easier to carry the ammo another way.

Which meant they had been in one hell of a hurry.

The table had been cleared before the inhabitants left, and Ryan hefted the tin box onto the rough, scarred top. It was lighter than he had expected and he found that it was more than half-empty. There were old photographs and papers jammed together in a haphazard fashion, some of which had succumbed to damp and mildew over the years and were stuck together and unreadable. Ryan pulled out some of the photographs and passed them to Mildred.

She thumbed through them and could see that they were a mixed collection of snapshots from the twentieth century. Some were old black-and-white photographs that had almost faded to sepia that she could pin down as being either from the twenties or the forties by the fashions and hairstyles. It had been a long time since she had seen such things, and it surprised her that she could still remember enough to place the period with such accuracy.

Others of the snapshots were in color and from the last thirty years of the century. These she was able to place and date with a much greater accuracy as the fashions and hairstyles were those during her time. In some instances she was able to identify the exact year from some seemingly inconsequential feature of the snap: a slogan on a T-shirt, a billboard in the background.

She felt a tear prickle at the corner of her eye. It had been a long time—too long—since her old life had tapped her on the shoulder in such a way. It was an ache that was painful yet at the same time pleasant: to recall those days reminded her of a part of herself that she had been forced to bury. To have that bubble to the surface was good. That it was still there at all was something of a miracle.

Yet as she looked at the snapshots, there was something about them that seemed odd. The people in them didn't appear to be related in any way and the locations seemed to be from all parts of the U.S., with no rhyme or reason to them. It was as though someone had just collected these photographs whenever they had come across them. Why? To recall a world they had never known? To satisfy their curiosity at what life had been like before the hardship they now endured?

Ryan was wondering much the same thing. The papers left in the tin box told him nothing. A collection of letters to and from people that appeared unconnected, pages torn from magazines, old newsprint that crumbled to the touch, half a paperbacked book and some invoices and receipts for products and services that had been obsolete for well over a century.

It seemed a completely random collection. But only half. What had happened to the top layers of the chest? And did they have any relevance to the mission of which the companions were now engaged?

It appeared unlikely, but this train of thought had its own reward. Scanning the walls, Ryan could see patches where some hangings had been taken down and carried away in the flight: but other things remained. Among these was a map of the area, drawn by hand. A scrawled note along the top edge read, "Trale from volcano to Ankridge," with a compass marking beside it.

"Who the hell lived here?" Ryan muttered to himself as he examined the map.

"Someone who could have been something at another time," Mildred murmured in reply, putting the photographs back into the chest.

Krysty joined Ryan at the map. "I'd like to know how accurate this is, and how they got to draw it," she commented.

"Figure whoever did it must have used the trail often, and not just to go to Ank Ridge and back. This takes us back past the slopes, and I think they must have scaled the volcano slope to get a good look at the territory. Think about it. It's flat all around here, and if you were to risk getting far enough up, you could see the surrounding area probably all the way to the sea."

"Look," J.B. interjected, indicating a point on the map just beyond where they now stood. He had joined them to examine the map and had been drawn to one particular spot.

"Fireblast, that's going to fuck things up," Ryan breathed as the implication of J.B.'s discovery hit him.

The Armorer's finger was on the part of the trail that passed Fairbanks. It indicated that the land had shifted, forming an incline that had collapsed into a valley. About twenty miles in circumference, it formed a bowl in which the ville of Fairbanks was set.

They would have to approach the ville from above and would be a sitting target as they descended the slope with little or no cover.

"Aw, shit, this is bad, isn't it?" Mildred moaned as she realized what had caused Ryan's exclamation. "It's bad enough that we were coming on them on a flat plain that didn't offer cover. Now we've got to try to get down into a valley where they'll be barricaded and we'll be in the open."

"Shit!" Jak exclaimed. "They know we're coming by now."

"Why?" Ryan queried.

Jak shook his head. "How easy see us coming over land? One hunter from here on ice, see us coming, know what happened in other villes... Not hard guess what we want. That's why they gone. Bet they gone to Fairbanks. With twenty hour start."

"Dark night, that ville's gonna be locked up tighter than a gaudy's pussy when you've got no jack," J.B. murmured.

"Say that one again," Ryan lamented. "So how we gonna break this to Thompson and Jordan?"

"Uh, carefully," Mildred said wryly.

THE REACTIONS of the three men who were leading the attack were certainly instructive when Ryan and the companions rejoined them and relayed what they had found, and the conclusions they had drawn.

Thompson was thrown. It was apparent that he hadn't considered that their force may be visible enough to give early warning. To him, the trappers and hunters who lived in the isolated settlements between the volcano's lower slopes and Fairbanks would be far too preoccupied with their every day existence to notice the encroaching forces. And even if they did, they could be taken by force and eradicated. The fact that Fairbanks may now be awaiting their arrival with hostile intent was a factor that he hadn't considered, and had no contingency plans to implement.

Jordan took it all in his stride. "So they will be ready for us. A sacrifice that is hard-won is all the sweeter. They will die a more noble death as warriors if it is battle, and not in a halfhearted defense of an attack from the blindside."

McPhee kept his own counsel, but couldn't disguise an askance glance at the chief and the stranger that suggested he felt that one was out of his depth, the other verging on insanity. McPhee had to follow the chief; the evidence of his own senses suggested that Jordan was what he claimed to be. And yet his seeming disregard for tactics beyond a plan to charge head-on into a glorious war that may result in a pointless and Pyrrhic victory suggested that he didn't have the grasp on reality that he suggested.

McPhee cast a surreptitious view around the tribe. Those who were close enough could hear what Ryan told Thompson and Jordan. To the companions, they would remain as inscrutable and unreadable as before, but to the shaman, who knew them well and was of them, it was evident that an uncertainty spread through them. They had a communication that was based on body language and the slightest of gesture; through this, the unease felt by those closest to the chief spread through the ranks.

Unease could mean vacillation at a crucial moment. The shaman was no fool. He was aware, even if Thompson and Jordan chose to ignore it, that many in the tribe were unhappy at having the strangers in the war party. Furthermore, he was certain that the trap in the last large ville had been down to McIndoe. The medicine man now began to weigh options in his mind. If the sec chief was against the outsiders, then perhaps he felt a lack of confidence with the chief and the supposed voice of the Almighty. Being sec chief, he would carry the support of most of his men and perhaps many of the other tribe members now that this latest revelation had sent a shiver through the ranks.

Perhaps it would be a good time for him to cultivate McIndoe. As a good pragmatist, McPhee was an old man who wanted to live to be a little older. Whatever that may take.

A FEW HOURS remained until they reached Fairbanks. As they marched, the companions became aware that they were slowly ascending the land-shift. It was a very small gradient over a long distance. This could account for why it was barely visible, as the distant horizon seemed to be stretching flat out in front of them. It would also explain why the bulky outline of a ville the size of Fairbanks was lost to them. All that appeared was another group of cabins that housed trappers, off to one side of the trail.

Thompson sent the companions off to recce the cabins: three, this time, with two cinder-block structures adjoining, that had housed livestock. All five buildings were empty and showed signs of being vacated with some haste. There was little else to see and no time in which to conduct a thorough search. This time, there were eight beds in the three cabins, and a greater number of dogs, perhaps some other livestock that had been loosed or taken. Two of the beds suggested that these trappers numbered children among them, and in view of what the Inuit would probably have done to them, Ryan was relieved that they had fled. To chill children in cold blood was against the grain, and he would have found it hard to hold back, even though greatly outnumbered, and he knew his people well enough to know that they felt the same.

They reported back the condition of the settlement and left it behind them, the mood within the tribe growing as dark as the skies above them, the hours of daylight bleeding fast away. To mount their attack by night, even if only by chance, would give them a greater chance of success, as it would mean that the night gave them greater concealment. And yet the tribe had been marching all day, and would fight better for rest, even if only a few hours. The companions were aware of the mood changes within the tribe and had noted the resignation with which Thompson had received the news of yet another settlement where the inhabitants had fled to the comparative safety of Fairbanks.

"Do you think he has a plan for the firefight, or are we just supposed to run, shout and shoot?" J.B. muttered to Ryan in dry tones as they marched.

"I don't think he'd know how to find his ass with both hands," Ryan replied. "But it wouldn't matter shit if we could rely on McIndoe. He's a good fighter and he will have thought about a strategy. Problem is, part of that strategy will be us getting our own asses hung out to dry."

At the head of the caravan, Thompson brought them to a halt. Jordan signaled back for Ryan to bring his people forward.

"It lays over the ridge," he said without preamble as they approached. "Like ye, I have never seen the place. The others are familiar with it, but before we plan, it would perhaps be as well to take a look."

Sounded like a good idea to Ryan, so he agreed, allowing Jordan to lead them to the lip of the incline. From the valley below, the glow of lamps lighted against the encroaching dark cast a faint glow in the air. Lowering themselves lest there were observers below, they approached the edge of the incline. It fell away relatively steeply, falling around fifty feet in total over a length less than a quarter mile.

Below them, in the basin of the valley, the ville of Fairbanks stood. It was their first sight, and whatever they had expected up to this point, those notions were now dismissed.

"It will be an intriguing challenge, will it not?" Jordan asked of them.

"That isn't the word I'd use," Mildred answered. "If they know we're coming—and it's fairly certain they do—then we are well and truly screwed.'

Chapter Sixteen

The sight that greeted them presented a challenge that would be, at the very least, formidable. At most, it would be a headlong charge into disaster.

Fairbanks lay in the bowl of the valley, a collection of about one hundred buildings, some of which were small shacks that housed only one or two, but the majority of which were larger buildings, some of two or three stories, that were either used to house several people or as places of trade and entertainment.

A faint buzz of music and chatter drifted up from the valley below, the lip of the incline cutting down on the harsh winds that blew across the plain, allowing the gentler currents of air coming from below to lift the heat of the ville, and the sounds of its life, until it reached their ears. The music was discordant, played on out-of-tune instruments, with singing that was even less mellifluous laid over the rhythmic base. The conversations that were carried on simultaneously formed an excited buzz. Words weren't discernible, but the tones and frequencies of the sounds betrayed a certain excitement that was running through the ville.

If only on a rough estimate, based solely on the buildings and the sounds rather than any sight of them, Ryan guessed that the Inuit were outnumbered by the ville people—perhaps as much as two to one. They had seen villes that size and with that kind of construction. The valley location gave it shelter, and the old predark buildings that had survived had been augmented by cabins and constructions that had added to the size and security of the ville. Fate had protected it when the earth shifted, and those who made their homes in this barren area had welcomed the slight respite it gave, banding together gladly.

It wasn't enough that they were outnumbered, and that the solid state of the ville gave it an impenetrable look, giving those warriors protection while the Inuit had to approach down the exposed sides of the valley. There was one other thing that made Ryan feel the whole mission was a suicide charge. A feeling he didn't experience alone.

"Someone chill me now, 'cause that's all we'll be doing if we take this on." Mildred sighed with a barely disguised exasperation.

"Thompson must have known. He must have. So why didn't he say anything?" Krysty added.

"Because we not come—make break and risk buying farm then, not walk gladly into chill," Jak commented before spitting heavily on the ground, the sputum acting as an emphasis to his disapproval.

"I can see why he wouldn't tell us, but did he tell you?" J.B. added, directing his comment to Jordan.

The stranger within Doc had stayed silent while the others had expressed their disgust. Ryan had been watching the old man carefully, to see if the shock would cause any more of Doc to try to break through. Possession or madness, he didn't care. The point was that inside the head now inhabited by the personality of

Jordan, Doc Tanner still lurked. They had seen a brief glimpse of him, and if he were to reemerge, then it would ease their attempts to try to extricate themselves—and the man himself—from their predicament.

"I had no idea," Jordan replied slowly. "They didnae tell me. From the way it was described, it was an ordinary wee town, not something that looked like Edinburgh ready for an English siege."

Ryan had no idea what that meant. Something that the personality calling itself Jordan had dragged from its memory centuries before. But there was no mistaking the tone and emotion of the voice in which he spoke those words. Jordan was having doubts about the success of the holy mission.

And, frankly, Ryan couldn't blame him. For the thing that made the ville of Fairbanks appear impregnable was the wall that stretched around the perimeter, forming a ring that had only one way in and one way out. It was not the first time they had come across a ville that was protected in such a way. Indeed, for a larger ville that had been built from predark remains and had been established since people first began to crawl from the nukecaust, it was an obvious move. But there had never been a wall quite like this before.

It had no sec posts. There was little need, as to try to scale it would prove to be impossible. The wall was partly constructed of rock hewn from the sides of the valley, and partly from huge blocks of ice that had been ripped from the land around. These rocks and ice blocks had been built into a construction that stood as high as some of the two-story buildings—perhaps forty feet, perhaps a little less, it was hard to judge when looking down into the valley—with jagged edges that would have given a plenitude of foot- and handholds if not for one simple precaution: when the wall had been built, it had been covered with water that had frozen into a layer of ice that now made the ascent of the defense nothing short of impossible. No doubt that, as the weather gradually chipped at the sheet ice, so it was replenished in those areas that the elements themselves didn't refresh. It was a bold move of simple genius. Using the constant low temperature to furnish a defense that did away with the need for manpower.

As for the only entrance, it consisted of a set of doors less than half the height of the wall, cobbled together from wood and metal sheeting. On each side was a tower with a covered crow's nest atop that housed—as far as could be seen—two men per nest. The doors looked flimsy in comparison to the wall, but then they didn't have to be strong. A force bottlenecked into attacking through this one spot would be easy pickings for both the sec men in the crow's nest and for any armed citizens who waited patiently behind the last line of defense.

Short of sending out parties to mine the wall, thus blowing great chunks from it to gain access, there was little that could be done to breach the defenses with any degree of success. As Ryan looked to his people, he could see that they felt the same way. Come to that, he could tell from the expression on Jordan's face that he, too, shared those thoughts.

But what was Thompson's great plan? Did he have one?

They had to find out. Ryan began to pull back from the lip of the valley. Unless the Fairbanks sec had sec scouts, they would be aware that the Inuit were com-

ing, but not that they'd actually arrived. The downside
to the ville's splendid isolation was that such a scout
party would be hard to send out covertly. It was reasonable to assume that they had some time in which to
rest and form a strategy.

So they'd better use that time wisely.

FOLLOWING RYAN'S LEAD, Jordan pulled back with the
rest of the companions and headed straight for the chief,
who was seated in a small group that also contained
McPhee and McIndoe as well as the sec chief's trusted
lieutenants. Jordan strode ahead of the companions and
heatedly began to shout before he was upon them.

"Ye did not tell me of the walls—like Edinburgh, like
Jericho. Saints alive, man, do ye expect us to shout and
the whole thing comes tumbling down upon the
enemy?"

Thompson said nothing. His expression betrayed little, but his frozen posture suggested he was taken aback
by the sudden explosive anger of the stranger.

It was McPhee who answered. "Surely the Almighty
will guide you in this, as he will us," he said carefully.
"Should you not have your own plans?"

"Plans!" the stranger roared. "How can I have plans
when I had no idea what the damn town looked like
until a few minutes ago? Ye people are the ones who
live here—"

"Then what about your mighty warriors?" McIndoe
cut in. "Isn't it time they proved their worth?"

Ryan found it hard to keep a sardonic smile from tugging at the corners of his mouth. He had to admire the
smoothness with which the sec chief had shifted the
whole responsibility of the attack and put those he hated

in the front line at the same time. It was just unfortunate for him that Ryan had a few ideas.

"There is something we can do. If—and only if—you've got anything more than blasters in your armory."

"Yeah, like some more of that plas-ex," J.B. added pointedly, having followed Ryan's reasoning.

"We have some plas-ex," McIndoe replied blandly, letting the implication drift past him.

"Good. Then we may be able to get this attack going," Ryan said. "If you've got the balls to help us."

"HOW THE HELL do I get myself into this kind of shit?" Mildred whispered.

"How the hell do any of us get into this kind of shit?" Krysty murmured by way of reply.

They had circled the perimeter of the valley and were now approaching the wall around the rear of Fairbanks, almost 180 degrees from where the majority of the Inuit rested, awaiting first light and the beginnings of an all-out firefight. They had scrambled down the incline and kept low as they ran across the flat valley floor toward the wall, armed with plas-ex and detonators.

They weren't alone. Ryan's plan had been simple and had quickly enthused both Jordan and the Inuit leader as a certain way to gain egress to the ville. McPhee had kept his own counsel, and in a sense Ryan didn't blame him. It was a strategy, but it was in no way a certainty to obtain the desired result. It was a possible solution, and—perhaps more importantly for Ryan's people—it would enable them to test the resolve of McIndoe and his sec force. Would they take this as a chance to try to eradicate the companions, or would they put that to one side and treat it as a chance to make their mission successful?

If the former, then it would be one-on-one, and Ryan's people could take on some of their enemy, sending a message to those who would try to take them out. If the latter, then it would mean that their attention was now focused on their primary objective. This being the case, it would possibly make it easier for the companions to snatch Doc and make their escape in the chaos that was sure to ensue.

Either way, it would have a bearing on Ryan's future strategy.

So it was that five parties of two were armed with what J.B. estimated as enough plas-ex to blow holes in the wall, making points of entry and possibly weakening the structure enough to cause a chain of collapse around the circumference. This last would be difficult to achieve. J.B. had little more than a glimpse at a distance, and in the dark, on which to base any calculations. Any success would therefore be more luck than judgment, and any resulting collapses beyond the points of explosion a bonus.

Mildred and Krysty were paired, while Jak and J.B. moved together. Ryan chose to go with McIndoe. It would give him a chance to sound out the sec chief. Four other Inuit sec warriors were paired.

Each team was given enough plas-ex to cause the requisite damage, and instructed on where to place it on the wall. J.B. was surprised to find that Inuit had a large stock of explosives, which he could only attribute to stockpiling from the villes they had earlier decimated. If nothing else, it explained why the sec chief had been so free with the explosive he had used to try to blow them all the way to the farm. The fact that he was now revealing this to them did little to allay J.B.'s concerns, although he could understand Ryan's tactic in trying to draw the hostile Inuit faction into the open, forcing them to either stand and fight or sublimate their hostility to the greater cause.

Regardless, Ryan arranged it so that each Inuit pair was split by a pair comprised of his people, and he and McIndoe made the most difficult assault of all: that upon the front of the wall, having to plant plas-ex as near to the entrance as possible without detection. The one-eyed warrior reasoned that this would be the advance that would determine how the Inuit sec man would play out the whole combat situation.

So while he and the impassive Inuit advanced silently down the slope, trying to pick out the few brief respites of shadow offered by the contours of the steep slope as they descended quickly to the valley floor, the other parties set off around the lip of the valley and began their own descents. Ryan used his wrist chron to count off the start times for those who had the farthest to travel, trying as best he could to stagger the parties so that they would be planting their plas-ex and setting their detonators with as much synchronization as was possible.

Mildred and Krysty, as the pair who had the farthest to go before beginning descent, had set off before any of the others, and by the time they were on the valley floor they were both beginning to feel the effects of the journey.

They came upon the wall without being detected. They could sacrifice speed for stealth as there were no sentries on this darkened side, the night being accentuated by the shadow of the rock and ice.

"Shit, I can see why they don't bother guarding this,"

Mildred breathed as she reached out to touch the surface of the wall. The ice covering the block construction was slick and beyond cold—it almost burned to touch.

"Bastard to climb, all right," Krysty commented, "but more to the point, how the hell do we get the plas-ex into the wall?"

"I was kind of hoping you'd tell me that," Mildred whispered. She stepped back and looked up at the towering construction. About five feet above her head, a patch of ice had cracked and fallen, leaving a crevice between rock and ice block that could hold a charge. The problem would be gaining the height. Climbing the rock would be impossible. Only one thing for it. "How strong you feeling, girl?" Mildred asked.

Krysty followed her eyes up to the point in the rock. "Why me? Why can't I be the one who places the charge?"

"'Cause I've got no Gaia power to call on if you dislocate my shoulder?" Mildred queried with a grin. "Besides, I called it first."

"Can't argue with that, can I?" Krysty murmured wryly. She dropped to one knee and Mildred clambered onto her shoulders. Steadying the pair of them, Krysty carefully climbed to her feet and advanced slowly, planting her legs apart in front of the wall to try to spread the weight and balance.

When Mildred felt that Krysty was solid, she carefully raised herself, one foot at a time, until she was no longer kneeling, but standing on Krysty's shoulders. She tried to balance speed with the desire to avoid causing Krysty pain—discomfort was an inevitability—and winced on her friend's behalf as she felt the woman's

shoulder muscles tense beneath her boots and heard
Krysty's breathing grow more labored.

Ultimately, it was simply a fact that Krysty was taller
and had a more developed musculature than Mildred.
It made sense for the smaller woman to plant the
plas-ex. But this didn't prevent a twinge of guilt as she
fumbled for the gap between the rock and ice, wasting
precious seconds. She gently prodded the pliable
plas-ex into the gap, then set the detonator before placing it in the explosive.

It was tempting to jump down and spare Krysty another second of agony, but she was aware that one
wrong landing could make things harder. A turned,
sprained or broken ankle at this point would really
screw things. So she lowered herself carefully, Krysty's
hands reaching up to guide her down.

"How the hell could you get fat on the slop we've
been eating lately?" Krysty gasped with as much good
humor as she could muster.

"Just my age, I guess," Mildred returned. She looked
along the curve of the wall. "Doesn't look like the tribe
is interested in getting rid of us right now. I just hope
they've got their charges planted."

"More than we have," Krysty said, dropping onto one
knee. "Think we can make enough of an impression
down here to get the second charge planted well
enough?"

"Just do our best." Mildred shrugged, joining her.

They chipped out a small section of the ice at the foot
of the wall, using a knife given them by Jak to dig out
the hard earth underneath the overlap of ice and lever-
ing up a section, almost snapping the blade before the
ice cracked enough to give them a small hole at the bot-

tom. Some of the charge would blow out into the earth rather than into the rock and ice, but there wasn't the time to make a further impression. They would have to hope that this blast, combined with that of the higher charge, would be enough to have the desired effect.

Charges now planted, the two women made their way back across the valley floor, keeping a steady pace. They needed to be swift, but the efforts of planting the charges had taken a toll and the ascent up the steep valley side would take no little effort. The rock and ice were slippery underfoot, with little to assist them on their passage to the top. Muscles in their calves and thighs burned with the effort of climbing such a sheer incline at such speed. It was with relief that they made the top, pausing for only a second to catch their breath before starting the long haul back to the Inuit camp.

At least they hadn't been attacked by rogue Inuit. Ryan had sent them the farthest, despite the extra effort, as he reasoned that the rear of the wall would be the safest spot. J.B. and Jak had taken an area that could still, at a pinch, be seen from the crow's nests. This demanded more caution and the greater stealth skills of the albino youth and the Armorer. Like Mildred and Krysty, they had found the most difficult part of the task was actually finding somewhere in the ice wall that would take the charges.

Once they had placed them, they had little problem in getting back to the base camp, where Jordan was waiting anxiously for them, flanked by Thompson and McPhee, who was now finding it hard to mask his skepticism about the whole attack.

Like Mildred and Krysty, they had encountered no problem with the Inuit sec men who had been dispatched at the same time, and figured as their distaff companions that the Inuit would save any attempts to be rid of them until the full-scale attack took place. Indeed, when they returned, they found that one of the Inuit teams had already returned. Before too long, the second Inuit team joined them, with Mildred and Krysty not far behind.

"Did ye do the job well?" Jordan asked each of them as they arrived.

"Did the job—have to wait to see how well," J.B. answered for all of them.

There was only one pair who hadn't yet returned. The companions exchanged wondering glances. What was going on? Ryan and McIndoe had the least distance to cover. What was keeping them?

THE DESCENT TO THE VALLEY floor had been painfully slow. With the Inuit camp enough distance back to insure that even the sheltered fires wouldn't cast enough of a glow to be picked up by the Fairbanks sentries, the last thing that the advancing pair wished to do would be to alert the men in the crow's nests by their own lack of caution. There was little that could be used as cover, and both men were frustrated by the lack of time as they reached the floor of the valley. In many ways, this presented the same problem magnified. The glow of light from the ville spread over the low gates and out across the valley floor.

There were, however, advantages to this. Beyond the cone of light, the contrast with this and the darkness was greater, which gave them some space in which to maneuver; and the sounds of the ville that also spilled out into the valley could possibly be so loud to the ears

of the sentries as to make anything on the outside hard
to detect.

Ryan's plan was simple. Each man took a parcel of
plas-ex and ran—on each side of the cone of light—
until he reached the wall. Once there, he found a way
to plant the explosive by a pivotal point—a hinge, say—
of the door, then get the hell back to rendezvous at the
point on which they now stood.

McIndoe eyed Ryan suspiciously, as though mentally checking through the plan for any possible catch
that may leave him exposed. He could find none, but
still he paused. Ryan wondered if the sec chief was trying to work out a way in which he could entrap his foe
and yet get away himself.

"Listen, you stupe bastard," Ryan snarled, patience
now gone, "I know you tried to chill us, and I know you
don't want us here. But what do you want more—for
your mission to succeed or to get rid of us? If we're still
standing at the end of the firefight, then we sort this out.
Until then, we're pulling in the same direction because
neither of us wants to buy the farm. Does that make
sense to you?"

If the Inuit was surprised by Ryan's sudden cold
statement of fact, he wouldn't betray his feelings. Instead he considered the words, then nodded briefly.
"Okay. I tell my men. Until we all last ones standing,
then we don't waste energy trying to chill you. But
after…"

"Good enough for me," Ryan snapped. "Now let's
get this done."

The two men parted company. Ryan's instincts told
him that he could trust the Inuit sec chief so far. The battle for Fairbanks, now they were here, was the greater

target. It was one factor less to consider. Now he could only hope that none of the Inuit on the explosives parties had been given prior orders to try to surreptitiously wipe out Jak and J.B., or Mildred and Krysty.

But there was little time to worry about that right now. Using the darkness along the perimeters of the light cone, and the cover of the noise, Ryan had soon made the wall. He discovered the almost glasslike ice covering and cursed to himself as he searched for cracks. He dare not try to force an opening, as he could see the men in the crow's nest from where he was standing. He edged closer to the wood and metal doors.

Here was opportunity. The roughly hewn doors were ill-fitting, and where panels of wood and metal had been joined together were seams large enough for plas-ex charges. The hinged sections were also poorly fitting, gaps appearing between door and wall.

His problem was to fit the plas-ex and detonator without being overheard or spotted by the sec men who hovered less than several feet above him. Despite the extreme cold he could feel the sweat gather in the small of his back and trickle down his forehead, stinging in his good eye and slipping beneath the patch into the puckered and empty socket, as he worked the plas-ex into the gaps, priming the detonator. He kept looking up, almost able to smell the musk of body heat and animal skin from the guards above him. He was sure that he had to be visible in the light, at least partially. Certainly, as he looked across the twenty-foot divide that was the double-door span, he could see McIndoe working feverishly at his own task.

The Inuit finished, looked across and spotted Ryan. He gestured him to move back into shadow as he withdrew.

Ryan placed the last detonator and stepped back, looking up as he did. The men in the crow's nests had their gazes fixed on the ridge that defined the height of the valley. It hadn't occurred to them to look down.

Breathing a sigh of relief, Ryan pulled back into the shadows and made his way to the point of cover where McIndoe was waiting.

"Careless for one who say so much the other way," the sec chief commented. "Come, we don't have much time. Others must be back by now."

Ryan checked his wrist chron. The Inuit was probably right. And daylight would come soon.

They began the ascent, each knowing that before they had time to rest adequately, they would once again be making the descent. But this time more openly, in an all-out attack.

Chapter Seventeen

Dawn broke on the Inuit as they began to separate and prepare for attack. They were still far enough from the lip of the valley to be invisible to the inhabitants of the ville below, and could move with some freedom as long as they kept the noise to a minimum, something at which the Inuit were adept.

Jordan and Thompson consulted with McIndoe while the shaman looked on askance. It seemed more and more obvious that the old man wished to distance himself from the leadership, lest anything should go badly awry. From their small grouping, the companions could observe this with impunity.

"Reckon Doc got strategy get this right?" Jak asked in a tone of voice that suggested it was the closest he would ever get to a rhetorical question.

"Who knows what's going through that mad bastard's head at any time?" Ryan replied. "It's not Doc who bothers me. What does Thompson know about this kind of firefight, and what is McIndoe going to do to help him?"

"You figure he knows what he's doing?" J.B. queried.

"Who? McIndoe?" Ryan allowed himself a short, humorless laugh. "I'd say that bastard knows exactly what he's doing. Question is, who's he doing it for? If he's gonna set up Thompson to take a fall on this, then where does that leave Doc?"

"Where does it leave us?" Krysty interjected. "We've got to get ourselves out of here, and try to get Doc before we hightail it. So if McIndoe decides that he's going to put us right in the firing line to buy the farm, then how do we get ourselves out of that—and get Doc into the bargain—without the Inuit turning on us?"

"If I knew that…" Ryan began, petering out with a shrug.

"So it's just a matter of looking for the chance and grabbing it triple fast, before they have a chance to figure out what we're doing, right?" Mildred asked. From her tone, it was most definitely a rhetorical question.

Before they had a chance to discuss the matter further, the conference group in the distance broke up and Thompson came bustling toward them, with Doc striding behind him. Trailing them, beckoned by the chief but showing a distinct lack of enthusiasm, came McPhee. He had the air of someone who would rather be anywhere else than here. McIndoe, watched by Ryan, moved off to start dividing the Inuit into combat units. On the faces of those closest to the companions he could see the set determination shine through their normally impassive visages as they watched their sec chief.

The way these people fought, they wouldn't rest until they enemy was chilled or they had themselves bought the farm in the attempt. A noble determination, but one that would cause problems when the companions were attempting to extricate themselves from a combat into which they had been unwillingly pitched.

By the time the trio reached them, Doc's long stride had put him in the lead of the group. The closer he got, the easier it was to see the messianic gleam in his eye. His mouth was flecked with white-foamed spittle at the corners, which flew in all directions as he began to speak. The fire of battle had already taken him over.

"Are ye ready? Are ye ready for the war to end all wars? We will save this tribe, and the Almighty will not have sent me in vain. Aye, I cannot tell ye how good it feels to be at the forefront of this noble cause. We have just been discussing tactics and the best way to attack these heathens and take them for our own. I want ye to be in the forefront of this with me, as I know deep in my bones that ye are the finest fighters I have ever had the opportunity of standing shoulder-to-shoulder with, and I know that together we can triumph. Are ye with me?"

"Slow down, slow down," Ryan said, gesturing to Jordan to calm down. "We will join you, but first we have to know what you plan to do."

"Aye, aye, that makes sense," Jordan agreed, nodding maniacally, his eyes betraying that he was hyped up beyond the capacity for rational thought. It was as though a bloodlust had already infected him, before the first shot had been fired. It was no surprise to the companions, particularly to Mildred, who had noticed this tendency to hysteria in Doc Tanner many times before. The old man's psyche was so fragile that it took little to tilt him over the edge.

The fact that Jordan was now reacting the same way suggested that there was more of Doc inside his head than they had any right to expect. This may be a good thing. It was extreme trauma that had brought out the

Jordan persona, so perhaps another extreme trauma would elicit Doc's genuine personality from within once more.

Thompson and McPhee were now with them, and had both noted the stranger's manic fervor. McPhee found it hard to disguise his disquiet with this development—in fact, he could barely be bothered to disguise his unease. But the chief seemed to take it calmly, as though this hysterical behavior were a necessary part of preparing for battle.

Certainly he smoothly took over from the overwrought Jordan in explaining the tactics to the companions.

"We split ourselves into small units, place ourselves around the edge of the valley, moving quickly before the sun is fully up and the plas-ex goes off. Once that's gone, then the fuckers down there will know we're here, so there's no point in hiding. We see what damage the plas-ex has done to the walls, and we try to get through any holes and go for the center of the ville, closing in and driving those we don't chill into the center, where we can fire them up."

"Burn them?" Ryan asked, aghast.

"Of course—that's the old way to sacrifice," Jordan replied suddenly. "We cannot build a wicker man in which to house them, but the city is their body, and so it is the same thing."

Mildred and Krysty exchanged glances. Both knew enough about predark religions and beliefs to know that there was a kind of logic in what Doc-Jordan was saying, but there was something about his driven demeanor that was worrying. This was a man on the verge of a complete mental collapse. And what of the hidden—or lost—Doc persona then?

But now there was little time to worry, as Thompson cut across the old man, keen to explain tactics—and the part the companions would play—before they ran out of time.

"You will come with us—" he gestured to himself, Jordan and the distinctly uneasy-seeming McPhee "—at the forefront of the attack. We will head down into the valley from this point and take the gates as they are blown apart, forming a spearhead into the ville. It is my place to take the head of the attack, and I want you with me as I trust Jordan's views on your capabilities. We have only minutes to prepare, so I leave you to brief your people and join us."

It was possibly the longest speech that any of them had heard the Inuit chief make since they had first arrived on the frozen wastelands, and there was something about the quality of his words that made the chill air of the Alaskan morning run even colder through their blood. In his own way, he was as driven as Jordan, and would willingly go to his own chilling to achieve his purpose.

Thompson turned and walked away, McPhee tailing him with a displeased frown tugging at the corners of his otherwise unreadable face. Doc lingered for a moment, and as he leaned in and spoke to them, there was an edge of his true personality that seemed to break through the thick burr of the Scot Jordan.

"I know I can trust you," he said simply, before turning and striding off in the wake of the chief and the shaman.

"That one crazy man," Jak said softly as Doc departed. "Like man wanting buy farm."

"Yeah, I know what you mean," Ryan replied in an

equally low tone. "If he's gonna be that determined to lead the line, then we're gonna have a hell of a job to get him and ourselves out of this."

"That's going to be a tad difficult if we're leading that line with him," J.B. said wryly. "It'll be all we can do to stop running straight into the farm."

"Yeah, we need to find a way to make sure that we don't head the charge," Ryan mused. "I guess what we really need to do is to persuade Jordan that his interests are best served if mebbe he isn't right at the front, but in the second wave. That way we don't walk headlong into the firefight and we can shelter him."

"Need watch our side, too," Jak added. "Fuckers not like us. Might have agreement with McIndoe, but not know if others keep to it."

"True, and I figure I can trust him, because the stakes are so high for him, but I can't be certain. We need to watch our own backs, mebbe take out some of the Inuit around us so we can clear a path to get the hell out."

"So what you're saying is that we need to watch everyone in case they want to chill us, and try to save some old buzzard who'll want to charge headlong to his own doom," Mildred summed up. "Shit, Ryan, you aren't asking much, are you?"

Ryan allowed a hollow, barking laugh to escape. "Put it like that, it doesn't sound so great, does it?"

"First things first," Krysty said decisively, cutting into the pensive silence that had formed in the vacuum behind Mildred's words. "Let's get Doc where we want him, and I think I may have an idea about that."

THE TIME WAS APPROACHING fast. Too damned fast for McPhee, who sat on his haunches, watching the preparations around him. The majority of the tribe had already dissipated into the half light of the approaching dawn, leaving a number who looked to his jaundiced eye like a pitiful few to take on such a monumental task as storming the gates of Fairbanks. McPhee was no coward. Such a thing was unknown among the Inuit, whose natural disposition was to fight until the bitter end. But there was a world of difference between being a coward and being practical. He was certainly the latter, and could foresee nothing but disaster. No matter how big the holes blown in the walls around the ville, they were still outnumbered and walking into bottlenecks that would leave them lined up like sitting targets.

McPhee just couldn't see the necessity of buying the farm for no reason other than a glorious folly. And this was looking more and more like a glorious folly. His attitude had been changing constantly, his position as medicine man, and the training from childhood that had entailed, clashing with his natural pragmatism.

The pragmatism was winning out. And he certainly didn't trust the outlanders. Why would anyone who you had tried to chill sacrificially then agree to aid you in your task? Because they were offered little choice? Perhaps. But surely that would mean their imperative was to get out as soon as a chance presented itself—as it surely would in the heat of a firefight.

So it was with a jaundiced eye that he saw Krysty leave their group and approach Jordan, who was seated with the chief. She began to talk, and even from such a distance, McPhee could see that her words were making an impression on the stranger.

He decided it would be best to be a participant in whatever was taking place.

As he neared them, he began to catch parts of the conversation. He came in just as Krysty was finishing a long, impassioned speech.

"…right for you to sacrifice yourself. After all, if you've been sent for a reason, then surely it would behoove you to insure that you can see through that purpose?"

"Aye, I can see what ye mean," Jordan replied thoughtfully. "If this is to serve some purpose, it would be ridiculous for myself and the chief to fall before the enemy afore any of that purpose is realized."

"But we have a duty—I do—to lead my people," Thompson said firmly. "I cannot stand down."

"But it would not be standing down," Jordan reasoned. "It would be about strategy, about being there at the right moment, when the people come together, and not about wasting your life before the aim is achieved."

"After all, have you come all this way for nothing?" Krysty added, trying to press the advantage. She could see a shadow of doubt cross the face of the Inuit chief.

McPhee smiled to himself. The fool was going to fall for it. He knew Thompson, knew that the woman had played on his sense of responsibility to the tribe as a whole. This way they would keep themselves and their friend the stranger from the front line of battle without appearing to lose face.

Certainly, it meant that the shaman trusted them no more. However, it would benefit him to play along with this.

"You know, what the woman says makes a lot of sense," he said smoothly as he approached. "We have our own task to fulfill with this sacrificial firefight, and we do not fulfill that by buying the farm at the first moment. If we do, then this whole mission is in vain."

Jordan looked up at the shaman. He wasn't alone in this, but it was his honest, open eyes that fixed on the medicine man. They were trusting, searching for guidance.

"Ye think that this is the right thing? I can see that it is, but somehow feel that I am letting down the people I have been sent to serve."

McPhee shook his head. "No, you would be letting them down by being chilled before we have a chance to make good the sacrifice, before you can save the tribe you were sent to save."

Jordan considered this, then firmly nodded. "Ye are right. I have a sacred duty."

He turned to Thompson. "We must not go at the head of the attack. We must hold back and follow the first wave, so that we can be there when our victorious forces round up those who we shall offer to the Lord."

Thompson affirmed this, and McPhee breathed a silent sigh of relief. For the moment he was assured of a degree of safety.

Krysty left them to return to the rest of the companions; but not without a sense of uncertainty. There was something about the medicine man that made her feel he was working to his agenda...and would have to be watched.

LIGHT SPREAD across the wastelands, wiping out the glow from the valley below. Day slowly moved from the watches of the night, and around the rim of the valley the war parties of Inuit warriors were ready. Gathered in small clusters, waiting at the points where the expeditionary forces had planted the plas-ex a few short hours before, they prepared for the moment when the timed explosions would rent the air, signaling their cue to action.

The sounds of a people waiting for attack came to them from the valley below, drifting up on the breeze: shouting, rough music, the clang of metal. The inhabitants of Fairbanks were on edge, unable to rest, knowing that an attack would come, but not when.

They knew soon enough.

The plas-ex detonators, timed to go off when the day had fully broken, did their work. A string of explosions, less than a few seconds between first and last, echoed around the valley, raising clouds of dust, rock chippings and ice as the explosive rent great holes in the fabric of the Fairbanks defenses. Sections of the wall began to crumble around those holes blasted, cracks spreading, rock grinding against ice as the weight of the wall forced great chunks of rock and ice to topple, triggering further cracks and falls. In some areas, holes blasted by the plas-ex were blocked immediately by falls of rock from around, then reopened as additional ripples of destruction washed away the blockages in waves of shock.

At the gates of the ville, the twin crow's nests were toppled by the blasts that split the metal and wood doors from top to bottom, splintering the thick timbers and sending these splinters on a deadly trajectory, chilling those who were nearest to the explosion. The tumbling nests spilled their screaming occupants, who hit the rock floor of the valley with bone-splintering force. The doors fell in, scattering those who were in the immediate area lest they become squashed like bugs beneath the great weight.

Behind the remnants of the wall, covered in dust, rock and ice fragments, the people milled in confusion. Some were blinded and deafened, concussed by the explosions, smothered in rock dust. They wandered aimlessly, not sure of what to do. They stumbled headlong into those who had been galvanized by the onslaught, and were now spilling from the center of the ville, crowding the narrow streets as they rushed to the ramparts, leaving the gaudy houses, bars, old buildings and newer shanties in which they lived to man the wall and defend their ville; to defend their lives. As they did, they hit those stunned by the explosions, falling over one another, fighting to get out of the way, to get fighting the enemy rather than one another.

It made them an easy target for the first wave of attack.

AS THE EXPLOSIONS SOUNDED, so the Inuit war parties moved forward to the edge of the valley. To this point they had stayed back, so that they couldn't be observed from any vantage point within the ville. Now this no longer mattered. The Fairbanks inhabitants knew they were being attacked and they knew that an enemy was without. Now was the time for the Inuit to press home the advantage the explosions and resultant confusion had given them.

From their starting points around the circumference of the valley, the Inuit moved in, men and women, dogs, sleds and livestock. They hit the edge of the valley and started the steep ascent, half running, half falling, the sleds and dogs tumbling over one another, the beasts whinnying and screeching in fright as they lost balance under their loads, rolling and tumbling before righting themselves at the bottom of the valley. The Inuit warriors also tumbled and rolled as they descended, but they put speed above their own safety, and trusted that they would hit the floor of the valley uninjured. As long as they were on the way down, then they had no shelter, and they were sitting targets for any sharpshooters who may be lining what was left of the walls or coming through the gaps to meet the foe.

Ryan plunged down in the second wave, alongside the rest of the companions, Thompson, McPhee and Jordan. He had barely a second as they reached the lip of the valley to take in what had happened to the walls surrounding the ville.

In this fleeting glimpse he had enough time to note that the majority of the walls had been reduced to rubble. The gates had blown off, and through the gap, beyond the dust that had been raised, he could see the milling crowds, unorganized and confused. He prayed that they would remain this way long enough for his section of the war party to hit the floor of the valley and either try to find cover or head straight into combat. If not, then they were exposed and virtually asking to buy the farm.

Their luck held. The first wave of Inuit tumbling in front of them hit the valley floor running, firing into the crowds as they ran, driving some back into the maze of streets beyond the rubble, cutting others down where they stood, while a few ran the wrong way, coming out to meet the enemy and firing wildly, unable to take aim or form any kind of battle plan. If they were lucky, a stray shell plucked at the layers of skins and furs on the Inuit warriors, perhaps penetrating enough to take them down, if not chill them. Others hit home on dogs or pack mules, sending supplies across the floor of the valley. But none halted the advance, and those few who dared to stand and fire soon found themselves cut down.

Ryan hit the bottom of the valley in a roll, the thick clothing doing little to stop the bone-jarring jolt of the icy rock as he impacted at speed, driving the breath from his body. He got to his feet, shaking his head to clear it, trying to breathe deeply but finding that he was stopped by what felt like his panga blade driven between his ribs. He gulped, his eye watering, the sudden pain making him fall to his knees. He prayed that he hadn't fractured ribs in the fall, making him a sitting target for any enemy sec. And then the spasm passed—painfully, but nonetheless subsiding. He was able to breathe again.

As he did, he cast an anxious glance around. He could see all of his friends had made it down in one piece and were advancing on the broken gates of the city. Krysty spared a fraction of a second to look back to see where he was. Satisfied that he was on his feet, she returned her attention to the battle zone ahead, knowing that just the one glance had been risk enough.

Ryan scrambled to his feet, not wanting to lose sight of his friends in the approaching melee. He could see Thompson, Doc—he couldn't think of him as Jordan right now—and McPhee ahead of them, in the middle of the second wave.

Ryan gained ground on them as he approached the opening to the ville of Fairbanks skipping over the wreckage of the crow's nests as they lay across his path, the bloodied, mangled remains of their inhabitants beneath, laying where they had been thrown before the wreckage followed them down, wiping out whatever chance they may have held of escaping the big chill.

The Inuit had wasted little time in driving the fighters of Fairbanks back into the heart of their own ville, the relentless onslaught of the Inuit taking them by complete surprise. They were still a mix of the dazed and confused, and the ardent defenders: but even these latter had some desire to stay alive and were stunned by the complete disregard of their own safety shown by the Inuit fighters. The tribe moved forward with no fear, with no thought for themselves. Their complete willingness to walk into a hail of fire to gain ground for those following was something for which the Fairbanks fighters had no answer. How do you stop those who didn't wish to be stopped?

As he crossed the line that had once been marked by the now-departed gates, Ryan had little doubt that the Inuit war parties around the circumference of the ville were having the same effect. Their relentless drive would soon compact the conflict into one small area. It would make a massacre easier.

But it would make grabbing Doc and getting out a lot harder.

Chapter Eighteen

If the days leading to this moment had seemed to blur into one, being nothing more than hard slog in an inhospitable climate, then from this point on it seemed as though everything was in slow motion, each fraction of a second forever imprinted on the mind, every image seared on the retina forever.

The adrenaline coursed through the veins of every man, woman and child in the ville of Fairbanks as it was engulfed in the bloodiest battle it had ever witnessed. The walls that had for so long been thought an impregnable defense were now irrevocably breached, and the people within were now besieged by an unstoppable force. No matter what they may have thought before this moment, there was no way that they could have been prepared for the whirlwind of death and destruction that now engulfed them.

The Inuit knew little of these people and how they lived: furthermore, they had no concern. They didn't care, and saw the inhabitants of the ville in the same way that those very people saw the sparse game that they hunted and trapped to eke a living off the unforgiving land.

Ryan and his people, too, knew little of what life had been like in the ville. They could surmise that these were people who lived hard and played hard: trapping and hunting, surviving on what little trade they could do with the few convoys that would come this far north, risking their wags on such hostile terrain. The buildings that now spilled forth fighters, or were consumed by fires started by blasterfire, hand-to-hand combat and grens were used as gaudy houses and bars, the flammable spirits feeding flames that licked at the outsides of the buildings, spreading along streets of old blocks and the ramshackle makeshifts that had been erected in the gaps from the rubble and wreckage.

The people of Fairbanks were mostly Caucasian, with a few who looked as though they may have blood that came from the Inuit or an associated tribe. They were not so well wrapped in furs and skins, betraying the fact that they had been inside but a short time before, forced out into the daylight by sudden attack, some clad in warm coats and furs, but most fighting the cold as much as the enemy.

They weren't so well prepared and neither had they the drive and experience of combat. These were people who brawled and hunted, but had no real experience in chilling their fellow man.

Although they outnumbered the Inuit warriors, they were no match and were easily pushed back to the center of the ville.

As the companions followed in the wake of the first wave of Inuit, there was little for them to do other than watch their own backs from those stragglers who had escaped the coruscating attack of the warriors. Few were left alive who weren't forced back, only small pockets of those who had taken shelter in the burning buildings. They were terrified and confused, appearing to fire wildly before being cut down by precision fire from their opponents. Others couldn't escape the buildings, and threw themselves from broken windows, clothes ablaze, to plummet one or two stories onto the sidewalks and roadways, where they lay broken but not yet chilled, the fires still burning on their bodies as they mewled and moaned. For them, a shell to put them out of their miseries was little more than a kindness.

The old buildings, battered by the nukecaust and then by a century of neglect in the harsh conditions, were easy pickings for the flickering fires that found plenty on which to feed. The ramshackle buildings that stood between the older, predark structures were constructed of materials that fed the flames, the fires greedily taking the fuel and growing with an incremental fierceness.

Behind them, whole boulevards were alive with flames, the smoke choking the already foul air, clouds of thick darkness hanging pall-like over the valley. Collapsing and ruined two-story structures spread their rubble across the sidewalks and beaten-up old street surfaces. The air was filled with smoke, the sounds of crackling flames, people and animals screaming, and the incessant, arrhythmic chatter of blasters firing from all points within the ville.

In truth, just getting out in one piece would prove difficult, let alone fighting the Inuit and trying to snatch Doc while the surrounding area was turned into an inferno.

ON THE FAR SIDE OF THE VILLE, McIndoe was leading his war party through the streets with a ruthless efficiency. His brief—as with that of the other war parties—was

simple. Overpower the opposition, drive them toward
the center of the ville, and chill immediately those who
would get in the way or would try to put up any kind of
resistance.

The Inuit sec chief had complete faith in his people
to complete the task. He may not believe in Jordan, and
be uneasy about the man's friends being in the war
party, but he was as good as his word when it came to
the firefight. His people were directed to forget about
the companions and to concentrate on their task in
rounding up the Fairbanks inhabitants for a ritual sacrifice.

As he marched, firing with unerring accuracy at the
panicking Fairbanks fighters, whose shots flew high
and wide, he kept his mind stoically on the task. The
difference between his people and those in the ville was
simple: the Inuit didn't care if they lived or died. If they
could survive, then good; if not, then it was the will of
the Lord that they be taken. The greater good meant that
a loss of life was no waste. So they did not panic as they
marched and fought. This gave them a greater clarity
and calm from which to make the right decisions—the
ones that, ironically, would keep them alive when the
fear of their opponents would cause them to be chilled.

Around his party, the ville was being consumed by
fire. If this was to mean that his people would also be
consumed—in effect, become as much of a sacrifice as
those they had come to claim—then that, too, would be
the will of the Almighty.

He led his people on, knowing that all the war parties would be acting in the same manner and that one
way or another they would give their thanks to the Lord
on this day.

McPHEE DIDN'T FEEL the same way, an ironic turn of affairs for one who was the spiritual leader of his tribe. But the old man had spent too long going through the motions, without even really thinking about the truth of his religion, that he now found himself looking at events in a different light to those who had kept their faith.

Perhaps it was simply a matter of spending so many years with no real sign that their Lord was anything other than a figment of someone's imagination generations before. Or maybe he was just old, tired and cynical. Either way, he could see nothing but bad coming out of this expedition. As he looked around him, firing on those poor souls who were desperately trying to get away from the Inuit onslaught, he found himself thinking of them as just that: poor souls. Not some glorious sacrifice for the greater good of the tribe. Shit, he'd long ago figured that they were on the downward slide. He'd seen others on the plains come and go with mutie shit that infected them after the nukecaust. Sterility was the best way, especially when you looked at some of the mutations that were fighting right now: shuffling on deformed legs, ignoring the pain of keeping up with others; or using vestigial arms to fire weapons that were made for normal limbs, bodies hunched to enable the action, and still achieving remarkable accuracy.

Yeah, they were good fighters, but they were on their way out. Nothing lasted forever. You only had to take a good look at the world before the nukecaust to see that. Some things are better left just to fade away. Maybe that's what should happen to the tribe. Rather than this last hollow sacrifice, where they would lose half their people—and for what?—they should retreat and go to live their lives in peace, hunting and enjoying their day in the sun until such time as there were none left.

Face it, that was going to come pretty damn soon as it was. He couldn't see them escaping being their own sacrifice. Not unless he could turn it around in some way.

FOR JAK LAUREN, this was indeed a strange experience. Following in the wake of the Inuit first wave, there was little fighting that the companions had to do. Instead, they were more concerned with keeping Doc in sight as the tribe war party swept through the burning streets.

Jak was used to being a warrior and leading the charge. His instincts, fired by the bloodlust and smell of cordite and chilled flesh around him, were yelling at him to step up his pace and step up to the base. He felt as though he should charge forward and join the Inuit horde as they drove their enemy back, chilling all those who were too slow to get out of the way.

Yet he could see that Ryan was holding them back for a purpose. If they were to seize Doc and try to get away with him, they would need to be detached from the main body of action. It was like hunting: you don't run with the pack, you stay apart from it, waiting for the right moment to dive in and take out your victim.

J.B. spent most of his time watching the rear. He had noted with a growing sense of unease how the whole ville seemed to be turning into an inferno around them, with the route they had used to enter soon being blocked off by a combination of fire and rubble. If they were to make their way out of here in one piece, someone had to work out a route. And if no one else had thought of it, at least J.B. was going to make sure that he had that angle covered. As they progressed, he kept his eyes on each side road and alley, making sure he noted how many were blocked, how many were still negotiable, and if possible how they all linked up. He wished to hell that they had been shown a map of the ville or had a chance to recce it before the attack. That way, he could be sure of leading them out. But the Inuit didn't seem to care if they got out alive.

J.B. sure as hell cared.

While the Armorer did this, Krysty was more concerned about keeping up with Doc, and how they would snatch him back. She was in the forefront of their party, level with Ryan, but keeping back from the Inuit who had gone in ahead of them. Even among the second wave of warriors, the natives had outstripped the companions in their desire to be part of this holy war. While Ryan wanted to keep Doc in his sights, there was no way he wanted to expose his people to any unnecessary risks, so he tried to keep their pace under that of their supposed allies.

Krysty could see that this was a delicate balance. They had to be able to reach Doc easily, but in his Jordan persona he was in the midst of the action, and it would be all that they could do to keep up with him without becoming sucked into the maelstrom of slaughter.

It was about waiting for the right moment. It was about choosing that moment.

But what if the moment wanted to choose itself?

What if it was about to do that right now?

THOMPSON WAS FIRING on those who came at him and directing his people to move those who remained toward the center of the ville. It was easy for the Inuit to run the Fairbanks people like a herd of deer. They were scared and would flee from any danger with no compunction.

The chief was worried about the fires that raged around them. He didn't want his people to achieve the aim of sacrificing others only to find themselves trapped and becoming a sacrifice of their own making. Yet he stubbornly held to the belief that he had to see this mission through to the bitter end. Although, it had to be said, there was a part of him that was beginning to worry if it was all folly.

He had believed in the stranger Jordan. Believed that he had been sent from the Almighty to save them from the slow and sterile chill of their tribe. Yet to look at the man as he joined the Inuit in action right now was to truly look into the howling face of madness.

Jordan was covered in blood and grime from the smoke, laughing and taking in great gulps of air that turned into choking coughs as the fumes reached down into his lungs. Yet this seemed to do nothing more than spur him to greater heights of hysterical cackling. He had discharged the shot chamber of the LeMat early in the attack, decimating a group of men who had rushed headlong into the Inuit party from out of a bar, carrying SMGs that they barely had time to raise before the lethal shot from the LeMat tore into them, the hot metal pulping their organs and splintering bone. Even those it didn't chill, such as the man whose right arm had been severed by the charge, hanging loose from a few tendons while he watched it dangle, a high-pitched wail the only sound emanating from his widened mouth, were soon cut down by Jordan as he strode into them with his sword stick unsheathed, the fine Toledo steel slicing through flesh as though it were nothing.

The ball charge had put paid to a gaudy slut who was almost naked, but who still had the nerve to carry a remade H&K MP-5 as she swung from the second story window of her blazing gaudy house, aiming to land on her feet to try to take out some of the opposition as she did. She had managed to let loose a brief volley of shots that had chilled two Inuit and wounded a third before the LeMat's ball charge ripped her open from thorax to sternum, the smashed bones making light of her internal organs and causing a shower of blood to shoot from under her surprised expression before she was thrown backward onto the sidewalk.

Jordan had laughed hard enough to choke, as though the sight were comical; Thompson admired her as a brave warrior buying the farm nobly, despite her near-nakedness, and couldn't understand what the messenger of the Lord could find so damned funny.

Now it seemed to him as though Jordan was nothing more than a madman who had led them into disaster.

The chief wasn't the only one thinking that way. McPhee, although he had no idea that his chief had changed his mind, had long ago reached this conclusion, and he felt that unless he acted now there was no way that any of the Inuit would escape a fiery chill in the Fairbanks inferno. To his mind, if he had to make Thompson stop, then he would have to take Jordan out of the equation.

Slowing, psyching himself so that he slowed mentally as well as physically, and trying to achieve a state of calm that would be miraculous in these circumstances, he raised his Lee Enfield .303 rifle and got Jordan in his sight. It may bring the wrath of the tribe down on him, but it was the only way to stop them dead, to bring them to their senses.

He squeezed the trigger and the rifle jammed. He cursed and wondered if maybe he'd been wrong after all. The blaster had been working fine since they had entered the ville, and for it to jam only when he was aiming at the man they suspected to be a messenger of the Almighty was something that made him think again.

No. It was too late for faith to strike him. Not now. He had to trust in his gut feeling to save what was left of the tribe, rather than place his trust in a madman who may or may not be sent from a Lord who no longer gave a shit about them.

The shaman moved through the crowds of Inuit who were sweeping toward the burning center of the ville, driving back those who were to be the sacrifice. McPhee increased his speed, elbowing and pushing his way past fellow tribe members who took his sudden enthusiasm for a flowering of his revelation. Let them think that, it would make his task easier. As he pushed his way through, he turned the rifle in his hands so that he brandished it like a club, the heavy stock ready to strike.

The laughing, yelling Jordan came into range. He was facing away from the medicine man, his white mane shaking as he cackled in the throes of madness. McPhee raised the rifle high above his head, bringing it down with the added momentum of the last step to take him close to his target. Thompson, standing beside Jordan as the blow began to fall, turned suddenly. Perhaps it was instinct, perhaps it was just something in his peripheral vision... His face, normally inscrutable, showed a sudden shock as he realized what was happening. Despite his views on the stranger being brought into doubt by his seeming insanity, the man was still a figurehead. He was the reason they were in the middle of an inferno, and Thompson knew that if he was struck down, then all meaning would be lost.

He knew this in less time than it took to blink an eye. Knew it and reacted. He tried to reach up to block the blow. But even the reactions of a hunter couldn't stop the blow entirely. His arm deflected the momentum a little and he felt his elbow jar heavily as the bones between that point and his wrist took the impact, shattering or cracking according to size. The mass of skins and furs covering his arm couldn't prevent it. McPhee's determination fed a fire to his actions that gave him incredible strength.

The deflected blow couldn't chill Jordan. Delivered straight, it would have shattered his skull, driving bone fragments into the brain and pulping it. The last-ditch effort of the chief had done enough to insure that that wouldn't take place, but nonetheless the blow was strong enough to push Jordan forward, splitting the thin layer of skin between hair and bone and rendering him unconscious. He pitched onto his toes, falling flat on the sidewalk.

All around the shaman there was confusion and anger. Those closest to the incident couldn't understand why their spiritual leader had turned on the man he had proclaimed as sent from the Lord. They also knew that their chief had been injured from his involuntary howl of pain as his arm was rendered useless. What should they do? Help the chief, or help the stranger, or chill the medicine man? Farther back, Inuit warriors knew something strange and very amiss had happened, but their view was obscured by those in front of them. They pressed up on those in front, who in turn were trying to stop themselves and others from trampling over Jordan as they attempted to lift him from where he had landed.

The moment had chosen itself.

FROM THEIR POSITION toward the rear of the Inuit, Ryan saw the movement as McPhee began to move forward. The shaman had been visible among the tribe as he still had his ritual vestments, which stood out against the heaving sea of furs and skins. He had been a useful landmark as to where Doc may be. Ryan knew that wherever McPhee was, then Thompson and Doc would be close.

The one-eyed man wondered what was happening as he saw the surge, then realized that it could be nothing good as he saw the shaman raise his rifle, try to fire, then turn it around like a club.

Without pausing to inform the others why, he began to move forward, attempting to push his way through toward the front of the crowd. He couldn't explain exactly why he knew the gestures of McPhee were aimed at Doc, only that some sense of danger told him that he had to act right now.

He wasn't alone in that. Krysty was already ahead of him. She couldn't see as well, but she sensed that the situation was changing rapidly. Her sentient hair wrapped itself around her skull and her neck, clinging to her in the manner that it only did in times of triple red danger. Jak, Mildred and J.B. couldn't see what was happening ahead of them, but they were clued into the fact that something was going down by one look at Krysty.

By the time that Doc had pitched forward, devoid of consciousness and with blood pouring from the wound on his head and down over his shoulders and hair, matting the white mane, the companions were fighting their way through the crowd.

J.B. kept one eye to his rear, trying to judge their chances of escape and to gauge what kind of route they could take. Things were going from bad to worse. Inside the skins and furs he was sweating, the air hot with the fires that raged around. Although the wind factor had been cut down by the fact that they were in a valley, still there was enough to spread the fires from building to building, street to street. Soon the whole ville would be nothing more than an inferno and they'd be trapped in the center of the blaze.

Dark night, they'd be lucky to get out of this one. But first they had to try to get Doc…

The sudden confusion had made this section of the Inuit invasion party seemingly forget all about the inhabitants of Fairbanks. They were jostling one another in confusion, trying to find out what was going on. For them, it was perhaps as well that the few survivors of their relentless onslaught had now drawn back toward the center of the ville, as they would have presented an easy target.

In truth, they were so distracted by their sudden halt that it was relatively easy for the companions to individually push their way through to the front of the crowd. They were not the enemy, even though they may have incurred some suspicion, so they were allowed to pass almost unnoticed.

Thompson was leaning over Doc. The old man was still and silent on the sidewalk. Ryan reached them first.

"What's—" he began to say, but was cut short by Thompson, who pointed to McPhee, now being held by two Inuit warriors.

"Him," the chief said simply. "He hit the messenger."

"Why?" Ryan questioned.

Thompson shook his head. "Think I know that? We've nearly achieved our goal, and then this."

"Nearly achieved what?" McPhee yelled, struggling against the two men who restrained him. "Achieved chilling the whole fucking tribe? In case you haven't noticed, this place is like a funeral pyre, and for more than just the people we came to sacrifice. If this is like a big wicker man, then we're trapped in the belly of the beast, as well. And it's all down to him and whatever he purports to be." McPhee, unable to gesture in any other way, spit at Doc Tanner's prone form.

Thompson stepped forward and struck the medicine man across the face with a back-handed blow that snapped the shaman's head back.

"Shut up. It was on your word that we started out here. You told me that it was the only way to appease the Lord."

"Me! You asshole, I was the one who had the doubts."

As the two men began to argue, and the Inuit looked on in complete confusion, the companions took the opportunity to slip closer to Doc. Mildred knelt beside him and examined the area of the blow as rapidly as she could.

"Hasn't fractured, by the feel," she murmured, running her fingers nimbly and expertly over the blood-slick skull. "He'll have a hell of a concussion and won't be able to move by himself."

"Fireblast and fuck it, it would have helped if he could have saved us carrying him," Ryan muttered as he settled beside her. "This is going to make it hard. What we really need is a bigger diversion than just those two arguing."

"Heads up, I think this might be it," Krysty said softly.

McIndoe appeared from out of the smoke, a couple of his most trusted sec men in tow. He took a long look at what was going on—the prone stranger surrounded by his friends, the chief and the medicine man arguing—and spoke in a tone that suggested he was less than happy with what greeted him.

"What the fuck is going on here? All parties have driven the survivors back to the center. They're all holed up on one street, a line of buildings. We've got them all pinned there. They can't get at us and they can't get out without being chilled. It's perfect for what we want. If we don't blast them, the fires'll get them. We just need the ritual. When you didn't arrive with the rest of the parties, we didn't know what to expect, so…" He shrugged, indicating he felt it was time for an explanation.

"I'll tell you what's going on," McPhee exploded. "We've run into a trap—a trap of our own making. Our own stupid idea, and we're caught like a deer in a pit. The fires will get more than the people of Fairbanks."

"But this is to save the tribe. To offer these people to the Almighty so that he can make us fertile again—" McIndoe began.

McPhee cut him short. "We're finished. All of us. We listened to a lunatic, and now we've got to face the fact that we're history. This isn't the rebirth of the tribe, it's our funeral pyre."

"Dark night, I wish he hadn't mentioned Doc," J.B. muttered as the attention of McIndoe—and, by extension, those others who heard McPhee—turned to where Doc had now been lifted up, supported by Krysty and Mildred. He was barely conscious, his eyes rolling in his head and only the faintest incoherent mumblings escaping his lips.

Jak, J.B. and Ryan flanked the women. They had hoped to at least start moving from the front of the crowd while attention was focused on the arguing sec leader, the medicine man and the chief. But McPhee's words had chilled those chances. If they could have just moved another twenty yards they could have tried to escape down a side street. As it was, they were backed up against a building that was uncomfortably hot from the fires that were reaching it, with no escape route.

"I knew you were trouble," McIndoe said, raising his Sharps rifle.

"Wait—what good will chilling them do?" Thompson yelled.

"None, but it can't hurt to take them with us if we're on the way out of here," McIndoe snapped back.

A wave of fear and anger swept through the Inuit at these words—as though it were no longer conjecture, but cold, hard fact that they were chilled meat—and Ryan could see his companions helpless before an onslaught of enemy fire, with nowhere to run.

They needed a miracle. They got something that was partway between miracle and disaster.

A loud rumbling filled the air. Already alive with the sound of yelling and screaming, and the crackling of both fire damage and blasterfire, it should have been almost impossible for anything else to be heard. But this was a deep, dark sound that seemed to swell from beneath whatever noises were going on above, until it felt as though it was making the very air itself vibrate.

"Oh, shit—it's all coming down," Mildred whispered. Ryan could barely hear her above the noise, but he was about to ask her what she meant when the sound—and its source—overtook them.

Desperation had fuelled one last act of defiance from the Fairbanks inhabitants who were trapped in the center of the burning ville. They had fired up the buildings in which they were now cowering, using all the fuel they could find, all the ammo and weaponry they possessed. It meant their own demise, but they knew that they were chilled anyway. It was only a matter of whether it was a quick chilling or one that was slow and painful.

Faced with such a stark choice, it was no contest. They had turned the street in which they were holed up like rats into a giant bomb. Once detonated, it had set off a chain reaction among those buildings burning nearby, the rubble strewed from the blast hammering into buildings made unstable by their own blazes, rendering them to the ground in their turn. Like a string of dominoes, once one building collapsed into another, it set those around it into a state of collapse.

The thick smoke was now overpowered, in its turn, by dust. Clouds of choking darkness began to engulf the Inuit and the companions as the buildings shattered to rubble around them and Fairbanks was razed to the ground.

The last they saw of McIndoe—or Thompson and McPhee—was the Inuit's surprised expression as his gaze was taken from his leveled rifle to the rubble that flew toward him.

Now it was all they could do to outrun the chain reaction. J.B. and Jak were off like rabbits escaping a snare, making for the street twenty yards to their left before the domino effect claimed it. Ryan helped Krysty and Mildred carry Doc, allowing Jak and J.B. to run ahead, scouting the route.

The Armorer had the layout of the ville as they had passed it in his head, and Jak was able to move more swiftly, telling him where once-open streets had already been claimed by fire and collapse.

With the roar of collapsing streets ringing in their ears, and the dust and heat making it hard to breathe, the three carrying Doc didn't know how they made it to the edge of the ville. There was no time to think, just to do. They kept running, somehow keeping their balance when stumbling, somehow breathing when the air seemed too thick with dust and smoke to be inhaled. It was blind instinct for survival that drove them. There were times when they couldn't truthfully say that they had seen Jak and J.B. guide them, only that they somehow knew where they were supposed to run.

Past the gates they had entered by; over the wreckage of the crow's nests; hitting the steep incline of the valley wall, now safe from the flying rubble but still trapped in the spumes of choking dust and smoke. They had to get up the side of the valley, to where the air was cleaner.

It was a blind struggle, one that seemed to take forever and no time at all. There was no meaning to time, only striving to survive.

Ryan had been flat on his back, gulping in clean air and hacking up smoke-polluted phlegm for some minutes before he realized where he was. He looked around.

The others were with him, all in a similar state of collapse. All except for Doc, who was still unconscious but now had the sweetest, most innocent smile on his face.

Ryan raised himself to his feet, feeling unsteady as the oxygen beginning to course once more around his system made him feel light-headed. They had ended up several yards from the lip of the valley, and they were fortunate that the winds were taking the smoke and dust away from them.

The one-eyed man staggered the couple of paces to the edge of the valley, so that he could see the devastation below. It was hard to make out through the smoke, but it seemed as though the whole ville had been flattened by the chain reaction. It was doubtful anyone else could have made it out alive. How *they* had, he couldn't tell.

He turned back to the others. They looked in no fit state to move as yet, but it was freezing up on the ridgeline, and they'd soon have to seek shelter. The early afternoon sun was already beginning to sink.

Shelter. Food. And a place to go from here.

Those would have to be attended to, and soon, but now, it was all he could do to stop from sinking to his knees and letting oblivion claim him.

* * * * *

Don't miss
ATLANTIS REPRISE,
the exciting conclusion of
the ALTERED STATES
duology, available in December

James Axler
Outlanders

CERBERUS STORM

SPOILS OF VICTORY

The baronial machine ruling post-apocalyptic America is no more, yet even as settlers leave the fortressed cities and attempt to build new lives in the untamed outlands, a deadly new struggle is born. The hybrid barons have evolved into their new forms, their avaricious scope expanding to encompass the entire world. Though the war has changed, the struggle for the Cerberus rebels remains the same: save humanity from its slavers.

DARK TERRITORY

Amidst the sacred Indian lands in Wyoming's Bighorn Mountains, a consortium with roots in preDark secrets is engaged in the excavation of ancient artifacts, turning the newly liberated outlands into a hellzone. Kane and the Cerberus warriors organize a strike against the outlaws, only to find themselves navigating a twisted maze of legend, manipulation and the fury of a woman warrior. Driven by power, hatred and revenge, she's now on the verge of uncovering and releasing a force of unfathomable evil....

Available November 2005 at your favorite retailer.